SCRAPERS

A Future Yesterdays Tale

Remi Zorne

Editing: J & S De La Torre, Robert Eversz, Kristen Holt-Browning

Book cover design created through Canva.com using Magic Media AI.

ISBN: 979-8-218-36255-3

To my parents, Jim & Sue, my biggest cheerleaders
and my lucky bamboo.

CHAPTER 1

Chicago, IL October 16, 2025

B rodie Frost rolled through the park just up from Chicago's North Avenue Beach on his World Industries Silver deck with the Red Ricta Chrome Cloud wheels. At 33, his skateboard had almost become a natural extension of his body. He took the relaxing way into downtown, swerving along the paths, popping 180's and tricks he'd learned as a teenager. His moderately short brown hair danced wild in the breeze. On that particular Thursday morning in October, just several days before his 34th birthday, Brodie was on his way to meet his older brother, Billy Wessner, who was also his proven adversary.

When Brodie got the call from him to meet, his first instinct made him wonder what the catch would be? When their father, Nathan Wessner, divorced their mom after high school, Brodie cut ties with Nathan completely. Soon after, Brodie changed his last name to Frost, his mother, Jaclyn's maiden name. Nathan had never been much of a father to him, anyway. Besides, life was much simpler not being tied to the menacing Wessner name. Even with all of that, older and wiser, Brodie felt maybe it was time to give Billy another chance and see what it was he wanted.

Billy was a corporate hatchet man, working for the highest bidders under the guise of 'marketing'. He snuffed out competition with stealth-like success and at a rapid pace. He was in the midst of working his way up the power chain at the Droshure Corporation with physical potency. Billy claimed he was in Chicago for business when he had asked Brodie to meet for breakfast. The invitation made him uneasy. It had been over three years since he'd seen Billy. Their relationship had never been a harmonious one. Being the oldest, Billy tortured him like the worst of siblings when they were younger, only easing up in the presence of most adults. After college though, their father got Billy a job at the Droshure Corporation, a toxic empire of chicanery that Brodie found to be the root of much evil.

Pulled from his momentary rumination by the shining sun and crisp autumn air, Brodie cut and shredded through the park. It was just before 10 and the lakefront was filling up with runners, walkers and brave surfers trying to hop the swelling fall waves pumping out on Lake Michigan. The day off from work found Brodie gently stoned and in a good mood, ideal conditions for whatever Billy had in store.

Just as Brodie landed a half cab flip, three masked strangers pedaling dirt bikes through the park interrupted his field of vision. He watched as they rode toward him, terrorizing pedestrians with yelps and ridicule, swatting a baseball bat at passersby. The bleached-out Halloween masks they wore took Brodie back to his childhood. All the way back to when Brodie was seven. It was the day Billy taunted him, to the point of dragging a dead racoon corpse across Brodie's shirt, after they'd chased him down. The whole time the childhood torture took place, Billy and his friends wore creepy, weathered Ben Cooper masks. In fact, Billy and his friends wore those masks year-round, wreaking havoc throughout the neighborhood.

Today, although Halloween was just two weeks away, the scene coming toward Brodie spun an unexpected knot in his stomach. It tempted him to turn back and go home, cancel the plan with Billy. But instead, he shook off the feeling and kept steady, well aware that paranoia was a frequent traveler for his thoughts when it came to family.

Brodie kicked up his board and caught it with one hand, as the two riders peddled within steps of him. The third, a passenger standing on the pegs of one of the bikes, took a swing at him. As Brodie ducked out of the way, all three riders hooted and crowed as they sped off, continuing their jubilant razzing through the park. Brodie dropped his board back down, pushing his foot heavy against the pavement, quickly making his way out of the park toward Michigan Ave. He wanted to get the meeting with Billy done and over with.

The incident in the park wasn't sitting right. It nagged at him as he rode on. First, the masks, but now he heard the popping crackle of what sounded like firecrackers banging off in rapid succession. Then, without warning, the ground shook underneath the wheels of his board, almost shaking him off, as a thunderous explosion rang out. Brodie hopped off his board as people came rushing from the downtown area, hurrying past him heading in the opposite direction. Their faces were covered with looks of panic. Soon sirens belted out in stereo as cop cars and ambulances rushed past in mass, speeding into the downtown.

"Hey, what's happening?" Brodie asked as he stopped a fleeing woman as she tried to sprint by.

"They're just shooting at people, I don't know," the woman said frantically, her hands shaking as she covered her mouth in shock. "I don't know what's going on." Her head on a swivel as she constantly checked over her shoulder with fear.

"Who?" As Brodie questioned, two black ambulances rushed past. Black ambulances meant deaths.

"I'm sorry, I can't stay here." The woman looked at Brodie, her eyes glazed over, glossy from panic. Then in a split second, she dashed off, heading away from the chaos with others, all trying to get to safety.

Brodie took in the horrific scene playing out in front of him as he got closer to downtown, tapping the back of his pants, making sure he felt the handle of his gun. After the assassination of the president and vice president two months prior, the country was on edge, fear and uncertainty were in full abundance. Because of that and the escalating unrest over the last several months, Brodie refused to go anywhere without his gun.

As he got closer to Michigan Ave, he saw more and more people, many injured, locked in confusion and terror, several others lay motionless.

"My leg, it's burning. Please help me," a man yelled up from the ground.

Brodie instantly went into work mode, crouching down to help the man. As he scanned the man's body, he saw thick shards of glass penetrating into his thigh, as blood saturated his pants. Brodie pulled off the man's belt and made a quick tourniquet just above the imbedded glass. He scanned the area for any available medics, all the while, concerned about Billy. The shooting had ceased moments earlier, but chaos was all around as people panicked, scrambling about searching for loved ones and safety. Finally, an EMT came to Brodie's side and took over.

Brodie dashed down two more blocks to the café where he was supposed to meet Billy, hoping to see him somewhere. But just as he reached it, he saw the front of the café and the businesses on either side had been partially blown out. The busted-out fronts had thrown bricks and glass out onto Michigan Ave. Bodies wailed in agony, strewn about the sidewalks and into the street. Blood drizzled off the curbs, pooling into the avenue. People stood locked in motion, baffled and in shock, while others worked to comfort and assist the injured and hysterical.

Out of nowhere, Brodie spotted Billy strolling down the sidewalk in a double-breasted suit, as if there wasn't turmoil all around him. Yet, as soon as Billy spotted Brodie, he awkwardly paused to give his coat to a woman panicked with fear. When he crossed the street and reached Brodie, his demeanor dropped flat.

"Are you ok? What the fuck happened," Brodie asked.

"Someone blew out the coffee shop, the restaurant next door and I don't know, look around! The whole street is blown to shit. It was fucked up. Then, it got completely silent and a couple of guys drove up out of nowhere and just started shooting," Billy explained. He rolled his eyes with a pacifying sigh. "But yeah, it's good you were late. It's also really fucking good I went around the corner to smoke otherwise I'd probably be dead. Just weird that you were late and all this happened," he raised his eyebrows at Brodie and pulled out a cigarette, lit it. He patted Brodie on the arm then offered him one.

"Hey, I'd be dead, too," Brodie said, waving his hands no, refusing the cigarette.

"So, what happened to you? Why were you late?" Billy prodded. "I'm kidding about you having anything to do with it, it was just weird."

The words took Brodie aback. The whole exchange was bizarre. Was Billy really accusing him of having anything to do with what happened? He studied Billy's face trying to understand the verbal charges as a wave of nausea consumed him. Brodie felt off center, his buzz was gone as anxiety tried to take over.

"What are you talking about? I almost got jumped in the park, Billy. People are hurt, come on."

"I'm just fucking with ya," Billy scoffed. He patted Brodie on the back, but he shook it off.

"We have to help these people," Brodie pleaded. "There's nothing funny about any of this. What is wrong with you?" Brodie's paranoia had been justified as he now wondered if Billy had tried set him up, lure him to his death. He couldn't stop replaying everything that had just happened.

"Let me run to my car and get different clothes. This is an expensive suit. I don't want to get blood all over it. That doesn't come out, ya know," Billy declared.

Brodie spent the next four hours tending to the wounded. To his relief, Billy never returned.

That evening when he got home, Brodie learned that similar attacks had happened in over twelve major cities and the news stories were still developing. Everything occurred within minutes of each other throughout the country. Of all the attacks, the only ones that were thwarted were in Colorado and California. No suspects were mentioned, but rumors of terrorism were spreading fast throughout social media. The death toll was climbing close to eight hundred and would grow well beyond that over the next few days. By the end of the weekend, all incidents were blamed on international terrorist groups, yet none of them claimed responsibility.

What followed over the next 3 months was a wave of panic and a country struggling to find a leader. In the wake of the attacks, several of the top politicians in line fell to political scandal. First the Speaker of the House was surpassed after a prostitution sting. Next, the role landed at the President pro tempore of the senate. That scandal bled much deeper as Devin Booker, who held the role, was sent to federal prison for reasons unknown before he even got close to being approved. Eventually, the position trickled down to the Secretary of State, Timothy Boobain. Mr. Boobain just happened to be a silent partner with the Droshure Corporation, one of the world's fastest growing robotic engineering corporations.

Just before Timothy Boobain got settled into the role of interim President, the class wars ignited throughout the country. With a culture of panic and unrest clouding over the US, people were frantic, willing to sell their souls to the devil for the security and protection of all they had worked for. Fear of gangs and more terrorism was thriving. Money meant protection and what President Boobain was ready to provide to those who could afford it, looked a lot like a strategic gentrification of the country. The rich got the *Corners Developments*, luxurious, gated communities that covered roughly 280,000 square miles of guarded lands created by the Droshure Corporation and its partners. Outside of those protected gates, the rest of the country suffered. President Boobain regulated natural resources, aid, electricity and water, putting strict limitations on what was available in the new slums of America, which was now referred to as the *Gutter*.

Instead of fleeing to one of the gated Corners states, like California where Nathan, Billy and Cece, Brodie's sister, lived, he went north to Wisconsin. The Droshure Corporation held the primary contract for the development of all the communities which were evolving into Corners states. They provided the residents with a sense of safety, connection and elitism. Brodie knew it all came at a price and not just a monetary one, at that. He and his friends in the Underground were well aware that the interim president and Jacob Droshure were corrupt and most likely responsible for everything that positioned Timothy Boobain into the role of interim President.

Living in the slums made it easier to plan for the revolution. The Underground could hide in plain sight, far from President Boobain's control. Aside from the black-market poachers and nationwide kill boys, referred to as the Splitters, who ran wild in the Gutter, Wisconsin was one of the safer states. The main reason that Brodie went to Wisconsin, though, was because of Nora, his ex-girlfriend, who just happened to be the love of his life. She was also an elite agent with the International Bureau of Investigations, the IBI. She was stationed there working undercover, owning and running a bar, just like any local civilian would. It was the perfect place for Brodie. He wanted to be far away from his brother and Nathan, and close to where he could make a difference, support the Underground resistance and be near Nora, even if they weren't together.

CHAPTER 2

Present day 2028 – Three years later

J ust before dawn, in a rundown suburb of Milwaukee, Brodie moved with purpose in the basement of a safe house. That day, the safe house was just a thirty-minute ride on his board from where he lived. Everything President Boobain had done caused a calculated genocide to slowly emerge. While there were hospitals in the slums, they weren't well-equipped and were filled with doctors that had been blocked from the Corners, who'd lost their licenses for one reason or another, or were appointed under Boobain's order. Supplies were never in abundance and were dispersed in limited capacity under the control of Boobain. This caused the need for the Underground to create their own medical teams within the slums. To remain untraceable, the safe house locations changed regularly.

Mother Nature roared outside, rattling the ceiling above where Brodie stood. There, in a large cement walled room just off the basement stairs, two bulky hunks of muscle kept guard across from him. In the center, with bloodied gloves and a surgical mask on, Brodie was in the middle of delivering a baby. He'd been told the woman was one of President Boobain's mistresses, but he never paid much attention to the details of strangers. In the Gutter, the less he knew the better. He was a bartender with a scalpel. Instead of serving up drinks, he served up anesthesia and healed the unwell. He was a surgeon for the Underground, a crime that could land him in big trouble, punishable under President Boobain's new laws.

When Brodie was little, he had learned that the truth, in a way, didn't exist. Only the perception of it did. The first time he learned about lies he was seven. Nathan had yelled at his mother, Jaclyn, then pointed to Brodie.

"He's a bastard and you're a slut," Nathan asserted. "You're not even my kid, you whiny brat." And in that moment Brodie felt relief, having no instinct to dispute Nathan's statement. Brodie was happy to not be genetically tied to him. He would soon learn that his mom, an established painter and artist, had been unfaithful during an overseas gallery show. Brodie was the product of that trip. "Did you love the guy? Were you going to run away with him?" Nathan hounded Jaclyn.

Brodie watched her hesitate, then before she could respond, Nathan slapped her across the face. "You're a slut." Nathan looked down to Brodie standing by the door and glared at him. "That never happened," Nathan said.

After that day, Brodie didn't waste time believing the words of most others. So, although the woman before him was supposedly one of Boobain's mistresses that had fled his hold, Brodie knew that people in the Gutter would say anything to get medical treatment and so would those who had been exiled from the Corners.

All of Brodie's patients came to him through the UDB, the Underground Database, so he did his best to fix them, regardless of story or identity. If he knew someone or didn't like the circumstances, he could turn down a patient and they would simply assign another surgeon. It had only happened twice since the country's divide. There were details

Brodie could learn from patients' words and stories as they babbled on under heavy sedation. All he needed to know this morning though, was that he was to deliver the woman's baby. After that, he would make sure that both she and child were healthy enough and given secure transport to a protected village when he was done.

As Brodie worked, his brown, looping curls dangled at the edge of his face shield. With his black, thick-rimmed glasses on, he was a doppelgänger for the late Buddy Holly, as his mother often told him. Though he wore long sleeves and a disposable smock, the tattoos on his forearms were just barely visible, along with the silver electrical tape wrapped tightly around his wrists. His parka, bag, and skateboard sat on a table across from where he worked.

Anonymity was important for surgeons like Brodie and medical staff in the Underground. Anonymity was safety. President Boobain had enacted a law that any non-appointed lifesaver in the Gutter caught helping someone who could taint the human gene pool or thwart the government's agenda could be punished by death, which included nurses and midwives. Brodie knew of several surgeons, three nurses and five doctors who had been killed in the last six months, so he had no interest in getting caught.

In front of him, the swollen red ankles of the young woman drove deep into the padded stirrups as she bore down at the edge of a reclined medical chair. At her side, a midwife sat gripping her hand. Brodie had worked with the midwife before. He knew her only by the tattooed flaming teardrop inked under her left eye. She was a stout, stoic, older Hispanic woman. They only spoke as needed, but Brodie liked working with her and knowing she was still ok.

The baby was crowning. As the midwife held the woman's hand tight, the muscles in her forearms flexed. With every painful push, the woman let out a snarly yelp.

"You need to keep her quiet. If someone hears, they'll call it in. They'll kill her and take the baby for use." Brodie spoke with purpose and warning.

The new government asserted that over-birthing was one of the main causes of sickness, mental disease, weakened immune response and diminished intelligence. If a person gave birth to more than two children, they could be arrested and forcibly sterilized. The woman lying before Brodie was on her third child. This, he knew from the intel he'd received. Now, she was under the protection of the Underground.

The midwife tried to muffle the woman's cries with her hand. Brodie glanced at the midwife as she locked eyes with the woman, trying to reassure her that everything would be ok. Brodie knew the woman had a 40% chance of making it. She was thin, frail and still detoxing from drugs. Now, with a baby, she would be a target. If any of the higher-ups in the Corners caught wind of her pregnancy, they would put a track out for her, especially considering the fact that Boobain and his wife were never able to have children of their own.

Brodie put his hand inside and carefully braced the baby's neck, guiding the rest of the tiny body out from the woman. Suddenly, the child's cry pierced off the walls. The baby was premature, but healthy. He had a much better chance of surviving than the mother, Brodie thought. The midwife took umbilical scissors, cut the cord, and placed it in a sealed packet. Brodie cleaned the baby off with purified water from a canister. The woman, exhausted, rested back as the midwife cleaned her up and helped her sip a cup of medication.

"It's a boy," Brodie said from across the room. He loved delivering babies, but under the circumstances, needed to remain measured and expressionless. He handed the cleaned-up infant to the midwife and filled out paperwork as they all waited for the afterbirth. Finally, he placed the mucus plug in a med bag and put all parts of the afterbirth in a chilled container in his backpack. If human tissue wasn't discarded or protected properly, it could be found and used for cloning, gene extraction or experimentation.

"You know what to do. Keep the room sterile and clean until the transporters come," Brodie said. "They should be here within the next two hours. They'll give you the names on this piece of paper. If they give you any other names, shoot them both. If that happens, text the phone number on the back of this paper. After you leave, you were never here. That goes for all of you."

Brodie handed the piece of paper to one of the guards, then removed his gloves, scrubbing the remaining blood and discharge from his arms and wrists, keeping his face mostly hidden. He pulled on a fresh pair of gloves and took out a phone, then snapped a picture of the two men by the door and another of the midwife.

Brodie took a picture of the mother with her baby and a closeup of each of them, separately. He drew a small amount of blood from the baby's heel and put it in a thumb size container. He packed up the last of his gear, threw on his parka, and grabbed his board. He walked over to the mother.

"You and the baby will be ok. Give the transporters the bag of medication and instructions. You will need that to survive." Brodie didn't feel it was a lie, there was still a slim chance she would live. The woman looked up to him and waved him close to her.

"Thank you. I will never let him go. My name is Roxanne Waters," the woman said. She spoke in whispers, keeping her words between she and Brodie. "My first son was shot and killed a year ago, then used for harvest. My daughter was kidnapped and taken for sex trafficking in the Corners. I was only with him to try to find her. I escaped five months ago. Someone needs to kill him. Someone needs to kill President Boobain," the woman said, exhaustion stealing her breath. Brodie didn't respond. "I'm naming my son Calvin, after you. The tattoo on your forearm. He will know you saved his life."

Brodie scanned the room to make sure he hadn't forgotten anything. How could he have been so stupid? Normally, he wrapped his forearms before working, covering up all of his identifiers, but today he must have wrapped too loose or too high on that side. He had a tattoo of Calvin, from the *Calvin and Hobbs* comic strip on his arm. His middle name was Calvin. When Brodie was eighteen, his mother told him his real father's name, Calvin Weston Truffant. The tattoo had a deeper meaning than it would appear. He needed to get out of there and not acknowledge anything. The woman would hopefully be on enough drugs for the next few days that they would erase most of her memory. Brodie went to the door. The guards parted and let him out as if he were a well-respected doctor. He quickly hustled up the stairs and disappeared into the quiet brisk morning.

Outside, smoky gray clouds draped the sky, hanging in limbo, waiting to rain or possibly snow. The air was thick with a soot that hovered, sticking to the skin. Brodie dashed through several rundown backyards and covered alleys like a track star. A few safe miles away, he stopped and unwrapped the electrical tape from his wrist. He took a piece of aluminum foil out of his pocket and unfolded it, revealing a small rectangular chip. He lifted a flap of skin on his wrist displaying a hollowed-out rectangle in his dermis layer. He secured the chip in the skin gap and lined the flap of flesh with super glue, locking it back into place. He threw down his skateboard and rolled closer to downtown.

CHAPTER 3

Hours later, Brodie cruised along the barren streets on his skateboard, while his buddy Marcus ran alongside him. Marcus stood at 6'2, was bald and had a full beard. He often wore a navy-blue beanie or trappers' hat like Brodie sometimes wore. Marcus was a cocoa skinned genius with a love for flames and the ladies. Though the morbidity of their reality clung to Brodie, Marcus appreciated the lawlessness and lack of demand put upon him when the country took a nose dive. As Marcus saw it, he was in full control. If he worked, he got paid. If he didn't want to work for a week, he didn't have to.

All around them hung the shadows of their past. As they moved through town, patches of grass sat sporadically sprouting out from the broken concrete, overgrown and dead. Within the last few years, the country had changed in a way most could never have predicted. Garbage fires flamed high in preparation for the cold evening, as the sun slowly inched toward its descent. Most of the homeless, which were vast, returned to their encampments and shelters, securing their safety for the night. The people that still held property in the Gutter rarely went out at night. When they did, it was in pairs. While Brodie was able to reside inside and remain moderately safe, many living in the Gutter were left to fend for themselves, seeking protection inside the shells of what used to be luxury and normalcy, now under the cover of cardboard, tents, churches and wooded parks. Most of the rampant violence had tapered off after the first year of Boobain's presidency and people were starting to get use to life in the slums, but being out at night would always come with a risk.

Brodie and Marcus were finishing up their day job. They were Scrapers. Flesh hunters, employed to scavenge for fresh dead bodies to harvest for parts. They worked for the Droshure Corporation. The harvested parts were used for synthetic development and genetic research at one of Droshure's many AI/clone plants. Given the amount of experimentation corporations were devoting to stem cell, AI, mind/brain manipulation and transplants, a fresh corpse could net a handsome wage.

Brodie slowed as he saw something sprawled out down a side road. Marcus turned back as he heard the skidding stop of Brodie's skateboard wheels. A body was collapsed across the vacant side street. It was a man. Brodie figured the man to be in his mid-fifties. They went to the body and Brodie set his tools down next to the terminated man. With thin medical gloves on, he touched the flesh. The body still held warmth, but everything else about the human shell before them was dead.

"My name is Brodie Frost, I'm a Scraper. Betrayer of my trade," Brodie sarcastically said the words under his breath. He sat his bags down and got ready to work.

"Dude, you sound like such a knob. You think I love doing this?" Marcus pleaded. When the two worked together, Brodie typically took the more complex extractions. Marcus might have been good with the ladies, but he was nowhere near as smooth with a scalpel.

Because of all of President Boobain's new laws, not to mention the natural progression of decomposition, Scrapers had to get to the dead quickly.

Every part had its time of expiration into rigor-mortis, not to mention the dark market poachers and hawks who weren't official Scrapers. The poachers and hawks were known to kill for parts, many sloppy cutters, often shredding the flesh and damaging anything of much use. Both the private and public sectors would take almost anything as long as it was live, usable tissue.

When Brodie scraped a plastic or cyborg, he called it in so the parts could be picked up by the Underground for research and investigative sampling. When it came to Droshure's payroll, Brodie was simply known as #184. The work was simple; pay for parts. If he ever got caught turning anything over to the Underground, he knew the punishment would be prison at best. He didn't care. Being able to help the Underground with any aspect of the damage that Droshure and Boobain were doing was the whole point of why he agreed to became a Scraper in the first place.

Marcus threw up a circular tent-like guard that was tall enough to hide their work but open, with walls short enough to see over. Brodie visually assessed the man's remains on the ground.

"Cardiac blow, you think?" That's what Brodie encountered the most, that and gunshot kills. Both Brodie and Marcus wore balaclavas covering most of their faces. Underneath his balaclava, Brodie wore a smaller mask covering his nose and mouth. He was obsessed with not being noticed and paranoid about accidentally leaving traces of his DNA anywhere.

"Yeah, that shit freaks me out," Marcus said. "One needle full of Zip, next thing you know, a few hours later, kaboom. That's why I stick to good ole reliable doggy style. I can keep an eye on the ladies and make sure they're not gonna dose me. I'm not gettin speared with that shit." Marcus laughed as Brodie shook his head in response to his friend's logic.

Zip was a liquid toxin that poachers typically used on bums. Some tossers, joy dolls and prostitutes made extra jingle (money) jamming Zip in johns so poachers could sweep in behind and get parts. It took dating and casual hook-ups to a heightened level of danger, to say the least.

"Not all blows are from Zip, some hearts just break down," Brodie said. "Either way, this guy's hearts no good, lungs are probably cashed, too. Skin isn't healthy, probably a smoker. We can grab everything else." He and Marcus continued their work with expeditious speed. Then Brodie heard that grumbling hum of the monitor drones, the same audible reverberations he'd heard in the sky almost every day since Boobain stepped in. "You see they started knocking down buildings? I heard anything over twelve stories is getting crushed so the monitors views aren't blocked." Brodie grabbed a packet and removed three Jamshidi needles. He aggressively jabbed one into the man's hip bone, drawing out marrow.

"It's just a scheme to make it easier for him to take over the land. Maybe someone will kill Boobain. I'm actually surprised it hasn't already happened. The guy's a loose cannon." Marcus said. He worked on the body, harvesting fat cells with a small vacuum like apparatus.

Brodie extracted the marrow from both sides, sealing it in protective packages, then into his med backpack. Afterward, he scanned the man's fingerprints onto a second phone he pulled from his coat pocket. As a member of the Underground, it was important to scan all available fingerprints into the Underground Database (UDB) with the hope that someday families of the deceased could be notified. He ripped the man's shirt open and put his scalpel to the chest. As he punctured the skin, browning blood breached the surface, slowly thickening. Before he made any progress, Brodie squeezed his eyes shut, trying to shake off the subtle stench that toyed with his olfactory glands. Ever since the COVID-19 pandemic of 2020, unlike others, his sense of smell had been significantly heightened. Unfortunately, he had forgotten his menthol rub and Marcus never used it.

"Do not puke, man. You need to swallow. Protect your DNA," Marcus said, laughing.

Brodie held his breath, gripping the scalpel, forcing his nausea down as he squeezed his salivary glands and tightened his jaw muscles. He couldn't stand the smell of death. As a surgeon, he could sense the odor, he knew the distinct smell of fluids as they drained to the lowest point of gravity in the body and started to pool. He caught his thoughts and rebalanced, finishing the cut. The two worked for just over an hour doing their best to cleanly harvest what they could use and carry under the cover of a gentle fog.

"Hey, we got company, someone's coming down the alley. You got your gun?"

"Always, just cover me. I need ten more minutes." Brodie stayed focused. He wrapped the parts he'd harvested in alginate gels and cool chem packs, securing them in containers. He scanned the sky, knowing the monitors were getting close, then peered down the alley to get a glimpse of the approaching stranger who he could now see was wearing a costume mask over his face.

Brodie had gotten used to the electronic hum that was now an almost constant vibration in his ears, a whole new kind of tinnitus. The monitors flew low, from the remote rural hills to the populated areas across the country bordering the Corners. Boobain's concern was not limited to the market poachers, illegal croppers and rebel rousers. His primary focus was the Drastics, those that had agendas against him and his corrupt government.

Brodie shifted toward the man's head, working carefully, harvesting the corneas. Sometimes they could be salvaged. His tool was homemade and jimmy-rigged. It resembled a high-tech melon baller.

"I think it's a Splitter. Hurry up, we gotta bounce," Marcus warned. Splitters were the villainous gang of savages running wild throughout the slums. Some were criminals, others deviant psychopaths', all considered serial killers due to the disturbing nature of the terrorizing acts of violence they carried out, simply for the thrill.

The pumping swirl of propellers pulsed heavy like a heartbeat from the sky, as choppers periodically flew patrol routes. Brodie finished scooping the corneas and put them in a protective medical casing. He made sure everything was secure, then dropped an acid solution onto the ground where any sweat or DNA of his own may have lingered, dissolving all traces of himself from the scene.

"Brodie Frost," the approaching Splitter announced. He walked tall, his legs stretching with each step as if he owned the pavement. He wore a ruby red Victorian winter coat, pinstriped black slacks and shit-kicker boots with metal tips. One of the Splitter's hands was hidden deep in his coat pocket, most likely with his fingers on a gun, the other was covered with a black leather glove. Behind the mask covering his face, the Splitters eyes stayed fixed on Brodie, paying no mind to Marcus.

Brodie kept his head down. He took off the medical gloves, replacing them with his everyday black ones. He kept his balaclava over most of his face, but removed the blue medical mask underneath and dropped it to the ground, along with the medical gloves.

"What do you want, man? You look like you're going to the renaissance fair," Marcus asked.

Just as the Splitter pulled his gun and lifted it in Brodies direction, Marcus drew his, forcing a standoff.

"People know who you are, Brodie Frost. Your ransom will set me up for life."

Brodie stood up and stared directly at the Splitter, not caring about the gun pointed at him. He drizzled gasoline from a small container over his discarded belongings on the ground and dropped a match. Proper disposal protocol.

"My ransom? What are you talking about, man?" Brodie questioned.

"You're the one that called the FBI on Billy Wessner, said he was responsible for the massacres of 25. Billy's a hero."

"A hero? Ha," Marcus interjected. "You don't know a thing about Billy Wessner. Anyway, that was years ago and it ain't true. Brodie didn't turn shit in. Now, bug off or my bullet meets your face." Marcus had a creative way of speaking to people. It was just what his brain naturally did with words.

Brodie wasn't the anonymous caller who had tried to rat out Billy after the shootings in the fall of 2025. It was their sister, Cece. After Brodie told her about meeting Billy in Chicago that day and how strange he was acting, Cece knew Billy had to be involved in some way. She couldn't help but call the FBI and CIA anonymously. It was a secret only she and Brodie knew and one that he would keep for life. He knew that if anyone found out it was her, she'd be dead before he could save her.

The Splitter kept his gun on Brodie, as he realized he was now stuck, clearly nervous about his next move. Brodie glanced up again, seeing that the monitors and choppers were out of sight. He had a window of opportunity, as they were momentarily hidden between the tall buildings that stood on either side of them. He nodded to Marcus and without question, Marcus dropped the Splitter with three shots.

"That's a new one. I guess your bro's telling stories, again." Marcus grabbed the shoulders of the dead Splitter and dragged the body into a hidden nook between buildings.

"Nah, just sounds like his fan club is growing. That's an old rumor. I'm not concerned," Brodie said, trying to play off the lie.

"Hey," Marcus looked at Brodie, "he knew your name. He said he could make money off your head. That's a new one. Just be careful," Marcus warned.

"Yep, I gotcha," Brodie said, dismissing any threat. He threw his skateboard down as they fled the scene with their goods. The hollowed-out carcass sat, stripped of any usable parts. The dead Splitter's body sat hidden, out of sight. Killing a Splitter to save your life was one thing, but to harvest a Splitter was a death sentence, just like gutting and harvesting a Scraper was. They were considered signs of war and neither Brodie nor Marcus wanted to start a war. "Hey, speaking of, you heard from Cece lately?" Brodie asked. "She hasn't been returning my calls. It's been like two months. We never go more than a few weeks without talking." If Splitters were seeking him out again, Brodie knew they might be trying to find the anonymous call tape too, if it was still out there. The whole thing made him uneasy and not hearing from Cece only made his worry grow.

"Last time we hooked up was before the assassinations. Like four years ago, when we were out in Vegas after your grandmother's funeral. Maybe she's just doing the Corners thing, working hard and living large. She messages every once in a while, but it's probably been a year. She is a gangster, just like you, you know that," Marcus said.

"Yeah, you're right. I'm sure she's just busy."

As a monitor drone hummed nearby, an alert sounded on Marcus and Brodie's work phone. It was their tracker. They needed to check in at a flash point. Scrapers had a built-in GPS for identification on their insert chips. Brodie didn't mind it. It was for their protection. Poachers would hide about, then swoop in, beat, or kill Scrapers and steal their goods, but they did their best to avoid the seasoned Scrapers that they knew were on the Droshure payroll. The poachers knew about the Scrapers track chips and knew they'd get shot if a monitor caught them mugging a Droshure Scraper. All scrapers had to check in and report within two hours of a scrape at flash points. If they didn't, a drone would locate them by chip. Early on, Brodie took the chip of a friend that was killed, Dave Collins. He was of similar height and eye color to Brodie. That's what made the Splitter's proclamation curious. How would they know who he was by name? Brodie couldn't shake the question.

"You think that guy saw a picture of me or something? How'd he know who I am?" Brodie asked as they made their way to the flash point.

"Don't do that to yourself, man," Marcus said.

Soon, the twosome reached a simple, steel pole with an 8 ½ x 11 metal box. As Brodie typed a code into his work phone, the metal cover lifted and a digital screen appeared. Brodie held his board as he lifted his wrist to the screen. Immediately, a full LED display appeared. It included his profile: [#184, Born: January 2, 1990, 38, 5'11, weight, heart rate, **MID-LEVEL SCRAPER**] along with a picture that wasn't him. All the stats and images were close, but none of it was Brodies. A green light flashed as a mechanical voice sounded, '**CLEAR. REPORT TO YOUR DROP WITHIN ONE HOUR.**' Once Brodie finished, Marcus held his wrist up to the visible LED screen.

They had an hour to get to Charlie, their drop guys place. As the roads became chunky and disrupted with death trap potholes, Brodie got off his board and secured it to his backpack. Once coveted neighborhoods were now littered with drug dens, pop up encampments, and quickly declining homes. There were still normals living throughout the Gutter, but they stayed in the smaller towns and rural areas, keeping far from any chance of trouble.

"Hey, I gotta pop in the store for a few things. Take the stuff and we can square up later, cool?"

"All good, bro. But you know Charlie gives a better price when you're with me," Marcus said. "That old dude does not like me. He only tolerates me because I'm with you."

"Charlie doesn't like anyone," Brodie said.

"You know he's keeping money from me, paying me low just because I'm not an 'official Scraper'," Marcus quoted with his hands sarcastically. "Just a measly apprentice."

"Let it go, dude. We won't be doing this much longer," Brodie added.

Brodie turned off, heading in the opposite direction from Marcus. A little while later, he walked into the Good Mart grocery store. Because of the chemtrail dump tests over the Gutter regions, unless a garden was inside a sealed structure and properly nurtured, fruit and vegetables couldn't be trusted and were potentially contaminated. Brodie knew the people that ran the Good Mart so he also knew the food was clean and freshly grown under cover. Some canned goods were smuggled out of the Corners and brought in, while other items were homegrown and made in the Gutter under strict and safe guidelines underground, unseen by President Boobain's flying spies.

Brodie scooted around the store, tipping back the fur-lined hood of his green parka, but keeping his mask up above the edge of his nose. In his cart he had water, iodine, salt, lemons, as well as a few chicken breasts, eggs, boxed brown rice and some arugula from the store's natural farm. He turned down the alcohol aisle and to his surprise, Nora, his ex, was standing just feet away from him. They'd split six months prior after dating for over five years. Though Nora had called him several dozen times during the last few months, Brodie never returned a single one. He was heartbroken and feared excuses and the friendzone. Avoidance seemed to be the best soother. But now, the explanation was right in front of him as she stood with Zoey, a woman Brodie knew Nora had previously been involved with. He tried to spin his cart around in the opposite direction, but it was too late.

"Brodie?" Nora spoke out. She was in her late forties, fit and only slightly weathered from duty and life. Brodie felt he knew her in her entirety, and in that knowing, he knew he'd never be good enough for her. When she had turned down his proposal it was all clear. He left before she could explain why. It knocked the wind out of him.

"Oh, hey Nora. Hi Zoey," Brodie squinted his eyes, trying to conceal his embarrassment and the emotion of his aching heart.

"You haven't returned any of my calls," Nora said. "I wasn't sure if you were ok. I was worried."

"Sorry. I've just been keeping busy. Marcus said he's been in. So..." Brodie paused.

It was awkward. He kept it to small talk as he maneuvered his cart past them, finishing his shopping.

When Brodie got home, putting his groceries away felt like it took forever, as he was once again lost in the history he and Nora had shared. Seeing her was tough, but just as he replayed the encounter for the eighth time, his private phone beeped. It was her. It was Nora.

'I need to see you. Can I come over in an hour?'

Brodie read the message a few times. He didn't know why, but this time he responded.

An hour later, Brodie let Nora in. She was wearing the flannel he'd bought her two years earlier. She threw her weathered, leather racer jacket on the couch as he stood, watching her. He waited for her to speak first, leaning against the kitchen counter across from her, but she just looked at him.

"So, what's up?" he asked.

"Why are you so mad at me?" Nora questioned.

"I'm not mad at you. We're good," Brodie said. "Being friends with you will just take some time. I guess you're back with Zoey. She's nice."

"Jesus Christ, Brodie," Nora dropped her head in frustration. "I said I wouldn't marry you because it would make you a liability, a target. But you just ran out. That's not fair. Then you don't return my calls? You know what I do for a living. Anytime we were lying in bed and it seemed like I was relaxed, I was. But I was also running twenty different scenarios in my head, making sure I had checked all the locks and camera's so that I wouldn't wake up to cold steel against my temple or you dead in my bed. If my guard is down, I endanger everyone around me, including you. I am an elite agent, Brodie. You know this. My heart would break if I lost you. You're an asshole for not responding to me for so long," Nora stammered.

"Marcus has been to the bar. He's told you I'm ok. Can't you just admit that you freaked out? You just don't think I'm the right guy. You weren't ready to commit to me, it's fine," Brodie said. He pushed himself away from the counter and got a glass of water.

"Brodie, I never freaked out. You will always be the guy. You've been the guy since the first time I met you," Nora said. As Brodie lifted the glass to his lips, Nora took it from his hand and placed it on the counter. Her dirty blonde hair fell in her face as she met his gaze. "If anything happened to you because of me, it would break me," she said.

Brodie took her face in his hands and kissed her.

CHAPTER 4

In the Corners

The sun melted into the brown, mountainous, landscape as most of the lights in the identical corporate office buildings went dim inside the small Los Angeles business park. Most workers had left for the day.

As twilight said its final goodbye, a businessman and woman exited one of the buildings and headed out to the main surface lot. When they reached the woman's car, strategically parked next to the man's, she grabbed his hand and put it between her legs.

"Follow me," the man said as he adjusted his growing erection. He got in his car and sped out of the lot, the woman trailing close behind.

The lot sat quiet as the security cameras continued their unobtrusive gaze. Eventually, a well-dressed older man strolled out of the same building and into the warm night air, an attaché case over his shoulder and a computer bag in his hand. He started toward his Volvo, whistling to himself.

Out of nowhere, a blue Mongoose dirt bike silently coasted toward the man. The only audible sound was the slow tempo of the chunky tire tread rumbling across the pavement. A passenger stood on the pegs, gripping the shoulder of the rider with one hand, and an aluminum baseball bat in the other. The driver of the bike had a backpack looped snugly around his shoulders. It was clear by their size that they were adults. Both wore black clothing with weathered Halloween masks covering their faces. As the noise of the bike's ticking chain grew louder, the businessman glanced over his shoulder. No sooner, the passenger swatted the bat at the business man. Ducking out of the way, he sprinted toward his car. Seconds later, the passenger hopped off the pegs and chased the man down. With one full swing, he swept the man's back leg with the bat, tripping him up, sending the business man skidding across the black asphalt.

Both riders off the bike now, one hurled a plastic bag over the business man's head, while the other grabbed the man's keys and wallet from his pockets. The driver's license had a special insignia on it, revealing the man's identity. His business card read – UN employee Nolan Petri - United Nations Division of Organized Crime & Human Trafficking. The biker held the card up to the sky.

"Billy," the passenger sharply whispered to the other biker. "It's him."

Billy, under the cover of a mask, gripped the bag tight around the man's neck, as the businessman passed out. Billy hit the button on the car keys and bolted over to the hybrid Volvo that beeped, while his partner in crime zip-tied Nolan's hands and feet. Nolan came to and tried to catch his breath, gasping for air as his eyes feverishly scanned the two men. Before he could speak, the other biker slapped duct tape over Nolan Petri's mouth. Billy drove Nolan's car over and the two dumped his body into the trunk of his own car, then threw the rest of his belongings onto the passenger seat.

"You ever say my name during a job again," Billy got in the other man's face, "I'll kill you myself. Now get out of here," he said. The other biker pedaled off the lot, as Billy walked around to the driver's side of Nolan's car. As he opened the door, a security guard stumbled outside, yelling from the edge of the buildings entrance. Billy, still under the protection of his mask, assessed the guard. After a pause, he got in the Volvo and sped off, removing all signs of what had happened. The security guard ran out at top speed searching in all directions for any clues or evidence. Nothing was left except the footage showing the two men under the cover of masks, but it wouldn't take long for them to figure out who was taken.

Later that night, Billy was having a little party at his home near the Bird Streets. The patio, which overlooked the city and offered a glimpse of ocean from the glow of the moon, was private and contained the standard wealthy bachelor pad amenities. Several guests played ping pong while others enjoyed cocktails at the edge of the pool. At the sound of the doorbell, Billy dashed inside to welcome more guests.

"Hey bro." It was Cece. She knew Billy was a creep, but at the moment she also knew it was best to keep him close. She knew Billy could ruin her at any time if he chose. She worked behind his back to get herself free of that hold, but felt it best to remain on his good side just a little longer. Cece was well aware Billy thought if he threw enough money at her, he could keep her content and under his control. It wasn't true, but she didn't mind the money so she played the game. The two shared an awkward yet playful, 'you're annoying', side hug.

Moments later, a bull of a man, Donte McKeon, walked in past Cece, not acknowledging her, and did a stupidly elaborate handshake with Billy. The two then hugged much more sentimentally than Billy and his sister had. As Cece walked ahead of them to get herself a drink, she caught Billy waving Donte into a side room. She shook it off and went out to the patio to find her friend Spider, who just happened to be a Splitter that balanced his time between the Gutter and the Corners.

Once they were alone in Billy's office, he dropped an envelope onto Donte's palm.

"Money for today's gig. There's a $5,000 Go-Card in there, too," Billy offered.

"Thanks, get what you needed?"

"It's with Droshure's team. He doesn't trust my guys to take it all the way, which is fine," Billy said. "I still get paid. Took off anything I thought I'd want ahead of time. Got a wicked Tag Heuer out of it. By the way, the kid you sent for the gig was close to getting a bullet from me. Don't send him out on my jobs anymore or I won't use you." Billy held his wrist up and showed off his newly acquired watch. "Anyway, check it out. Nice huh? Let's get you a drink."

When Billy and Donte returned to the main room, Cece was standing by the patio door with one of the faded out vintage masks over her face and a well-poured glass of wine in her grip.

"How does this thing even fit your face anymore? Why do you still have this, you weirdo?" she said, pulling the mask off, hurling it at Billy.

Spider stood next to her and took her hand. Everyone knew of Billy's wraith and it was obvious Spider was trying to steer Cece clear of it.

"Where did you find this? You know not to go through my stuff," Billy scolded.

"It was sitting on your dresser. I needed a sweatshirt you freak, calm down," Cece said.

Billy's eyes stayed fixed on her as he laughed, mimicking her. "Donte and Spider have ones just like it. I guess they're freaks, too," Billy asserted.

"Whatever Billy, Spider knows if I ever saw that weird shit around, I'd throw it out," Cece responded. "I still have nightmares about those stupid masks you and your friends wore when we were kids." She turned to Spider. "Do you know he use to come into mine and Brodie's rooms in the middle of the night wearing that shit and just stare at us. You're such a freak." She took a hearty sip of her wine. "Hey, you got any coke?"

Billy didn't like it when Cece acted as if he were off or defective, as if she was better than him.

"I do but you can't have any. Let's get fucked up, except for Cece. You're on wine punishment, no coke for you," Billy said proud of the penalty. He drizzled out a line of coke in front of her and sniffed it up with a smile. She didn't care. Spider would get her a toot.

Fifteen years earlier, when Brodie was overseas in Spain for a semester of college, their father, Nathan, moved Billy and Cece to California, abandoning their mother. Shortly thereafter, Nathan divorced her over Skype. Nathan never like Brodie and Brodie never liked Nathan. Billy, on the other hand, took notes, admiring his father's ability to get what he wanted at any crime or cost. Their father was a smart sociopath, a master embezzler. That was how he got the attention of Jacob Droshure and Timothy Boobain. Jacob Droshure hired Nathan Wessner without meeting him face to face to become the company's CFO as well as, Droshure and Boobain's personal accountant.

Before Timothy Boobain became President, both he and Jacob Droshure equally owned the Droshure Corporation. When Boobain went into politics several years later, he remained a silent partner. Billy, ever the proud pit bull was able to take care of a more pressing vacancy, that of their obstacles architect, their hitman and cleaner. Billy was the one they called when a situation needed resolving under the radar and untraceable, such as the Nolan Petri situation he'd just taken care of. It wasn't that Billy and his father were that close, it was that they were of the same breed, same blood, both sociopaths. They spoke the same dysfunction. Billy was well aware that if he physically stayed close to his father and the two men, he could move up the corporate ladder and eventually surpass them. A plan that he had carefully constructed years ago.

The crushing wave of destitution that swept across the US was a success, in part, because of what Boobain and Stoyton Society had hired Billy to do that day in October of 2025. The events that he helped choreograph that day would saturate history books for decades to come, trailing right after the assassinations of the president and vice president.

Soon after, the people's fear cleared a perfect path for Boobain to become Interim President. His immediate priority was to gentrify the country under the guise of safety and security, catering to those who could afford it. The rich welcomed the Corners Developments, as it promised security and elite living, to the point they nearly begged for it. Boobain and Droshure didn't exactly care about safety, it was the financial benefit and power they were ultimately after. Billy's father was one of several financial brains that moved money for them and their partners without a trace.

Early after the first Corners development, Billy reached out to Brodie and tried to convince him to work for a hospital there. Brodie never responded. That was Billy's last attempt at trying to 'help' Brodie. He knew if he got Brodie to the Corners early on, it could work to his advantage, but after the October massacres, Billy was certain Brodie was the one that named him as a person of interest and considered Brodie his enemy even more than he had before.

With Cece in the Corners, having a role on the philanthropic side of the Droshure Corporation, Billy kept her close, asking about Brodie just infrequently enough for her to think he might care.

Just then, Spider handed Billy two shots and kept two more for himself, tucked between his fingers.

"Got some bad news," Spider said as he downed one of the shots. "A Splitter I know was killed earlier today. Told his friends he was going out to kill the guy that ratted out the Maestro, to show you honor. That's what some of them call you in the slums, ya know. The Maestro," Spider smirked. "Anyway, he turned up dead. Thing is, he told his buddies the guy he was going after was Brodie Frost. Your brothers' names out there, Billy."

"I don't care if his fucking picture is suspended from the sky. I hope they smash him. Where was this?" Billy downed the two shots, coked up, hanging on the response.

"Someplace in old Wisconsin, Madison or Milwaukee, maybe?" Spider said, tipping back his second shot. "You better think about this. If you don't put word out, they're going to kill him for you. Some of these nut jobs will do anything to be on your team," Spider said.

"Oh, you're thinking I care if they kill him," Billy snickered. He patted Spider on the back then disrobed down to his underwear and did a cannonball into the pool. With his company cheering him on, several women stripped down and jumped in after him.

CHAPTER 5

B ack at Brodie's place, he took Nora's hand as they went down to the underground parking structure of his condo building to her maroon Yamaha R6. She knew how to drive a car extremely well, but in the Gutter, she felt she was less of a target and less catchable on a cycle.

"So, what are we doing?" Nora gazed at Brodie

"You tell me. You know what I want," Brodie said.

Nora's head dropped as she charmingly grinned. She took his hand and studied his face.

"I want to be with you. But, I'm not marrying you until all this with Boobain is resolved," Nora said. "A revolution is about to begin. The people want their country back. It's too hard to be happy right now. I just mean, sometimes it makes me feel guilty."

"It shouldn't," Brodie said as he pulled her close by the hips. "There will always be something going on. I just feel like you lost your ability to be happy because of your work. I don't want you to become numb."

"I have no control over that. I wish I did, but it's how I was trained," Nora said. "It's how I stay alive."

Brodie closed his eyes and leaned in, bringing himself closer to her atmosphere. He knew her job was what made her human but it was also what made her so closed off, at times. She lifted her face to meet his, grazing her lips against his, feeling the softness of his mouth as they sought solace in the final embers of their earlier sexual escapade. Nora backed out of his grip and got on her bike.

"When will I see you, again?" She said the words half joking, knowing he detached when his insecurities got the best of him.

"Just stay. You can stay forever if you want. You know that." Brodie caught himself smiling to the point he could feel air brushing against his open mouth. He hadn't smiled like that in quite some time.

"I need to talk to Zoey. She just got in two days ago. She's not going to be happy, but I need to ask her to leave. Come by the bar tomorrow if you can, prove your word." Nora leaned to the side and gave him one last hug, then peeled up out of the parking structure.

Twenty-five minutes later, Nora was home. She tried to slip in unnoticed as her part-time lover, Zoey, was fast asleep in the bed. Knowing today would be goodbye, Nora kissed Zoey on the shoulder, then rolled over onto her side, facing away from her. She tried to force herself to sleep, but wasn't having much luck. She was restless. And now, after just hooking up with Brodie, she couldn't stop replaying their encounter.

Life had slowed down for Nora when Boobain came into power. The IBI (International Bureau of Investigations) had been watching him for years because of his connection with the Droshure Corporation, while she was working other cases out of the country. Once he came to power, though, Nora was posted stateside and had been for the last three years. She was one of several props spread throughout the Gutter and the Corners. They were tasked with monitoring the human trafficking around their respective areas, keeping an eye out for Splitters, Corners spies, and any other atrocities that took place under President Boobain's authority. After years of working undercover all over the world, she was back in the USA with a gig as a bar owner in the Gutter, just one state away from where she grew up.

Nora leaned back on her elbows and stared out the window, through the swaying sheer curtains. On occasion, she heard the howling echoes of coyotes and barking strays fighting for territory and dinner scraps. For the most part, people in the Gutter stayed under shelter and out of sight best they could from sundown to sunup. Outside, Nora could see the lone car that had been watching her place for months. While he was watching her, Nora's team had eyes on the car, watching him from their hub location in Switzerland. They tracked full audio and activity not only of Nora, but of all their agents in the field. Nora knew at some point she'd need to take care of it, make the car and the driver disappear, but it wasn't time just yet.

Nora was the same age as Zoey. She wasn't interested in a relationship and Zoey expressed the same intent. It was a friends-with-benefits situation, though she knew Zoey hoped it would evolve into more. The two met and dated early in Nora's IBI training. Zoey was a secretary at the time, which meant she was a level one agent. Even though Zoey was supposed to visit for a few more days, the sight of her now weighted Nora with a heavy sense of guilt. Yet, Nora couldn't stop thinking about Brodie and what happened.

Brodie was the primary reason she had taken her current assignment. She had other good options, but it was the most important option and it kept her close to him. They met via a one-night stand when Brodie was in college decades earlier. Then five years ago, when Nora was visiting her brother, they ran into each other at a bar in Chicago. Their friendship quickly turned into an undeniable love story.

When they dated it was good. He did his job, she did hers. They had their time together and the distance when she was on jobs wasn't an issue. But when Brodie proposed, Nora was certain she loved him, but couldn't wrap her mind around colliding her job with marriage and the current state of the country. It gave her instant anxiety. After that, Brodie went into a funk. All of that was why what happened a few hours earlier confused her so much, but it was a welcome confusion.

Nora got up and wandered barefoot across the hardwood floor to the kitchen. She checked the gravel lot that sat outside the bar. Zoey's Mini Cooper was parked near the door. Nora's bar was rigged at every turn, inside and out. When the assignment was needed, they bought a rundown bar just outside of downtown. Why Milwaukee? Chicago was almost as bad as Creepers Row. It was overrun with gangs and crime, to which the IBI had undercover agents entrenched. Most in the slums avoided major cities, unless they were involved in the lawlessness and disorder.

Milwaukee and other smaller cities gave the IBI the luxury to embed all the security equipment they needed, yet still remain inconspicuous. Secret cameras, bugs, trackers, VPMs (voice pattern monitors), along with RHC scans for detecting RICs (Robotic Implanted Clones) that sat hidden in plain sight. It was a simple watch post. It wasn't for nothing though, the intel Nora and the other teams across the slums had collected so far was helping the IBI narrow in on the identities of corrupt members of not only Boobains team, but the Stoyton Society, as well. Stoyton's 'Order of the Realm', as they referred to themselves, were the IBI's primary target.

The Stoyton Society was an elite, secret society of extremely wealthy international moguls playing a real-world game of Risk. Nora had been briefed on their agenda long ago. First create a desire for things that beautify and simplify life, ways for people to covet security and vanity with implants and inter-body upgrades. After that, the dependence on those once coveted luxury items would kick in. No longer a want, but a need, to the point that the people wouldn't be able to live without those now needed elements. Stoyton's ultimate plan was to create the perfect kingdom on earth through dominance and control. The exploitation of the human soul. And their plan was working. People were falling for it, forgetting that gluttony was just like any other drug and one of the seven deadly sins.

It had never been easy for Nora to get close to people. She rarely let her guard down. She was paranoid about getting executed in her sleep. She had come close her first few years as a Nitzer scholar, shacking up with randoms as missions concluded, during downtime. Unfortunately, one of her conquests wasn't so random. He was hired to kill her and steal her electronics for intel. She smashed his face with the sharp edge of a hotel alarm clock and jammed a pen into his jugular.

With Brodie though, Nora felt a level of comfort and intimacy she'd never felt before. Zoey had been a good distraction for the last few days, but seeing Brodie confirmed that she was nowhere near being over him and inviting Zoey up had just been cruel. Nora's internal ruminating was disrupted by the sound of passing drones. Though her windows blocked out their ability to pick up any sight or sound inside her bar or home, the noise still agitated her.

Zoey stirred, turning to Nora. It wasn't a smile on her face that Nora saw, though.

"Can't sleep, can you?" Zoey mumbled. Groggily, she adjusted herself up to sitting, covering herself with the sheet, her bare leg dangling out over the bedside. "I know you snuck in after 3. You could have just told me to go home after we ran into him. I could even smell him on you when you came in, that hiker, woodsy, beer smell he must wash with for whatever reason."

"I am sorry. I was only going there to talk. I didn't realize how late it got," she said. She reached to Zoey but was rejected.

"Nora, cut the shit. I know you slept with him. Seriously, why did you even have me come here?" Zoey questioned her as she retrieved her clothes.

"I'm sorry. I had no idea we'd run into him. I don't know what else to say," Nora felt like a jerk but the words came out of her mouth defensively before she could stop them. "You know, the way you two have concerned yourselves with each other over the years is amazing," she said. She got out of bed and found Zoey in the living room, dressed and ready to leave.

"And you're so innocent. I'm out, this is too much. I don't want to be his stand-in, anyone's stand in. I love you, but I'm not an idiot," Zoey said.

"This has nothing to do with you. I told you I wasn't good for anything serious. I honestly thought he and I were done," Nora said.

"When you invite me here, then literally leave me in your bed to go fuck him... its shitty, it fucking hurts," Zoey said, patting at her heart. "Like, I feel actual pain." She walked to Nora and took her face in her hands, kissed her blankly, then let her hands drop. "It's not fair for you to still be in love with him and play with other people's emotions. Figure it out. And, if that means you have to flip up whatever rock that man-child decides to hide under, which he'll do again... I know you're strong enough. I'll call you in a month. Try to keep yourself safe," Zoey said. She didn't let Nora come any closer as she slipped out and left as the sun was just starting to rise.

A few hours later, an alert woke Nora. She got dressed and ran down the back hallway of her home, through the corridor between her house and bar, then downstairs into her safe room. To the outside observer, the bar and house were separated by several hundred feet, but the secret tunnel below ground level connected the two structures. When she sat down and clicked open her computer, it showed every room on her property, including the exterior perimeter surrounding the bar and house for a quarter of a mile out.

As Nora logged in, a scroll rolled across the bottom of the screen with updates and active situations. *A UN worker had gone missing, Nolan Petri. And two more Scrapers had been found dead in South Dakota.* Nora took note and continued her checks. When Scrapers were killed and harvested, then left in plain sight it was a warning. Typically, it happened when Scrapers were hiding people or playing both sides, doing things the Droshure Corporation didn't tolerate.

Nora read the story twice. Most didn't know that the Splitters were on Droshure's payroll. Why he would have one group on his payroll attack another could only signal one thing, that something bigger was coming. On the camera's, she noticed three patrons at one end of her bar doing shots. Nearby, she spotted a Splitter wearing some version of steampunk kill-boy attire with sunglasses covering his eyes, drinking a whiskey on the rocks. It was Dusty, one of her contacts, another IBI agent who was undercover. Nora patiently watched for the other patrons to finish their drinks and stumble out into the high noon sky. The Shadow Box, Nora's bar, was mostly locals, low and formerly middle class and harmless, along with a handful of people that stayed in the outer lands of the Gutter and fellow Gen X'ers occasionally coming in for the music and ambiance

Nora finished her entries and quickly shut down her system, leaving the cameras and surveillance programs running. She made her way into the bar through the exterior door. Within minutes, her bouncer, Motor, a brick of a man with Fabio long dirty blonde hair, locked the door as the staff of two sat down at the opposite side of the room, also undercover, level 2's. Nora stood behind the bar, in front of Dusty.

"You get the flag on the dead Scrapers in South Dakota?" Nora asked.

"Yep, and this hasn't hit the wire yet, but a Scraper from the area was murdered by a couple of Splitters three days ago in Chicago. Guy's name was Zyron Blake. They gutted him for parts and hung him by his feet outside a W hotel known for housing traffickers. Apparently, he's been sending info for over a year to some big wig with the UN that's been investigating Droshure and Boobain. He's not with IBI, it's not our agency."

"Did you get any records?"

"No. I had a team at his place as soon as I could after we left, but he didn't save anything. I was there when it happened. We surprised him. The Splitters I was with were already on his computer when he arrived. I was told we were just going to rile him up. During the fight, he was able to smash the computer. But either way, he must have put everything on a shimmer days before or something, to a secret drive, then dissolved the original. Splitters got some papers, but I saw them. Nothing important. There's a party at midnight tonight. A bunch of them will be there. I'm going to see what else I can find out," Dusty said.

"Just be careful. Do you know if he was talking to the same UN guy that's missing?"

"Not sure, but it'd be pretty ballsy for Droshure's people to kill this Zyron guy and send this kind of message to international power. They could have kept him alive," Dusty said. "I'm working to find out what their next plan is."

"All right. Keep me posted and keep your lines clean," Nora said.

"Just make sure you tell your Scraper friends to be careful, especially the ones that are helping the Underground. Splitters are getting cutthroat and careless. Boobain and Droshure's orders. They're getting paranoid and want no secrets. Keep an eye on any new faces in here, anyone that starts to behave suspiciously. And I'd think about getting rid of your friend down the street."

"Might be time. We have Scrapers out there, right?" Nora asked.

"We do, but they're nameless for their safety. I know who some of them are, only for protection as much as I'm able. Droshure has people working for him and they aren't always easy to spot. Some are well-dressed Corners stiffs, sleepwalkers in suits, and others might be blatant Splitters who want to be seen. It's the ones in between we need to stay alert for."

"I agree. Anything else? You want another drink?"

"That's all I got for now, but I'll take you up on another whiskey," Dusty said.

Nora fixed him another drink and signaled to Motor that they were done. He unlocked the door to the bar just as Nora took a seat in a corner booth. She lit a cigarette and pulled out her worn copy of Gillian Flynn's *Sharp Objects*. True crime was her distraction of choice. She secured her line and sent Brodie a message to come to the bar when he could.

CHAPTER 6

B rodie scrambled through a rundown sub-division decorated with worn and crumbling homes and fourplex apartment structures. Trash and garbage rested, strewn about the landscape. Grocery carts sat parked in front of homes in place of cars and SUVs for transport. Dangling shingles gripped onto the wind, as roof tiles and pieces of siding had become lawn ornaments long ago. Brodie skated down the main street running through the neighborhood, passing a group of teenage punks doing whip-its. A dozen cans of generic whipped cream stood lined up on the ground close by. One of the punks hocked a wad of phlegm in Brodie's direction as he went by.

"Hey gramps, can I get a ride? You ever hear of a car, ya loser?" the kid said.

Brodie continued past with a grin. He planned on riding his board until the day he died.

Finally, he turned a corner and emerged onto a main road at edge of a gas station. Broken-down cars with shredded and exposed wiring, along with old non-electric car parts sat scattered along the fringes. Old-school lights spelled out G-A-S S-T-A-T-I-O-N, flickering in Dayglo orange. The

G was burned out, along with one of the T's, while the other letters leaned south courtesy of rusted-out screws. Stray cats wandered across the gravel and dirt lot. Not much else was nearby. A vacant church, a store front and what used to be a boutique hotel, now inhabited by dealers all could be seen down the street as tweakers wandered in and out.

Mandates had been passed by President Boobain making electric cars the standard in the Corners. Pre-2024 manual automobiles were no longer sold and it was illegal to drive any non-electric car in the Corners. In the slums, that was all some could get their hands on, but Boobain made sure gas was expensive and always in low supply. Public transportation was available in certain areas, but rarely reliable. A few of the skeptical elite held on to their gas cars for their own peace of mind, storing them with friends still in the Gutter on the outskirts, running them off of carefully produced ethanol. Marcus and Brodie didn't bother with cars. Marcus had his motorbike and Brodie felt safest on his board.

Brodie slowed to a stop and stepped across the gravel lot toward four gas tanks sitting at the center of the station, all with padlocks on the handles. Next to one of the tanks, nestled on a folding chair sat Marcus, dressed in a zipped open puffy winter coat and gray striped auto mechanics coveralls. He sat reclined with his feet resting on top of an upside-down, rusted-out steel drum, sucking down the last bit of a joint with a roach clip. No customers. He was bored out of his mind.

"What up?" Brodie asked as he took Marcus's joint out of his hand and pulled a drag from it.

"What up, man. Nothing going on here. And she's driving me crazy. I don't know why two people have to be here. Nobody buys gas anymore." Marcus nodded his head toward the station building.

Inside the small building, Brodie caught sight of a haggard, hefty woman sitting at the counter. Through the window glass, he could see a roughed-up copy of 'The Secret' under her tight hold. Marcus scowled at the woman for a second. She noticed and flipped him off, then returned to her reading.

"She's got a crush on me," Marcus laughed.

"I'm sure she does," Brodie said.

Marcus flicked his nearly cashed joint toward the gas tanks, flirting with an explosion. He smiled at the clerk, just in time to catch her now on her feet. At the door, she stood ready to cuss him out. He waved, then focused his attention back to Brodie. As he stood and turned, the grip of a pistol could be seen edging out of the deep, back pocket of his overalls.

"I'm on my way to see Charlie, we on for beers later?" Brodie said.

"Yeah, Colorform at 5, cool? There's a chick that goes there that I'm kinda into," Marcus said.

"Works for me. I need your opinion on something anyway. Hooked up with Nora last night. I'm supposed to stop by later, but I'm kinda freaking out," Brodie said.

"Wait, you what?"

"I'll fill you in when we get there. Gotta get this stuff in the big chiller." Brodie didn't want to get into the details there. "I promise, I'll tell you everything. Just let me get this to Charlies."

"Just be careful. If that Splitter knows who you are, I'm sure others do, too," Marcus said.

The two slapped a handshake and Brodie was off down the road on his board before Marcus could question him any further. Marcus pulled out another joint, scraped a wooden match across a rock from the ground, igniting it. He sent the lit match twirling like a baton, in the direction of the gas tanks. It bounced off one, onto the gravel. The out-of-breath clerk hung her head out the door.

"Goddamn it, Marcus! Knock that shit off, yer gonna blow the God damn place up," the woman hollered. Marcus shrugged his shoulders at her. He sat back down, put his feet up and puffed away on his joint.

"And wouldn't that be a dream," Marcus said.

Brodie punched in the gate code and circled to the back of Charlies house. There he was bent over, muddling around in the temperature regulated, greenhouse. Charlie was the drop guy. He worked for Droshure, too. Scrapers and traders got their harvested parts and dropped them off with guys like Charlie. In turn, the drop guys had pickups every 7 hours with the warehouse boys and runners who would then transport to Droshure's clone factories and RBF's (robotic blend farms).

Charlie was a feeble man. At sixty-seven, he was mostly skin and bones, except for his bulbous boiler of a belly. He was dying of cancer and he did not give a shit. His garden consisted of tomatoes, carrots, lemons, a little bit of ginseng and a small isolated section inside for his marijuana plants. Brodie had been going to Charlie from the first day he scraped a few years ago. He had come to care for him like an uncle. Charlie saw Brodie as a number but also took to him a bit, often referring to him as, "kid". To Charlie, Brodie was the kind kid, the Scraper with a skateboard that sometimes brought him food, blankets and supplies.

Early on, Brodie mentioned in passing that his father worked for Droshure, but as things continued to escalate in the country, he never mentioned it again.

Charlie got up from the garden, almost toppling over, and hobbled to his bee boxes. The stench of musk and body sweat followed in his wake. Each step came with a grunt, as pain was a part of his daily life. Brodie threw a pebble across the cement patio with a grin, startling Charlie. He turned and saw it was just Brodie.

"Jesus Christ, kid. Don't spook me like that. You want me to crap my pants?" Charlie closed one of the bee boxes, put his gardening tools down. "How is it out there?"

"Kinda slow, but it's fine," Brodie said.

"Kinda slow? Tell that to those fucking poachers. They're nicking our product, gonna run us both out of business. You need to be looking for product, always," Charlie said through bouts of coughing.

"Body hunting isn't exactly my thing," Brodie said. "Besides, Scrapers going outside of their order lists risk punishment." Brodie did go hunting for bodies with Marcus when they worked off the Underground's drop list.

Occasionally, when they found a body that wasn't on Droshure's inventory yet, they took the parts for research and identification with the Underground. Charlie didn't need to know any of that.

"Whatever, let's get down and weigh your stuff, get you paid," Charlie said. Brodie offered him an arm, but Charlie wouldn't have it.

They went to a hidden area in the backyard as Brodie lifted a hatch covered by a patch of grassy turf revealing a set of stairs. Brodie grabbed the rest of his things and headed down the staircase beneath the patio, flicking on a light. Charlie followed behind, clutching the metal rail for balance. When they got to the basement it opened into a small interim chamber where they put protective medical smocks on over their clothes, plus stocking caps and booties for their feet. Everything in the room they were about to enter needed to remain sterile. Charlie pushed a button as the sealed doors opened. The two then went through a second secure glass door and into the work lab.

"I delivered a baby boy yesterday," Brodie said. Four metal medical slabs, several refrigeration coolers, and bundles of medical and hazmat containers surrounded them as he carefully began to remove the contents of his packs.

"You gotta stop doing that crap, saving lives. They catch you delivering babies..." Charlie shook his head in disapproval.

"They won't catch me. Besides, I'm a surgeon, there's an oath to help," Brodie said as he helped Charlie prep his cuts from the day.

"You *were* a surgeon. You quit. You're a Scraper, now. So, get that oath out of your head, kid or it'll get you killed."

"All of a sudden you're all preachy and shit," Brodie laughed. "Come on then, cranky man, let's get on with it." Brodie was proud of the set of eyes he'd scored from his find. He had a quick and steady hand and was a clean slicer. Before he knew it, Brodie was lost in the old days when he did surgery full-time, helping people.

"Hey, kid, wakey wake," Charlie snapped his fingers in front of Brodie.

"Sorry," Brodie said.

Charlie had a hankering for talking company right out the door. He was a lonely old man who liked to complain. He had an adult daughter living in California. His wife had divorced and forgotten about him long before the split. Brodie thought he didn't like people but it was all part of the façade. Charlie liked having people around to talk at, but he would never admit it. Most didn't like to stay. Charlie had about a dozen people that dropped with him. Other than that, his company was limited. Normally, Brodie would stick around for a beer and chat him up, but he wanted to get done and meet Marcus.

"Hey, you think any more about getting some meds from Droshure? Might take away the pain." Brodie helped get everything scaled. He watched Charlie wheeze through his mask, putting on his magnifying specs, scrutinizing each part.

"Look, I know all about the bits and pieces they're putting in new medicine. All that tracking shit. I don't want to be any less myself than I already am. I have my drugs. I don't want their shit," Charlie said. He had a steady supply of street drugs and marijuana plants and that was all he wanted.

"Well, it's always out there for you."

"Here, I can't give you much, but the eyes and the marrow will bring a nice stack. Just remember, if you're off it can cause a mutation, which means they have to scratch the batch, terminate and incinerate the product. Costs too much and means less money and electricity for us in the slums. You know they make the poor suffer first. We don't want them to find us unnecessary and just start using the trash cutters. You road walkers are much more efficient."

"Seriously, my cuts are fine. Why you busting my chops?"

"I'm not, kid, you're one of the best," Charlie said. "I'm just saying stay cautious. I'll give you 17k for the lot, including that crap you wasted your time getting. They only really want eyes, marrow, stem cells and vitals. The fat, too, but it's not worth the carry for price." Charlie coughed, patting his chest. Brodie knew that when Charlie was crabby and in pain, he offered less money.

"I'll take it. Have a seat, you seem tired today. I'll clean up and get everything packed," Brodie said. Though they both had masks on, he was a little nervous about Charlie contaminating things with his cough, or worse, picking up a final virus from body tissue that would end him.

"My goddamn ribs feel like they're sitting in a block of broken glass, of course I'm tired."

Finally, Brodie had everything cleaned up and ready for the runners. They went out through the secure room, into the change room and removed their med smocks and gear, disposing of the items in the incinerator. After all was burnt to ash, they headed upstairs, Charlie's lungs whistling a melody with every step. As he pushed the door open to Charlie's house, Brodie was hit with the smell of incense, patchouli, he guessed. Charlie disappeared to another room, only to return with sixteen wrapped stacks of one hundred dollar bills and a seventeenth stack of mixed increments.

"You know these are only really good in the slums, right?" Brodie inquired.

"You want half on a Go-Card, then? Trackable and hackable? I'm guessing not, so shut it. I gotta take a piss, but I want to ask you something. Don't leave yet." Charlie teetered off, making every attempt to avoid falling over.

"Fine, but hurry up." Brodie wanted the work day to be done. "You want me to get someone out here to clean for you? Or is that lady still coming," he yelled out.

"She still comes. Droshure's people send scrubbers once a week. No way I'd let those market rats in here, anyway," Charlie yelled back.

Brodie wandered around, peeking in cabinets mostly filled with honey jars. He reached up and grabbed two small ones for himself, sticking them in a clean part of his backpack. He wandered out to the patio and waited. Charlie's place wasn't the most popular spot to be leaving since some knew what he did for a living. For bandits, it was a good perch to wait in order to knock a Scraper for the jingles, the money. Finally, Charlie stepped outside.

"So, what you need, Charlie?" Brodie asked.

"You ever think about working in the chop shops? You know, at the RBF's putting all these parts back together in their dummy gardens?" The way Charlie spoke, Brodie knew it was a serious inquiry.

"You mean, do what goes completely against both of our philosophies? No, no thanks. What I do is bad enough," Brodie said.

"Hey, I have to ask. Everyone I recruit, I get a little tip. You might want to think about it. Big money, set for life. Plus, you wouldn't have to worry about getting killed, you'd be working inside a harvest yard."

"Charlie, no thanks. I'm not interested. Why the push? I never thought you'd be trying to sell working at those clone farms, so, what's up?"

Charlie paced, walking in circles, letting out gas as if it were bird songs, not even aware. "I have to ask. I have to keep an eye out for their recruitment list. I got wired your number along with two others. They said you guys had wanted skills and instructed me to try to get you all to level up. I'm sure they got eyes on me. I just don't want to get shot."

The Underground had been trying to recruit Brodie, aka Droshure #184, because of his skills and ability. He would be an asset working at the human plant, closer to the action, but he wanted no part. The further up the Droshure chain he went for the Underground, the more obvious he felt he would appear. It was way too close to his family. In Brodie's free time, he'd processed several cyborgs, mutants, and plenty of half-breeds running wild in the slums, all government experiments gone wrong. He'd taken them fully apart and rebuilt them in the Undergrounds labs to learn the elements and study the depth of inhumanity in their construction. There was no way he would go work up the line. He'd be too obvious.

"Well, at least do me this. Go see my guy Potter at the edge of the market. He'll have a car for you. Things are heating up. For some reason Droshure's interested in you. If and when there's a revolution, you're going to want to be able to move fast. Besides, you look out for me, you're nice to me. I want to help you out however I can. They're starting to blow up Droshure's stuff and when he fights back it will get ugly." Charlie got a pen and scribbled

Potters location on a piece of paper as phlegm-filled fireworks flew out from his mouth with every cough.

Brodie picked up a towel and threw it to Charlie. "Cover your mouth." He watched as Charlie scribbled out barely coherent letters. "I'll get the car, thank you. And you're right, shits starting to get a little weird. Watch your back."

"Keep yourself safe. I'm not going to be around much longer and I want to help those that I can." Charlie handed Brodie the piece of paper.

"I appreciate it. Take care of yourself. I'll be by in a day or so," Brodie said.

Brodie put the paper in his pocket, got his stuff and left. He watched Charlie through a back window as the old man grabbed a baggie and a spoon from a drawer next to the sink. Charlie poured a few small rocks onto the spoon and grabbed a lighter. It took him several tries to muster the strength to ignite a flame, but he eventually did. He sizzled down the rocks to liquid and drew the fluid up into a syringe. He tried to pull his foot up close enough to inject the needle between his toes but he couldn't. Brodie was tempted to go back and help, but instead, turned and left. There was nothing he could do to save Charlie.

As he traveled back down to the sidewalk, Brodie's phone flashed an alert.

CHAPTER 7

Audrey stretched out in bed and noticed Billy wasn't there beside her. Curious about his whereabouts, she ventured out into the living room and saw him planted in front of several tv's, sitting in his boxers. The international stock markets scrolled before his eyes like an infinite grid of information. None of it included American stocks. Not since Boobain got the US kicked out of most international markets.

"Hey, I know you're stressed, but you should get some sleep, Billy. We have the tour in six hours," she said. He acknowledged her with a grunt and kept his gaze fixed forward, examining the constantly changing data on the screens. "Did you hear me? We have the tour today and that matters more than your stocks. Do you want me to go without you?" Audrey ran her fingers through his hair trying to gauge where his attitude was at. He swatted her hand away.

"Knock it off. This is my project. I'm the one that set this all up. Why don't you go back to bed if you're so worried about it?"

"What is your problem? We started this together. My name, my Droshure name got us in the door," she said.

"I just mean it was my idea, my creation, my notes and my plan. A plan I had long before you came into the picture." Billy didn't miss a beat.

"Wow, tell me how you really feel," Audrey said. "Why are you being such a dick? What do you want from me?"

He picked up one of the phones beside him on the table and grinned wide. He lobbed it to Audrey and she caught it.

"Call him," Billy said.

"Your brother, again? Why would you draw attention to yourself right now, Billy? The fact that you get a boner from pranking Brodie is a little psycho."

"If you love me, just do it." Billy knew what he was doing, playing another one of his games of control. Audrey found Brodie's number on Cece's old phone and called, putting it on speaker. After several rings, Brodie answered.

"Hey C, where've you been? I've been trying to reach you for weeks," Brodie said on the other end. "Cece? Hello?"

Audrey held the phone out, away from her ear, keeping her gaze blankly fixed on Billy. She smiled and drew the phone closer to her lips to speak, but Billy snatched the phone and hung up.

"You have no idea how much that turns me on."

"You're sick," Audrey said. She took him by the hand and pulled him into the bedroom. "Come back to bed. We have to be ready in 4 hours and it takes an hour to get there." She stood at the edge of the bed and pulled her nightshirt up over her breasts and bent over at the waist with a naughty grin. Billy spanked her bare ass, clutched her at the hips.

"That a boy," she said.

Later, an hour outside of LA, Billy and Audrey walked through a massive underground hangar. In one section, an incased and protected assembly line of prosthetic limbs moved on conveyer belts as manufactured artificial fleshy upper and lower arms dropped into large bins. Nearby, several other 3-D printers and contained assemblies ran on auto as lower and upper legs, hollow fleshy torsos, and most of the other parts it would take to create a human shell moved down a line.

Across the room, there was a secure steel door with a sign hovering above it that read 'RealPro2'. A twenty-something, pony-tailed, design engineer pointed out different areas of the hangar, explaining to Billy and Audrey what else was going to fill the structure.

"This area just houses the fleshy bits, so to speak. Hands and feet are developed in another room because of the tech hub in the digits. We're still waiting for the Board to decide where they'd like the GPS installed, most likely pectoral muscle. They've taken the modifications that were primarily QL enhancements for the mentally disabled and are already testing the upgrades and implants," the hipster engineer explained. "Currently, there are 150 vets and 100 elders with dementia whose families have agreed to let them participate and be activated. All have signed the NDAs and given full body approval for the GPS implant. It might seem like the so-called Skimmers were a huge failure, but the data collected from their malfunctions immensely accelerated the fine-tuning of this round of implants and enhancements we're currently testing. In appro..." the lanky engineer paused, looking at Billy, waiting for him to answer his ringing phone.

"Excuse me," Billy said as he stepped to the side for privacy. "Hello?"

"Billy, it's Roach, just wanted to inform you that all is set to go with the Needles plant," the voice on the other end said.

"Ok, it's gonna leave tracks to the Underground, right?"

"Exactly, as you requested," Roach said.

"Call me when it's done." Billy hung up and rejoined Audrey just as the engineer was handing her his business card.

"Everything all right?" Audrey asked.

"Better than expected. Handing out cards I see. I'll take one, too." Billy touched Audrey on the small of her back for ownership, as they continued forth.

"Over there is where you'll have the automatic distribution center most likely. We're just happy that our design will work for your product and goals. We're pioneering the automated production centers that will only require human intervention twice a week, plus on call staff and remote technicians to monitor in case there are malfunctions with the AI staff," the engineer explained.

"We get it. We know most of this. We broke ground on the RPI Health-care Spa premiere location," Billy said. "We want people to think they are going for a relaxation treatment that they will emerge from feeling youthful, enhanced and refreshed. We're taking the fear out of going to the hospital so it feels more like going in for a simple upgrade," Billy paused, waiting for someone to praise him. Instead, Audrey picked up where he left off.

"Eventually, we will want to move everything technical overseas. We'll keep the manufacturing in several secure plants in the middle regions of the country, fully safe and secure, obviously. But for now, this is perfect for where we are with the full scope of the project," she said.

"I just want to remind you again of the NDA and other confidentiality forms your company signed regarding this project. I'd hate to see the contract get pulled," Billy said.

"There is no need to worry, sir. The only people that I've spoken with on this are those on the project, the head of operations and the CEO. In turn, the CEO directs the teams but gives no information on who the client is. This is a strictly need-to-know basis. We've worked on several international and government contracts in the past so many of the older folks working here are familiar with the *'don't ask questions, just do your job'* motto. We want to ensure you one hundred percent anonymity. None of the current non-tier 3 employees know exactly what the product is and they don't know who the client is," the engineer said. "They want to get paid, so they know they aren't to ask questions."

Just then, Billy got a text from Spider, simply worded *'Everything's set with the drop guy.'*

"Well, we're looking forward to meeting in two months with your bosses to tour the underground AF hangers we acquired in China. We are set to release the Living Solution within six months so everything has to be ready. Six months after that is released, we expect to launch phase one of RealPro. Your bosses know what comes after that. And just keep reminding them no helping hands from Denmark. Denmark, bad, China, good," Billy's ego came through as he tried to flex his authority at the wickedly smart young engineer. He knew the engineer was far more intelligent than he was, but he didn't need to accept that.

"I got a glimpse at the test commercials for the Living Solution from my bosses. It's a great spot. I have to ask, who is that gorgeous woman in it?" The engineer caught Billy off guard with such a benign question, sacrificing the moment for superficial desires.

"I can't tell you, but if you're lucky," Audrey said, "maybe someday you'll get to meet her. We're going to walk around a bit."

Billy awkwardly took Audrey's hand as the two wandered the across the 'in development' Innovation Production Center, checking things out. Billy gripped her tight.

"Now, you're hitting on people in front of me?"

"Look, I know a lot more about these products than you think. I know you may not be a fan, but I'm still Jacob Droshure's daughter and with that comes knowledge and some power," Aubrey pulled her arm from Billy's grip. "Don't forget it."

CHAPTER 8

The setting sun faded, as Brodie made his way to Colorform, one of the few bars that had managed to retain its original ambiance throughout the class wars, storms and the countries divide. It was an edgy and dark industrial club. Most of the patrons were an urban blend of plastic posers, sellouts and goths that just loved the vibe. A small population came for the betting rooms in the back. Brodie just liked the beer list.

He turned a corner and saw the multicolored neon letters spelling out, *COLORFORM*, hanging, half lit. Beneath it, Marcus stood puffing on a joint, in between flicking matches off his teeth. Five rusty stick-shift cars and two modern sedans sat parked on the plot of dirt that half mooned around the bars entrance. Parked in front, a Neptune blue Porsche Taycan was parked just to the side of the door.

"I'm ready for a beer," Brodie said.

Marcus craned his neck, making sure no one was around, then walked around to the hidden side of the Porsche. "I gotta take a piss. I wonder whose piece of shit this is?" Marcus took a leak on the car's front tire. "Fuck these rich Corners fucks," Marcus laughed. He zipped up and rejoined Brodie at the door.

"Don't forget to wash your hands, dude." Brodie stayed away from him, exaggeratedly avoiding Marcus as they walked in.

"Right, cuz it's not like there isn't piss along the walls all over the slums. You got your stupid gloves on anyway," Marcus playfully reached out at him like a zombie.

Inside, Brodie scanned the bar. Modern house music barreled out over the speakers, bumping against the walls as several grooved out on the dancefloor. Neon edgy, red, green and blue lighting decorated the club. A soothing soft blue lounge area arched just off the dancefloor with several couches partially hidden from view. People stood in gaggles conversating and flirting, while others relaxed. Dressing to impress was a thing of the past in the Gutter. Now days, people dressed for comfort and in whatever they could get their hands on. After the split and rich flight to the Corners, many in the Gutter raided homes and acquired plenty of clubwear, but no one was judging anyone on appearances in the slums.

Two back betting rooms occasionally released the noise of booing and cheers from ongoing college and professional basketball, baseball and international soccer games on huge screens. Football was no more because of how dangerous the game had become. There were fewer colleges and fewer professional teams, but the demand to watch something, to have something to root for, grew even higher after the country broke apart. Colorform was full of nooks and crannies that allowed patrons a cool space with discretion and the freedom to do what they pleased, be it drugs, betting or other publicly inappropriate, illegal activities.

Marcus chatted up the bartender as Brodie sat half paying attention, his eyes wandering across the room, taking inventory. He thought about Nora and their interaction. At the end of the day, she was on a major operation and the timing probably wasn't right. He wasn't giving up, but he was preparing for rejection, he functioned better that way. It was all a cluster in his head, but his thoughts broke apart as he noticed someone across the room.

There on one of the lush couches in a partially visible nook sat Donte, Billy's friend and comrade, wearing a double breasted, pin-striped suit. He sat reclined with his arms over the back of the couch as a trampy scab's face bobbed up and down in his lap. From what Brodie could see, her face was drug punched, might have been the lighting, though. Brodie turned away, hunching forward at the bar, hoping to go unnoticed. He glanced back over his shoulder, only to realize he'd been spotted as Donte pointed at him. Donte zipped his fly and threw a few bills at the scab.

"Ah fuck, I can't believe that assholes here," Brodie said.

"Who?" Marcus turned around and scanned the crowd.

"Donte McKean, the loser in the suit. Probably his Porsche you pissed on. He's been friends with Billy since college. He was always fucking with Cece, being all handsy and shit, trying to pressure her into stuff. Back then, a couple times I told him to back off," Brodie said, looking over his shoulder, again, then leaning in towards Marcus. "When he didn't, I broke his nose. A few months later, he and his friends beat the shit out of me while Billy just laughed. Mind you I was like a junior in high school. I still have a scar on my chest from the beatdown. He's a Corners guy. I think he works with Billy for Droshure. But," Brodie shrugged, "maybe he's seen Cece." He spoke fast as Donte was approaching. He stepped up with a mouth full of horse teeth and slapped Brodie on the back. Brodie stood up before he could do it again.

"Brodie fucking Frost. What are you doing in this shit hole?" Donte asked, not caring about the response. He slammed his hand on the bar, barking at the bartender. "Hey shakes, order for McKean ready or what?" The bartender flashed Donte a dirty look.

"You seen Cece?"

"Sure, seen her and a whole lot more," Donte winked at Brodie.

"Right, that's why I saw you talking to your girlfriend over there, you run out of Corners tricks?" Brodie said not wanting an answer.

"You're a funny little fuck," Donte said.

"Seriously, why are you down here? You live in California. What's your business?" Brodie asked.

"Free country, plus I'm cleaning up after some loser Scraper, Zyron or something. The dipshit committed suicide. You might look into it." Donte chuckled at his own words, overconfident and far too proud of his wit.

"Everyone knows he got diced by Boobain's kill boys. His crew is getting sloppy," Brodie said.

The bartender returned with a bag of synthetic, microwaved food for Donte. He snatched it up and turned back to Brodie.

"Well, I didn't kill anyone and I don't give a crap who did. I'm just here to pull his stack." Donte pulled a French Fry out of the bag.

"Some Corners chick said the same thing yesterday to one of my buddies. So, I'm wondering what are you guys' fishing for? Whoever killed him, already took his stacks so it can't be about the money. I heard everything was gone." Brodie stayed focused on Donte, not breaking eye contact. Marcus was at his side, watching the two men, knowing at any point punches might be thrown.

"Hey, you had your chance to be on the other side of this. Could be working in a Corners hospital right now making big dime instead of playing Operation on the scum and trash dolls living down here."

"There's no way I'd work in one of those clown shops you guys call hospitals."

"You're delusional."

"Look, have you seen my sister?" Brodie asked.

"Well, well, well. I guess you really haven't heard from her. The plot thickens," Donte toyed with him. "Your sister is a drunk, she's a tosser. Stand still long enough and your bro will be dropping her off on a corner... NOT in the Corners."

"She's not a tosser. You saying she's working for him?" Brodie could feel his body tighten and swirl with anxiety.

"Hey, get pissed if you want," Donte spoke in between exaggerated bites of French fries, "but she's a tosser. She just gives it out like candy," Donte said, heading toward to the door, but Brodie blocked his way. They stood nose to nose.

"My sister wouldn't even sit in a room with you. The scabby flopper that was nose deep on your dick five minutes ago, that's more your level. Ceces got more class than to be with you," Brodie said.

"She's trash, Brodie. A drunk party bumper. Your bro has parties, she locks in the clients. Man, the last time I had her, those sweet hips rockin' in these hands," Donte cupped his free hand in the air as if it was an ass cheek, then smiled. "Might not be her favorite push, but she sure likes my stacks enough to ride my di..."

Before Donte could finish, Brodie's fist was following through on a well-placed punch that kicked heavy into Donte's face. He held his cheek, impressed by the effort. Brodie took the opportunity to pull out his phone and take a picture of Donte's face.

"Marcus, this is Donte. Donte this is Marcus. Now tell me where she is," Brodie said. Marcus, trying not to laugh, extended a hand to shake, but Donte slapped it away.

"Taking my picture? You always were a fucking weirdo." Donte spit blood onto the floor, inches from Brodie's boots. He stuck his fingers in his mouth, pulling out a back tooth that had become a casualty of the punch. Brodie and Marcus didn't move, waiting for Donte to answer. He licked some lingering blood from his lip. "If you're patient enough, I'm sure your brother will toss her out with the rest of the trash and she'll be swimming down here in the Gutter soon enough. Don't ask questions you don't want the answers to. Now get out of my way." Donte tried to maneuver past Brodie toward the door.

"Where is she?" Brodie pleaded, but Donte ignored him, pulling out another fry. Brodie swatted the bag away as fries fell to the floor. Donte caught Brodie's hand and punched him in the stomach. Brodie stomped Donte's leg by the knee, sending him off balance, but Donte had a good three inches of height on Brodie and recovered quick. He grabbed a nearby pool cue and cracked Brodie in the ribs. Before things could get worse, Marcus pulled out his gun and aimed it at Donte.

"Time to leave, big guy," Marcus said, simple and matter of fact.

Donte shook his head laughing at Brodie. "You're nothing, Frost. You wanna find your sister, call your brother and schedule a dip." Donte pushed the door open and left. Marcus and Brodie followed him outside and snapped another picture, this time of Donte and his car, license plate. "Fuck off, Brodie," Donte said, flipping him off as he got in and peeled out of the lot.

Brodie and Marcus made their way back inside the bar and sat back down.

"What the fuck was that, dude?" Marcus asked.

"He's just as big a psycho as my brother, but dumb as a brick."

"You really think Cece's been with him?"

"I don't know, but I'm going to find out," Brodie said, still taken aback by what had just happened. He sent the picture of Donte and his plate with a description of both to Krispy, a good friend of his. Many didn't know it but Krispy was like the Al Capone of the Gutter because he was so heavily connected. "I got a call from Cece in the middle of the night and she said nothing. Somethings not right," Brodie said, his escalating frustration now visible as he slammed his beer.

"Jesus man, what the hell," Marcus said. "So, what else was it that you wanted to talk about?"

"I ran into Nora and Zoey yesterday. She came over two hours later and we hooked up," Brodie said.

"Wait, they both came over? You're living my dream."

"Just Nora," Brodie said, coddling his ribs with one hand.

"Well, I don't think they're together if that's your concern. Pretty sure Zoey just got in a few days ago. You're on your own though," Marcus laughed, shaking his head. "I told you not to ghost her after she turned down your proposal. Obviously, she's still in love with you."

"She told me to come by today. That's all she said, swing by if you get a chance. I'll go tomorrow. I mean, what if she says it was a mistake?"

"Come on, we're going over there. I'm not listening to this shit all night." Marcus stood up, threw some bills on the bar and put his coat on.

"Dude, no," Brodie said.

"Let's go."

"Nope, can't. I'll go tomorrow," Brodie was adamant. "I'll let her know. I'm all beat up. Just sit and have another beer with me. I gotta make a quick call, though. I'll be right back." Brodie got up and went to a far corner of the bar, cleared his private line and dialed. He cupped his sleeve around his phone to muffle his voice from anyone that might come close.

"Hey Krispy, it's Brodie, I need to place an order."

"I got your pictures. Name it," Krispy said on the other end. His tone was flat but his focus was steady and could be heard through the phone.

"Names Donte McKean. Left Colorform about five mins ago, prob headed back to the Corners. He's got info on my sister. He has information I need. New Mod Blue, sweetheart, Porsche Taycan," Brodie explained.

"I'll put my crew on it. Pick up or delivery?"

"Pick up."

"Done. I'll make sure it's stored in a special place. Come by tomorrow after 9pm and I'll have information on where to pick it up. It's party time," Krispy said.

Brodie hung up his phone and ran a shiver on it. It was a program that dissolved the call data and all traces of anything sent from his phone, leaving it only accessible on Krispy's end.

Later that night, Brodie returned to the seventh-floor condo he called home. It was secure and filled with mostly over 55'rs, a quasi-retirement residence. The riff raff didn't bother with the elderly. Old parts weren't worth as much. For that reason, Brodie remained hidden. The roof top community room and deck had been permanently closed. Before the newer monitor drones started popping up, he and Marcus would sit up there late at night and search the sky for stars with a few beers and forget about reality for a while.

Brodie plopped down on his couch and cracked a beer. He grabbed his Rubik's Cube, twiddling it around to fully solid sides, while he tried to hush his thoughts. He didn't believe a word Donte had said. He needed to find Cece and he knew Krispy would come through. He just hoped it would be sooner rather than later. If Donte had answers, Brodie would stop at nothing to get them.

The Gutter was becoming a place where Brodie could no longer hide in plain sight. The safety was wearing off quickly, especially given what the

Splitter from the other day had said, that word was spreading that number 184, the skateboarding Scraper, was Brodie Frost, 'the guy that ratted out Billy Wessner'. Even if they didn't know he was Billy's brother, they still pinned him as a rat.

Brodie tossed the almost finished cube onto the coffee table and stretched. His body cracked and popped from wear and tear. He turned, searching out the window for the night. It was dark. Streetlights automatically went off at 8pm to encourage obedience. Being out at night required a gun, a mask, and a means of communication, in the event that something happened. Brodie hated what Boobain had done to the country, but he was trying his best to never let it keep him from some resemblance of normalcy.

He sent Nora a message letting her know he would come by after the sun came up. Within seconds, she responded with only two words 'be careful'. The simplicity of it threw him off. Normally, she would want to clarify the time or if it would be at the bar or her house. The brevity of the message made him nervous, but ruminating on it would have to wait in line. He needed to stay on task. He clicked around on his computer, searching on the InterWire, trying to find any clue about what his sister might be up to or where she might be.

Before he got too involved, he grabbed a hoodie from his room. His bed was a black metal platform frame with a king size mattress resting on top of it. He'd built it mostly from scratch right after the split using materials from abandoned homes. He made secret compartments underneath the frame to hold two hand guns, several cases of bullets, two gas masks and two fully stocked doomsday survival backpacks. One was for Nora. On one of his bedroom walls rested a poster from the 1950 World Cup in Brazil. He hadn't played soccer in years but the poster reminded him of back when things were normal. The rest of his walls were bare.

He lived as simply as he could, knowing that things could escalate into a revolution at any time. That was the best-case scenario. Worst case was that Boobain would go mad and decide to terminate everyone in the Gutter, noxious gas, diluted water supply, perhaps. It was the reason he had all of his routines. Clean filtered water, clean food, clean air. When he first moved in, Brodie had stolen fifty carbon monoxide detectors and left them outside the doors of his neighbors, anonymously. He'd even gone so far as to have Marcus help him inspect the HVAC systems in his complex twice a year, making sure the air quality was decent. He felt he was doing a good job of protecting the elders in his building.

Finally, he sat back down and pulled up his messages. He clicked his fizzle into motion, blocking hacks, tracks and viruses. He was on the secret messaging site of the Underground. It was safe, and once he viewed the messages, they wiped automatically as if they'd never been sent. But still, Brodie didn't want to take any risks and layered his protection.

He had four messages. The one that caught his eye was a video sent from one of his allies, Dodger. He clicked on the link and a video appeared. It was a commercial. A beautiful, blonde woman with perfectly proportioned assets and flawless skin slowly strolled through a meticulously manicured garden park. It was Cece.

'Hi, my name is Karen Russell. Let me tell you a secret. I'm closer to 60 than 40, but you'd never know it because I look like I'm 30. Now, let me ask you this, are you sick of being tired by noon, gaining weight after eating the foods you love, not getting a full night's sleep, catching colds, diseases, even not being able to please your man, or vice versa guys? Well, I am the Living Solution and you can be, too. I'm not talking about living forever. I certainly don't want that. Believe me, I've thought about it,' Cece said as she walked through the park, talking to the camera. *'But what you see before you is the new way of aging. The Living Solution brings with it a long, healthy*

and happy life. With scientifically designed genetic modification supplements and inserts composed specifically for your individual DNA, health goals and body design, you can finally start living the life you've worked so hard for, the life you deserve. The scientists at the Droshure Innovative Science & Technology Labs have studied for decades to come up with a safe and effective, personalized supplement that in tandem with ideal homeostatic programming inserts, pledges just that. Trust me, I am the Living Solution.'

Brodie couldn't believe what he saw as the woman's image froze at the end of the commercial. Immediately, he knew it was Cece. It didn't make sense, though.

"This can't be real?" Brodie was in disbelief. She looked made up, almost a plastic. Her hair was dyed. She appeared different than the last time he'd seen her, just a few years ago.

When they spoke six months ago, she made no mention of Donte or of being in support of enhancement blenders. She certainly didn't give the impression that she was going to be part of a commercial promoting Droshure's crack pot science. It wasn't her thing. Brodie recalled several conversations making fun of plastics, as she called them. The made up, liposuctioned, filler infused people she'd see wandering about in the Corners. Plastics had a different glow, an unnatural one. Women willing to inject whatever it took to keep their husbands or catch the wealthy mogul, anything to stay young and desirable. Neither she, nor Brodie wanted any part of that world.

Cece couldn't stand the Boobain regime, but she'd told Brodie she'd become dependent on the money she was making. She smoked pot, dated tradesmen, and hated the politics and the fake people. She was more like Brodie, both in her interests and demeanor, than most realized. The only part of her that was like Billy was her hunger for money. She hadn't learned how to be modest, like Brodie had. But then again, as a woman, her opportunities were much less financially beneficial than his.

Brodie closed his portable, as a picture on his nightstand caught his eye. It was the only picture he still had of his whole family. He pulled it close, absorbing how happy he looked in it. He stood in the front, away from Nathan. Brodie smirked. Even as a kid he was a nerd, with his crazy curly hair and thick-rimmed glasses. Now, they were the only kind he'd wear. He flipped the picture over. Their ages were scribbled on the back; Billy, 12, Cece, 10 and Brodie, 6. It was long before everything happened, way back when they were the complete mirage of a happy family.

Brodie picked up his phone, cleared a line and called his mom. After Nathan divorced her and left Jaclyn with nothing, she moved overseas to Spain and started painting, again. Not long after, she remarried. An immediate upgrade. The male voice that answered was one Brodie found comfort in. His mother never took his calls. She was still mad at him for not going overseas with her when she left. But knowing his convictions didn't align with Nathan's was something she had always loved about Brodie. He was her brave little boy, but she also feared that his bravery would lead him into harm's way.

"Can't sleep?" The baritone voice belonged to his mother's husband, Izzy. Shortly after Jaclyn landed in Spain she met him, a furniture maker. They've been together ever since they first locked eyes, almost 11 years now.

"Hi Izzy. Any chance she might talk to me?"

"Hey, sport. Sorry, she's having a low day today. But, if it helps, she always asks how you are after you and I talk."

"Is she still painting?" Brodie asked.

"Yep, she has several pieces for you when you come. You know, she'd love to see you. That's all she wants."

"You guys know how it is here. It's going to be awhile." Brodie hated not seeing his mother. "Has she talked to anyone else in the family?"

"Yourself and Cece are the only two she acknowledges as family. We haven't heard from Cece for few months, but that's not out of the norm," Izzy reassured.

"Well, tell her I love her and I miss her."

"I will, glad you're keeping yourself safe. I've said it before, if you need transport here, I can get you on a plane," Izzy said.

"Thank you, and thank you for being there for her. I need to be here right now, but soon. I promise. I'll call again in a month or so. I love you and please tell her I love her." Brodie hung up the phone feeling empty.

When Brodie was little, Nathan threw all of his mother's paintbrushes and her easel into the firepit when she was out of town. That was after he found out about the affair. After that, Nathan didn't let her travel without him and sold her painting studio in Chicago. She became a woman that lied to herself every day to avoid reality. Brodie always thought her loyalty was to Nathan, but he later realized it was to her children.

Brodie held the picture, fighting through his past. In a knee jerk reaction, he shredded it into several pieces, then sent them scattering across the room like confetti. Annoyed, he retrieved the pieces from the floor, pouring them in a drawer.

CHAPTER 9

J ust before dawn, Nora rolled out of bed. Discretely, she peeked out the window at the car sitting down the road. She sent a message through her device, then threw on some black pants and a black shirt. She secured her pistol in its holster and grabbed a pair of black gloves and her midnight-lava-black helmet. She dashed down the stairs and into a closet, pushing aside some coats. She traced her palm along a now visible sensor in the drywall, then pushed it ever so slightly, lifting the back wall of the closet up like a garage door. She disappeared down the covert subterranean hallway ramp to a garage where her motorcycles and two cars sat parked. She picked her black Kawasaki Ninja for the early morning mission. All the labeling had been painted over and hidden so it was just black and gun metal silver, void of identifying markers.

Nora wormed through a snaking tunnel until she emerged a block away, seemingly out of nowhere. As the motorcycle hummed quietly in the darkness of the predawn sky, she exited and rode along a gangway to the street. Moments later, she was right behind the car that had been parked across from her place for months. She silently rolled up to the driver's side and fired two shots. She pulled out a black walkie talkie.

"It's done. Coordinate 24R 947C. Confirmation of termination. Scrub the car. It's probably bugged," Nora said.

She peeled off around the corner and disappeared into the city for an early morning ride.

CHAPTER 10

Shortly after sunrise, Brodie shivered as he woke to a chill, noticing a frost that clutched his windows from the outside. It had snowed a few days prior, earlier than normal, but quickly melted, only leaving a dusting of leftover powder. The sun pierced in, but brought with it, no warmth. With regulated heat on the water and heating system, the residents had to do their best to stay warm. In fact, everyone living in the slums was in a similar situation. President Boobain regulated anything he could, creating near unlivable conditions for many, especially through the Midwest winters. Brodie left blankets for different tenants at random times.

He rolled out of bed and showered. His sleep the night before hadn't been great. His mind was wide awake, trying to reconcile the interaction with Donte. His eyes caught sight of the dried blood locked in place on his knuckles. His head gently pounded, steady. Brodie put on his Carhartt beanie, pulled up his gaiter and wrapped a scarf around his neck for extra heat. Though he was use to wearing his headphones and listening to music, he left them at home. He needed to be alert and ready for anything. Brodie grabbed his gloves, his sunglasses, and this time left his favorite green parka hanging in the closet. Instead, he grabbed a black one that he hadn't worn since the prior winter. He double checked everything and made sure he had his gun, then trekked out into the day.

Brodie traveled down the side streets on his skateboard, trying to avoid the fulltime hustlers and beggars. Though he lived in the Gutter, fairly safe areas still existed when the sun was up. He cruised down the center of the road, past hollowed out apartment and condo complexes. Even so, some in the communities continued to gather weekly for group cleanups, removing downed tree branches and debris from storms and vandalism.

The ordered killing of a Scraper stuck in Brodie's mind. The poachers were easy to spot and fend off, but if Scrapers were being targeted by Splitters, Brodie knew he had to stay as covered up and inconspicuous as possible, even in daylight. He needed to change his routine and so far, he was doing an ok job of avoiding as many recognizable patterns as he was able.

A few blocks from home, he eyeballed the camera's that adorned the street corners around him. Some had been spray painted over by taggers and rebels, while others hung, fiercely observant. He and Marcus had mapped out all the cameras that had been covered or shot out and created less surveilled routes for them to travel when possible. The camera's that did work, were able to tract for a distance of 1200 meters and swivel 360's, recording activities and facial recognitions. A full face was required for the recognition to work, which was why Brodie and many others living in the Gutter kept their faces partially hidden and almost always wore sunglasses in public.

Brodie sidestepped a parade of blowing rubble and continued toward the market. An older man wearing a stained and tattered business suit stumbled across the street toward him. The man's hair was slick and oily, completely disrupted and sticking out in all directions like a rooster's tail.

The man starred at Brodie, babbling incoherently, staggering towards him. Brodie covered his nose as he caught the stench of booze belching out from the man's pores as he came closer. He did his best to avoid the stumbling drunk, but still, the man tried to grab a hold of Brodie's arm as he passed.

"You think I'm drunk, but I am not drunk. No sir, captain," the drunk slurred out. "Can't you feel it? It's in my skin, the worm in my blood. I got the android fever. It's in my brain. You wait, they infected me and put them electronic track worms in my body. They see everything, everything!" the man yelled out, flailing his hands. "They watch. Don't think they don't watch. They know who I am. They know who I am, so now they know who you are, too." Brodie walked past the man, yet he kept yelling in Brodie's direction. "Clean your blood, captain, or they'll find you," the man yelled, impassioned.

Brodie kept his focus forward and continued on his way. Android fever was the aftermath of privately funded experiments done by Corporation X, as they referred to it in the court documents. Brodie knew the topic, experimenting on humans. It wasn't that uncommon. It was just usually in the spirit of extending life, not disrupting it. There were rules, but Brodie felt it was more like, soft suggestions. He had gotten a small education in med school on bacterial nanowires and all that stuff. Sars, Corona Virus, all the way back to Polio. It was one class on the history of Viruses and Immunology. It made him afraid of people for a little while, but he still wanted to save lives. So as anyone would do, he went about his life and eventually as days passed the fear turned to caution, then intelligence, then wisdom as he kept up his education. The wisdom he gained was the sole reason he joined Doctors without Borders and served for three years in his twenties. He still wanted to help people. He just didn't need to be around them afterwards.

The research head and primary founder for Corporation X didn't start off evil. A Reiki master and energy healer, Tobias Wright, was young. The Underground suspected that he simply got the wrong offer at the right time. He fell to temptation and soon enough Corporation X was working with Droshure as a subsidiary and introduced a conductive bacterium into the bodies of over 1,200 unsuspecting Las Vegas vacationers and locals within one months' time. It was not contagious, but it left lasting physical and mental damage on those that hadn't died from it. The intent was to be a sleep regulator. However, because the sample of people weren't assessed for anything, not health, statistics, nor blood type, it was a flawed experiment from the start. It produced little success and served as the opposite. the inhalant not only disrupted sleep, but also created a chemical imbalance in the brain that proved fatal for many.

Brodie had several friends who at one point, were in school for bio-medical engineering who had seen successful trials abruptly end and dis-appear. And to the contrary, trials that displayed a multitude of problems swiftly moved through the chain and hit first, the pharmacy, then the Off-the-Shelf markets. Those friends left their programs. A few became waiters and teachers, some nurses, while others revolted against the Gov-ernment and big pharma getting involved in the grass root movements trying to expose the truth.

Brodie kept moving. Android fever wasn't contagious but it sucked Brodie's energy to be around those that suffered from it. He passed a few open stores, but supplies were scarce and generic, potentially tampered with. The hours were random and the products were made cheaply and in mass. Unless people worked for Droshure factories, they didn't take their jobs seriously. Many places still open in the Gutter couldn't attract steady workers. Most rarely showed up on time, if at all. Only a few could be trusted not to steal during their shift, never to return. Because of looting and the ever-growing homeless population, businesses that could afford it, hired protection to guard against robbery and looting.

Finally, Brodie reached the Rail Market, an open bazaar much less appetizing than the Maeklong Railway Market. The stands sat along the looping track of a short-lived and failed HOP streetcar route through downtown Milwaukee. It was filled with vendors, hustlers and dealers. Everything from used clothes and furniture, to grabs of drugs, vegetables and weapons could be bought for a price, or swapped for goods or sex. Weapons were strongly monitored in the slums, so the selling of them was under the cloth, meaning only asked for by code and sold under the table. A buyer wouldn't know if they got the product they asked for until they reached a private, hidden area. The Corners did everything in their control to keep the lower class from arming themselves and rising up. Still, Brodie didn't go anywhere without at least one gun on his person.

"Hey baby, come have some fruit? I give you more for better, cutie. Plus, plus." A weathered woman selling old dresses hustled her pitch to Brodie as she ruffled her skirt above her knees. Down the street, a bundled-up elderly woman readied as Brodie approached.

"Hey, come here. I have shoes for you. Your feet will feel very nice," she said.

Brodie stepped up, scanning the selection, Nike, Adidas, Clarks, a plethora of different brands. All of them used, some worn out and stinky, others practically new. Most of the goods sold at the market were things found in vacant homes throughout the slums. Brodie inspected a vintage pair of red and white checkered, slip-on Vans and sized them up against the base of his boot.

"You know where I can find Potter?" Brodie subtly asked, keeping his gaiter up just beneath his eyes, but still making eye contact.

"You want Potter? I got what you want right here. Why you want Potter? He no good, but these shoes will make you happy." The little old woman smiled a grin that was minus a few teeth as she tried to sway Brodie into a purchase.

"It's business. You know, jingles." Brodie shook the palm of his hand, as if it was full of change.

"Ok, fine. He's down four stands across the block. Tall, stupid white boy by the stand in front, red hair. You ask him," the elder said.

"Thank you," Brodie extended a twenty dollar bill her way, holding up the pair of Vans. With thick knit gloves on, the woman snatched the money from Brodie.

"Ok, ok, go on now," she said as she fanned him off.

Brodie walked away with a smile. He enjoyed the reminder of how nice it was to talk to people in random conversation. It was an infrequent occurrence since the split. A good interaction with a stranger could turn his whole day around. It made him think of his childhood, being nine years old and having a bike to ride down clean streets with full green trees arched across the roads. Every neighbor knew the whole block. Lawns were lush and manicured, houses were intact. Block parties were in full effect every month. Being able to block off side streets without a permit or any concern for reckless drivers. Games of kick the can and cartoon tag lasted far into the night without any fear of crime.

Once the class wars hit, after the October massacres of 2025, houses were burned for fun as Devils Night became a monthly event and stretched throughout many areas of the Gutter. As soon as they could, people flocked to the new Corners developments faster than they were available. For those who couldn't afford it though, human trafficking sky rocketed as people were being stolen and sold internationally for the sex and slave trade. Everything was open for barter and loot. Though law still existed, it was subjective and came with judgement and a price at Boobain's order. The poor knew it and tried to revolt, but it failed. At least it failed the first time.

Brodie glanced over as a noise fell into his ears. Standing there was a skinny white kid of about sixteen, bouncing a dirt-stained yellow tennis ball against a building. Kerchunk, kerchunk, snapped into his ears. The kid's hair was dyed a Raggedy Anne red, dark roots spilling out. The teen was antsy. Brodie could see the kid gauging if he could get him to buy something. Two black plastic garbage bags filled with hats sat on the folding table near him.

"Hey man, you wanna buy a hat?" the kid asked.

"You know where I can find Potter?" Brodie asked, disregarding the kids initial question.

The kid caught his ball and skip-hopped over to Brodie, acting sketch, twitchy proper.

"He's right down the alley, sir. Just knock twice. Hey, are you a digger? Do you scrape?" The kid danced zig zags in front of Brodie as he spoke, unable to stand still. Almost tripping over his words.

"I'm not a digger. You know where he is?" Brodie made sure his face was still hidden behind his buff.

"I know you're a digger, bro. You got the look. I wanna scrape, too. You know who I can talk to? I got mad wicked speed, yo. I'm lightening quick. Come on man, help me out," the kid stumbled out the words.

The kid was too eager. Brodie knew he was either on the chisel or special K, both far too easy to find in the Gutter. Chisel was the latest dust of choice. Brodie never tried it, had only witnessed friends on it. It heated up the body and gave a vibrant feeling as if your body was filled with glitter, like a human snow globe. After the high, you would unexpectedly get the swerve. With the swerve, first came the body tremors, then came the massive, immobilizing chills and dizziness, coupled with a skull cracking headache.

"Come on kid, where's Potter?"

"Whatever man, fuck you. Guys a shady fuck, anyway. Blue door on the left, halfway down the alley. Knock twice only, asshole," the kid mumbled, defeated.

"What do you mean he's shady?" Brodie stuck a twenty-dollar bill at the kid.

"Guess you're about to find out, bro." The kid snatched the twenty and went back to bouncing his ball, done with Brodie.

Brodie thought about leaving. Maybe this was a bad idea. It made him second guess his choice. Ah, paranoia. He shook off the suspicion and knocked twice on the blue door.

"Yeah," a baritone voice said behind the door said.

"I'm here for Potter, Charlie sent me." The door opened and a large man with gargantuan biceps was standing there. He wore a sleeveless T-shirt with a daisy on the front that read '*Pluck You*'. His hands were sullied with car grease.

"Are you 87, 243, 184, or 168?" The man read off a list on a clip board.

"184," Brodie said.

"I'm Randi, come on, Potters over this way." As Randi turned back briefly to observe Brodie on their way to Potters office, Brodie noticed Randi only had one ear. The other had just the internal loop, no ear lobe or external ear flap at all. A cochlear implant sat imbedded in the open gap. Brodie's mind played out scenarios of how Randi had lost his ear as they made their way across the warehouse. It was large and plain with light gray walls, no windows in the makeshift mechanics' lair. A few junkers were being rehabbed by some guys on the other end of the warehouse floor. The place didn't appear big from the outside, but inside it was massive. Randi knocked on an office door.

"Potter, 184's here for a car, one of Charlie's guys," Randi said.

"Let him in," a voice said as Randi pushed the door open. Potter sat finishing up a call and waved Brodie in, offering him seat and a cigar from an open box. Brodie took one and sat in the executive leather lounger. Potter lit the cigar for Brodie, just as he ended his call.

"Ok, sorry bout that." Potter sat back in his chair, almost ogling Brodie with a smile. "So, you're the guy. It's you. I honestly didn't think you'd show up." His orange disheveled hair was only a slight distraction in contrast to his high-end attire.

"What do you mean?" Brodie asked, realizing he had taken his buff down to smoke the stogie.

"Don't worry man, you're protected. I'm friends with your guardian angel," Potter said.

"I'm confused," Brodie said, caught off guard.

"Charlie told you he was getting you a car. He was trying to set you up. The old mans lost his crackers. There's a list Boobain sends to all the drop guys in the slums twice a month, full of Scrapers he wants watched, brought in or killed. You just happened to land on it this time," Potter paused to take a drag off his cigar. "It just means there's some suspicion around your activity. They probably don't know who you are, so it's not about you, per se. It's just a little elevated with you in particular because of the chatter the Splitters are chirping. Charlie might act tough, but he's afraid they'll kill him if he doesn't oblige. So, he agreed to set you up." Potter grinned at Brodie, as he puffed on his cigar.

Brodie shook his head. "I don't understand. I've done nothing but help Charlie," he said.

"The world doesn't work that way, my friend. Now, under no circumstances do you remove your scarf or face covering when you leave here or in public. We make nice in here for a bit so it doesn't look suspicious. Then I'll sneak you out."

"Why would he set me up? He'd never let Droshure get to him," Brodie said.

"Man, everybody is hawking Scrapers right now. The G wants you guys followed in case you're trading intel, like that cat they killed. And maybe he had no choice. But guess what, lucky for you, I like your protector a lot more than that grumpy geriatric. That's who you need to thank. Her team caught the intel. How, I have no clue."

"This is messed up. Charlie's been like an uncle to me." Brodie remembered Nora's message. Maybe he should have called her back sooner.

"Times change, my friend. It's what's happening everywhere. Trust no one. Anyway, I'll send out someone who looks enough like you. One of our Qwins. They'll stay on plan and mirror your pattern, behavior and take most eyes off you and redirect to him. We even gave this cat a skateboard. So, stop riding yours. Your Qwin's car will be tracked, which he knows. He doesn't know who you are and you won't know who he is. He gets paid to be a diversion. I'll even send Charlie a message that you were as excited as a baby with a bowl of Jello over the new car. Tell no one you were here or about me, cuz you weren't here."

"I don't get why people are suddenly on me," Brodie said.

"Don't worry about the why's. People do stupid shit all the time. Charlies got hidden folders on every body that comes through his doors. He's a weird fuck, not the helpless sweet potato that you think he is. There are some pretty dark reasons his wife and kid left him."

"So, you know who I am?"

"Do I know your name? Yes, but that's irrelevant. Do I know someone who wants you protected? Absolutely, and because of who that is and her relationship to me, I now want you protected, too," Potter said.

"You're not going to get called up for this?" Brodie asked.

"By who? Look, because of what I do I get to toggle between worlds. And I'm a good pretender. Government lets me slide cuz they think I'm monitoring all of you in the Gutter. In truth, my guys run reels, the Qwins and the bots run cars around and I send the G fake footage. They're too self-involved to question it. Nothing said in this room is heard. Even if the room is bugged, it's intercepted before it leaves these four walls. As long as they 'think' I'm tracking folks, all is good," Potter said. "Hit that stogie deep, get some flavor. It'll cut some of the anxiety you're feeling. This happens on occasion, you're definitely not the first to be set up."

"Hey, I have to take you at your word." At that point, Brodie had no clue who Potter was. He was still unsure if he was going to walk out of his office alive. He took a few strong pulls from the cigar, then without warning felt a little wide-eyed and woozy, yet more relaxed. He blinked to lock his focus back in.

"A little stronger than your norm. Cubans, I have a ton. My father was an arms trader back in the day. When he passed, he left half a garage full to my brother and I. Gave us a little bit of leverage after the split. I'll give you a box," Potter rested back in his chair.

"So, what happens now?" Brodie was screwed. Too many things were coming through, making him think this might be his last day.

"I'm gonna walk you out my private door. Your Qwin is going to come in here through a different private door after I get you out of here and I'm going to walk him to the cars. Then he's gonna take a ride, go to some of the places you go, at night he'll park by one of the half-way decent buildings across town from your area. He'll be discreet but visible enough to keep the spot on him, not you. You're going to go about your business, but you need to avoid your common haunts and habits for a while. Most importantly, keep yourself covered. Scrapers can't be fucking around right now. Just keep busy and do not go anywhere near Charlie's again. Your angel already has someone going to recover your file from his place today. No more contact with Charlie, no more scraping for Droshure. Not right now. Not for a while." Potter was friendly but stern in his delivery.

"All right," Brodie sighed. "I get it. I appreciate this." Brodie stood up. He felt trapped. The perspiration on his palms pushed heat and sweat from his skin as his anxiety swelled. If he was going to walk to his death, he wanted to get it over with.

As soon as Brodie got far enough away from the building, he pulled the box of cigars out of his back pack and flipped it open, inspecting the cigars. He took one out and as he passed some bum warming their hands by a trash fire, he set the box of Cubans down near them and walked on without a word. Brodie gripped his hood and tugged it down over his face as far as it would go, yet allowing him to still see. Something was building around him. He needed to switch up everything.

CHAPTER 11

H ues of scarlet and plum fueled the Los Angeles skyline as Billy sat in the dark, several screens flickering with activity in front of him. The warmth of the early morning air soothed his face. Fixated, he replayed the same loop of footage over and over. On screen, somewhere above Summit County, Colorado, a government helicopter hovered over a snow filled mountain range, toying with an avalanche. Down below, seven masked skiers swerved new patterns down a mountainous peak. The news reporter explained that a request had been made for the skiers' IDs. This was standard procedure in marked gray zones that encroached the Corners borders. One skier held an object up towards the sky. Instantly, as if a giant was swinging it around by its tail, the chopper twirled in circles. Nose down, it viciously spun, smashing into the mountainside. Video of debris garnishing the area was caught by a homeowner a fair distance away. A contact number appeared at the bottom of the screen for anyone with information regarding the incident.

Billy picked up his phone and dialed.

"It's Billy Wessner for President Boobain," he said. He stood up, waiting to be transferred. At that moment, he turned at the noise of the bedroom door opening. Audrey walked in, still in her silk pajama bottoms and tank top. Billy covered the phone with his hand.

"Did you see the crash in Colorado?" Audrey asked.

"I'm calling Boobain right now."

"Do you know those skiers? Were they your hire?" Audrey asked, kissing him good morning.

"You think I'd arrange for one of Boobain's government choppers to explode? Now what would be the benefit in that? But seriously, I can't take credit for this one." The mischievous grin on Billy's face made it hard to discern the truth. Plus, he knew at least one of his phones was most likely bugged.

"God, you're a menace," she whispered in his ear. Just then Billy's demeanor changed as he put his finger up and spoke.

"Tim, what the hell is going on? Did you see the crash? If your teams can't protect my teams from things like that happening, how am I supposed to ensure their safety?"

"Who is this?"

"It's Billy Wessner, sir. You seriously don't know my voice by now?"

"The crash doesn't concern you, Billy. We use your teams when we have to, last resort. Up to this point, our security has been exceptional."

"Are you kidding? That's what I'm worried about. Droshure's plants are getting annihilated, several just this week." Billy said, grinning through his performance of outrage.

"You need to scale down your attitude," Boobain sternly demanded. "This is being handled. You're on a need-to-know basis. You're the one that set that parameter when you agreed to do this work."

"Well, I hope your guys are taking this seriously. That happened right near the coordinates to the (USCD) Underground Smart City Development project. Stoyton's one of your biggest investors and I know they wouldn't be happy if anything disrupted the region."

"I shouldn't even be speaking with you. That's for both of our protection. I've got a ton of shit to manage right now. If you want to help me, head over and check up on Jacob, he's supposed to be handling the fallout. If he's incapable, that may be your window, but for now I need you to go through Jacob. Stoyton doesn't need to know about any of this. Got it?" Boobain was pissed.

"Yes, but just remember, they're one of your biggest investors and I got them for you. I'll head over and see Droshure in an hour or so." Billy hung up the phone and pulled Audrey in by the hips.

"That guy is such a dumb prick. If I can pull this off, a seat at the Stoyton table is worth the world. You get ahold of your hacker for the UN guys computer? No one can get through the ghost holes on his system," Billy said.

"Not yet, none of my European contacts recognize the guy's name. Christopher Scott may be an alias. We don't even have a picture. My people are looking, though, asking the right questions. If he's out there, they'll find him."

"With all the guys you slept with in London, none of them can find this guy?" Billy thought he was being funny. Audrey didn't.

"Maybe it's time you find someone else on the DQ to hack in, you know?" Audrey said, pissed. "Someone working against my father or one of your Splitter buddies, because I don't feel like helping you when you act like an asshole."

"Calm down, I was just kidding. Spider knows two internationals we're bringing over that can probably do the job, but it will be three days to get them here. Worst-case scenario, there's a hacker in Creepers Row who will be able to find this Christopher Scott."

"My darling," Audrey said patronizingly, "those people are far less than human. They can't be trusted for shit."

"If we have to, we can accelerate the hits on the other two UN folks who worked with this guy, but we're not quite there yet." Billy grabbed his coat. "I'll see you back here later, I'm heading out. Now don't go bang my dad while I'm gone."

"Do you know how deranged you sound? It was your sick idea, anyway. I need to see him at least one more time to get Boobain's banking info."

"You're right, you're right. Good girl." Billy smacked her on the ass with a wink, and headed out.

"Billy, do not do that. I'm not your fetch dog or your whore. You really don't need any more enemies right now, trust me."

Billy roughly grabbed her by the face, but she jerked out of his grip and slapped him.

"Be careful," Billy said, smiling at her fury.

Later that morning, Jacob Droshure sat in his office skimming documents while Nathan, Billy's father, sat across from him, quiet as a mouse, drifting off as his elbow repeatedly slid from the arm of the chair. Meanwhile, Billy lingered about the room, pacing like the cokehead he was, waiting for Jacob to finish pretending he was important. Jacob Droshure was a stout, robust man of average height. He knew the part, but wore the ambiance of someone who was losing their grip, always sweating, hands always tremoring. The Colorado chopper crash looped on the screens in front of them intermittently mingled with footage of an exploding clone plant. Billy obnoxiously tapped his foot, trying to spark a reaction. Unfortunately, he could tell from the aggravated glares that he was only annoying his father.

Outside the tinted windows, five stories down, the streets were alive with wealth and safety, oblivious to the chaos unfolding around them. That would change within hours. They had no idea that what they had put their stock in, would soon crumble right under their noses. High-end boutiques, fancy restaurants and luxury hotels filled the heart of the Corners communities. Unlike the Gutter, the camera's that guarded the Corners were welcomed, at least the ones that were visible to the naked eye. California was one of the first fully locked states. The whole circumference was bordered off unless you were a resident member of the Corners, a paid for status.

At least three other states were right behind them, close to locking borders. The more they expanded the Corners, the more destruction there would be in the Gutter. Billy knew luxury would always be desired by the wealthy. It was an excellent vocation. Now that the middle country had been decimated and left to flounder, there was no turning back for Corners residents. There was nowhere else for them to go.

Billy knocked on Jacobs' desk. He had a plan in his head and until it was fully executed, his brain would be on full speed. He needed to hurry this up.

"Tick-tock, Jacob. What the fuck is the delay?" Billy said.

They were interrupted by a knock on the door. Just then, a voice came over the intercom.

"Sir, there's a Tony Flicker from the Davis County Plant here to see you." Jacob pushed a button on his desk and his office door opened. Seconds later, Tony Flicker rushed in, red-faced and panicked. His eyes bounced between the three men in front of him.

"Um, sorry Mr. Droshure, sirs," Tony said, acknowledging Billy and his father, along with Jacob Droshure. I got a direct order from my superior to report here per President Boobain. I'm Head of Operations at the Davis County Plant in Utah." Tony, nervous as hell, swiped glistening sweat from his forehead with the sleeve of his jacket.

"Why are you in my office, Tony?" Jacob flexed his authority as his eyes hunted Tony's every move. Billy watched him belittle Tony, a simple, innocent worker bee doing his job.

"Sir, one of the security helicopters exploded near Summit County early this morning and President Boobain expressed concern to my superiors that someone may be trying to penetrate through the Colorado Underbase. There is concern about the Davis plant and all those bordering Colorado. Several alarms have gone off in the last two weeks and we haven't been able to identify the cause. My superiors request that you send a Sweeper unit to cover the plant." Finally, Tony stopped moving, out of exhaustion from speaking.

"Take a god damn breath, Tony. I already know about Summit County. Tim sent you here because you're having alarms?" Jacob smirked, patronizing the man. Billy couldn't stand the way Jacob thought he had more power than he truly did. If Billy wanted Jacob's job, he could kill him right then and there and get away with it. Jacob liked to embarrass the weak. A simple bully. Billy was much more subtle with his trickery.

"Yes sir, this is under President Boobain's order. My bosses are meeting with him after the press conference. That's why they sent me. Because of the recent protests and last week's explosions," Tony paused, mentally regrouping. "Sir, it's one of our largest locations. President Boobain must feel it's important, and I agree." Tony waited for an answer.

Jacob stood near the window, distracted by two buxom beauties strolling past, a few floors below. "Look, I don't know why Tim didn't just call me, but I'll ask him that myself when I talk to him. I'll send the team over tomorrow morning. If we find nothing, I'll make sure your employment is terminated. You'll be relocated out of the Corners." Jacob gave Tony a dismissive look.

"The guys just doing his job, Jake." Billy interjected, but Jacob paid him no mind. "Do a full sweep, Tony. Jake will get a team out there tomorrow morning. He hasn't had his coffee, yet." Billy nodded his head for Tony to skedaddle.

"I understand, sir. Thank you." Tony rushed out the door.

Jacob was back at his desk, standing, glaring at Billy, waiting for Billy to look his way.

"What are you staring at me for?" Billy smirked.

"Don't you ever try to out rank me in front of anyone ever, again. Yes, you're fucking my daughter and yes, you've done a lot for this corporation and Tim and I, but do not take my generosity as authorization."

"It's fucked up of you to even bring Audrey into this, Jake," Billy said. "But seriously, why ride that guy like that? He's just doing his job. Which, looking at the news, it's more than either of you are doing. And as far as taking you for granted."

"Now you're a bleeding heart? You are so full of shit. That's not going to work on me. You're a snake and you always will be, it's why we hired you," Jacob said.

"Whatever," Billy smirked.

"It's up to you, Billy. I could have you arrested and behind bars in five minutes if I wanted, have them drop you in the Gutter."

"But you won't. Stoyton would be all over you. I'm an independent contractor, now. You might have hired me, but now I ultimately work for the people that run you and President Boobain. Don't forget that. You rat on me, this whole empire crumbles because of the secrets I know." Billy was fired up. It took restraint for him to not clock Jacob Droshure in his weathered face right then and there.

"God dammit, Billy. Why didn't Tim just order the god damn sweep himself if he's that concerned? I'm sick of feeling like his little servant. This is my company, that is part of the deal." Jacob said the words like a pouty little child. Billy loved watching his ego whirl about like a chaotic tornado. With every moment of friction between Timothy Boobain and Jacob Droshure, Billy felt his power rise. He had no interest in running the country, he simply wanted to use the people that ran it to get his higher objectives through unnoticed, and his plan was working.

"You have a crisis on your hands. You were the one who was supposed to establish the surveillance on the vehicles. It was your error that got that chopper blown up. Mr. President has to run the country, or at least pretend that's what he's doing. If you let him get to you, you will lose the battle. Just get it taken care of," Billy said. Just then, his phone went off. "Call a sweep team. Start there and stop worrying about what I'm doing. Now's not the time for you and Tim to sword fight. If it's not there already, get a military unit to survey the area over and around Summit County for anything that might be detected." Billy stood at the door.

"Fine, but once this is all resolved my goal is to never see you again."

"Be careful what you wish for, Jake, that might come true in all the ways you don't want it to. Oh, and thanks for having my back, dad," Billy said.

"You're on your own, kiddo," Nathan said, steering clear of any engagement.

CHAPTER 12

B rodie was still shaken with the reality of Charlie's betrayal and the
video of Cece. As soon as he got what he needed from Krispy, he
was taking off to get her out of the Corners, there was no way she'd be
anywhere else. There wasn't enough room in his thoughts for Charlie or his
health anymore. Maybe Charlie had no choice. Maybe Droshure wants all
Scrapers watched. Either way, the last twenty-four hours had left a burning
storm rumbling inside Brodie. Nothing made sense.

When he got home from Potters, Marcus was waiting outside resting
back on his Triumph Thruxton.

"Man, is it good to see you," Brodie said. "I'm losing my freaking mind."

"What's going on?" Marcus was genuinely concerned.

"You can't go back to Charlie's, ever. He's not safe. He tried to set me
up, but apparently, I have a guardian angel. It's gotta be Nora."

"You serious?"

"Yeah, I'll explain."

"You wanna skip the drop sheet?" Marcus turned his bike off.

"No, I gotta stay busy till Krispy's tonight. He's having a party," Brodie
said. He kept his gaze on Marcus, trying to assess if he could truly be

trusted. "Ok, here's the deal. I think Cece's in danger. After what Donte said last night, I had a chat with Krispy to try to get some info. Soon as I know where she is I'm going to find her. Let's go, we can cover a few places today," Brodie said.

"Wait, slow down. You're going to the Corners?"

"I'm going wherever Cece is. I've got Splitters coming for me and with Charlies' set up, I'm better off gone anyway," Brodie said.

"Get on and let me see the drop sheet." Marcus handed Brodie a helmet and glanced at his phone, reviewing the coordinates. Twice a week, the Underground sent Brodie and a few other double agent Scrapers a secure list of suspicious behavior sites with potential death drops that required investigation. Scrapers referred to the list as a Drop Sheet. Brodie got on the back of Marcus's bike as the two sped off, weaving through alleys and side streets. Today Marcus knew his mission. It was to keep Brodie safe and alive.

Far across town, in a rundown, formerly wealthy suburb, Marcus skidded the bike to a stop as they parked just at the edge of the neighborhood. Bundled up, they began their trek into the area. Both were strapped. Things were escalating and they were as prepared for the unknown, as they could be. It was freezing out. The cold, while an irritant, provided a bit of distraction.

"But why would Charlie want to track you? Doesn't make sense," Marcus questioned.

"I couldn't tell ya. Remember that baby I delivered the other day? I didn't tell you but it was one of Boobain's mistresses. Anyone in that room could have ratted me for the coin."

"Well, maybe Billy's getting crafty," Marcus said. "Maybe word got around and someone told him who your drop guy was. For the record, you never told me you delivered a baby. You don't tell me that stuff. So, was Boobain's piece pretty?"

"Very, but way worn. If Boobain finds out she had his kid, she's dead."

So far, Brodie and Marcus had gone to three houses, but they only found one body which was already scraped to the bone. The other two houses resulted in nothing. As they walked the sidewalk, Brodie spotted an old woman peeking out from a second-story window as they passed. With full gear on, they weren't identifiable. Brodie wasn't worried about her. He appreciated that she had survived and found shelter at her age.

"So, you're really gonna take off to find Cece? You really think she's in trouble?" Marcus asked.

"I don't trust Billy. And if what Donte said is true, I gotta get her out of there."

Marcus stopped walking. Soon after, Brodie did, too.

"It's not a good idea. But, if you're going, I'm going with you. You're my best friend. Do not protest." Marcus smiled and held onto Brodie's shoulder, face to face, acknowledging that he was serious.

"All right, thank you," Brodie said, nodding his head yes in appreciation.

"Now let's finish this shit up. It's cold," Marcus said rubbing his hands up and down his arms, trying to keep warm.

The two took off down the street like vultures scavenging for prey, reaching the last address for their work day.

"You snake that coot from last night?" Brodie couldn't help but ask.

"Her names Jeanine. And I'm more like a python, my bro." Marcus widened his hands, exaggerating the vastness of his cock.

"You're nuts," Brodie laughed. The camaraderie he felt with Marcus was like no other. Marcus felt more like a brother to him, than Billy ever had. He knew Marcus was trying to distract him until they went to Krispy's. It was helping.

"That's right, loco in la cabeza," Marcus laughed.

They walked up a tar blotched driveway of cracked concrete. It was one of the few houses on the block that looked somewhat intact, which meant someone might still be living there. Brodie and Marcus walked the perimeter, their eyes peering into windows as they passed, arching up on their tiptoes. They weren't just looking for tenants, they were scoping for squatters and hawks, too.

Marcus picked the backdoor lock and the two cautiously entered, guns in hand at the ready. Brodie felt cool air brush against the exposed bits of his face the moment they stepped in. The heat was off. He flicked the light switch up and down, nothing happened.

"I'll take the upstairs," Brodie said, taking two steps at a time, securing his Maglite headband. Quick and diligently, he checked all the nooks and crannies, making sure no one was there. Brodie checked bedrooms and closets, as Marcus did a similar inspection with the basement and main level.

"Clear up here," he called. But then something caught his eye as Brodie peered back into one of the bedrooms.

"Clear down here, two bodies in the living room. Couple in their thirties, you want the guy or the chick?" Marcus questioned.

"I'll be right down," Brodie yelled.

Brodie couldn't help but notice the dangling handle inside the ceiling of one of the bedroom closets. The immediate urge to check it out came over him. He jumped up and grabbed the handle, as the accordion staircase unfolded in front of him. He scrambled up and scanned the attic, shining his Maglite along the borders of the room. There in between the wooden beams, tucked in with rolls of pink fiberglass, sat a partially hidden body.

Brodie carefully scooted over to it, checking for vital signs, sweeping the mouth for anything that may have been jammed inside. The man's hands were missing, cut clean off and nowhere in sight. Brodie pulled the body close to the staircase and left it at the edge. He slid back down from the attic, closing the hatch.

"Hello? Brod, you good?" Marcus yelled up, again.

Seconds later, Brodie came trotting down into the living room with a few T-shirts and a sweatshirt in hand to find Marcus already working on the man's body.

"Had to take a piss, thank God the plumbing still works. Thought you might want this stuff, too." Brodie tossed the clothes next to Marcus on the floor. He knelt down next to each body and scanned the fingerprints of the young couple into the UDB.

"The man has a gunshot to the head. She's got two to the chest, some bruising. I'm guessing joint suicide or something. Can kind of tell from the point of entry, the hold on the gun wasn't super stable. I don't know how much we'll really get off em. Been dead over a week, I'd guess," Marcus said.

"We'll get something off 'em. I just wonder why no one else was here?" Brodie said.

Marcus shrugged, not caring, and continued working. He slipped on his gloves and doubled up, putting a protective guard over his gaiter as he worked. Brodie caught Marcus out of the corner of his eye, watched as he made a smooth incision down the man's chest with an electric handheld scalpel.

"Your cuts are getting better."

"If any vitals are good, I'm scoopin em," Marcus said.

"It all goes to the Underground. Besides, no vitals from these two, been dead too long."

"You know they told Samson he can't slice anymore?" Marcus spoke.

"Samson's with the internationals, he's just gathering data. He could care less. That's why he can't slice for shit," Brodie laughed.

"I had no idea. I like that guy," Marcus said.

"He's a good dude, a master hacker, too. I'm sure he accomplished what he needed to. Don't share any of this, though. I don't want to see him end up on the hook." Brodie spoke firmly as the two continued working, both men periodically scanning the scene, keeping their eyes on the windows.

Marcus finished packing the bits he'd gotten off the body. Afterwards, he took the man's finger, cracked it, put a tincture on it and smoothly twisted. With the grip of his glove, he worked the man's wedding ring off his finger. He scooted to the woman's hand and did the same, removing her wedding band. He shoved the rings in a small plastic bag, then into his back pocket.

"Couldn't have waited till I finished? You need money that bad?" Brodie asked. "Ah, I don't care. Take em. If you don't, someone else will." Most Scrapers looted. Brodie didn't know why he was busting Marcus's balls. He couldn't bring himself to take anything other than clothes off the dead, and that didn't happen often.

"Look, this is 500 minimum to the right buyer. It's like Storage Wars, you never know what gems you'll find in the burbs, plus we're not making anything off the parts. I gotta get something out of this." Marcus finished cleaning up and checked out the window. "Hey, we got a car coming two streets down. We don't want company." He kept his eyes on the approaching vehicle as he disposed of his medical gloves and replaced them with his cycle gloves.

"I need you to keep watch down here. I found a body in the attic and I wanna give it a quick check," Brodie requested.

"Fine, the car passed by, but you gotta hurry up," Marcus urged.

Brodie flew up the stairs like an Olympian to the attic closet. He grabbed the handle and shimmied up. He roped up the body with twine, then heaved it down the ladder, into the room.

The body seemed a day or two old, still fresh. He figured this body might be the reason why the house was on the drop sheet. If suspicious activity was picked up at a location, that was all it took to make the drop sheet. The man was in a suit, mid-fifties. The skin at the cut sites where his hands were removed was brutally shredded, not clean, but choppy hacks.

"I'm going as fast as I can," Brodie yelled down.

He opened the clothes, rummaging for other injuries and cause of death. The skin on his chest was blotchy, slowly turning to the greenish opaque color of death. With his hands severed and missing, there was no way to identify the man. He scanned for any way to identify the man. Brodie double checked the mouth.

"Rookies. You always knock out the teeth," Brodie said softly to himself, smiling.

He pulled out a quart size container, then another half the size. He covered the man's top teeth with putty and once the teeth were covered, he closed the man's jaw, creating an imprint. Brodie secured the imprint in a container and pulled out a small camera, taking several pictures of the man's open mouth. Seconds later, he reviewed the images through his phone. As he zoomed in on one, he noticed an odd-looking cavity in a back molar. Brodie grabbed a tiny pliers, braced his foot, carefully pulling the tooth out from its root. No sooner, he noticed a tiny computer chip awkwardly wedged into the tooth where a filling would normally sit. He got a small baggie and put the tooth with the implanted chip inside, sealed it up, and put it in the inside zipper pocket of his jacket.

He rolled the body over and noticed two blunt force wounds on the man's back. As he did, a small device tumbled out from the man's waist.

Several clicks were audible as Brodie spotted the thumb size camera device. Shit. Though Brodie had a mask on, his eyes could be seen, his glasses, too. Within seconds, he stomped the ankle of his boot into the camera, destroying it. He snapped a few more pictures of the decaying remains, then smashed out the rest of the teeth, proper protocol. Brodie wiped down any trace of himself, then lit the man's clothes on fire best he could, using some nearby paper and his lighter. He flew down the stairs and got Marcus.

"We gotta get out of here, I'll explain on the way. I started a fire upstairs but I need you to do your magic and make sure the place is torched to the ground."

"Done," Marcus said.

"You're my ride or die, man. Thank you," Brodie said.

Brodie bolted upstairs and lit several more fires. When he got downstairs Marcus was waiting for him in the kitchen.

"I turned the gas on but, we'll see." Marcus spliced a sweet spot in the gas line, letting the two ends dangle onto the floor. He pulled out a spray bottle and saturated the kitchen with rubbing alcohol. He turned on all the burners and the oven. "Grab your shit, we're out," Marcus said, excited. He loved a good rush. The two men grabbed their scrapes and ditched out the back door. Once back on Marcus's bike, half a mile away, they heard the blast from the home exploding.

After Marcus dropped him off, Brodie got cleaned up, grabbed his old puffy brown coat, snatched a clean balaclava off a shelf and headed right back out into the afternoon. With his gun secure, he rolled through the city on his board, down the less monitored streets. Finding that camera fueled him. His chunky glasses had been his best accessory, now they had become the one thing that made him identifiable. Brodie couldn't wear contacts. They agitated his eyes. He figured all he could do was hide himself in plain sight. Then it hit him, what an idiot he was. As he passed by an unattended trashcan fire, he chucked his skateboard inside. He warmed his gloved hands as he kept his eye out for Splitters and monitor drones. He made his way to Nora's bar, his mind racing with anxiety the whole way. He needed to give her the chip. Brodie didn't need another target on his back. He knew Nora would know what to with it.

CHAPTER 13

In the back office of Current, a snazzy high-end restaurant just off Rodeo Drive in Los Angeles, Billy was mid-pump, thrusting into a biracial buxom beauty, Omari, perched on the edge of a desk. His phone chimed for the third time. Being the man that he was, rather than stop, Billy climaxed expeditiously, then stepped away from the beauty, sweaty and out of breath. Still in the thrill of it, he took in the view of Omari as she cleaned herself up, clearly disappointed with the abrupt release. Billy glanced at his phone.

"Sorry about that, duty calls. Emergency conference call. Shits starting to get crazy so be careful about who comes in. I'll swing by Tuesday for a plate. Save me a table?" Billy stepped into the bathroom and glanced back at Omari, playfully pleading.

"I'll have a table for you after you come back and screw me properly," Omari said with a slight South African accent. Billy put a $1000 Go-card in her hand, which she whipped back at him like a frisbee.

"Stop giving me money, I'm not a whore." Omari got dressed, changing back into her high-end attire with the sophistication of the successful restaurant owner that she was.

"What? I'm just trying to do something nice for you."

"Then don't cum in five minutes next time, how's that for nice?" Omari replied as she fixed her make-up.

"I'll make it up to you." Billy kissed her on the cheek, then left. He wandered through a hall that landed him out onto a back alley near the dumpsters. With his phone piece resting in his ear, he placed a call.

"What's up, Troy?" Billy asked.

"Hey, you know the NP37 dump the other day, the thing Droshures all up in arms about? Well, I'm calling you first, mostly cuz I can't stand that guy."

"I know about it, but I didn't arrange the dump. What's up?"

"The body was found. Droshure knows that part. Someone was at the house today where they dumped the body. Whoever did the dump put a camera on the body and it was triggered a few hours ago. That's the part Droshure doesn't quite know about, yet. I got a Splitter headed over there right now to check. I'm sending the feed it picked up. It's just under 2 mins long and a bit blurry. I tweaked it and lightened it up as much as I could. If you zoom out, you'll get a little better view of the face and what the guy did, but he's mostly covered."

Billy maneuvered his phone to reduce and zoom out, displaying the picture more clearly.

"Why wouldn't they just get rid of the body and destroy it? Burn it? Fucking idiots," Billy reviewed the images as he spoke. "Wait." Billy recognized Brodie's eyes and glasses instantly. "Did you send these to anyone else?" The day was turning out to be a curious one for Billy, and not in a good way.

"No," Troy said.

"Is this everything you got, what you sent me? There are no other cameras?"

"Yes, this is all, just this feed. This is the only camera that triggered at the location. No clue if they put more out."

"Droshure's teams are so fucking sloppy," Billy raged on. "This is why you call me first. When people take orders from Droshure they screw shit up and the wrong people get killed. Do you think there were any other cameras? That's what I need to know."

"Billy, I wasn't there. I said nothing else triggered for that location so I'm guessing nothing else is there. I monitor the cameras and alerts with nine other guys. I just figured you'd want to know," Troy said.

Billy paced back and forth, trying to figure out his next move. He was baffled by the fact that Brodie even crossed paths with Nolan Petri's corpse. Just the vision of Brodie's mostly covered face with those stupid glasses staring back at him, fueled Billy. Their cat and mouse game started long before the October massacres, but this ignited things to new heights.

"Ok, I need you to send me all footage you have on Nolan Petri at this location, then destroy it. Check with the rest of your team to confirm there were no other camera's. It's a direct order so if anyone asks, you just say it malfunctioned. I will back you one hundred percent. I just need this footage completely wiped. For you, it never existed. I'll connect with you and compensate your efforts."

"I got it. I'll check with the team, then delete the stream file for this location only."

"Perfect. Thanks, Troy." Billy was ready to hang up. "Just make sure you send me everything you have, then destroy it. Looks like whoever it was took something from the mouth before they knocked out the teeth."

Billy hung up. He was pissed. He hadn't talked to Brodie in two, maybe three years, since right after Boobain took office. All he knew was that Brodie wasn't on the right side of his plan. He had Cece under his thumb, but Brodie was a becoming a big problem. Sure, he dressed like a silent, tough guy, but Brodie was always for the greater good, never the greater gain. Billy starred at the paused image of Brodie, wanting to slam his phone to the ground. Instead, in quick instinct, he punched a nearby dumpster, splitting his knuckles, igniting crimson splatters.

"How the fuck did these morons forget to sweep the mouth, Jesus Christ. You always smash the teeth out. Fuck." Billy sent two messages and jogged over to the valet to retrieve his car.

By the time Billy walked into the conference room, it was filled with VIP's and haughty moguls. There were a few faces he recognized, cleaners like himself but much lower in status and title. But the room was mostly stacked with people that Billy otherwise would never be introduced to, just threatened with by name. And there, front and center sat three nerds in lab coats, the inept trio tasked with inspecting the body of Nolan Petri. Jacob Droshure stood at the head of the room holding court, fists clenched at his sides, red faced. His executive assistant stood next to him, younger and better looking, waiting to jump in when Droshure started to fade.

Billy didn't care that the Petri dump had caused this much of a ripple upstream. It wasn't his problem. Droshure hired his own team and Droshure was the one that screwed up. The only thing that concerned Billy was Brodie. If he was there and actually found something on the body, that would be a big problem and Billy knew it. It was the job of the lab nerds to do the full scan, skin to bone. Their error may have been the only bread crumb Brodie needed to cause a tsunami of destruction for Boobain, Droshure and everyone else involved. Billy took a seat, crossed his legs and waited for the clown show to begin. He needed to make sure they didn't have any screen shots of Brodie. In the back of his mind, he was running through the quickest way to find him. Cece would be the easiest route.

"I need everyone to shut up. Now, who was in charge of inspecting the body of Nolan Petri?" Droshure's millennial assistant shouted out. Droshure put his hand up to silence the room.

"Uh, we were on the medical side, sir." A lanky lab coat stood up and spoke, nervous. A man and woman rose alongside him. Droshure stared at the threesome, examining their fear.

"Was anything found on the body?" A wealthy German board member sitting in the front row turned and asked the lanky lab kid as if he was speaking to a child, slow and over articulating.

"Sirs, we examined the body as we always do. Same procedure." A nervous gulp erupted from the man's throat as he swallowed, audible to all in the room.

"Well, clearly not as you always do because the slides you showed Mr. Droshure and I an hour ago from the intake revealed the body had a device of some sort embedded in the mouth on your heat scan. How do you idiots not remember to knock out the teeth? We wouldn't be here if you had done your job." Droshure's executive assistant berated them. "The man's hands were severed. Did anyone even get his fingerprints? Do we even know if this guy was Nolan Petri?"

"Sir, the hands were severed at time of death. Standard procedure. One was brought with the body that was used for identification. As well, we have the pictures and results of the identifying scan done by the capture team. The item in the mouth appeared to be a simple cavity. I needed to leave the room briefly for a call and I was under the impression my team did a thorough inspection of the teeth and mouth after we noticed something, as with all standard procedures."

Billy tried to contain his frustration. He texted Troy, getting confirmation that all footage had been destroyed, but Troy wasn't responding. The moment he looked up to Boobain and saw a fuzzy picture of Brodie's face in front of him, he knew Troy had fucked him over. The only thing that mattered was the highest bidder. Billy thought it was him, but apparently not. Three blurry slides of Brodie were shown. One was of him knelt over the body and another with his hand in the mouth. The third was clearly when Brodie noticed the camera and crushed it with his foot. Billy watched the science nerd search for the words to lead him out of this mess, still attempting to save face in front of his team.

"Hey, three stooges? So, none of you checked the fucking mouth after something was detected?" Droshure's executive assistant said the words through gritted teeth. The lab geeks glanced at each other, all hoping to deflect blame. The room remained silent with no response. "Get the fuck out." The assistant pointed to the door. By this time, Droshure's face was blazing, he was ready to pop an artery.

Billy watched as the three couldn't get out the door quick enough.

"So, who dumped the body?" Billy asked. "Why wasn't it burned?"

"My head of security supposedly sent one of our top teams to dispose of the body. But clearly not." Jacob showered a storm of spit with each consonant. "This incident cannot go beyond these walls. We cannot be tied to Petri's murder."

"You realize your team has put your company and the whole project at risk?" Billy stood up and walked to the front of the room.

"This won't come back to us. Say what you need to say, Billy. You could have swept the mouth just as much as they should have," Droshure injected.

Billy reached for the remote and took over. He tilted his phone sideways and soon pictures of Nolan Petri appeared. Pictures taken prior to the dump, during the kidnap and execution Billy was a part of, along with pictures of the body when they first brought it in to the science labs for inspection. One of Nolan Petri's hands sat intact in a baggie next to the body on the slab.

"See how the body isn't touched except for where we whacked him for capture and kill? His clothes are still on. See how the hands are severed and there is a red piece of paper on the chest? That piece of paper is what notifies the lab inspectors of all need-to-know details, including the fact that it was a VIP to examine closely and dispose of the body. No one should have directed them to hide the corpse in the Gutter." Billy took the images off the screen, closed his phone and handed the controls back over to Droshure's assistant. "You have to cremate, always."

"At that point, the inspection team scans the fingerprints to confirm identity, then destroys the severed hand. Did that happen?" Droshure asked.

"When we picked up the body, the hand was still in the baggie with the body," a fit twenty-something jetted the words out, caring more for his life, than anything else at that moment. "We incinerated the hand on our way to dump the body. We went to the dump site and Eric kept getting spooked. He hasn't done many dumps in the Gutter. He was supposed to set the house to burn."

"So, that Eric, the guy that just ran out of the room with the lab idiots wasn't qualified to do the dump, but you neglected to let your superiors know that you had concerns?" Droshure's assistant questioned.

"No, sir. I thought he would be fine. We dumped the body and the driver waited in the car. We hid it in the attic and Eric said he set the house to blow. We were together the whole time," the nervous young cleaner said.

"Well, guess what?" Droshure's assistant proposed. "You fucked up. You and everyone involved mangled this operation. Remove yourself before I have you physically removed." Quickly, the cleaner scrambled out of the room.

"We have no data. Three blurry slides. We can't rely on anything any of those idiots told us except that soon people will know there was a hit on a UN staff member," Droshure said.

"It is rumored that there may have been a data chip. Is this accurate?" one of the investors asked.

"Guess whose job it was to find anything on the body? The three dip-shits that just ran out and if not them, the two dopes that dumped the body," Droshure yelled at the other cleaner heading for the door to leave.

"Several teams are still working to get into protected files. Most likely, whatever was taken off the body either had a code or back up of the protected files, something. Or else why would it be there?" Billy asked the question rhetorically, standing up from his chair.

"We have nothing. We got word thirty minutes ago that the house was burned to the ground. No body, no chip, no more clues. All we have is this shitty footage. I don't care what it takes, but I need teams putting this footage together so we can get a clear face. We have to find this person," Droshure said.

Billy got up and left without waiting for the meeting to conclude. Droshure came hobbling out after him.

"Billy, stop."

"Why would you think it was a good idea to call those people into a meeting for that?" Billy asked. "Now they know you're weak. You just exposed your flaws by displaying that clown car of idiots in front of the investors. And now everyone knows there might be a chip. If anyone of them finds something and decides not to turn it over, your power shrinks immediately."

"Stop acting like you're not at fault here. Your team could have swept the mouth, too," Droshure said.

"The chip that I didn't know existed? I wasn't hired to give the guy a physical. You hired me to track him, get his electronics and any other information off him and kill him. That is what I did. The mysterious chip, that ball was dropped by your teams," Billy said.

"Forget the damn chip for a minute. Does the person in that picture look familiar? A professional?" Droshure worked to compose himself and try to give Billy a little respect, best he could.

"You can barely see anything. You know, Jake, if you don't trust me, I'll tell Mr. Boobain that I'm out. You and your missteps are becoming a liability not just to this operation, but everyone lingering around the edges of it. Yes, someone found something on that guy. At your pace, you'll never find out who," Billy shook his head in disbelief. "If Nolan Petri did have data on his body, anything that can incriminate any of us or this 'Corners' project, it's your coffin, and I'll help them put you in it. Bottom line, you should have hired a better team to scrub and dispose of the body. Why on earth would you have them dump this guy in the Gutter when there are plenty of deep lakes? This is your ego's failure."

"I didn't know the details of the dump. I usually don't. And let's just think about this. These days anyone can fabricate lies on data," Jacob said.

"The data recovered on this guy's computer leads us to ghost holes. There are certain files that we can't access. Look, work with me. People talk. Let me take the lead on this, I'll find the guy. You just keep your people working on the ghost holes," Billy decided to play nice with Jacob. Up to this point, Billy had gotten away with being labeled a prick and a derelict, taking care of the big wigs dirty business, but he never left a footprint. Right now, though, until he or Audrey got the banking information off his father, he needed to play the game. He needed to keep the Droshure empire and Boobain up and running. Once Billy got his money and Stoyton said his work was done, Droshure and Boobain could crumble.

"Fine. Do what you do. Get one of your teams on this and have someone type up what's been found on the computers so far. Get it to me in an hour. Clearly, the security I've put my faith in doesn't deserve a prayer. We'll reassess the threat level tomorrow." Jacob patted Billy on the shoulder. "I'm sorry. You do good work, I'm just pissed about all of this, Boobains been on my back about everything."

"It will balance out, Jake. We'll take care of it." Billy left and his mind immediately went to how he would find Brodie before anyone else got to him. Billy knew calling him would be too suspicious, he hadn't done that in years. And after what happened the day of the October massacres, Billy knew Brodie would never trust him, again. Cece was his quickest key to Brodie. But first, he needed to get word out to the Splitters, increase the bounty. But if found, he needed to be brought to Billy only, preferably alive. If anyone would kill him, Billy wanted to be the one to make that call.

CHAPTER 14

B rodie stood outside, nervous but grateful to see Nora. With Charlie's betrayal, he was starting to question everyone, even those he trusted, but not her. He didn't like that she had to protect him, but he knew why she did it. Though paranoid, Brodie tried to take people at their word. Nora had warned him about that several times. It was no longer a safe way for him to live. He needed to be cautious of everyone.

The deep, hyperactive throttle from the speed metal bass of Atari Teenage Riot pounded out into the parking lot. Brodie stretched his arms, cracked his neck side to side and pushed the heavy brass door open. His ears were met by screeching lyrics and echoing loops of chaotic jungle drums running laps around the perimeter. He scanned the room like a pro. He hadn't shaved in a day and remained mostly covered, doing his best to stay alert and ready for any potential threat. A mini mosh pit was in progress, five patrons strong. Brodie fought the urge to join them and let loose.

Nora's bar held a certain 90's anti-establishment new wave charm. It made Brodie feel comfortable and at home even though it wasn't his generation. He caught Marcus out of the corner of his eye, across the room sitting quietly, his hands surfing the body of a strawberry blonde coot in tattered pleather pants. Her black and purple-rimmed left eye shined out at him across the room like glitter. Brodie flagged Marcus over and caught the bartender's attention for a beer. He watched as Marcus tried to shift the woman off his lap, but she was all over him. Brodie couldn't help but smile. He continued his visual search for Nora, but again was distracted by Marcus as the strawberry blonde, annoyed by the dismissal, leaned in to kiss Marcus but instead, chomped her teeth next to his earlobe, teasing that she might take a small bite. Quick to react, he held his hand up, keeping her at bay as she barked at him, then threw her hands up. Free of the woman, he sauntered over like Shaft.

"Why do you bother snappin at those coots? I swear you're gonna wake up with..." Brodie teased.

"Don't you worry about my wood," Marcus interrupted. "Besides, point out a chick around here that doesn't look like she's got a boggy marsh? They aren't here. Nora is the rare exception, my friend."

"That is so not true," Brodie laughed. "You see Nora?" Brodie asked.

"She's around somewhere," Marcus turned to face Brodie. "Hey, shits getting heated, people are snooping about that house fire. I stuck around out of sight to make sure it burned fast and as I was leaving, car full of Splitters came through, right up in front of the house. It was pretty crumbled down at that point, so I think we're good, but what the hell was that about?" Marcus asked.

Brodie scanned the bar and finally spotted Nora by the door confronting an ox of a man. "There she is," he said, whacking Marcus on the chest, pointing toward the door.

As the bar went silent, Brodie saw Nora's fist slam into the flesh of the towering, burly dude. The cracking noise of her knuckles crushing into his cheek bone was audible, to the point that Brodie and Marcus winced. The burly man held his bloody face with one hand, grabbing out at Nora's shirt with the other. She caught his wrist and with one swift crank, twisted it 180 degrees, only going to the point of excruciating pain, not destruction. Instantly, a stream of piss soaked through the man's pants, trailing down his legs as he dropped to his knees in pain. A splattering of blood on Nora's favorite blue Henley and cargo pants caught Brodie's eye. He zoned in on her as she nonchalantly swiped at the stains with her free hand, annoyed. She eyeballed the ogre, waiting for his next move. It appeared the action had stopped as Motor, being the bouncer, stood holding the door open for the disruptive man to leave.

"So, you honestly think Charlie's working for the other side? I still don't see why he'd be trying to fuck with Scrapers. He'll be dead in a week if he keeps it up." Marcus quickly realized Brodie hadn't heard a word. His eyes were still fixed on Nora.

Brodie started to get up just as the burly guy got to his feet, but Nora drove another punch into his face. After, Motor grabbed him by a tuft of his ratty goatee and pulled him out of the bar.

"Bye, bye," Nora said.

"Hey, missy. You shut up. Leave him alone." The words barked out as a drunken woman staggered over from the dance floor. With smeared lipstick and Smurf-like baby blue eyeshadow, the woman aggressively stumbled back and forth toward Nora. Caked out on drugs, her finger swiped rapidly like a windshield wiper in front of Nora's face.

"Out of here. You and your fucking drug-dealing boyfriend aren't welcome back. You're on my list and I'm reporting you both." Just outside the door, Nora waited for them to walk off her property. When she walked back in, she spotted Brodie at the bar. The sound of clapping startled her as the bar patrons applauded her success. She took a bow as whistles of approval rang out from the fifteen people inside.

"All right, all right, back to drinking. Shows over," Nora grinned.

"Man, I'm screwed." Brodie watched, as she headed for the backroom unable to wipe the grin from his face.

Nora couldn't help but smile back at him, but then shook her head 'no' in a shame-on-you manner.

Brodie could tell the fact that Marcus knew Nora and he had just hooked up, might make things awkward. But then, as he flicked a match to the floor, Brodie saw his gaze return to the strawberry blonde coot he'd been chatting up earlier.

"Come on, you're not seriously thinking of snakin' that? We're hitting the road after Krispy's. We gotta stay focused." Brodie glanced over at the woman.

"Me? You gotta stay focused, besides, she's cool. I like my Gutter babes. I'm much more worried about you these days," Marcus laughed.

"You don't need to worry about me," Brodie said.

"Really? I beg to differ," Marcus looked at him exaggeratedly. "What about the Splitter that would have shot you if I wasn't with you? The body you found? Charlie? Seriously, whose body did I torch in that house, Mr. I'm fine?"

Marcus lit a match off his teeth and threw it to the floor, then lit a joint.

"Don't know, don't care." Brodie's attention was on Nora as she came from the back room, her cheek starting to bruise from the scuffle. First thing he needed to do was give her the chip he found.

"Marcus, you know I love you, but please stop throwing matches in my bar." Nora snatched Brodie's beer and took a much-needed swig. "Mr. Frost, now that you are here, I can tell you both why I called." Nora gave Brodie another scolding glance. He understood the look right away, he'd seen it before.

"I was trying to get here, but things kept coming up. Truth be told, I've had the worst twenty-four hours I've had in a long time."

"What was going on with the knob shine at the door?" Marcus asked.

"The asshole's been selling dirty juice in here. Then he reached into Bobo's register, tried to grab some cash. Bobo's seventy-one years old. That guy's lucky Motor didn't just shoot him."

"Dirty juice?" Marcus questioned.

"Looks like clean Hemolife, the supposed blood of the young, anti-aging juice. What that guy was pushing is dirty plasma, unscrubbed, unclean, mixed with crystal light, or Kool Aid, who knows what else. Droshure lets it float around the Gutter hoping it will kill off the poor. It gives the same immediate jolt, but it hasn't been filtered, so it's infecting people with all sorts of things that makes em sick, kills them. It's gray market shit," Brodie said.

"Jesus, ok," Marcus said.

Nora leaned in closer to Brodie and Marcus. "You guys know a Scraper named Zyron?" Norah whispered.

"Yeah, he's around. Don't know him well, though. Kind of stays to himself," Marcus said.

"He's dead. No doubt in my mind it was Droshure's people," Brodie said in a whisper.

"I got word that a couple of Splitters did it. Gutted him, then hung him by the feet like a carcass. Rumor is he was working both sides. You guys hear anything like that?" Nora kept her voice low, her eyes scanning across the happy dancing crowd in her bar. With Motor around and Dusty across the way, she felt more secure having the conversation.

"It's not the type of thing we'd talk about at random. That gets you killed. Most flippers don't announce it. For all I know, Marcus could be working both sides. They get orders and they carry on," Brodie said.

"I heard him at a bar once, bragging to some plastic blondie about how much money he was making off Droshure. I didn't think nothing of it.

Figured he just meant with scraping. That was about seven months ago, though," Marcus said.

"You guys need to be careful. With the whole revolution kicking up, people want Boobain out. Boobain wants the Gutter wiped, that includes any Scrapers that seem suspicious. He wants the land, and I don't want either of you to come up missing," Nora said.

"Doesn't matter if shit like this happens or not, there's always risk. I've killed three Splitters and two poachers trying to shake my goods, just in the last two months. It's no joke out there. Brodie here said he's not Scraping anymore. Our boys retiring," Marcus said, slapping Brodie on the back.

"Good, you have to be safe. This is why if I contact you, you need to let me know you're ok," Nora said sincerely. "If I have to take my teams time to make sure you're ok, it's not gonna be a good look for me. This is all getting very real."

"You knew about the car, didn't you?"

'Yes. And you should have better instincts. Neither of you should be accepting favors from anyone right now." Nora gave them a sobering gaze, then walked off to wait on a customer.

"What exactly happened with you two the other night, anyway?" Marcus asked with a chuckle. "I haven't seen this side of her. She's really worried about us. You must have given her the ole big dipp..."

"Leave it alone. She and I will figure it out," Brodie tried to laugh. He couldn't focus, not until he got the chip into Nora's hands and more importantly, out of his.

"Look, she's in the middle of an assignment. You gotta give her some slack, she only turned you down cuz she's trying to protect you," Marcus said. He flagged Bobo over to get two more beers.

"I'm supposed to be the one protecting her," Brodie said.

"Whatever, screw that macho bullshit," Marcus shook his head.

This time when Nora came back over, Brodie got up.

"Hey, I gotta give you something. Can we go to your office," Brodie asked.

"Sounds kinky. Can I come?" Marcus joked.

"Meet me in the back," Nora responded.

Moments later, Nora and Brodie went into the backroom and shut the door. Fully sound proof, bullet proof, yet comfy. It was outfitted with two small couches, a coffee table, desk, chair and a secret stairway.

"Whatever you have to tell me, it's fine. I've gotten used to this," Nora said.

"Don't say that." Brodie took her hands and sat her down. "This has nothing to do with the other night. I shouldn't have walked away from you when you said no, either. But, that's not what this is about."

Brodie pulled the baggie with the tooth out from his pocket. Nora watched as he twisted the top off from the bottom. The small chip revealed itself. Nora took it out of his hand.

"Where'd you get this, whose tooth is this?"

"Marcus and I swept a few spots from the drop sheet earlier. There was a dead couple on the main floor, murder-suicide. The body this belonged to was tucked in the attic, nothing usable but a fairly fresh kill. The hands were cut off, but the teeth were still intact. I don't have the equipment to guarantee if I opened it, it wouldn't trigger a fizzle. I don't know what's on it," Brodie said. "Nor do I want to."

"Gotcha, I'll take it downstairs and my team can check it out."

"The other thing is that when I rolled the body over, a tiny camera dropped from the guy's waist, at least that's where I think it came from. It was motion triggered. I could tell it was clicking images or something. I don't know if it caught me or not. I was covered, except for my eyes, but

I had my glasses on. My point is, whoever killed this guy might have my image somewhere. I smashed it as soon as I saw it," he said.

"Droshure's put the press on Scrapers. Too many of them have been busted leaking info, ending up dead," Nora emphasized. "You have to be smarter than that, Brodie."

"I'm being very careful. I told Marcus he can't go back to Charlie's."

"Jesus Christ Brodie. Charlies, now this?" Nora went for the button to display the staircase, but Brodie stopped her.

"I don't want to see it. Just let me know if its anything I need to know about. For all I know, the guy was a P.I. and its some Corners celebrity plastic cheating with a gutter pro."

"Just promise me you'll lay low while I figure this out? And return my calls," Nora urged.

"I can't make that promise. I need to find my sister," Brodie said. "I'm meeting a contact at Krispy's in an hour. I put a track out last night after I ran in to this guy that knows where she is. Some Corners stiff that's in good with Billy. He said she's a tosser, that Billy's got her under his thumb. Like he's turning her out for tricks and clients."

"Brodie, it isn't safe for you to go running around," Nora said.

"I need to find her and get her out of the Corners, especially before the revolution." Brodie moved toward Nora and took her face in his hands. He kissed her. "I need you to be ok with this. It's my sister."

"I'm not. When are you leaving?" Nora questioned. "I'm going with. Let me call my contacts and see if they have anything. What's the guy's name?"

"Donte McKean, but my guy is on it. Don't risk your team," Brodie pleaded. "I'll call you when we leave Krispy's. That I can promise. And however you know that Potter guy, thank you. Once again, you saved my life."

"You sure Krispy is safe?"

"The safest," Brodie said, heading toward the door.

"Just be careful. And if you leave without me, on this quest to find your sister... you shouldn't bother finding me if and when you get back," Nora said. Brodie was caught off guard by the statement.

"I won't leave without you. Marcus is coming, too." Brodie kissed her and left the room, headed back into the bar. When he didn't see Marcus there, he finally spotted him on the dance floor with the same strawberry blonde from earlier rocking out to *Spin Spin Sugar* by the Sneaker Pimps. Brodie sat down and ordered two more beers. Soon enough, Marcus returned.

"I don't know man. Wildflower Suzie is super dope." Marcus was grinning ear to ear.

"Nora's coming."

"You mean to get your sister? Well good, we'll need her help." Marcus put his arm around Brodie and raised his beer to toast. "To sex and survival."

"To luck." he toasted Marcus back. "And to Wildflower Suzie."

Ten minutes later, Brodie saw Nora come back out to the bar and flagged her over.

"Hey, we gotta get going. I'll let you know when we leave Krispy's. I might not have service there. If you don't hear from me, give it an hour," Brodie said.

"Shit, I forgot we're going over there," Marcus said. He glanced over to Wildflower Suzie. Brodie waited as Marcus chatted her up and got that number, happily securing it in his back pocket, before returning to Brodie. "Ok, now I'm ready."

As he and Marcus walked toward the door, Brodie spotted a man across the room dressed in red slacks, a snug black T-shirt with a Victorian jacket hanging over the chair, talking to two people. He had a tattoo on the top of his hand and a thick gnarly scar up his right pointer finger, almost splitting it in half. Brodie went back to Nora, whispered in her ear. She looked over her shoulder to the guy, discreetly. It was Dusty, but Brodie had no idea he was one of Nora's contacts.

"He's a Splitter. He's in here every now and then. My team keeps an eye on him. I can't make them all leave. It would look suspicious. They just come to dance and rage, anyway. It's not like I'm playing Taylor Swift in here," Nora said.

Brodie knocked on the bar. It was a secret way for him to ask if she was ok. Nora returned with one knock which meant yes, and mouthed 'I'll be fine'.

The setting sun brought the chill of night with it. Brodie and Marcus, covered in their winter gear, moved through the biting cold air toward Krispy's place. Those that lived on the streets were winding down for the night, securing their safety under the cover of blankets, cardboard and whatever else they could find. Brodie and Marcus turned a corner and headed down a graffiti splattered alleyway toward the back of a moderately tall building. At each edge of the alley, two monsters of men stood watch outside their SUVs, providing security. They let Brodie and Marcus pass. Soon, they came to a metal door with a padlock on it midway down the alley. Brodie picked the lock with two small sticks he retrieved from his jacket. An audible click was heard as Marcus lifted the lock and pulled the door open.

Krispy always had different obstacles for people to figure out in order to get into his parties. Pick a lock, climb through a window, go down a short tunnel on hand and knee, kick a door in. If someone couldn't figure out the obstacles, his security bulls would remove them from the property for the night and they'd have to wait for the next party. The apartment complex and the buildings surrounding it had been abandoned two years prior, but a few drug dealers had taken up residence under the watch of Krispy Spade aka Kristian Bowie Spade, one of the biggest dealers in the Gutter and Corners.

Brodie and Marcus were greeted outside Krispy's door on the seventh floor by two topless and very tall Spanish beauties holding AK47's.

"Hola Lola," Marcus said to one of the women, kissing her on the cheek.

"Hi guys, go right in," Lola said.

"I see you're both freezing, you want my coat?" Marcus winked as he glanced at their rigid nipples.

"He pays us well to keep our tits out, watch the door and greet folks. Besides, it's not that cold, we've got these to keep us warm," Lola said, massaging her AK47.

"And we got great tits. Who doesn't want to show off great tits?" The other gal spoke the words in between snaps of her gum, looping it between her tongue and teeth.

"I'll catch you on the way out to discuss which one of you is having my babies," Marcus joked.

"That would cost you a lot more than 500 bucks, sweetheart." Lola held the door open for them and winked. Brodie laughed, pulling Marcus inside and away from the ladies.

Krispy's place took up the whole seventh floor. The area he opened for his parties was slightly sullied and had two-bedrooms, two bathrooms and a huge open living room. He took ownership of the whole building and used the 10th floor for his office. His watchdogs had their perch and kept an eye out for trouble from the roof. The scramble rooms took up the top three floors above Krispy's office. What Brodie liked about being there was that all electronics were shut off, meaning Krispy's place was rigged as a cold zone.

The whole building was encased in a Faraday Shield and all Wi-Fi was blocked. The only systems that worked were those of Krispy's team. Camera's, phones, anything connected to Wi-Fi, 8G, was blocked from the whole perimeter and interior of the building, excluding the top floor. Krispy had access throughout, but all others systems were jammed at the door. That meant if Brodie was there and someone recognized him, they wouldn't be able to report it until they left. It also meant if he was in danger, he couldn't call for help.

He and Marcus made a beeline to the kitchen and were met by three huge generators set side by side, like kegs of beer.

"Jesus Christ, where does he find this shit? I don't know why he doesn't rig the system in the basement, tack the ropes and power the whole place instead of using these shitty generators and making everyone walk up seven fucking flights of stairs." By the time the words came out of Marcus's mouth, the lights had already flickered twice.

"It's so he can see who's coming and going, besides he doesn't want his life to look too glamourous. He's got these mirrors and shit set up on this floor so his team can see everyone, at any moment. He doesn't need to tack into shit. Plus, he's a perv, he likes watching people bang and stuff. He's got every inch of this building covered." Brodie reached in the beer-packed fridge and grabbed three cans out. He shoved one in his pocket, gave one to Marcus and cracked the third open for himself.

"Bit of a madhouse in here," Marcus laughed.

On the surface, Krispy was a sleazy megalomaniac, but underneath the exterior, he was Brodie's most loyal and knowledgeable contact, excluding Nora. Brodie didn't like referring to her like that, though. Krispy tracked everything he purchased, drank and ate, scanning it all through a high-tech food scanner on the sixth floor, checking for toxins, trackers, bombs and parasites. He never took food or drink that was handed to him. He was paranoid and suspicious of everyone, partly because of the drugs he did, partly because of the work he did. That's why he was so scrappy, he barely ate. He no longer trusted reality.

Krispy traded for the food scanner by selling drugs to an FDA agent friend. Brodie knew Krispy sold to a lot of people, didn't matter if they were with the Underground, simple plastics, Boobain's people, or even President Boobain himself. He didn't ask, nor did he care as long as he got his money. Krispy was a connector, but he was very selective about whom he kept company with, even those invited to his parties. Everyone invited was either a friend or someone he wanted to watch, observe. Deep-dive background checks were done on everyone he interacted with, both personally and professionally.

Brodie saw the muscular beanstalk of a dope man holding court across the room. Black metal screens with invisible blocking sensors covered all the windows, but one. That one was specially made with the sensors infused through the glass. It was the only window to see out, but no one could see in. Brodie's eyes looked out at the trail of small garbage fires along the sidewalks, then scanned Krispy's pad. His condo resembled a furniture store, in that the furniture was nice, but completely mismatched in pattern. Most of it had been stolen from upscale vacant homes early on, after the split. Krispy called it, dystopian chic, and it was.

If there was one thing he and Krispy had in common, it was paranoia. Brodie looked around at the vagrants that made up the party of misfits.

It wasn't just homeless floaters. Krispy's reach was far and wide. It was a mishmash of creative types, posers and plastics, along with some chest puffing business workers from the Corners. Brodie hated the scene, but he needed to get the information from Krispy and stay on his good side. Unfortunately, Krispy didn't like to be rushed. He only talked business after being in someone's company for at least an hour. He told Brodie that he didn't trust eager people, said it was a sign of guilt and deception. Then he'd carry on about Buddhist mentality, say we are not of the capacity to control the outcomes of others. So, Brodie needed to be patient and just keep an eye on the room until Krispy called him over to talk. Keep his buff up over his face as much as he could, in between sips of beer.

"Lotta chokes and posers in here tonight," Brodie leaned over to Marcus.

"Hey, lonely hearts bring big bucks, guys a great business man," Marcus said. "It's like drugstore speed-dating in here. For every one of these Corners tools that Krispy gets laid or sells some jolly to, he's making hard bank. He could live in the thrill on a yacht off the coast of Positano if he wanted to, but this is what he chooses. Why?"

"He's got his reasons. Besides he's getting tape on folks, filling up his blackmail stash. After he's got what he needs I'm sure he'll disappear," Brodie said.

"Truth."

Brodie and Marcus meandered through the room, watching as scabby coots got high off the jolly, then passed them over to a squeaky-clean white-collar Jones. Two guys and a giddy young chick sat hunched forward on a couch, engrossed in a story Krispy was spilling. At forty-six years old, he looked like a burned-out Alice Cooper, his foot resting up on the edge of a coffee table as if he was ready to sing 'Schools Out'. Wearing green cargo shorts and shell-toe canvas sneakers, he leaned toward his audience, skin glimmering with sweat, eyeliner running trails through the wrinkles comforting his eyes. His long, gray hair was roped in a ponytail, and a checkered fanny pack dangled from his waist. Brodie called it Krispy's golden codpiece. Inside, he kept his drugs, stash, cash and pistol.

Brodie noticed Boss, one of Krispy's security guys, across the room. He stood at 6'8 and was thick as a boulder. He remembered the night Boss shot a guy's hand clean off after he tried to touch Krispy's stash pack. The guy's hand was left hanging by a string of tendons and ligaments.

"Hey, never mind the suits, I haven't been around this many hot bendies in forever." Marcus eyed up a well-dressed, sexy plastic in a Prada skirt.

Brodie pulled Marcus over toward Krispy, waiting for him to finish his story. He was right in the middle of taking a hit of Liquid K when the woman in his fan club pulled out an old Polaroid camera as her shrill voice cut across the room.

"Let me take a picture of you, Krisp," the caked-out woman blurted out. She jumped up and down with lucid excitement, as her breasts bounced all about, then without warning one bounced right out of her shirt, drawing attention to the necklace of hickeys sucked around her neck.

"No pictures, scamp, put your tits away," Krispy said as he continued, not missing a beat.

"Oh, come on, let me take a picture of you," the woman pouted.

"Fuck off," Krispy said as he took another hit.

"Come on, just one, pleeeeeaaase? You're so fucking badass." It was clear she was trying to prime him for free jolly.

Krispy grabbed her camera and slammed it to the ground, bits of plastic broke, flying about. As he stomped on the remaining pieces, his eyes caught Brodie and Marcus nearby. He looked to the woman and softly, spitting venom said, "there's your fucking picture, fucking trying to get me captured. No one takes my picture." He snapped his finger in the air and immediately a man removed the woman from the party. Then, suddenly glee covered his face as he turned back to Brodie and Marcus with open arms and walked over.

"Hey, it's Digger and the Flame Boy, what's up my friends? Glad you finally made it over. Feels like forever." Krispy patted the guys on the back. He wore veneers that were never set quite right in his mouth. The fake set rested slightly off, forcing him to talk with an impediment, which Brodie thought was one of the coolest accents he'd ever heard.

"Hey Krisp, where's Marley? I didn't see her," Marcus inquired.

"Shit man, one night she just flew away like a little fucking bird," Krispy said. "Got pissed and said I needed to get political, smashed my 70-inch tv. I told her all I needed was to get paid and laid. She shot a beer at my head, bought a fucking gas mask, said she was going to save the world and took off for California like a week ago. Like she was going to go burn her bra or some shit. As if we can't watch the whole fucking world from here. Fuck California." Krispy puffed his chest as if he was invincible, impressed with himself for having gotten all of the words out.

"Black tongue Marley? She left you to go protest? She stopped doing Ice?" Marcus couldn't believe it. Marley loved her drugs even more than dick...and Marley love dick.

"Seriously, guys, it was madness. She stopped like a fucking cold turkey," he said. "Something triggered her. You know, maybe these Victorian Splitter clowns banging shit and knocking on folks, spooking people. That shits below my concern, but maybe she felt like she had to fight. I would protect her from the world. God dammit I fucking miss her."

Brodie could see genuine emotion on Krispy's face, he was struggling without Marley. He looked wounded, high as hell, but wounded.

"She'll regret it. Protesting's for the birds," Marcus said.

"She is a bird, man, my bird," Krispy replied.

"Ah, she'll be back Krisp, don't worry. She loves you. Besides, it's good she's getting clean," Brodie said.

Krispy took off to greet some guests as Brodie lingered about. Marcus worked the room and approached two finely dressed plastics from the Corners. Brodie had met his share. They were rich chicks from the Corners who had a lot of work done on them, who sought out tunnel parties. That's what they called the gatherings held by rich dealers and influencers living in the Gutter. Brodie was already bored with the scene and growing antsy. He went toward the door to go outside and check his phone quick, but his path was blocked by the silhouette of a woman.

"Hey, why you in such a hurry?" the woman asked.

Brodie fended off the dancing fingertips crawling toward him as the woman reached out for his shoulder. Up close, he saw the touch came from an average brunette. Fake tits but 'only to accommodate her frame', Brodie guessed. She wore a stylish wide legged Kalvin Clein jumper, the affordable Calvin Klein knockoff, with very impractical stilettos. Brodie could tell with heels that high and cleavage that deep, she was from the Corners. Women didn't dress like that in the slums unless they wanted trouble or were packing heat and not afraid to use it.

"Not in a hurry. You want one?" Brodie pulled the beer out of his pocket.

"I don't drink beer," the woman said. She pinched her thumb and pointer finger and drew them up to her lips, mimicking smoking a joint.

"Gotcha. You a friend of Krispy's?" Brodie pulled a rolled joint apart from several clustered in a baggie and gave her one. He lit it for the woman as she burned the paper halfway down.

"Sort of. Let's just say you and I probably know some of the same people. I've seen you around." The woman said the words in a seductive whisper, as she blew rings of smoke from her mouth.

"I don't think you have," Brodie's eyes smiled back, his balaclava still covering the bottom half of his face.

"You should take that down from your face and enjoy yourself. Life is short." She eyed him up head to toe, her gaze lingering around Brodie's cock. She wasn't enough to get him excited, but enough to distract him from his boredom and paranoia, momentarily.

"You came all the way from the Corners for a party," Brodie said.

"I have clients that need things. I come in to get those things for my clients and a little something for myself. Seems like you'd have a nice face under there. Why so shy?" The woman swayed her hand across the denim of Brodie's pants, brushing against his hips. He firmly removed the manicured fingernails and hand from going too far. The woman quickly spun around and managed to rub her ass against him before he grabbed her by the waist and moved her off him. He was over the party, but the woman only took his action as playful. He was ready to go, but he couldn't rush Krispy. He peered over at Marcus who was dancing with a plastic.

"You work for Droshure or Boobain?" Brodie asked.

"Why would you say that?" The woman squinted her eyes at Brodie, seductively pouting.

"Everyone from the Corners ultimately works for one or the other, even if that's not who writes your paycheck. It all comes from the same bank of dirty money," Brodie said.

"Oh, honey, let's not get it twisted. I work for myself," the woman said, slightly offended. "And before you get all coy, you should know that just because you're famous doesn't mean I have the desire or the financial need to deal with some preoccupied emo punk, just to get some dick. Plenty of dick here. You have…"

Krispy walked up with two bouncers who interrupted the woman and grabbed her gently by the arm, removing her from the party. Krispy put his arm around Brodie, guiding him out to the hallway and down to a smaller studio unit. Once they were alone, Brodie took down his face cover as Krispy's demeanor changed.

"They'll take care of her, probably just give her a memory block, make her forget the day. You know, she'll forget being here," Krispy said sounding a lot more sober than Brodie thought he was. "More importantly she'll forget she ever saw you," Krispy calmly said. "Sounded like she might know there's money on your head. They'll drive her car to the edge of the Corners, put her in it. She'll wake up not knowing what happened. No harm, no foul."

"Thank you."

"My uncle Tommy, tracked down your boy, Donte. They nabbed him on his way back to the Corners. They have him in Creepers Row and he's all yours when you get there," Krispy said.

"That's the best news I've heard all day. I owe you big time, Krisp."

"You don't owe me a thing, man," Krispy patted him on the shoulder. "Just don't tell anyone I helped you out. I need people thinking all I am is a big dope man that throws killer tunnel parties. You're my amigo. You saved my mom's life. Besides, you pay me back by keeping my secrets and staying alive," Krispy said.

CHAPTER 15

Billy got up from his leather lounger as the doorbell rang persistently, accompanied by several knocks. He knew by the impatience that it had to be his father. As he opened the door, Nathan stood with the disposition of an annoyed sloth. Cece was already sitting comfortably on the couch across from them with a displeased grin, never having been much of a fan of either of them. With a glass of wine under her grip, she was doing just fine and entertained by how important Billy always thought he was.

"What is this about Billy? I'm going to be late for a meeting," Nathan said.

"Yeah, bro, this better be good." Cece was a little drunk but fully intact and not being held captive in any visible capacity.

"Droshure has a big problem, but you two need to know something before they do. Follow me."

The two trailed Billy through his place, past several bedrooms, into his back office. He leaned over the keyboard and tapped on a 50" screen in front of them, making the images of Brodie largely visible. He played the short string of footage, as Nathan and Cece hovered over his shoulder trying to get a closer view.

"Who is that?" Cece asked. She recognized Brodie instantly but said nothing.

Billy enhanced the images and the footage appeared even larger.

"Who does that look like to you guys, the glasses, the fucking mole under the left eye?" Billy asked.

She was well aware of the rift between Brodie and Billy. She chose to remain expressionless until she heard the rest of Billy's pitch. Without realizing it, she took a step back, which didn't go unnoticed by Billy.

"Enough with the riddles. Who is it and why do I care?" Nathan asked.

"That's Brodie, can't you see it? When's the last time you talked to him, Cece?" Billy turned his focus to her.

"I don't know, two months ago, maybe. He hasn't called me back but he goes off grid sometimes, why? Where's the picture from?"

Billy got Cece a new phone over a month ago and put one of his burner phone numbers in as Brodie's. So, any time Cece tried to call or text Brodie, the calls and messages went to Billy. He took her old phone under the guise of disposing it, but had been messing with Brodie ever since with prank calls. Billy knew exactly why Brodie hadn't called her back.

Moments later, the screen showed a blurred Brodie bent over, knocking the teeth out of Nolan Petri's corpse, then noticing the camera, just as the footage fizzled out and went blank.

"So what? So, it's Brodie, who cares?" Nathan said.

"Remember the UN guy, never mind. Point is, it's clear that Brodie got something off the body of a VIP. Droshure's idiots dumped the body in a random house in the Gutter. Wisconsin for some asinine reason. It's hard to make out, but the tech is sure there was some devise Brodie took from the mouth before he knocked out the teeth."

"This is trivial to me. Why do I care? Besides, even if this is something, it doesn't connect to me in any way." Nathan was as kind as he was patient, neither were part of his construction.

"You should care because right now we have that fucking United Nations guys computer and the documents have Droshure and Boobain's name all over them. You know what we don't have though? The code to the ghost hole on his computer," Billy spoke aggressively, frustrated. "That means we have no way to find out what else is on the computer and no way to know what else they have on us. None of Droshure's teams can extract it. No one seems to be able to track down this Christopher Scott, whose name comes up as a contact all over the documents. I'm going to tell you once, dad. Do not trust Jacob, not anymore. And if Brodie or this Scott guy have dirt connecting Stoyton to Boobain or Droshure, everyone and everything we've been doing dies."

"Don't be so dramatic, you sound like Brodie right now," Nathan said. "This is your problem. And I'm not like you, my work is done behind a desk. If that's Brodie and he was close enough to that body for them to snap footage and you're worried, bring him in. Make it about family. And send Cece to hustle around and find this Christopher Scott."

"Ha, hey, I'm right here. I don't work for you guys and I certainly don't 'hustle' for you guys," Cece said.

"You relax," Billy said to Cece. "You have a couple more marks to clear from your blemished record before you're clean, so just sit tight. I still own you. Jacob put out a tag for capture alive to all Droshure Scrapers and Splitters to have him brought to me. Most don't know he's your son or my brother, so that helps us." Billy couldn't stop pacing. Any other adversary would be fine, but Brodie triggered him in a way no one else could.

"He's never been my son," Nathan said.

"Oh God, dad. Get over it, he's almost forty fucking years old." Cece rolled her eyes. "I swear you two are ridiculous. Brodie can't stand either of you as much as you can't stand him. I'm going, I have a date." She slammed her wine and grabbed her coat.

"Cece, if you leave, I'll have you brought back. I need you for a party, some of these guys might know this Scott person," Billy said.

"She's high, again. She can't be trusted like this, anyway. Let her go," Nathan said.

"She knows too much, dad."

"God, I can't stand the two of you when you're together. And you don't even like each other," Cece snickered, shaking her head, annoyed.

"Hey, I am the reason you were even able to negotiate your title. So, dial down the Wonder Woman attitude unless you want to join Brodie once we lock him up," Billy said.

"This isn't even about Brodie," Cece demanded. "And you don't 'own' me, so fuck you for that. If you wanna take over Droshure's company, stop acting like a bitch and just do it."

"Find out what Donte knows. He goes back and forth to the Gutter all the time," Billy said.

"I can't stand that sweaty leech. Isn't there anyone else?" Cece put her coat on.

"Just call him, he knows you and he likes you. Or go see him," Billy begged. "Dad and I need to go about our business as if this was just a random guy. If you hear from Brodie, you better fucking let me know right away. I just need you to do this for me, please."

Cece stood by the door, having confiscated one of Billy's bottles of red wine for her own.

"If I hear from him, I'll let ya know. Thanks for the wine," Cece said, shutting the door behind her as she left.

CHAPTER 16

B ack at Krispy's, he hit a button on what at first seemed to be a simple wall. A secret compartment opened out like a drawer. He grabbed a small envelope and handed it to Brodie.

"They've got your boy in Creepers Row. Here's two lesser traveled routes where my uncle has protection watching for your passage and some other intel he thought you might need. He said the Row is littered with Splitters. Open your bag." Brodie complied, swinging his backpack around to his chest, unzipping it. Krispy pulled out some poorly bleached-out vintage Halloween masks. "Looks like the Flintstones or something. All this mask shit is kinda stupid if you ask me, but right now, it's what'll keep you alive," Krispy laughed.

"Nice," Brodie said, taking a closer look at one of the masks.

"When you get near Creepers Row you put these on. There are four. Whoever you're with, you all need a mask. This is how Tommy's people will know you and know where you are. There are tracking sensors in each mask. This is how you'll draw the least attention from other Splitters, too," Krispy assured. "If you stop too long, my uncle will send for you. Anyone asks, you just say you're from Ohio or some shit, traveling through. This is how you stay alive."

"I appreciate this," he said sincerely.

Brodie knew he could trust Krispy. They had known each other for over a decade and Brodie had literally brought him back to life on more than one occasion. He was Krispy's personal medic and their friendship carried with it an unspoken loyalty. Right after the class wars, Krispy called Brodie in a panic. His mother was ill and needed treatment. Over the next several weeks Brodie visited her almost daily. In Krispy's eyes, Brodie saved her life. Unfortunately, six months later she was killed. Went to the grocery store and her body was found down an alley three hours later.

"Say no more. Now, you know your bro's got his flies out buzzin around for you, right?

"Yeah, it's ok. I have some things in place if needed," Brodie said.

"All right then, let's go get caked, my brother. Don't rush it, leave in the morning. Logical progression, my friend. Never rush anything important. This is your life. Go in there, I'll be back in shortly." With the envelope resting deep in Brodie's pocket, he went back into the party alone. Krispy would come back in from a different area moments later.

"We gotta go," Brodie said as he found Marcus chatting up a plastic.

"Seriously? But my stick, my lonely sti..." Before Marcus finished his sentence, he glanced up and saw that Brodie was serious. Marcus leaned over to the woman, kissed her on the cheek, and took her card.

"Gotta go baby. Mom called, dinners ready," Marcus said.

Brodie and Marcus stumbled through the brittle night air on their way back to Brodie's place. He still had his wits about him, but Marcus was pretty lit. They trekked out in the cold, winding through a trail of alleys, passing drunks, bums and night walkers. Fires flared for warmth but other than that, the night was filled with darkness. Brodie mentioned that they needed to get to Creepers Row, making Marcus swear not to tell anyone.

It was just a click after midnight, as the wind snapped at their faces, moving them both closer to stone cold sober.

"Nora just texted. She's meeting us at my place. I had no signal in there. Some chick was all on me, told me I was famous. She said it like it was a curse," Brodie said.

"Dude, chicks will say anything to get on you. I'm sure she didn't mean anything by it. Not everything tracks back to Droshure and your brother," Marcus said, struggling with the words.

Brodie shook his head at Marcus, then smiled wide.

"You're so right. Fuck 'em," Brodie put his arm around Marcus as they walked.

Suddenly, a howling screech caught their attention. A shrill cry of pain rolled out into the air. Brodie put his hand on his stomach as a knot twisted through it. They just needed to stay focused and get to his place, the environment around him was taunting him, though. The concrete walls they passed oozed with the stench of freshly splashed urine and stale garbage, musky air. A busted-up Amtrak train car sat, splattered with graffiti, half on and half off the tracks. The welcome aroma of marijuana seeped out from the open cracks and crevices, smothering the stink in the air.

Another audible shriek cut out, swimming through the alleys. This time, sounding much closer. As the two paused, another yelp lashed out into the atmosphere like thunder. Brodie put his finger to his lips as they inched closer to the alleys corner. They peered around and saw three Splitters dressed in their blacks and Victorian garb, military shit kickers on their feet, brutalizing a couple that was motionless on the ground.

The threesome had vintage British Army S10 gas masks on. Most didn't know the identity of the Splitters, but the Underground did. The Underground had identity charts with pictures of faces, specific characteristics, height, weight, and nicknames used for each Splitter in their respective regions. It was rare they would be 'in uniform' without something covering their face, almost always some sort of mask. Brodie knew most Splitters wore old, bleached out masks, anything from Halloween to masquerade to home-made thrown together face covering, anything to hide their identity. Tonight, the fact that this group wore gas masks gave Brodie the impression they were high in rank. Only high-ranking Splitters were allowed to wear gasmasks of any kind.

Brodie stood, frozen in motion, waiting for his mind to force his body into action. Nearby on the ground, the woman's body was sprawled out, disjointed, already beaten and bloodied. The Splitters whaled on the man on the ground and hadn't noticed Brodie and Marcus approaching, yet. One of them raised a hand and struck the man with a thick live wire, as sparks showered out. The Splitter whipped the wire against the ground like a lasso, getting off on the jolts, finally noticing Marcus and Brodie charging toward them. Marcus and Brodie grabbed anything available to break up the kill jam. Brodie grabbed his gun, aiming it at the Splitters.

"Get the fuck off them." Marcus dashed toward the Splitters, trying to scare them out of action.

The lead Splitter, Bugs, lunged his thick boot into the dead man's face, then as if to taunt Brodie and Marcus, flexed his muscles like a gorilla. Brodie shot him dead, not wasting time. Marcus got to Bugs and removed his gas mask, then took his weapons and wallet, as one of the Splitters disappeared to the edge of the alley. Brodie got into a fist battle with the remaining Splitter, Joke. He was bulky with overreaching upper traps and thick hulky arms that kept the Splitters neck locked in place. He tried to fight Brodie, but Brodie got him to the ground and ripped off his gasmask. Lucky for Brodie and Marcus, Splitters were chronically less likely to kill with guns. More often, their fetish was beating people to death, taking lives with their bare hands.

The third Splitter came back, catching Marcus off guard, knocking the gun out of his hand. The Splitter lunged at him with a broken bottle, slicing through his coat and across his forearm. It didn't faze Marcus, as he followed up, whacking the Splitter in the face with a nearby building brick, sending him to the ground. Marcus ripped off the Splitters mask as the Splitter managed to knock him over. The Splitter scrambled to his feet and ran before Marcus could get up and take aim.

Marcus turned at the sound of grisly growls and saw Brodie, buff now down around his neck exposing his face, cut up and battered, with blood drizzling down the side of his face like icicles. He had the second Splitter to the ground, gripped by his hair, beating him on autopilot.

"Brodie, stop! He's dead." Still holding his gun, Marcus tried to help him up off the Splitter, but Brodie shook him away.

"I'm fine." Brodie looked to the couples' mangled bodies. Then, abruptly let go of the Splitters hair and dropped the lifeless body to the concrete. Brodie's head was in a swirl. All the anger he had stored up over the past few years had been unleashed in a fury of rage. He looked around, noticing the Splitter he had shot, dead on the ground.

"Where's the third?"

"He ran off," Marcus said. "You sure you're ok, man?" Marcus extended his hand and this time Brodie took it and got up to standing.

"I'm fine," Brodie said. "We gotta get out of here. That's Bugs I shot, I didn't know. They'll be back to find out who did this."

Just as Brodie and Marcus reached the end of the alley, a voice yelled out as a figure stepped into view from the shadows behind them. It was the third Splitter standing at the opposite edge of darkness.

"You just killed my comrades. Bugs and Joke were important leaders. Consider yourself marked for death, Brodie Frost. I will kill you and your friend," the third Splitter proclaimed. The Splitter stepped back in the shadows, once again hidden in complete darkness. His hyena-like laughter bounced out along the concrete walls. "You will die soon, Brodie Frost, we know who you are," the Splitters voice trailed off.

Hearing his full name out loud and clear threw Brodie off. This was the second time in 2 days. He was starting to realize the severity of everything going on.

"Let's go," Marcus said. "We gotta get out of here." Marcus grabbed Brodie by the coat as the two ran off toward Brodie's place. They needed to throw off anyone who might follow them. If there was one thing they both knew, it was that word would travel fast and more Splitters would be hunting for them.

"This is what they do," Brodie yelled. Dirt and blood still covered his buff and face.

"He's going to bring more back. I guarantee it. You know that guy's name, the one that ran?" Marcus said, nose to nose with him. Brodie finally made eye contact.

"I think it's Ryder." Brodie sprinted off but Marcus grabbed him by the coat, again.

"Hey, we have to stick together. Your bro put a tag on you. We have to be careful."

"I needed to see Krispy. You wouldn't have been able to stop me."

"You think whoever is involved in all this didn't have eyes on me torching that place? The Splitter you just obliterated, that's Bugs. The other guy you killed, that's Joke. They are high up in rank. You don't leave my fucking sight. You lost that privilege with your silence," Marcus demanded, frustrated. "We have to get you Underground. They can protect you."

Brodie, scratching his arm, didn't want to hear it.

"We have to go to Creepers Row, that's where I get information about my sister. I don't feel safe anywhere so it doesn't matter where I go. I need to get her out of there," he said.

"Dammit, Brodie, you said it yourself. They will torture and kill you," Marcus said.

Brodie didn't care, he took off running. Marcus sprinted, trying to keep stride next to him, both on guard like Dobermans.

"We can get you to the Underground. I'll go find your sister. I'm advising against you going to your place, they might be waiting," Marcus said.

"Fine, you've advised me, now clear your conscious. I'm getting my stuff and leaving. I've got enough connections to get ID's, gear, and scribblers. I've already made the calls." Brodie tried to slow his thoughts and took a breath. "Look, Cece is all I have left and I have to make sure she's safe." Brodie threw his hands up. He'd made up his mind. "So, are you gonna go with me?"

"Of course, you're my best friend." Marcus didn't want to go, but there was no way he'd let Brodie go alone.

"Good, I can use your help." Brodie continued as he caught a glimpse of the bloody mess on his gloves and clothes. He shivered as the cold sweat on his skin collided with the brisk chill in the night air. With his fists still clenched and his hands unsteady, Brodie tried to pull his body out of shock. He needed to be solid for what was ahead. He could tell Marcus felt helpless, but this was just how it had to be.

As they neared Brodie's place. Marcus ran the perimeter while both kept watch, guns drawn. Brodie knew Marcus was a ride or die friend and that he would do the same for him, but Marcus had something Brodie had envied since the day they met. Optimism. Marcus went to surf in California with Brodie, long before the class wars. Brodie made him come along to stop in at his dad's place. Marcus witnessed every insult chucked in Brodie's direction from his father and brother. As if being a surgeon was a career for the meek, not a man's job. Marcus knew the family history. He'd even dated Cece casually, which was why he knew the importance of finding her.

Brodie swiped his access card as they scurried inside his condo building, fingers cautiously on their triggers as they ran up the winding maze of stairs. Finally, at his door, Brodie fumbled with his keys, losing grip as they clattered to the floor. Marcus swooped them up and unlocked it. Brodie's thoughts were two steps ahead of his actions as he glanced around. Fiercely numb, his adrenaline still pumped like an angry drum. Never would he have imagined his brother would go to such lengths, as to put a bounty out to the Splitters. But Marcus had warned him about his family long ago, as did Nora, but that was when Brodie was still hopeful that he might regain some semblance of normalcy, at least with his siblings. That was before Billy set him up that day three years back in October, when the attacks happened.

Brodie crossed the threshold of his condo and caught sight of Nora standing up from his couch. Several backpacks and a few totes sat packed next to her. He struggled to know what to say. She had warned him about something like this happening, over and over. He watched her eyes scan his body with trepidation, then lock in on his bruised and bloodied face as he removed his buff.

"What happened?" Nora said as she scolded them both with her eyes.

Brodie wanted to respond, but his voice was lost. With every attempt at words, the letters fell apart on his tongue. He grabbed his stomach and ran for the bathroom, barely making it to the toilet, as he slammed the door shut with his foot and puked. Brodie had never felt more afraid of dying, the thought made his mind skip for a minute as he sat on the bathroom floor, gripping the sides of the porcelain bowl.

"What the hell happened, is he ok? Why isn't he saying anything?" Nora asked looking to Marcus. Something hadn't gone as planned. She could tell.

Marcus tried to get Nora to sit down.

"I'm not sitting down."

"We ran into some Splitters on the way back. You remember how Brodie always puked when he first started scraping?" Marcus asked, trying to slow his adrenaline. "His anxiety is high like that again, the last few days, its fucked right now. I have never seen him kick the shit out of someone like that before."

"He got in a fight?"

"The Splitters, Joke, Bugs, and Ryder on the way back from Krispy's. Joke and Bugs are dead. I'm sure Ryder is gathering the gang. Brodie's contact is holding some Donte guy from the Corners in Creepers Row. He wants to go now. If he would have been alone, he'd be dead. They would have killed him," Marcus said.

"I'm going with him," she said. "I just- I'm trying to think about the best option. They're going to be looking for both of you."

"Everything is starting, Nora, you know this. He thinks if they're willing to go after him, they're holding Cece, too. What did he need to talk to you about alone the other night? Did it have to do with the house where he found the body? Did he tell you he had me burn the place? Ever since then, shits been getting upside down."

"I'm going to check on him." Nora went and knocked on the bathroom door, gently pushed it open. Brodie was sitting on the closed toilet, his bloody shirts and coat on the floor beside him, trying to get his thoughts to stop spiraling.

"Are you ok?"

"I don't know, anymore. We have to go, though," Brodie said.

He stood and turned on the faucet, splashed water over his face, rinsing off the blood. He winced as the water stung each fresh cut. He sat again, as Nora grabbed a washcloth and gently dabbed his wounds.

"Have you tried to get a hold of your sister? Are you sure she isn't just busy?"

"Nora, please don't do this. I can't get a hold of her. I have tried everything. Something is not right. Please just trust me."

"Well, that chip you found has information on it. It's like the key to a master database of information. My guess is that Boobain had the guy you found, Nolan Petri, killed. He worked for the UN. He was investigating Boobain and Droshure, part of a bigger investigation into Stoyton Society and other international oligarchs that are involved in some dark stuff. Boobain's a small piece, but that's usually the easiest way in, through the weakest link," she paused. "I need your understanding that once we get your sister out, I'll have to question her about your family, Droshure and Boobain. Just to see if she knows anything," Nora said.

"What do you mean hold her?" Brodie washed up as Nora talked.

"Brodie, she's been living in the Corners for years. From the outside, it seems she and your brother get along just fine. This could all be a set up. You need to understand that and take this seriously."

"She wouldn't set me up," Brodie said. He turned off the faucet and looked at Nora. She put her hand to his face, again. He removed it, but didn't let go. "Whatever you need to do, I get it. We gotta get on the road."

"I don't think it's a good idea."

"You don't have to come with. The revolution is starting," he explained. "Krispy told us his lady went with a huge group to the edge of the Corners to protest. Hopefully that will provide a good distraction. The timing for me to go into the Corners is perfect. You said it yourself; this revolution has a global reach. That's where the focus and concern will be. Not on us."

"My team is still decoding the last few encrypted files on the chip. They'll alert me if there is anything we need to know." Nora kissed him gently on his split lip, a part of her not wanting to let him do any of this. They stood face to face, wishing they could disappear. A knock on the door disrupted their moment.

"Hurry up guys. If we're doing this, we gotta go now," Marcus demanded.

Nora opened the door and went out to the living room.

Brodie went to his bedroom and shut the door, locked it. He peeled off the rest of his clothes, now seeing the full wreckage done to his body. He touched his ribs with a wincing jolt of pain, recoiling. He was sure at least one was bruised, if not several. Whatever this was, he knew it was just the beginning. He put on clean clothes and got himself together.

Back in the living room Marcus and Nora packed up some food and final supplies.

"Is he gonna be ok?" Marcus asked.

"He's shook. Sorry if I was rude, I'm just worried about him," Nora said.

"I'm glad you're coming." Marcus knew her history, that she was International Bureau of Special Investigations (IBSI), Nitzer Scholar Class 5, deep cover, so deep she didn't exist for years, literally untraceable.

Brodie grabbed his laptop, along with some eater ointment for tracker burns and infection, flare sticks and pepper bombs. He flipped his mattress up and pulled two gas masks out from the underside of his bedframe. A red one he had gotten Nora for her birthday and a dark neon blue one for himself. He packed the masks, laced up his Doc Martens, threw the bag over his shoulder, and opened the door. He dropped his arm, scratching again, then walked into the living room

"Is there anything else you guys aren't telling me about what's going on?" Nora probed.

"You know everything I know. Actually, you know more than I know," Marcus said.

"Brodie, you're not leaving our sight," Nora said. "What he found at that house, it's with my team. For all purposes, neither of you even knows it exists. Make sure your lines are secure."

"I got a Yogi- nothing gets through," Marcus said.

"I've known how to get through a Yogi for years. Just clear your line and keep all communications to a minimum," Nora said. She wanted to trust Marcus to be smart.

"I'm not even telling anyone I'm leaving. You got nothing to worry about with me," Marcus said.

"All right, let's trash the place, whoever's coming is coming soon," Brodie said.

Marcus grabbed a lamp and bashed the base of it into a nearby desktop monitor. Brodie looked at him.

"What? You got what you need in your bags, right?" Marcus kicked in a small 36-inch monitor with a grin. Nora shredded the couch cushions, removing anything she found hidden inside, all the while watching the interaction between Brodie and Marcus.

"Fine, trash it all, but don't burn the place down. I mean it. The people that live here are people I look out for. They don't need disruption. Anything we need to burn, put it in the plastic bags and we'll get rid of it on the way." Brodie peered out the window. He couldn't shake the feeling of doom. He didn't see anything suspicious outside in the darkness, just can fires and the occasional car. He prayed that the clear path he saw in his mind was real. He prayed no one would pop out as they pulled out of the garage. He prayed he wouldn't be dead by morning.

CHAPTER 17

Hours before dawn, Nora and Brodie quickly lugged their backpacks and three green military bags down through the tunnels under Nora's bar, out to an underground lot where her black Mustang was parked. Marcus stood against the car, smoking a cigarette.

"I'll load em up," Marcus said.

Brodie and Nora ran back inside. Once upstairs, another car approached and parked in the lot. Soon, Motor got out of his car with his long hair rolled into a Chonmage and a buff covering the lower half of his face. He and Nora quickly hugged.

"Brodie, you know Motor. Thanks for coming so quick. We have to get on the road before sun up." Nora paused, giving Motor a second glance. "I don't think I've ever seen you with your hair up, looks cool." Nora clapped her hands. "Ok, chop, chop we gotta hustle."

"Any special instructions or just the usual routine?" Motor knew the drill. Nora had vetted him before she hired him. He was an agent, just a lesser class, more muscle, than mole, but his intellect was not to be underrated. He did a superior job protecting Nora and watching her back.

"No Splitters in here unless they're with Dusty," Nora said. "Even still, keep an eye on him. If anyone asks, I have a cold, that includes Dusty. No clones, no plastics. I need you here 24/7 until I return. Absolutely no one in this office, including you after this moment. If things get flipped, there's money under the two middle floorboards in my bedroom along with a safe spot to meet six months from today. If there is a danger observed, the team will contact you. Don't mess with any screens or camera's if you see them. Leave them on their timed hours. My team gets the feed and if they're turned off, an alert will be triggered and a Finder will come. If shit really goes down, burn the place to the ground and let the boss know."

"Just be careful. Contact me if you need assistance," Motor said, taking the keys.

"Thank you. And don't lose this," Nora said, handing a phone to Motor. "It's the only way I will be able to reach you. Lock up after us, make yourself at home. I owe you big time."

Nora threw the backpack over her shoulder and tossed a small satchel to Brodie. Motor walked back out to the bar and as soon as he was out of the room, Nora and Brodie went down through the tunnel and back out to the car. Motor knew there was a tunnel, he just didn't know where it was or where it led.

Marcus kicked a busted area of loose gravel back and forth, anxious, as he puffed away on a joint, his other hand gripping his gun. As he saw Nora, he flicked the joint and hurried to help with her final bag. Marcus treated her like his sister and also, like a lady. She didn't mind it at all.

"Six hours to Jonas, two hours before sun up. It'd be best to get to Creepers Row before dark if we can," Brodie said.

"Ok, you in the back," Nora looked to Brodie. "You need to stay in the car and out of sight at all time, unless we give you the ok. Keep your face covered with a buff, or whatever. Keep a hat on. Don't get out of the car unless we tell you the area is clear. You can't be seen."

"I got it, I got it," Brodie said.

"You took your ID chip out, right? Empty nest is best, you won't even register as being in the car," Marcus said. "I took mine out at home and left it."

"It's out, it's empty. And I have these, we'll need them in Creepers Row." Brodie opened his backpack giving the two a quick glimpse at the masks Krispy provided.

"Those are awesome," Marcus said, impressed.

Nora put the car in drive and the three sped off into dawn.

The threesome drove into morning, heading toward a sky that resembled the 'Scream' painting. It hung, eerily decorated with gray splatters of polluted clouds drooping from above like a frown. Marcus worked on his computer in the front, scrambling signals all the while reviewing maps, alerts and documents that Brodie got from Krispy. In the back, Brodie sat, quiet and seemingly in the midst of deep contemplation. His eyes followed the landscape, bland and simple, as it morphed through different shades of depression. Each town had its own flavor of misery.

Brodie hated that he was so morbid about the environment around him. It saddened him, but he refused to let people see much of that side of him. It was possible that there would be no reckoning and the country wouldn't return to normal. It was possible that the outcome of the revolution would be nothing but many, many deaths. But Brodie knew now wasn't the time to lose faith.

When the morning came with anger, Brodie tried to think back to the things of his past that made him happy, a beautiful tree to climb, birds, laughter in the park, even playing hacky sack with his mates when he was in Spain for a semester abroad. Unfortunately, what he saw through the filter and freedom of his twenties, now revealed the true vulnerability of any dreams he had left.

It was too early for most of the vagrants and grifters to be out taking their post, so the streets were fairly empty. This morning Brodie found peace in the quietness outside, as he kept his window cracked. Hope fluttered, taunting him like a high school crush. It seemed lost at so many turns, but it wasn't forgotten, not for Brodie.

A few cars passed them here and there, as they traveled along deserted highways and through sparse, abandon neighborhoods to get to Jonas. The tin of Choppers and drones glistened as the early morning sun slivered through billowing clouds, kissing the metal it pierced. All seemed calm for the moment, but the three remained constantly at the ready.

Suddenly, Brodie smacked his arm again, scratching feverishly, like a junky, as if he was trying to claw through his own skin.

"Hey, pull over a second," Brodie said. He shifted in his seat, trying to figure out how to calm the burning under the skin of his arm.

"Right now?" Nora asked, unsure.

"Yeah, just do it if you can. The Choppers are long gone." Brodie pulled a switchblade out from his back pocket and released a small scalpel. Nora turned down a vacant side street and pulled over. Brodie threw the door open and swung his legs out as the thick rubber soles of his Doc Martens hit the pavement. He rolled up his sleeve just above his elbow. Nora put her arm over the seat to see what was up.

"What are you doing?" she asked.

"I think Joke got me with a beetle last night, feels like someone's drilling fire into my muscle." Brodie took his scalpel and punctured the skin on the underside of his forearm, just below his elbow. He made a small, one inch long incision.

"If they tagged you, we'd know by now. No one's been following us." Marcus peered over, observing Brodie.

"You said Ryder got away. I'm sure they've contacted Billy," Nora said.

Brodie pinched the skin at each side of the incision as blood drizzled down from the corners. He put the flame of his lighter right up to the new gap in his flesh. A near microscopic, carbon fiber black beetle comprised of other soft scrambling metals weakly crawled out from Brodie's skin. He gripped it tight between two fingers, like a tick and held it up. Mechanically, it tried to scramble, but was malfunctioning, defective, moving slow and disjointed.

"I must have damaged it scratching it. It had to be Joke's, so it's possible the others don't know about it. He might have been the only one tracking it. Here." Brodie dropped the gnarly beetle into Marcus's palm. "Flame up, my friend," he said.

Marcus was already out of the car as he examined the spybot, holding it close to his vision. He set it on the ground, crouched down and lit it on fire. Seconds later, with an underwhelming pop, it exploded with a tiny flame, then disintegrated into black dust like a smoke bomb. Marcus hopped back in, impressed with the gadget.

"I forgot all about those, I used to dip those in acid and go out to the clubs. I would get so high, it was fantastic," Marcus laughed. "I tracked my trips," he said deep in memory for a moment.

"It will itch for a little while. Flush it with clean water and rub the eater on your forearm. There's a tube of it in my bag. It should kill the toxins and microplastics," Nora said.

Brodie wrapped his arm with a breathable bandage, seeming unfazed. It wasn't his first track. "Did you call Jasper?" Brodie tried to ask the question casually. Jasper was Nora's ex-boyfriend, but he was also elite military and as much as Brodie hated hearing about him, he knew Jasper could help them.

"Brodie, he knows the Corners. So, when I give him the word, he'll meet us in Nevada. If we need to change plans, he can adjust quickly. He can set us up with everything we need to get in unnoticed."

"Wait, we're going to California? Like those Corners? What happened to Creepers Row?" Marcus was confused.

"Info is in Creepers Row. My sister is most likely in California. My buddy Mentos, little brother Chavo is a hacker and will get us into the Corners and any facility we need. He's on call for the next few days. He's hacked into their security systems many times." Brodie hoped it wouldn't come to that. He was hoping Cece was just off with someone else, away from the Corners.

"Well, I guess we'll know soon enough. Can't turn back now," Marcus said.

Brodie left it at that. He didn't say much else as Marcus and Nora made small talk, working out details. The more he got a grasp of the plan, the more he felt back in his own head. The shock from the night before with the Splitters was dispersing into his past.

They turned off the deserted highway and drove for another eighty miles until they reached a dense forest. As the road turned to dirt it led them straight into the woods, guiding them to a large metal gate. Brodie got the ok, then got out of the car and jogged over to a small electronic box next to the gate. He typed a code into his phone, then held it up to the box as the gates parted. He got back in the car as they pulled in, the gates rapidly closing behind them. After a short distance, they reached three long, two-story hangar style warehouses and an old farm house.

Once parked, an older man walked out with blue neon goggles dangling from his neck. Simply dressed in jeans and a T-shirt, he picked up his pace and trotted toward the car with a huge grin. A woman walked out behind him. With his buff still covering most of his face, Brodie hopped out and the two men embraced.

"Oh man, Jonas, it's so good to see you," Brodie said. "Hey, Deya." Marcus and Nora were out of the car and in protection mode, keeping a watchful eye on Jonas and his wife. Their eyes scanned the perimeter, staying fully alert.

"I'm sorry to hear about Cece, sounds like you have bigger problems, though. You sure you don't want to hunker down here for a bit? I hear your brother's got money on you, a little higher stakes this time. Stay for the night, get your head straight," Jonas said.

"I wish we could, but we need to keep moving. Safer that way. You know Marcus, and this is Nora. This is my good friend, Jonas and his wife, Deya."

"You sure you can't stop in? I made sandwiches," Deya said.

Back toward the buildings a short distance away, a kid around twenty strolled out from a metal side door. With short spiky dark hair, wearing black jeans, he flipped open a Zippo and lit a cigarette. Brodie noticed him, immediately.

"We just stopped to get supplies. We can't interact with anyone." Brodie skimmed the grounds, making sure his buff was pulled up to his eyes. "Who's that? How many you got working here now?"

"A solid fourteen, most of them live here. Some travel on the weekends, see their families, parents, kids," Jonas said. "Lane over there, he's been here for about eight months. Good worker and knows his way around artificial intelligence like I haven't seen in a while. Only time he leaves is when he takes his crotch rocket zipping around. The kids been dating one of the girls here, she's a little older. Both of them, two of the smartest." Jonas looked over his shoulder toward Lane. "He keeps us up to date on all of Droshure's body blending and upgrade crap, too. Enough about that, you sure you can't come in and eat?"

"We really can't," Brodie said. "We only have about five minutes for this. We need to get to Cre..."

"We need to get to where we're going," Nora said, cutting Brodie off before he could finish.

Brodie heard himself say the word. Shit, even though Jonas was going to monitor their movement, it was supposed to be in real time. No one was to know where they were headed, not even those he trusted.

"I'll pack the sandwiches to go, wait here." Deya hurried back toward the farmhouse.

Jonas flagged Brodie to walk with him toward another car. When they got there, Jonas handed him a black over the shoulder pack and a set of keys.

"The IDs are in here, there are five. All are marked for full perimeter access throughout the Corners. I'm tracking 'em downstairs so I'll know where you guys are. I got this car for you. Plus, erasers and anything else you'll need are in this small duffle. Give me what you have and I'll burn it. Your biggest problem is your face, they'll be looking for you. Grow a beard, dye your hair, do whatever you can to alter your appearance. There's a set of contacts in the bag. If they don't bother your eyes, put them in. They block scans, too, so you won't register as a warm body if the monitors do a pupil scan." Jonas looked at Brodie and sighed.

"You're getting all James Bond with this shit. I appreciate the hell out of you, man. Thank you, seriously, but we're sticking with the car we brought," Brodie said.

Just then, Lane finished his cigarette and started to jog over.

"Get that guy outta here," Nora said to Marcus, as Brodie took the que and got back inside the car before Lane arrived.

"You need help with anything, Jonas?" Lane asked as he reached him. Nora discreetly snapped a data scan of him as they all kept a close ear on their conversation.

"No, we're good. Head back on in, I'll be there in a minute. When you get a second though, can you check the scanners on the Kentucky line? We need it clear and open for some guys coming in later tomorrow."

"Sure thing," Lane said, nodding in agreement, then with a spin, he turned and ran back inside.

Jonas waited for the door to close then wandered back over to the threesome.

"Sorry about that," Jonas said.

"No worries. Thank you for everything. We owe you, just say the word," Marcus said.

"Just keep him alive, you all stay alive. If it doesn't feel right, don't do it," Jonas said.

As they drove off, Jonas hit a remote in his pocket that opened the gate as he saw them approach it. Seconds after they passed, the gate quickly closed behind them.

Back on the road, Marcus drove as Brodie scanned intel that Jonas included in the bag. The car was quiet, no one spoke for a while, each lost in their own thoughts. Brodie stopped reading and looked up. He needed to distract himself from the intensity of the situation.

"Marcus, you ever been to Creepers Row?"

"Never. How much longer till we get there?" Marcus spoke the words in monotone, lifting his hands like Frankenstein.

"You shouldn't mock that place. It is filled with sicko's and criminals, the boogeyman. We have about four and a half more hours," Nora warned.

"We need to minimize the chit chat soon. If you see anything weird, don't taunt it, Marcus," Brodie said.

"For real?" Marcus asked.

"It's not a fun place," Nora said.

Brodie knew all about Creepers Row. Back when he worked at the hospital in Chicago, just before the class wars and the split, he and his fellow physicians would get patients in with horrendous wounds. The worst of them were transported in from what use to be Gary, Indiana, the area now referred to as Creepers Row. As they healed, Brodie would sit with the patients as they told him their stories. He had a good bedside manner back then. Right after the class wars, he still had a handle on hope and happiness, meditating for an hour if not more, every day. But then, Brodie became more and more distracted by the escalating decay around him, unable to shake off the heaviness.

He looked out the window as they passed run-down fast-food restaurants, abandon amusement parks that looked more like the devil's carnival, hollowed out skyscrapers and strip malls, the parking lots now tent encampments. Garbage cans that started overflowing years ago, now served as grills and heating units. Boobain had zero concern for keeping the Gutter clean. People burned the trash, but with that came a noxious and at times, toxic stench. It was the best they could do. Brodie closed his eyes and tried to meditate, waiting for those calming color swirls, trying to trick his body back into homeostasis.

"We're losing daylight. Just be prepared for night prowlers," Nora alerted.

"At least we're getting close," Marcus said, not wanting to scare himself with what may lie ahead. "So, where's the rest of your family, is your brother still in the states?" Marcus asked Nora.

"Mom's still in Portugal, in Lisbon near the beach," Nora responded. "My dad and his current wife moved over there long before the split to help her. The accident left her paraplegic so she's in a wheelchair, no feeling from the waist down. She refuses any stem cell trials, regeneration dopes and any other research, but she has an amazing doctor there."

"I didn't know she was paraplegic. I don't know if you ever told me that," Marcus said.

Light rain fell as the day was clouding over and coming to a close. Occasionally, they passed through rundown towns, dysfunctional farm communities, along with the occasional cluster of tents overflowing out from under highway bridges.

"She was working a story in Sudan. An explosion hit and she was blown seven feet back. The blast completely mangled her legs. My dad and his new wife moved from Greenland to be with her even though they divorced, like twenty years ago. They take care of her, see her almost every day. It makes me feel better knowing they're all together," Nora said. Dusk loomed ahead as Nora glanced at the gas gauge. "We gotta get gas and fill the cans next place we see. We don't want to get stuck in Creepers Row," Nora said.

As they spoke of Creepers Row, Brodie's fears haunted him like a rabid dog. For a moment, he wished he had told no one and taken the trip alone. Even though he'd been there, it had been years.

"Marcus, choppers and drones don't fly over Creepers Row because they just shoot 'em down with old military equipment. NAFO doesn't drive through there anymore because some of the bridges are sensor rigged to blow any vehicles weighing over twenty-five hundred pounds. Women don't typically go in, either, so while you guys are watching me, we need to protect Nora, too," Brodie said. He knew the stats and the dangers of the area and didn't need to state them out loud.

"Very few women living in there," Nora said.

"Right after the class wars, everyone went ape shit and over five hundred women and like two hundred men were raped, dismembered and left roadside just for trying to drive through," Brodie said. "I worked on a lot of people with horrific wounds from the derelicts living there. They don't just kill people in Creepers Row. They make a craft out of it. Rumored to be a group of serial killers that found each other prowling the area."

Brodie noticed Marcus pull out a cigarette and reached his hand out for one. Just then, something squealed out in front of the car and across the road. It moved in a blur, too fast to comprehend exactly what it was. Nora jerked the wheel, but kept full control of the car. All three at full attention, spinning to scan the atmosphere around them to see what had zipped past.

CHAPTER 18

B ack at Jonas's farmhouse, night fell and the glow of Lane's cigarette contrasted with the overcast yet, partially starlit sky. Everyone was inside and many were already in bed for the night not long after sundown. Jonas leaned outside the door.

"We've got a car coming," Jonas yelled to Lane. "There is no communication on their arrival. Don't let them in. I'm going downstairs to alert the cover and check the mirror." The mirror was just that, an invisible square that hovered above the property and recorded everything below, right side up. "I'll talk with them over the intercom first." Jonas retreated inside as the brightening beams of light from the approaching car came into sight from a distance. Lane jogged the short distance to the gates, looked over his shoulder and made sure Jonas was gone. Standing near the gates in the dark, Lane waved at the car, signaling them to wait as he turned and ran back inside.

Lane quietly passed Deya in the main room along with a few others, listening to music, winding down for the night. He skipped down the stairs spinning a silencer onto his gun, then secured it behind his back as he shuffled in to find Jonas. There he was, checking equipment and assessing data on the screen for the arriving car, while keeping an eye on Brodie's position. He pulled up the track on a small laptop, then glanced back feeling a heavy presence behind him. He nonchalantly closed off of Brodie's position.

"Are they trying to get in? What did they say to you?" Jonas asked.

"They needed directions. Their phone died an hour ago. They're trying to find some farm."

"They'll be on their way any second," Lane said, walking up behind Jonas.

"Ok, everything else looks good," Jonas said. He kept glancing over his shoulder, uncomfortable with Lane towering behind him. Just as he started to get up, Lane raised his gun and shot Jonas in the back of the head.

Jonas fell forward awkwardly, but was able to hit the scramble key. Instantly, the mother board fried out, sending sparks flying and wires singeing out on the small laptop. He reached for the main system keyboard and was able to at least start a system wipe.

Lane pushed Jonas's body to the floor and grabbed the zip from the sparking laptop as flames flared out. He pulled Jonas's phone from his pocket, then went to the camera and hit a button as the gates rose and the black luxury sedan pulled in and onto the property. He ran upstairs, then out to meet the sedan.

Just as he did, the car door swung open as Billy stepped out, his face fully covered with a mask. Spider and two other Splitters followed suit, all with guns in hand and their faces covered.

"Most are sleeping but there are a few in the main living room," Lane said.

"How far away are they?" Billy asked.

"They left here about two, three hours ago. I called as soon as I could."

"You get the tracker on the car?" Billy pressed.

"I tossed a frog. I think it got on there. They wouldn't let me get close to the car, though," Lane said. He stepped back and glanced over to the house, then back at Billy. The Splitters and Spider took their cue and made their way inside. "Jonas hit a scramble as I shot him but I got the current coordinates. I'm pretty sure we'll still be able to track them." Lane tried his best to sound capable.

"Where was their car?" Billy asked.

Lane walked them over to the area. "Their car was parked over here, and like I said, it was a black mustang," Lane said.

Billy activated the flashlight on his phone and scanned the graveled area where the car was supposedly parked. There it was. Billy pointed to the ground.

"Pick it up," he said. Lane's face filled with panic as he scurried over and picked up the frog tracker he had intended to stick to their car. "Didn't stick, did it."

"No, I guess not," Lane turned down. "I swear I saw it stick. I'm sorry, we still have the zip drive. We can salvage something from it. I promise I can find out where they're going," Lane said, trying to justify his use. He handed the zip drive to Billy.

A straight-faced Billy pulled out his gun, pointed it steady at Lane, just as two gunshots echoed from inside. He lifted his mask, staring at Lane. "Look me in the face and beg," Billy said.

"I can hack back into the tracker. I know the system. I can get it back online," Lane said, his hands up, as if he was getting arrested. "Come on, Billy. I can help you guys. I'll do whatever you want. You gotta give me a chance. Please, I can tell you who was with him."

"Who was with him?" Billy paused, taking his aim off Lane momentarily.

"It was a woman, forties maybe, brown hair, pretty. She looked military. And a guy, same age I'd guess, dark skinned, hat on. One of those winter hats with the flaps," Lane said, stumbling through his words, hoping it would be enough.

"It's called a trapper hat," Billy said flatly, unable to show any emotion other than disappointment. He shot Lane without question. His limp body hit the ground. As the warehouse door opened, Billy pulled his mask back over his face.

"Everyone's been taken care of inside," the Splitters said. Two got in the front as Billy and Spider got in the back. Billy handed him the zip drive. Almost immediately, Spider was tapping away at the keys of a small laptop at a secretary's pace. Billy slammed his hand into the side of the car.

"Get me back to the airport and get a car headed to the tracked spot. I want to know who you get to follow them, names, everything," Billy said. "We know what direction he's headed and the car description. Get a license plate and get teams in that area there, now." Billy pounded his fist against the car interior.

"I took Jonas's shirt. If they hugged, his scent might be on there," one of the Splitters said.

"I'm not looking for a cheating wife, you fucking moron." Billy scrunched his face, annoyed. "Give it to me." He took it and threw the shirt out the window.

CHAPTER 19

T he threesome continued on their journey, nearing Creepers Row. Out of nowhere, the car swerved, as if the pavement was rippled with grooves. The car jerked back and forth ever so gently, the force enhanced with each gust of wind.

"Skimmer?" Nora asked, surveying the area.

"That'd be my guess," Brodie said.

"I thought I saw legs. What the hells a skimmer?" Marcus asked.

Brodie watched as uncertainty covered Marcus's face. He gripped the gun resting in his hand, ready to fire.

"You know about Skimmers, dude," Brodie said. "Ex-criminals and homeless extracted from the prisons and the streets for testing like five years ago. They were intended for rehabilitation and programmed with basic target chips, infused with adrenaline lines. A DARPA project for the military that Boobain's team hijacked and re-purposed. All the tinkering screwed up their upgrade programming and fried their brains, turning them into human speed zombies." Marcus listened intently as Brodie spoke. "The government didn't know what to do with them, so they dropped them all in Creepers Row. Thought if they killed them, it would be all over the news as a failure, considered genocide," Brodie said.

"They all have chips imbedded, like a shock collar, and if they breach the perimeter of Creepers Row they get an electric shock. That's why you don't see them all over the slums. Most don't make it out," Nora added. "There are other places like Creepers Row, misfit colonies, where they dump the human aftermath from their experiments to try to live and survive. They're all over the world. It's just not advertised."

"I remember hearing about the beginnings of those trials right after I got canned. It's only been like six years since they booted me from DARPA. I do miss that place, just not the bureaucracy of it," Marcus said.

"There'll be one running rogue down the street and it'll just splat, smash, straight into a moving car," Brodie said.

"Hey, gas," Nora pointed. "Buffs up, guns out." She pulled over into a barren, rundown gas station.

Brodie pulled out his phone.

"Who are you calling? Come on, Brodie, we gotta focus," Marcus said trying to help Nora keep him on guard.

"Just thought I'd try to reach my sister once more," Brodie said.

"Please tell me you have a block on that phone?" Marcus said.

"I have a block on all of my phones, they point to a CH in Puerto Rico."

"Good, no more calls. Do not try to call your sister. Let's make it out of Creepers Row and go from there. You sure you still want to go through with this?" Nora looked back at Brodie. He seemed distracted, fidgety. It made her nervous.

"Yes, I do."

The gas station stood by itself along a fairly desolate stretch of road. They parked right next to a padlocked gas pump. Brodie was sick of wearing his buff, but knew it was crucial. Under Nora's watch, he got out and stretched his legs, listening as the wind whistled through the trees. A few middle-aged guys loitered, laughing together, drinking forties in the covered entrance of a church splattered with graffiti half a block up the street. Brodie watched them, almost jealous of their freedom.

He secured his gun, as Marcus walked toward the station hut. The stench of sweat and garbage caught Brodie's nose as he grimaced. There was a clerk sitting behind the counter, feet up with a shotgun resting at his side. The clerk jumped at the clang of the doors bell and grabbed the shotgun, meekly pointing it at Marcus. Brodie started toward the door, but soon enough, Marcus flashed a thumbs-up back at them.

Seconds later, the half toothed young punk wandered out with Marcus, shotgun in hand, the nose dragging in the dirt behind him. A large hooped key chain dangled from his belt loop.

"How much y'all need? It's getting dark. I'm closing up soon." Gobs of tobacco bounced up from his gums, rolling over the edge of his lips like an oil spill.

"Your pumps work, right?" Marcus questioned, eyeing up the kid.

"I'm here, ain't I? People sure ain't coming for the moldy food. It'll cost ya about a hundred bucks to fill that car of yours. You pay me first, cash. No electronic phone, Go-card bullshit." The kid stood with all of his 140 pounds clutching his 5'11" frame, trying to beat the fight against episodic gusts of wind.

Marcus pulled out a hundred-dollar bill as Brodie got back in the car before they approached. The punk was more focused on checking out Nora, anyway. He examined her up and down, as Marcus stepped in front of him, blocking his view, waving the hundred in his face. The kid snatched the bill and unlocked the pumps, still ogling Nora at every opportunity. Though her face was mostly covered, he greeted her with a kinked-up grin. The punk stepped back as Marcus, gloves on, pumped the gas. Nora didn't take her eyes off the kid or her hand off the gun in her partially visible shoulder holster. It was making the kid nervous, but that didn't stop him from gawking at her.

"Don't know where yer heading, but y'all want to be careful. The Row's just up the road about an hour or so. Y'all best be avoiding it, unless you want them perverts to git a holda yer female here," the young punk said, making an attempt at chivalry.

"We're not headed that way, we're headed south, Ohio, but thanks. We just needed gas," Nora said flatly.

"Just saying, I can smell you from here, ma'am. And if I can, they most definitely will be able to," the kid said.

"We appreciate the warning, friend." Marcus finished pumping the gas and filled the containers. He stuck an extra twenty in the kid's shirt pocket as he padlocked the pumps.

"Y'all be safe. Nothing be no good out here once the night turns black. The darkness around here, it'll eat yer soul." The kid meant it sincerely. He quickly locked the gas tank handle and turned back and headed inside, locking the door.

They could tell by the wave of nervous displeasure that covered the kid's face that he'd probably been through a dance or two with the wicked.

Dusk faded to night and conversation ceased as they neared the edge of Creepers Row. Brodie assessed Nora and Marcus in his mind. Mentally, he tried to insert himself into their heads to know what they were thinking. Either of them could be tricking him, waiting for the right moment to hand him over or kill him for the coin. Brodie knew wasting too much time with paranoia would get him killed. He needed to trust Nora and Marcus, plain and simple. His chest got tight as his lungs squeezed shut like an accordion. He took a deep breath, forcing them open with a massive exhale. He needed a distraction.

"Can I have a cigarette?" Brodie asked.

"Windows stay up. You ok?" Nora questioned, knowing his response would be a lie.

"Yeah," Brodie said, affirming her intuition.

The weather turned erratic. Sleet fell in sheets, splashing sideways as the wind spun up making visibility worse. Brodie appreciated the distorted view, it made the quest seem less real for a bit, more like a bad dream.

Marcus lit a joint, cracked the window as his face got sprayed with rain. He stretched his hand back and squeezed Brodie on the arm with a smile. "This is where the fun begins, right? Riders on the storm."

"Goddammit you guys. Windows up. I'm not messing around," Nora ordered.

"We should put the masks on, too. This is how Tommy will know us." Brodie handed the bleached Halloween masks to Marcus and Nora, then put his on. With sunken eyes, a hobo's five o'clock shadow and a drunken smile, the Fred Flintstone mask fit right in with typical Splitter's garb. For now, the masks would make the threesome blend in.

Up ahead, flaring lights caught their eye as a gigantic neon green Trojan horse stood two stories tall with partially shorted-out neon-orange flames shooting out from its nostrils. Crumbling structures and busted out storefronts drizzled with satanic slurs and graffiti lined their approach. The massive abandoned industrial park filled with towering smoke stacks puffed out across the wide river from where they were, the black soot clearing a path for itself to reach the sky's limit.

Some of the more creative deviants that lived in Creepers Row stayed together and stayed hidden across the river taking full ownership of the factories. They were the mad scientists and genius's cast out from society, deemed crazy or too radical for the real world. They felt safest in the factories, hidden from the psycho's dwelling in Creepers Row and far from the plastic people and corporate vipers in the Corners. They were first to get to the factories when the split happened after the class wars. They grabbed the abandoned factories and protected the surrounding area like the mafia, creating a man-made river around it and hiring the most loyal beasts of men to keep watch. It was likely that the next AI pioneer, currency mogul or natural chem entrepreneur resided under the masquerade of Creepers Row insanity in those factories.

Brodie knew one guy that lived there, Linus. He'd met him several times overseas when he did Doctors Without Borders. Linus was a robotics engineer, training medics on new tech. A few years ago, shortly after the political assassinations, Brodie ran into him at a random bar in Montana on a medical run. Linus told him all about the factories and some of the geniuses that lived there with him. He offered Brodie a room, but Brodie preferred his freedom, even if it was in the slums.

Rain-soaked stray cats and dogs scurried across the streets as rodents swam up from the sewers. Brodie felt his hands dampen and swell as he rubbed them back and forth on his pants. For a split second, he felt the road roll and warp around him, swaying his vision back and forth like a hammock, bending his perception of what was really in front of him. He felt his stomach spin, unsure if it was just him.

"Is it me or..." Marcus started, but Nora interrupted him.

"It's the toxins in the area, just keep watching for trouble," Nora said. "It's not lethal, just keep your buff up. Worst it'll do is make you feel a little high or paranoid. Give you a slight headache."

A car erratically sped up alongside them. A long-faced guy with a Lincoln beard hanging far below his neckline flicked his tongue in and out, trying to see through the tinted windows. He rolled his window down and put muddied hands up, grabbing at the air. He shook his face back and forth, tasting the falling rain on his tongue, as if his face were between a woman's breasts. The splatters of rain cleansed grime from the man's grungy face. They couldn't see inside Nora's car, but that didn't deter their madness. A pixie haired chick rolled down the backseat window. She took a puff off her cigarette then chucked it out, sending it against the tinted back window, bouncing off and down to the ground. The driver swerved the car back and forth, dangerously close to Nora's car, pacing them, trying to knock them off the road and into the swamp running alongside them. Eventually, the car of randoms sped off into the bleak darkness with stuttering accelerations.

Just as they were calming from the skirmish, something struck the back window, delivering a small spider crack. They searched around for a culprit but the object was nowhere to be seen. The environment around them was changing. They knew they were in Creepers Row. They watched as the few drifters that were on the streets appeared as if they had escaped from an asylum, med-stepping, drenched and unfazed by the weather, most carrying heavy artillery over their shoulders or on their person. Some hovered and dwelled in the nooks and crannies getting high, others simply trying to keep safe and warm. The car continued on, embarking on the dead city, one that had no law, no morals.

"Take a right up ahead." With the map resting on his lap, Marcus pointed toward what appeared to be a road leading to nowhere.

They made the turn and got a closer view of the industrial park across the water. Brodie now saw that it was bookended by two abandoned casinos at the shoreline. Flashes of red, white and yellow sporadically zigzagged past in the night, down by the water and through the woods along the road. Coupled with the movement, came cackles and sharp cutting screeches that seemed to vibrate against the car windows.

"Zero service here. Good news is it means if anyone was tracking us, they lost the signal miles ago. I'm switching to ghost," Marcus said.

The car passed a concrete mausoleum. Off in the distance, zombie-like figures staggered about with scarecrow stiffness. A few miles later, as the rain eased, Nora pulled the car into a humid, fog filled area that mocked a ghost town. Three neglected Craftsman homes sat grounded along an otherwise empty stretch of road. Something rocketed past the front of the car. It was the silhouette of an old man, but it passed by too quickly for Brodie to be sure.

He kept his eyes fixed on the exterior, watching for trouble as another blurred figure whizzed into the woods, speeding parallel to the road. Brodie wiped his eyes, searching again, trying to track the movement. A damp mist swelled outside, forcing the inside of the car to turn humid with a thick and balmy air. Brodie wiped sweat off his forehead.

Nora turned into a ramshackle neighborhood. To the left of them, along the shoreline, tents and makeshift homes sat scattered. Debris blew up in spirals colliding with drizzle as the wind increased. More adult-like figures spun past the back of the car, quicker than a human could be capable of, bumping off the trunk as they passed. Nora caught sight of Marcus readjusting the hold on his gun.

"Easy on the guns, Marcus. They're harmless," Nora said. Just after she did, lightning speared through the sky in front of them, belching out a thunderous chaser.

Finally, they pulled into a large, overgrown cul-de-sac lined with four structures. There were two church-like buildings and another that mimicked a small, rundown Bedlam. Crossbones, wolf carcasses, and other, possibly human, knickknacks garnished the lawns. Brodie could smell the stench, sticky in the air. Death oozed from the ground, smelling of moldy meat and spoiled sweat. The fourth structure was their destination.

"The firehouse, pull in over there, right in front," Brodie said.

Nora could tell he was ready to get out of the car, stretch his legs and walk around. He was never one to sit around and do nothing so being in the car this long was against his nature, but she knew he would do whatever it took to get to his sister.

As they pulled into the driveway, the firehouse door opened and Tommy, an older man with a cowboy hat on and a cane in hand, limped toward them, but not for lack of muscle on his frame. Brodie assessed him, figured him to be around sixty. Tommy looked enough like the picture Krispy showed him, like an older, more put together, version of Krispy. His appearance was rustic, but clean. His long beard was rolled up, intertwined through a wooden bead, nestled under his chin.

"I'm Tommy," he called out. "Hurry on inside."

Brodie studied Tommy further, evaluating his potential for betrayal. He grabbed his bags and quickly made his way to the door, waiting for Marcus, Nora and Tommy. Through the fog, Brodie could barely make out the outline of two punk hillbilly types sitting on the trunk of a car, outside one of the church-like houses across from Tommy's firehouse. Their existence was confirmed only through moments of lightening and the orange glow of their cigarettes pulsing in the night.

"How'r ya doing, Tommy? Who's your new friends? I can smell every inch of her all the way over here. I'd love to see a pretty face. I can trade ya for her," one hillbilly said. He let out rapid wolf howls that distorted with the wind.

"Mind yourself, Lodie. These are my friends. Don't forget our arrangement," he said. Tommy went inside last, double bolted the door and punched a code in to reactivate the security system. Instantly, a light lit up the circumference of the property. Brodie turned at the sound of the heavy steel bolts sliding into place.

"Those friends of yours?" Brodie asked.

"Let's just say people like that are an unfortunate but harmless part of the landscape around here. The other two houses are mostly undercovers posing as derelicts. You're safe here. But we should make this quick. From what Kristian told me, people are looking for you."

Brodie walked into the main room, impressed by the wall of camera's covering the exterior, along with the approaching road. Weapons sat in bundles along the perimeter of the room, along with ziplocked packets of intel and instructions taped on top.

"Hey, thank you for doing all this. I owe Krispy, I mean Kristian my life for helping with this." Brodie extended his hand, but Tommy, though friendly, didn't take it.

"You are a wanted man, kid. You've got a serious fan base. I called Niko Finch, one of my guys working undercover for Boobain. He said Droshure and your brother are willing to do whatever it takes to get you to him. What is it he thinks you have?" Tommy asked.

"He enjoys throwing my life off kilter. Sibling stuff, I guess," Brodie replied.

"Seems like more than that. Anyway, most of Boobain's top guys had a FluxR implanted into their body. It's a human scramble program. Like an internal Faraday box. It's in trials with the military right now," Tommy explained. "Somehow most of his top team got the option to trial it. It's possible your brother snagged one for himself. Any trace that locks onto a device on their person or tries to body scan, the FluxR scrambles, bouncing the signal to a tower in the reverse direction. People have been trying to track his movements but he shakes it pretty quickly."

"Everyone seems to know where he is. People see him, but he's good at disappearing. Always has been," Brodie said.

"And truth be told, my crew could care less about your brother. We're more focused on taking down President Boobain. If helping you find your sister doesn't interfere with our mission, as a friend of Kristian's, I am happy to help. Some dangerous people are just better dead than alive. Now, your father, he's been funneling money for Droshure and Boobain since long before the class wars. Stealing money from the people. How'd you end up with such a wicked family?"

"Nathan's never been my father, we don't share the same blood," Brodie said.

"Well," Tommy clapped his hands together, avoiding any further unnecessary awkwardness. "I'll get Marissa, she'll take you downstairs. We need to keep you in motion. You stay in one place too long, someone's bound to find you. I'll stay up here with your friends and keep an eye on the cameras."

The décor inside Tommy's home wasn't at all what Brodie expected. The rough, decrepit, haunted firehouse exterior was in full contrast to the Zen-like open layout inside. Stacks of maps, data and diagnostics sat sprawled out in organized chaos on a large dining table. Firearms sat at rest, strategically placed throughout the room.

"So, you're prepping for the take back?" Nora asked.

"My team leaves tomorrow night for a mission. They stay close. Most of our prep work doesn't take place here. There is zero service, it's where I live. My camera's run off my own grid, as are my communications. I've got an arrangement with the Mensa nerds across the water. They make sure my grids work. I can't speak for Lodie and the boxheads outside, but in here, you're protected." Tommy paused, now studying Nora.

"Thanks for doing this, Tommy," Marcus inserted.

Tommy nodded in Marcus's direction but returned his gaze to Nora. "I've seen pictures of you. A few years ago, but I never forget a face. You're with an agency?" Tommy said the words as he kept his gaze toward Nora.

"It is possible." Nora was friendly, but chose to remain anonymous. She didn't feel the need to offer up any information, or even speak much more at all. This was about Brodie and his sister.

"Marissa, Marissa baby, they're here," Tommy yelled out. "Oh, I almost forgot. Here's his chip, you may need it for access." Tommy handed Brodie Donte's tracker chip, which was wrapped in aluminum foil inside a small, palm-size Faraday bag.

Moments later, an athletic fifty-something looking woman with the body of a kickboxer came into the room. She swiftly pulled her gray, billowing curls into a ponytail and stood next to Tommy.

"Hello, hello," she said in a sing-songy, motherly way. The hint of an Argentinian accent was easily detected. "I'm so glad you made it safely. Are you ready to get some answers from your special guest?" She kissed Tommy on the cheek before waving Brodie over, guiding him toward the back of the house.

As they started down a back staircase, Brodie was hit with the stink of stale body odor, that of a meathead's gymnasium. Once downstairs, two brawny security thugs stood guard, while two others, twins, sat on folding chairs across from a punched-up Donte.

Brodie felt his body tense up at the sight of him. Donte was right there. The key to finding Cece was sitting in front of him with his arms bound, mouth gagged and blood seeping from his face.

"He's all yours," one of the twins said.

CHAPTER 20

Billy cruised through the old Universal Studios lot in his Porsche and pulled up to the valet. He launched his keys to a part-timing college kid and went inside an Art Deco office building. As he rode up to the seventh floor, his eyes scanned the cityscape through the glass elevator panes. Long before the split, the Droshure Corporation had been a silent, but major, partner in Comcast and Universal Studios. Comcast was no more, but the land and property had grown to become far more valuable than Comcast had been worth. This was the corporate headquarters for the Droshure Corporation. All significant meetings with shareholders, political dignitaries and foreign diplomats took place here.

Billy smirked as he took a mental inventory of all the money that had been through the doors. Even though he carried out most of the dirty work that resulted from those meetings, Billy had only been invited to the building three other times. He was treated with more of a back-of-the-bar, dark-alley transaction type of respect. Everyone needed him, but most didn't want to be seen with him which was good because he despised most of the people he did work for. He hummed along to Alanis Morrissette's 'Ironic' as it played from the elevator speaker.

To Droshure Corporate elites, Billy was a necessary accomplice. He made things happen without leaving a trace. What Droshure didn't know was that Billy didn't sleep much and because of that, he was an avid reader. He knew he was just as smart as Brodie. What made him different was that he didn't need to flaunt his intelligence. It was one of his secret weapons. He thoroughly researched every company he did work for. For Billy, it was 100% about power and control. Notoriety was fleeting, but power was a coveted commodity. Nothing got him off more than having the upper hand.

When Billy moved to California with Nathan and Cece, before he was invited to work with them, he read everything he could get his hands on about Droshure Corp and its board of directors. He started from the company's inception, back in 2006, shortly after Hurricane Katrina and the non-existent recovery efforts. That was how Billy discovered the Stoyton Society, buried deep on the DarkNet.

In 2018, it was Billy who brokered the deal for Droshure to acquire the Comcast lot along with the homes that surrounded the perimeter. Now, Boobain used the facility for news modification. When Billy found out from a contact in the Gutter that the Underground was tagging the Corners media that was put out by the Droshure Corporation, he looked into it. He and a hacker friend found out they were tagging everything with an identifier and running it through CoreBase encryption software, one of the leading deep fake extraction programs and adding an untrackable disclaimer about modified truth. Billy was the hero and the one to refer them to DeckSpin, a deepfake software application that was much more sophisticated and the preferred choice of those on the darknet. It was far more impenetrable than the aging programs of Google and the like. Billy referred to the whole thing as 'the fool's delusion', referring to those that were living in the Corners.

The elevator doors opened and Billy emerged out on to the top floor. He made his way to the conference room and knocked. As he pushed the door open, Jacob waved him in, taking his eyes off the screen in front of him, momentarily. He was in the middle of flipping through papers, toggling his gaze back and forth, tracking multiple computer screens projected on a white wall. The images displayed in front of him replayed underwater data of stealth activity picked up by sonar tracers. Billy watched with a curious eye as sweat dropped from Jacob's red face, onto his hand. Jacob's rising heart rate appeared to be flooding his arteries, taunting his blood pressure like a tidal wave.

Billy went to the window where, from blocks away and several floors up, the muffled chants of protesters could still faintly be heard through the glass. Like any society, there were those that supported the borders of the Corners and those that felt the borders were inhumane and nowhere near a democracy.

"Doing ok, old man?" Billy asked.

"Tim will be here any minute. He's the one that wanted you here. We have a meeting with investors later."

"Lucky me. Why you being hostile?" Billy asked. Jacob ignored his question.

The office door swung open with such a force that the doorknob left an imprint on the wall behind it, reverberating as Boobain charged in. He walked right up to Jacob and threw printouts of several reports on the large desk in front of him. Billy tried to conceal his pleasure at the aggression. He sat down as Boobain got so close to Jacob that his breath appeared to cool the clammy beads of sweat on Jacob's forehead. Billy wanted to bet on it, which bead would dampen the critical papers first.

"You told me you had control of this," Boobain said, speaking to Jacob.

"Are you serious? It's 4,000 AI RMs and blends out of a fleet of over one hundred thousand," Jacob said. "I tried to get your attention before. You're the one that blew it off. So focused on Nathan and getting your money to the right banks. You're the one that wanted to be President. I've only been doing what you told me to do, what I've always done, run my business, our business." Jacob tried to play it calm and collected, but Billy heard the quiver in his voice. Jacob Droshure was losing it.

Boobain's face flared red as he listened to Jacob babble on, trying to explain himself out of trouble.

"Is this about the..." Billy tried to interject.

"Stay out of it, Billy. Jake here thinks he's living on fucking Fantasy Island. It's not just 4,000, it's 14,000. We only have 106,000 on hand and in trials. You don't even have the correct figures. You think I have time to come here, with all the presidential duties I need to be focusing on? You think this is a good fucking look?" Timothy Boobain shook his head with frustration. "Two hours ago, there was a massive breach at the Davis County plant. The plant that Jake here, was supposed to check two months ago. These people are joining hands and blowing up everything we've created. That screws us, that screws our plan and it costs money. Every god damn explosion costs us money. Can't you hear them outside? Those are our people, the one's we convinced to move here. They are slowly turning against us each time these mistakes happen."

"Hey, we could have done this much quieter," Jacob conceded. "Incorporating the presidency into this plan was all your idea, not mine."

Billy's eyes followed Boobian and Droshure back and forth like a tennis match. Finally, Jacob went to the window, peering out at the city, then locked eyes with Boobain, again. It reminded Billy of the fights between his parents when he was little. He pondered why he was there.

"Do you guys want me to leave, maybe be alone?" Billy joked, starting to get up. They both ignored him.

"That's our country, right there. You're forgetting your credo. Rich people like being rich. Rich people like keeping losers out of their neighborhood. Rich people like life to feel safe and protected."

"Blah Blah, get to the point," Boobain demanded.

"They still want that, Tim. That's not going to change. They are addicted to elitism," Jacob said. "This whatever, supposed revolution, it's a fad, a TikTok trend. If they want to take selfies and brag about being a part of protests, I really don't give a shit. They don't really want this uprising to succeed. They like their life in the Corners, they just don't want their neighbors to know how greedy they are. Get a drink, get a fuck or whatever it is you need to do to stop acting like we didn't plan for hiccups. The clone plant isn't a problem. We'll just build a better one. None of this is a problem," Jacob said.

"You're not thinking straight," Boobain said. "I canceled today's meeting. We need to have answers before we waste our investors time, especially Stoyton."

Jacob walked over to Boobain and put his arm around him, patted him on the back, though not without it being shirked off. Jacob poured two cocktails from a fancy crystal decanter that was worth a small city. "Have a drink." Jacob handed Boobain the glass, which he emptied before it had fully set into his grip. Boobain grabbed the remote and unmuted the news.

"He's right, Mr. President," Billy said. "This stuff is going to happen, it'll pass. You're forgetting the bigger picture. The wait list for Corners SafeCity developments is longer than when the first one was available. You've got people that already live here on the wait list to upgrade to the newest communities. This is an opportunity to strengthen the plan. But if you panic, you're going to cause your people to panic. That's when they will revolt against you and win." Billy walked over and made a drink for himself, realizing no one was going to do it for him.

"Are neither of you fucking paying attention to what is going on? Especially you, Jacob. That's your god damn job," Boobain barked.

"I do my job and you do yours and run the country, or Corners, or whatever it is you do," Jacob said defensively, then took a sip of his drink. Boobain glared daggers at him, then took a step back and walked over by Billy, finally appearing amused, insanely amused.

"Don't you realize that there is information floating out there on both of us and everyone we've been doing business with? That includes you, Billy. Stoyton will pull out of this if we can't find this little hippie fuck overseas that has the missing part to this computer file. We are not the bosses in the bigger picture here, Jake. Stoyton controls everything. You need to be afraid of them. Your special teams can't get the job done, anymore. Billy doesn't ask questions. He gets the fucking job done. Utilize him," Boobain demanded.

"Thank you, Mr. President," Billy said, flattered and carefree.

"No offense Billy, but are you fucking serious?" Jacob scoffed. "He's a lunatic. Look at him. He's ten times as dangerous and ten steps ahead of you at all times. I brought him on. Don't fool yourself into thinking he's more loyal to you than I am. Most likely, he doesn't give a shit about either of us."

"You just called me a lunatic?" Billy said, ignored by both men.

"Yeah? Well, he's put out more of your fires than you realize, saved your ass more than you know. Now come on, I need you to handle this," Boobain said.

"Entertain me, what has he done to save my ass?"

"There wouldn't be a chip floating around with sensitive data on it if you would have just let him handle the UN guys disappearance from A to

Z. I should've bombed the slums, released a virus when I had the chance. Now they're doing just as I thought they would and trying to rise up and erase everything we've accomplished. We should have gotten rid of more of them." Boobain was now close to punching Jacob or flipping a desk.

That's what Billy wanted. The only reason he secretly had a few specific plants blown up, in the midst of the Undergrounds revolutionary chaos, was to set up the system to need his creations. That was his main job for Stoyton Society, set the stage. All Billy wanted out of it was to be the top global dealer of vanity and Stoyton was giving him the opportunity. The fact that these two men were about to implode all over each other's egos in an orgasmic death just invigorated Billy more.

Jacob threw his hands up, "Welp, you can't just obliterate half a country of people, Tim. Look, we've been in the corporate world for decades," he said. "You and I both know it's a slow, methodical process to manipulate a large population toward what they need. Calm down, think this through. We can't overreact or, like Billy said, we're done. I'll give you that, Billy," Jacob said.

"Oh Gee, thanks," Billy responded.

Boobain's phone rang. He took the opportunity to step outside without excusing himself. Jacob downed his drink and poured another, shrugged his shoulders in a, 'whatever', manner as he mumbled to himself. Billy's text notification went off. He absorbed the message and responded with a click, then put his phone away. He smiled at Jacob, amused by his unraveling.

"What are you looking at?" Jacob grumbled.

Minutes later, Boobain stepped back in.

"I want you to go to Boston," Boobain said to Jacob. "Get to the Rustopf industrial park. Make sure everything is running ok, full security check, no breaches. Get your best team and take them with you. Someone is working against us and I want to know who. I want all of their communication stopped. I want all of this mayhem stopped."

"Come on, the location is fine," Jacob said. "People riot, it's not a big deal. Have Billy go. He's not trying to run the nation's corporation."

"Billy is needed elsewhere. He's fixing your fuck up." Boobain filled his glass and took his drink off the bar. He calmed down, reconstructed his demeanor. "Jake, I wouldn't ask you if it wasn't necessary. Put in your time, prove to me you want this to work as much as I do. Billy was just in Colorado last month. We're all doing our part. Just step up."

Billy loved a plan that required no action on his part. He wanted to applaud himself, but that would be too obvious. Part of the reason he was drawn to this in the first place was because Boobain and Droshure were easy marks, perfect stooges. Stoyton Society had his back as long as he got them what they needed. Jacob and Boobain were just means to a greater end.

"Fine. I just think it's a waste of my time." Jacob avoided eye contact with Billy from that point on. "I gotta take a leak." He walked to the door, as if waiting for an arrow to pierce him in the back.

"I'll have Jenna arrange your flight plans," Boobain said, as the door shut. Bored amusement covered Billy's face as he let out a simple snicker. "This isn't funny. Do you think he knows?" Boobain asked.

"Probably. I think it's hysterical that you're thinking of killing the only guy that knows your organization inside and out. I certainly wouldn't risk my life to rescue you from this shit storm," Billy confirmed.

"He's being careless. I don't trust him anymore," Boobain said, frustrated. "You think he's got something to do with the breaches? Someone is leaking information and he's the one that was in charge of the dump."

"I don't think Jacobs your adversary. An idiot maybe, but murder won't look good. Send him to the Corners in Vermont, forced retirement. Make him sign an additional NDA." Billy didn't care what happened to Jacob but killing him seemed excessive. Either way, he was going to be removed, which was one of the things Stoyton wanted.

Boobain got right up in Billy's face. He grabbed him by the collar as hard as his aging body could. "You would be nothing without either of us. Just remember, you're here because we allow you to be."

"Easy, Mr. President," Billy said removing Boobain's hands from his collar. "You're losing your edge. One minute you guys need me, the next minute you're calling me an idiot and insulting me. I am not challenging you. But I am one of the sole reasons you've gotten as far as you have. Just remember, there's a big difference between desperation and madness. Be sure you know which you're fueled by before you fuck with me. If it wasn't for me, the stint, the shootings that aligned everything to be ready for you to step up, it would have never been pulled off." Billy got up and went to the door. "Do what you want with Jake, matters not to me. In fact, I don't even want to know," Billy said. Just then, Jacob came back in the room. Billy patted him on the shoulder as he passed by. "Oh, and Jacob, have a safe flight." Billy left.

CHAPTER 21

B rodie's eyes hunted Donte for answers. The history between them came flooding back as his body grew rigid with anger. He lifted his shirt up, revealing the four parallel lines scarred into the right side of his chest from the fork.

"Remember this, when I was seventeen?" Brodie asked. "You and your buddies did this because I stood up for my sister. The same person you called a slut. You tried to force her to have sex with you back then. You tried to rape her. She told me. She thought you were a joke. That's how I know she would never be with you in any capacity."

One of the twins took the gag out of Donte's mouth, then stepped back into the shadows, letting Brodie have his time.

"You'd be surprised. Wealth changes people. Your sister is no exception," Donte sneered, then spit built up saliva onto the floor.

"You're right. Money certainly does change people." Brodie paced as he thought about Donte's response. He was hesitant to begin. Torture was not his forte. This would be his first attempt at it. He'd killed before but that was for survival and the protection of himself and others, but never torture. He glanced over his shoulder. Marissa sat off in a corner, legs crossed, patiently monitoring the situation. It was time.

As Brodie walked closer to Donte's face, Donte spit another glob of phlegm, this time in his direction, landing it just at the shoulder of his shirt. Without a word, Brodie calmly removed his top shirt. Marissa came over and took it for him. As she walked back to her chair, Brodie punched Donte in the face.

"Where's my sister?"

"I don't know, probably banging some guy," Donte said, recovering from the punch.

"You asked for me, remember? I want to know exactly where she lives. I want a state, city, street, an address, a floor." Brodie squatted down, face to face with Donte for a moment. He retrieved a rusted-up blade from his backpack. He waved it in front of Donte, turning it at different angles, assessing where to begin on Donte's face. "You know what I do for a living, right?" Brodie asked. Donte rolled his eyes, mockingly. "Tighten his ropes, put that thing back in his mouth so he doesn't bite off his tongue."

The twins tightened the twine around Donte's hands and feet. He yelped as the rope shredded through the top layer of his flesh, ripping the skin. One twin stood behind Donte, bracing his chin so that he couldn't move his face. He jerked and yanked about, trying to break free, but the twin's hold was solid.

"Just scream when you're ready to tell me where she is. Or blink, either is fine," Brodie said. "Don't jerk your head, though, it could change your face."

Brodie held the knife just above Donte's left eyebrow. He pierced the skin as a thin stream of blood swam down, drizzling past the corner of his eye. Brodie put the blade closer to Donte's hairline and increased the pressure. The knife slid under the flesh, filleting the skin, as the flap of hair held on, secure only by a small connected strip. Every muscle in Donte's body visibly tensed up as he grunted through the bit in his mouth, slobbering spit out from the corners. Brodie pulled the bit out and tossed it to the floor.

"Something to say?"

"She's in Mono Lake at the Roslyn Estate," Donte said, gritting his teeth with pain.

Brodie grabbed the loose tuft of Donte's hair and pulled it, ripping it further from his scalp, but not detaching it just yet. Blood curtained out over Donte's eye and down his face, dripping off his chin. Brodie rested a gloved finger on the exposed tissue of Donte's scalp.

"This is your frontal lobe. Do you know what this part controls?"

"I can't fucking see and you're giving me a goddamn science quiz?"

Brodie rested the knife on the floor. "Fuck it, I'll just keep ripping until you give me an honest answer or bleed out." Brodie grabbed the flap of hair and gently pulled it back as Donte wailed out.

"Zephyr Cove," Donte screamed out in pain. "She's in Zephyr Cove, in Tahoe. The residential building at your dad's headquarters, the Dison Complex on the eighth floor. I swear to God."

Brodie noticed urine puddling on the ground beneath Donte. He let go of the chunk of flesh and hair.

"Look who belongs in the Gutter now." Brodie sighed, dropping his head back, thinking. "A woman once told me that you must ask a man a question three times before you can trust that he's speaking the truth. So, consider this the third and final time. Then, think hard about how much pain your body can withstand before it dies?"

"Look, that's where she is. It's gated in the Corners, one of the elite regions. There's two corporate towers and one residential tower. Come on, Brodie. I can help you. I'll take you to her. I swear, just stop."

"We found all this in his pockets. Is this your clearance?" One of the bodyguards walked over with a thick wallet, cellphone and some business cards. He pulled a gun from the back of his pants and put it to Donte's temple. "Is this Dison place where you live? Will your badge give them access to that building?"

"Yes, it will work. I don't live there but I have access to the buildings."

"Why did my brother put a track on me?" Brodie grilled him.

"Because you ratted him out about the shootings," Donte said.

"Errrr, wrong answer. Try again," Brodie said.

"I don't know. I swear that's all I know about," Donte pleaded.

Brodie threw a punch, crushing Donte's cheek and jawbone. Donte's head bobbed from the blow. His face was almost indiscernible with smeared blood and swelling. Brodie stood back, watching as any remaining color drained from Donte's face.

"Try again," Brodie requested.

"I swear to God, that's all I know." Donte stuttered as sweat and spit collided with his pain and aggression. Brodie waved his hand in a forward motion, signaling to Donte that he needed more. "You want me to say he hates you? Fine, Billy hates you. He sees you as an adversary. He's obsessed with your failure. He thinks you're a piece of shit and a loser... so do I. Is that what you wanted to hear? He fucking hates you." Donte dropped his head, exhausted.

"Bingo. I'm done with him. Do whatever you want to him. Thank you for helping me." Brodie put his hands together and bowed to Marissa and the twins in thanks.

"We'll take care of this and be up in a minute," she responded. "You go on up, no need to see this."

Donte heard the words and began twisting and squirming, more aggressively than he had before, realizing his fate.

"Brodie please, come on. Brodie! I can help," Donte begged, panicking for his life. "I swear to God, please just let me go. I'm no good to you dead. I'll give you whatever you want. I know things."

Just as Brodie reached the top stair, two gunshots startled him, then he heard the weight of Donte's body drop to the ground.

Brodie moved as if on a conveyer belt and made his way to the bathroom and washed the coagulated blood off his face and body. He tried to steady his hands, but they wouldn't stop shaking. He pressed them on top of the vanity, trying to make the trembling stop. The more he scrubbed the blood off, the more frantically his hands shook. The rest of the crew was waiting for him, ready to go with a backpack full of supplies from Tommy. He dug in his pocket and pulled out all of Donte's items and badges. Most importantly, Donte's chip. He wrapped it in an additional layer of foil to block any signals.

Before he knew it, Nora came in the bathroom and shut the door.

"Have a seat, we gotta bleach your hair quick." Nora had a jug of Clorox in her hand. She set it down and grabbed a towel, placed it around Brodies neck. She grabbed his head and pushed it into the sink, getting his hair wet.

"Easy, wait, you can't just put bleach on my hair. That'll burn my scalp." Brodie lifted his head from the sink in protest.

"Sorry, it's been mixed," Nora grinned. "I should have told you that part." Nora put on rubber gloves, then stopped short of bleaching his hair. "Can you trust me? May I proceed?" Nora looked at him, wanting his ok.

"I've always wondered if I could pull off the platinum look. Go for it," he said.

Brodie came out from the bathroom twenty mins later with a fresh platinum short cut. He pulled his gaiter up, then slipped the Flintstone mask back over his face, and threw his hat on and his hood up. Following suit, Nora and Marcus put their masks back on, too. Once ready, Tommy cautiously opened the door.

Across the way, as some of the fog had lifted, Lodie and two other Splitters were visible, standing at the edge of Tommy's drive. Dunny, the leader, wore a t-shirt, a black, gothic utility kilt with steel toe, and side buckle Moto boots. Many of the leaders across the Gutter wore the black utility kilt, along with the vintage British S10 gas mask, but today the three Splitters had nothing covering their faces. Lodie's face was covered with deep scars and threatening pock marks.

Brodie, Marcus and Nora had their hands on their weapons, ready to draw as they quickly made their way toward the car. Nora and Marcus stayed in front, doing their best to block Brodie from the Splitters view. Seconds later, the twins came out from Tommy's house and stood in front of the Splitters, putting a barrier between the two groups. Nora kept watch while Marcus made sure Brodie got in the car. Once in, he looked out the back window as the Splitters tried to wander closer breaching the driveway.

"Come on boys, mind yourselves. These are my friends, you let them pass," Tommy said. The Splitters were outnumbered but they didn't seem to care as Tommy pointed his shotgun at them. "You got your pay this month, now step back. Go on home"

"What er you guys doing here?" Lodie said, monotone and robotic, no affect. He got on his tiptoes, peaking over the twins' shoulders, speaking to Marcus and Nora. Lodie gazed at the windows, but his vision was no match for the tint.

"We're leaving," Marcus said, his gun aimed at Lodie.

Lodie smiled large, revealing a gold grill encasing his upper teeth. It drove Brodie crazy, waiting in the car. He felt like a sitting duck. He wanted to help, but needed to let this play out.

"We're just leaving." Lodie physically mocked Marcus, putting his hands on his hips. The Splitters behind him snickered like mountain boy derelicts, cheering on their mate.

"Lodie, no trouble." Tommy stepped off the porch. Another Splitter walked over and stood next to Lodie, as he swung the bat, winding up to throw it at the car windshield, teasing them.

"Precious cargo, huh," Lodie said, licking his lips not breaking eye contact with Nora. He tilted his head, peering at her sideways, as if to study her, as if that's what it took for him to see straight. All he could see was her eyes but he was locked in, mentally handling her.

"Hmph," Dunny assessed Marcus, then Nora. Only a few feet away, he stuck his tongue out and went in to lick Marcus's face. Without hesitation, one twin pushed him back as the Splitter fell to the dirt, still holding a thick chain in his hand. He howled out like a wolf, never breaking eye contact. Within seconds, he flipped back up to standing. "You got real pretty eyes, boy. Why don't ya show us what's under that mask of yers, Freddy?"

"We don't have time for this," Nora said.

The twins held the Splitters back, waiting for Tommy's ok to do more. Dunny stared at Marcus, eyeballing him, ready to punch him in the face. He slammed the thick chain in his hand to the ground like a whip. He smiled fake, like he was fixing his hair for a date.

"You think I'm trouble, Freddy? I ain't trying to hurt no one, I just have a feeling your friend hiding behind that window, well I think he could make me a rich boy. And I'm pretty sure that's who me thinks it is," Dunny said. He jumped and drew his gun, as the sound of Marissa's shotgun firing rang out into the sky.

"Next one's at you, Dunny. Let them pass," Marissa said.

"I will kill you slowly and enjoy it," Dunny whispered in Marcus's direction. "Then, I'll kill your friend for the bounty. Maybe not today, but sleep with those beautiful brown eyes open, honey. You don't want to be lost in my dreams."

Just as Nora and Marcus went for their guns, Marissa fired off five shots, killing all of the Splitters dead.

"Thank you," Nora said, impressed. "Please be careful. I'm guessing more will come here," she warned, securing her gun in her chest holster.

"Expect trouble on your journey, word will travel fast. Crazy protects the crazy around here. I only killed them to delay the inevitable. Boys, get rid of these bodies," Marissa said.

"She's right. You need to move, every second counts," Tommy said. The muscular twins retrieved the bodies as Marcus and Nora got in and started the car.

"Thank you for everything. I'll be in touch," Brodie said through the now open car window.

"Just be safe, there's bound to be trouble. Those aren't the only one's around here. Keep those masks on till you're long gone from here," Tommy suggested.

As they pealed out from the dirt lot heading back onto a true road they were, once again, met with haunting wails and howls echoing out from the creatures of the night.

Hours later, traveling with the hue of the approaching sun at their backs, the group was quiet, all exhausted, doing their best to remain on guard. Brodie took a deep inhale then released it as he glanced out into the dark, following the red glow of the nearby dawn in the wing mirror.

"I have a contact coming up. We can switch cars. Tommy set it up for us. We can't take a chance with whoever got word to those Splitters," Brodie said.

They would get more sun than rain today, Brodie hoped silently to himself, might be a good sign. But just like that, the red morphed into an ashen gloom as the wind picked up. Brodie tried to shake the torturing of Donte from his memory. He didn't know how to be ready for what was to come. He was familiar with the Gutter and how to disguise himself and defend against anything he might encounter, but this was new territory. What if the car got flipped, or someone just shot a missile right at them, not caring if he lived? Would he be worth as much alive, but maimed? Marcus turned the radio on and flipped through the scrambled noise, which broke Brodies analyzing.

"Trackers," Nora said, turning the radio off.

"Hey, we could..." Just as Marcus started to speak something bumped off the car with a heavy thump. It was a body, one heavy enough to jostle the car off its path, temporarily.

Nora stayed focused. Brodie watched as her grip tightened around the wheel, her neck muscles strained as she kept her head forward, eyes on the road, hitting the gas, speeding away from the carnage.

"Oh shit," Brodie said.

Up ahead of them in the road, a car full of hoodlums came into view, stopped in the middle of the one lane highway facing them. A woman with a Betty Boop mask on sat seductively on the hood, shredded fish net stockings covering her legs. Sparkling, tight whore's attire barely covered the woman's body. Next to the car, two men wearing Pantalone masks stood, pistols aimed at Nora's car. As they fired, a bullet pierced a front headlight. Marcus leaned out the window and fired several shots back at them, hitting one of the front tires, sending Betty Boop sliding off the hood of the car, onto the gravel at the side of the road.

"Everyone duck," Nora yelled. The wheels spun against the pavement and the car shimmied as she floored the gas pedal to its max. The audible zip and ting of bullets rang out, yet they were unable to do much damage. Marcus leaned out again and fired off several more shots, finally landing one in the sweet spot, as the car burst into the sky.

Hours later, the need for speed had passed, leaving them momentarily out of danger. The rain had subsided and the night sky was nearly gone.

"I'm going to rest my eyes a little," Brodie said. He closed them shut. He was sick of seeing the world. He wanted this adventure to be over. He could smell the tobacco from Nora's cigarette. He took a deep inhale, then exhale. The toxic aroma relaxed him as he started to drift off.

"So how do you know this Jasper guy we're meeting?" Marcus asked. "You've heard of Jasper. We dated a long time ago. We're in the same industry, he was an even higher rank than I am, but he works on contract now. Long before the split, he was missioned overseas. We just didn't see each other enough. Eventually, we..." Nora trailed off.

Pretending to be asleep, Brodie listened from the back. But before he knew it, he was running through a dense forest. All around him, yips and screams echoed out through the trees. He was in Creepers Row. He could smell the punch of shit and rotting flesh. How the hell did they get back there. Maybe he was dead. Maybe the carful of Splitters actually killed him. But then he heard voices whine out his name behind him. Branches crunched and crackled on all sides. He slowed at the noise, feeling surrounded. Startling him, to his left, Cece and Nathan emerged from the woods, sunken eyes, rotting teeth, tweaker scratch marks up and down their arms, yet expensively dressed, caked out on Dotties. They held hands as they laughed, pointing at Brodie as if he were a piece of melting art.

"Brodie, get it together. You're not real, you never were. You can stop running," Cece said. Then slowly, she morphed into Nora just long enough to confuse him, then back to Cece. She and Nathan, chuckled, full-bellied, as they reveled in their elation.

"Soon as I found out you weren't mine, I had ya cropped. You got scraped. You can slow down, you're done. That ain't yer body and it certainly ain't your mind. You do not exist," Nathan said.

He and Cece laughed hysterically, then disappeared from Brodie's vision in the blink of an eye. He stood in the woods alone, listening to the peaceful sounds of nature. Slowly, a clear plastic film encased his body and crept over his face, distorting his vision. He gasped as he felt his airway closing, blind pressure over his face and body. He jerked, waking up, grabbing at his face, trying to remove the film as he pulled the Flintstone mask off. His eyes bolted open as he saw Marcus looking at him from the passenger seat. His hand caught Brodie's, stopping him from grabbing at his face.

"Brodie, what's going on? Wake up. You were dreaming," Nora said.

"What the hell? How long was I out?"

"Maybe fifteen mins," Marcus said.

"I thought we were back in Creepers Row," Brodie was out of it, still catching his breath, calming down.

CHAPTER 22

B illy couldn't sleep. He sat on the patio, squinting his eyes, searching through the phone in his hands. It wasn't his, it was Cece's old phone. A thick, open book rested face down on the side table next to him. Across the country, the sun grew higher in intervals. He thought about Brodie and tried to get into his head.

Billy moved to LA six months after he finished his graduate program with a Masters in International Business & Marketing from Pepperdine. It only took a few months of being back in Illinois for him to know he couldn't stay. His parents had waited for him to get home from college to announce their divorce. They didn't wait for Brodie to finish his semester overseas. Billy knew his father never recognized Brodie as his son after finding out about the affair and that's why he didn't factor him into the decision.

In the Midwest, Billy quickly grew antsy, creating boring marketing plans for family friends that lacked any substance. He had never been a fan of the Midwest and the feeling was only enhanced by his return after college. The women he met cared more about having their heels match their sports jerseys, than they did about shaving their legs or their 401K.

Billy had the smarts, but he certainly wasn't the charmer that Brodie was, nor was he friendly like Cece. He didn't indulge in wasteful conversation or overemotional people. He felt Brodie was the king of both. Billy liked convincing people that they needed things, he liked to fuck and he liked creating and selling ideas for far more than what they were worth. That was also the reason why he couldn't sleep this particular morning. Brodie was messing with his future and not knowing where he was or what he was up to had Billy's head spinning.

"Babe, what's up?" Audrey appeared at the other end of the patio deck and dove in the pool. Bare-skinned, she swam the length underwater, finally emerging, resting her arms on the ledge in front of Billy.

"Can't sleep. Thinking about Brodie. Wondering what he would be doing in Creepers Row. The info we got from the farmhouse finally picked up a track and a couple Splitters reported to Spider that there was an incident. My brother was identified wearing some fucking mask by a car full of vagrants in Creepers Row, but by the time the other team got to the area, there was no sign of any Splitters and no sign of Brodie. They're just gone. Now, four hours have passed and no word, nothing. Spider hasn't called, I hear nothing."

"You really think your brother is that big of a threat?" Audrey never understood Billy's obsession with him. "What could he possibly have?"

"The thing about Brodie is that he lies. He tells people he's never fired a gun, but when he worked in South Africa with that Doctors without Borders thing, he told my mom he had to take a weapons class before he even left. He gives off this fucking emo, righteous do-gooder persona, but he's just a stoner blessed with intellect and a steady hand. He's no better than me. If he got any evidence off Nolan Petri, it may not only screw Boobain's plan, but I guarantee it will be the end of my work with Stoyton.

They will see me as a joke. Don't you get it? Brodie will do whatever it takes to ruin me."

"Well, maybe if you stopped fucking with him. It's not like you're innocent," Audrey said.

Billy got up, walked to the pools edge, and squatted down, putting his hand in her face.

"Right. Like he wasn't fucking with me when he called not only the FBI, but the CIA and who knows wherever else and gave my name as the mastermind behind the shootings," Billy sighed. "He thinks I was setting him up to die. It was just a fucking test. I wanted to see his reaction, how he would respond. His response was betrayal."

"Your tests are going to get you killed. You're testing Cece, Brodie, your father, even me. Fuck, Billy, this isn't a game. You need to stop doing so much coke. It's making you paranoid," Audrey pleaded.

Billy leaned down and got head-to-head with Audrey, kissed her lips gently. He took one of the phones off the table and held it toward her. As she took it, he poured a dash of coke onto the divot between his thumb and pointer.

"I like my white thunder dust. Now, call him. Just do it for me. Put it on speaker and call him. If he answers, hang up." Billy couldn't sit still. Dancing around, excited to prank Brodie.

"Why are we doing this, again? The first time you were drunk, the next five times we were high and messing around, but you keep calling him. What's your endgame with this?"

"It's Cece's old phone. If he sees she's calling, he'll think she's in trouble."

"You don't think he already thinks that with your fucking hang up calls? What's it accomplished? You still don't know where he is."

"Just fucking call him."

Billy knew Audrey didn't like the game. She didn't see the point. That didn't matter to him, though. It turned him on to get her to do things, it was that control, again. Plus, he didn't want Brodie to think he had the upper hand. He knew Brodie was snooping around, trying to get in touch with Cece. He knew it by the messages Brodie would leave, asking if Billy had gone crazy. Now, with everything the Splitters reported, it was time. Brodie would screw up and forget to scramble his line or something and walk right into the palm of Billy's hand.

"Put it on speaker." Billy watched her hit the button. He wanted to know she wouldn't turn on him, that she was still one hundred percent loyal to him. She was right, another test.

"You know, you could just call him from your own fucking phone and talk to him." It rang several times, then went to voicemail. Audrey hung up and went to the call log. "Thirty-seven outgoing calls to him just in the last two weeks?" Audrey smirked, disgusted, as she chucked the phone at Billy, sending it bouncing off his leg, tumbling out of reach, plunging into the pool to her delight.

"What the fuck?" Billy jumped up, waiting for her to get his phone.

"You're psycho, you are acting like a juvenile little asshole. You don't think that calling him this much just might make him suspicious? Jesus Christ, Billy. Now isn't the time to flare your sibling rivalry. Stick to Stoyton and don't worry about this Boobain shit. Do not fuck with my success."

Billy rolled off the edge of the patio into the pool, ignoring her, diving down to retrieve the phone. He sprouted out of the water and placed it to the side.

"Baby, go get a container and some rice for me," Billy said.

"Get it yourself, I'm finishing my swim."

Billy scooted out of the pool and dashed inside to gather the bits and pieces for the makeshift phone revival kit. When he came outside, he saw the carnage of the smashed phone in pieces on the concrete.

"Are you fucking kidding me? I can't believe you did that!" Billy yelled at Audrey as she wrapped her towel around her waist.

"It's not even your god damn phone, Billy. Now don't call him anymore or I'll tell my father everything. Just remember, there's a million Splitters that would love to see you knocked off your perch."

"Well, first of all, I don't give a fuck about your father. He's a small turd," Billy said. "Secondly, come on, calm down. Let's just fuck."

"Go fuck yourself, I'm going to Pilates. I need to be away from you for a little while."

Billy said nothing, just watched Audrey as she swayed her hips, shaking her heart shaped ass as she stomped inside. He sat back down and opened his computer and searched Brodie's name on Boomerang. Nothing came up under Brodie Frost. Billy scanned the horizon as if the answers were hidden in the skyline. He searched Marcus Etienne. Billy had met him a few times when they were younger. Another loser like Brodie. What came up on Marcus surprised him.

"Not just a dumb stoner after all. Father was an engineer at Bugatti, mother is the famous French author Jean-Cherie Etienne, blah blah blah. Wait, what have we here? Fired from DARPA, busted on dope charges. There he is, that's the guy I met." Bored and wired, he went in his office and locked the door.

Thirty minutes later, with his naked ass to the door, Billy clutched the hips of a leggy blonde bent over in front of him. The woman gripped the window sill as Billy pumped his way to climax. As he finished, he caught his breath and stood tall, cracking his back and releasing the woman's hips from his grip. She had perfect breasts along with a perfect voluptuous body.

"Was that nice for you?" the woman asked with low inflection, monotone, with robotic enthusiasm. She swiveled her head 180 degrees to face him.

Billy chuckled at the question, putting his boxers back on. She grinned seductively. He went over and put his arms around her, searching for something under her hair, at the nape of her neck. Finally, he pressed a partially embedded, illuminated blue power button. The woman's body went limp in his hands, like a sack of potatoes. The flat smile stayed fixed on her face like Botox. He hauled the limp humanlike body over to the large closet in his office and folded the doll over, putting the pleasure toy back into a large, sealed, container and hung it on the rack. He shut the closet, securing it with a palm lock.

Refreshed, he started bouncing back and forth, as if preparing for a fight, punch, duck, jab, jab. He was ready. He poured out another line of coke and sniffed it up. He keyed in a code to block his number and dialed.

"Hey Brodie, it's your brother, Billy. I wanted to see if you've heard from Cece. I left her a couple of messages, but she hasn't called back. I'm just hoping no one did anything to her. Again, it's Billy. Call me back."

Billy hung up. He left no call back number. "Stress on that mother fucker."

CHAPTER 23

B rodie sat in the back of the car, antsy, trying to move into a comfortable position. Nothing seemed right. He needed to stay on guard and comfort wasn't a part of that. The car traveled through a small town with signs of vitality and life. Several women stood in gaggles, saturating the sidewalks. They held their signs high, demanding proper schools for kids. Public schools were against President Boobain's platform. Most schools in the Gutter closed down after the class wars, not only due to the lack of electricity to power them, but also the lack of supplies. Most importantly, though, the risks teachers and children faced getting to a school had become too high. Trafficking in the Gutter was rampant, not just of drugs, but of women and children, too. That left homeschooling as the only option, which not everyone was equipped to pull off. In between the women, elders went about their morning walks, weaving around the homeless and agitated, who were camped out along the roads, staging protests of their own.

"You think they're ready for the revolution?" Marcus asked.

"I certainly hope so. I'm sure some of them have been holding those signs up since the day the country split and they had their rights and utilities regulated," Brodie said.

"Check in with Jonas," Nora got off the phone and cut in, signaling to Brodie.

Word of the potential revolution was traveling fast. Brodie didn't know if it would do any good, but seeing that people still had hope motivated him. The Undergrounds main concern was restoring order and taking Boobain and his corrupt enterprise down. The cast of characters included Brodie's father. The people Nathan Wessner embezzled from and for, was in part what kept him protected for so long. In truth, he was a quickly aging heartless old bore of a man who could make money disappear and multiply depending on the request. He was tolerated for his intelligence. His time would come.

"We need to dump this car and get to Tommy's contact. Jonas is dead," Brodie informed, as he ended his phone call. "A few at his facility were killed and several wounded. Deya, his wife and their daughter were upstairs when she saw Lane kill Jonas on the cameras. She tried to warn everyone, but they hid when they heard the gunshots. She saw Lane let a car full of Splitters in. A man got out of the car in a suit, she thinks it was Billy. They talked, then the man shot Lane. This is so fucked. She alerted the Underground and a team is there now, wiping the place. They'll find them a safe house."

"I'm one step ahead of you," Nora said. "I got us a safer option. Marcus is going over the route now."

"Well, it all makes sense now that we keep running into Splitters," Marcus asserted.

Brodie wasn't surprised. It seemed something was up with the kid from the moment he walked outside. Thank God he turned down the car,

Brodie thought to himself, replaying that stop over and over in his head, trying to identify the mistake.

"I just got an update. Three more Droshure RM plants have been wiped out with minimal casualties. Small ones. Four teams were able to get behind Corners gates without detection. Word on the street is they're hoping to take Droshure tonight or tomorrow, capture, not kill," Marcus said.

As they passed through a small town, now far from the vibrant city, Brodie could see what everything had done to the people, as bums and beggars roamed like zombies, no longer aware of purpose. Malls and playgrounds sat busted up and disheveled, overgrown with garbage and unkept foliage. Left behind stuffed animals and toys now rested partially buried in the dense grass and weeds. More and more, though, they were seeing protesters in support of the revolution. On occasion, they'd pass a basic coffee shop or grocery store with bars on the windows and security out front, but open at least. Signs offering free coffee and clean water for protesters hung in the windows. The security allowed some to carry on about their business throughout the last three years, making the best of what little they had left, trying to keep hope afloat. Nothing was new, but at least many structures were still standing. Nora pointed to the gas station as they pulled in.

"Can I get out and stretch my legs, please?" Brodie asked.

"Stay with him, Marcus. I'll be right back," Nora said.

She jogged over to the gas station and went inside. Marcus and Brodie stood with hoods up and buffs covering their faces, watching her talk to the cashier through the window. She put something in her pocket, then walked outside and around the corner with the cashier, out of sight. Brodie rested against the car, as Marcus pulled his buff down just enough to puff on a cigarette, an energy drink in his hand. Brodie looked back to the gas station just in time to see the cashier return, no longer on the phone.

"Hey," Brodie said. "Where's Nora?"

"Give it a minute. These are her people, I'm sure she's fine," Marcus assured Brodie, then offered him a cigarette.

"No thanks. Hey," Brodie took down his buff and looked at Marcus.

"What's up, man?" Marcus smiled, glancing curiously at Brodie.

"You mad at me? You know, for dragging you into all of this," Brodie queried.

"You didn't drag me into this. This will be over soon. And no, I don't think you're crazy for trying to find your sister. I'd be doing the same if I thought my sisters were in danger. Don't give it a second thought."

Just then, Nora pulled around from the back in a black BMW M8 Gran Coupe with tinted windows, waving her hand to let them know it was her.

"Transfer only what we need and get in," Nora said as she parked the car next to hers. "They'll hide my car for us."

They quickly grabbed everything necessary and moved it to the BMW, then sped out of the lot.

"We have another 4 hours to Winnemucca if we can keep a good pace. Let's do our best to make sure the scrambles are working. I'll drive. Marcus, stay on your laptop and keep up the magic. The car has a built-in Vesper-Dome, but we still need to scramble," Nora said.

"Vesper? A bit risky, don't you think?" Marcus asked.

"Not for what we're doing, they don't know or care. Besides, the foreigners I work with are my allies," Nora responded.

Brodie watched the interaction between Marcus and Nora, realizing he was with two of the smartest people he knew. If something happened to either of them it would break him. He should have never let them come with him. He should have done this on his own. Casualties were building.

After being back in the car for an hour, Brodie's skin grew warm as perspiration grew wet and clammy along his brow. His throat felt as though it was sealing closed.

"Hey, guys, can we stop? I need some fresh air," he coughed to clear his throat. He thought about just throwing the door open and jumping out. Maybe he'd be just as safe on foot simply traveling along bike paths and through tunnels, toward the Corners. First, he'd grab his bag, all of his supplies were in his bag. It wouldn't work. He needed to catch his breath.

"We gotta keep moving. Crack a window, we have to get to the Cat House and meet Jasper," Nora explained.

"There was a plane crash. Was headed for Boston, it's rumored that Droshure was on the plane, but they're not sure." Marcus read from his laptop, then wiped the information branch from his system.

Brodie didn't like the answer from Nora. His chest felt tight. He adjusted his buff, wiping sweat from his forehead, then pulled it down from his mouth, around his neck, cracking the window. He felt claustrophobic. Just then, his non-secure phone sounded an alert. He had a message. Somewhere along the route he missed a call. He put his phone to his ear and listened, as his face went pallid.

"That was Billy. Said he didn't know where Cece was. Told me to call him but didn't leave a number. After what Donte said, I trust Billy even less than I did before," Brodie said. "He's trying to trap me."

"All the more reason to get this over with. Billy's a psychopath," Marcus said.

Maybe there would be a way for Brodie to sneak off and ditch them both at the brothel. He could take care of things alone. The closer they got to the Corners, the higher the stakes felt and the more he worried about Marcus and Nora. He studied her face from the reflection in the rear-view mirror, getting lost in their history. She caught his gaze and smiled with her eyes.

"You doing ok?"

"Yep," Brodie said. He was detaching, preparing to flee. He half-smiled back, hoping she couldn't feel the weight of his thoughts. He pulled his buff up back up above his cheeks, attempting to hid any expression. His face grew flush, as his heart galloped right behind the swell, building steam. He could hear his pulse stampeding in his ears. He took a deep sigh, puffing his chest in and out, trying to catch his breath, not realizing how audible his anxiety had become.

"Give him a water, he's freaking out," Nora said.

"Drink this and stick your head between your knees. My nana always had me do that." Marcus grabbed a bottled water out of a bag and handed it back. "It works."

"I'm fine. I'm here for this." Brodie drank the water. "Can I see the map?"

Marcus handed it back to him. He studied it as if it might be the last time he'd see it, still on the fence about going solo.

Finally, they passed a large weathered and worn sign that read, Winnemucca, Nevada and pulled off 80 to the main street through town. The posts that held up the sign were covered in rust. The car cruised down the road as the landscape morphed into that of a well-preserved, yet small and vacant town. Several empty hotels and casino's straight out of the 1900s wild wild west stood with busted out windows and wide-open doors as periodic dust balls tumbled out from the inside. Tipped over video poker machines and slots could be seen through the open, blown out doors, all the money looted years back during the class wars and riots.

A shirtless old black man with long hair and a gray beard walked down the main street pulling a red wagon, its only passenger, a car tire.

Up ahead five teenagers sat atop the cement edge of a deteriorating surface lot's ledge, three girls and two boys. With their feet dangling, all five holding up blank signs. As the car neared, they hopped off the ledge and stood at the side of the road. Marcus rolled down his window.

"What's going on, there's nothing written on your boards."

"We ain't got nothing to write with, man. Everything's dried out. You know about the military testing around here?" One of the girls hopped down from the ledge and came closer to the street curb.

"Sure, everybody heard about it, you confirming?" Marcus inquired.

"No way, man! It's a lie. They ain't testing shit. They're saying that stuff so people freak out and stay away. They're doing it all over the slums. Every now and then, they come round and poison the cattle, put stuff in the fields so people find dead cows, dogs and shit, thinking it's in the air," one of the boys said.

Nora had Brodie grab her backpack and hand it forward. She took it and pulled out a small electronic meter and held it out the window, to the sky.

"They're right, AQI is 68, that's pretty good."

"Ain't nothing wrong with the air here. Boobain just wants the land. They're fooling everyone. We've got a garden and a well that's been keeping us strong and healthy. We're trying to tell people the truth so they come home, but people avoid the area," the boy said.

"They just think we're stupid teenagers. Decks almost twenty-three. He made us a greenhouse two years ago," one of the kids mentioned. "I can't tell you where it is, but as long as we don't eat the poisoned animals, we're ok. We go to Reno once a month for what we need. Limited electricity but we gotta stay here and let people know."

"You seen Rolly when you drove in? The guy with the wagon? He set up residence in the best estate just off main street. People who pass through just think he's just a bum. You know, dumb and stupid," another girl said. "He used to be a chemical engineer, worked for Dupont before they shut down. He's been taking notes and pictures of the folks that are doing the poisoning. Testing the animals that are dying. You remember that name, Rolly Leblanc. He's gonna turn it all into a book when Boobain goes down. It'll expose the rest of 'em, too."

"Where are your parents?" Nora asked.

"Decks parents died during the shootings on dark sixteen back in 2025'," an older boy and the leader of the squad of young adults said. "Katie and Julies parents are in Alabama on a commune near the ocean. Sue got separated from her folks. My mom is living a delusional life of ignorant bliss in the Corners with her new husband." The irritation from his mothers' choices could be seen through the boys' facial expressions, what was left unsaid.

"We think Rollys got a secret underground lair under the casino over there, where he stores everything. Anyway, there ain't nothing wrong in Winnemucca. Everyone can come home," the teenage boy said.

"We'll spread the word, guys. Stay safe." Nora shouted, as Marcus flashed them a peace sign.

They pulled off and continued on their way in route to the whorehouse, now seeing the small town through different eyes. The roof sat partially peeled off the old Scottish Inn. Several of the other bakeries and restaurants still stood, but with water damage and partially collapsed roofs.

"Boobain is nuts," Marcus said. "They all are. Weeding out the weak, broke and needy, just so he can rebuild some perfect sterile little psycholand haven. This is horrible"

"It's so much more than that, but," Nora added, "you're on the right track."

As they drove back onto the highway, they passed a large, worn-out billboard with two gigantic red tomatoes on it that read, 'Squeeze em, fresh tomatoes in 20 Miles.' The upper corner of the sign wilted over like a flower, hanging down from weathering.

Nora continued, and within fifteen minutes they found themselves in the middle of nowhere, open landscape. Even still, it felt much cleaner than what they were used to. The air was warm and refreshing. The sun was finally shining. A land without many inhabitants, left for mother nature to regenerate. Brodie and Marcus rolled down the windows for a moment, feeling the sun on their face and the warm breeze against their skin.

"It's gotta be just over that hill toward the high brush and cactus fields. Jasper said there's a lot of Boobain's upper-tier military that come here so we need to stay on guard. Buffs on, windows up." Nora said the words matter-of-fact while checking the gun in her ankle and shoulder holsters.

"I've never been to an actual brothel. Is it sloppy like the Gutter mop shops?" Marcus asked.

"Mop shops?" Nora said.

"That's what he calls the Peep and Play jerk shops in the slums," Brodie said as Nora rolled her eyes.

"Are you guys going to be able to stay focused in there?"

"Yes, mom. We promise." Marcus turned back to Brodie with a grin, "boobies," he giggled like a juvenile.

"Seriously?" Nora playfully whacked Marcus on the chest with the back of her hand. "Ok, Jasper said it's kind of off on its own, a little hidden. He said after the hill there's a shallow valley and then we'll see an old sign for it. It's called Charlotte's Web," Nora said.

Up ahead as they declined into the valley, just past a strategically planted ring of trees for protection, a large burgundy Victorian house came into view surrounded by five small cabins. As they approached, four armored black military-issue Mercedes Benz SUV's, two other luxury cars and a silver, stealth-like 442 muscle car with tinted windows sat parked.

"What the hell are we getting into," Brodie said eyeing up the military Rovers.

"That's Jaspers car. I'll go in first and make sure everything's good." She turned back to Brodie. "We're going to make it. You're going to have to start believing that for this all to work the way we want it to."

Nora parked close by the 442, keeping some distance from the military vehicles. The threesome prepared to go in, guns at the ready.

"Wait for my signal," Nora said. With her balaclava up to her eyes and her hand on the grip of her gun, she got out and cautiously walked across the dusty lot toward the door to Charlotte's Web.

CHAPTER 24

Billy sat at the bar inside Current. A tall bourbon with a slice of lime resting steady on the rim sat in front of him, next to a half-eaten plate of Bolognese. Casually dressed in jeans and a V-neck sweater, he stared intently at the baseball game playing on the tv screen hovering just above the bar. A thump caught his ear as Spider walked in and sat down next to him, also dressed in plain clothes, no mask. His serpent-stranded DNA tattoo sat visibly wrapped around his index finger. Billy acknowledged him with a nod, but kept his eyes forward.

"Who's winning?" Spider asked.

"I haven't been paying much attention." Billy signaled the bartender, tapping the rim of his glass, thirsty for another. "And whatever he wants."

"Old Stumps Nut Job if you got it," Spider said, turning to face Billy. "So hey, I've got some not-so-great news."

"What now?" Billy kept his eyes fixed on the game he had no interest in.

"No one has been able to locate them," Spider said. "The teams said the last signal was in western Kansas. One of my guys went to the spot they were last tracked. There was nothing. No clues on where they are."

Billy said nothing and tossed back the last swig of his drink before his next arrived. Outside the tinted shades, the silhouettes of shouting protesters stomping past were visible, their voices sporadically audible through the glass.

"Teams are all over the Gutter looking for them. It's not for a lack of trying. He's not in Wisconsin anywhere. They're just being too careful." Spider waited for Billy to respond but his silence continued. "You gotta give me something, Billy. What's the move?"

"That idiot Lane should have shot Brodie when he had the chance. Why are none of these people competent when it comes to fucking finding him? He's not a superhero. It's not like he's riding in an invisible car. This is the fourth or fifth group of Splits that have dropped the ball," Billy said. "There's no way he'd leave the country. He'd never go without Cece."

"What makes you think your bro would even do something with whatever it is he found? It could be nothing. Who knows, maybe he'll bring it in and get the cash or try to find you," Spider said, trying to calm Billy.

"Say that stupid shit one more time. Seriously, I'm not in the mood," Billy said. "What you fail to realize is he watches me, fucks with me. For all I know he's coming to kill me. Get that through your fucking head." Billy looked over his shoulder, having been reminded of his own mortality.

"They'll find him. You have the best teams out looking for him. I'll escalate the search, just understand, everything's getting crazy. More protests are popping up, people are starting to revolt. It's getting messy," Spider said. He thought twice about what he was going to say next, first looking down, then back to Billy. "Look, a lot of these guys are chasing the money. You might need to pay them more if you want a better result. Right now, Droshure is the highest bidder for Brodie. They don't know he's your brother, but he's the guy they're looking for."

"I'm heading to Colorado in an hour. I might be there overnight. I want you to call me the minute someone has eyes on him. Pay them more, threaten their lives, whatever it takes to get him to me."

"It'll happen. I'll make it happen," Spider said.

"Swing by and check up on Cece, make sure she isn't acting weird. The last thing I need is her working against me, too." Billy took the fresh drink in front of him and poured it down his throat. He got up from the table and headed to the front door. "When I get back, I'm staying with her in case he shows up."

"Hey, come back a second." Spider stood up, he had yet more unkind information to communicate.

"What?" Billy was getting sick of surprises.

"Some of the Splitters you had working for you have been talking shit. They've been saying you're taking advantage of their work. That you're a hack and a high paid, psycho punk. Some might be looking to take you out. Just watch your back." Spider warned.

"Let them fucking try," he said. "Get a meal, put it on my tab." Billy walked out the front door. His paranoia dropped as his ego swelled at the mention of a threat, now growing unafraid of anything, stepping into the road, joining a passing protest.

CHAPTER 25

Nora's fingers brushed against the pistol in the holster just inside her coat as she neared the door of Charlotte's Web. As the door pushed open, she drew her gun just before landing her eyes on Jasper's face as he strolled out toward her in a military uniform. He stood at 6'0 even, his hair disheveled and pulled back off his face, landing in length somewhere around his chin. He held his hands up to single it was him as Nora put her gun back in the holster.

"Sorry, I saw you coming, you just beat me to the door. Where's Brodie?" Jasper asked.

Just past Jasper, a scantily dressed pleasure dame in burlesque lingerie was getting up from the couch. The bodies of two dead military men in uniform lay partially hidden behind an adjacent bar.

"They're coming. Marcus is with us. He's safe." Nora held the door open and flagged the guys to come in. "What's going on with all the bodies," she nodded toward them. "Didn't wanna wait for us to have some fun, did ya," she smirked.

"Dead Corners guards, three more upstairs, two in the lounge. Just making sure it was safe," Jasper confirmed. "You said this needed to happen fast. One of the guys is in his briefs cuz I took his uniform and ID. I swept all the cabins and we'll stick the bodies in there so everything's clear. Two of the girls are watching the cameras and will let us know if anyone's approaching, but we gotta move quick."

The burlesque beauty sauntered past and put her hand on Jaspers back. "I'll leave you to your business. Thanks for the advice. I'll let Charlotte know they're here," the woman said as she disappeared around the corner.

"Thanks, Lucy," Jasper said.

"That's my Jasper, always looking out for the ladies," Nora said.

"Always, I'm a bit of a big brother around here. She's got some boyfriend troubles," Jasper said.

"Working here? I totally see why," Nora responded.

"All right, calm down. You look good by the way," Jasper complimented. He leaned in and kissed her gentlemanly on the cheek.

Just then Brodie and Marcus walked in. "Howdy," Marcus said.

"Hey guys, I'm Jasper," he said tapping on his own chest then continued with direction. "First thing that needs to happen, and quickly, is find a guard and get his uniform on. Take everything out of his pockets, pass cards, phones, all of it. Don't forget their chips. It will get us into the Corners smoother. If you need a blade, let me know," Jasper said. "Then we need to get the guards into the cabin so if anyone comes in here, there's no trace. The girls will pull the SUVs underground."

Marcus and Nora took off upstairs to search for the guards and uniforms, while Brodie hung back. He went to Jasper and put his hand out to shake, surveying the dead guards before him, trying to gauge whose uniform would fit him.

"I just want to thank you for helping me. It really means a lot and..." Brodie tried to make good eye contact with Jasper, wanting to come off sincere, but before he could finish, Jasper pulled him in close.

He inched right up to Brodie's ear. "If anything happens to Nora, it will be a problem for me. She hasn't survived this long just to be a casualty of some sibling rivalry. So, if I ask you or your friend to do something, I need your word that, without question, you and your friend will comply." Jasper took a step back, smiling, penetrating Brodie's gaze, assessing his reaction time.

"Absolutely. You have my word. She insisted on coming. I'll do everything in my power to keep her safe." At that moment Brodie realized this had become bigger than simply rescuing Cece. He needed to stop feeling sorry for himself and step up.

"I'm not mad at ya, buddy," Jasper said. "I'm just saying, she's in it now. You need to be 110%. You need to protect your people," Jasper winked at Brodie.

"I get it. I would give my life to save Nora," Brodie said.

"Good, because I'm doing this for her, because she cares about you. I work under contract now, for myself. It's too hard to know who to trust. But if I'm taking the time to help you, I'm helping you all the way, until you're all safe." Jasper put his hand out, waiting for Brodie to meet it with his own and shake in solidarity. "We good?"

"Yes, and thank you," Brodie responded.

"Awesome, cuz if not, I'd have to kill you and your friend." Jasper bellowed out with a chuckle just as Nora walked in the room, catching the tail end of Jaspers pressing, rolling her eyes.

"Cool it, Jasper. Brodie, get a uniform on. Clocks ticking," she said. "Are these women lounging around here safe?"

Marcus came back downstairs to the main room, geared up and ready for instruction.

"Yes, they're as safe as Brodie and your friend Marcus here. The ladies working were handpicked by yours truly for the utmost security," Jasper attested. "Marcus, if you don't have superglue for the guard's identity chip, let me know. I have a ton in my bag. One other thing, do not make any phone calls or communication while you are here. One thing I can't let any of you do is put this place in jeopardy."

"Nora had us turn off all electronics thirty minutes before we got here," Brodie said as he returned from the bathroom in full military garb, making him look like true Corners military.

"Alright, we need to hide the bodies before we head out. Marcus, you can help me get them out to the cabins. That way I can fill you in on the plans. Nora, you and Brodie get the bodies down here from upstairs. Wrap em, no blood on these floors. Keep guard and go over this map, it's our route in," Jasper said handing them a copy from his pants pocket.

The map had a direct route into California, into the Corners community, right up to the building where they believed Cece was being held. Jasper marked and outlined their path and possible danger spots, safe houses and current protest hot spots. He also marked all the areas they should do their best to avoid.

"You good?" Brodie asked Nora, touching her arm. He wanted to pull her in, hold her and make her feel safe. Instead, he took her hand. "I will do everything in and beyond my power to keep you safe."

Effortlessly, Nora leaned in and kissed him sweetly on the lips. "I know you will. Let's just get this over with," she said.

Finally, Jasper returned to the main room. "After we leave here, do not show any affection or tendency toward each other. Any of that will make you both a liability to the other. This is a rescue mission, stay focused and it'll be a piece of cake," Jasper directed. "Marcus went to use the can. If you two haven't done so, now is the time."

Brodie watched Jasper as he leaned against the stair rail by the door, driving gloves poking out from his pants pocket, looking very Sundance

Kid, circa Robert Redford. Brodie needed to get his shit in gear. In that moment, he realized how much everything that had happened since the split distorted his confidence. He had wasted so much time staying in the shadows, saving lives behind walls and gathering data. He needed to be Jasper's ally, step up and make sure everyone got out of this safely.

"Hey, let's get these last bodies into the cabin. Can you carry the tiny guy?" Jasper nudged Brodie.

"Yeah," Brodie said confidently as he scooped one of the guards' bodies and waited for Jasper to grab the other. The two quickly got the last of the bodies out of the house and into the drop hole of one of the cabins.

Jasper yelled out for Nora as he stood with Marcus and Brodie. Just then, a beautiful, mocha-skinned woman with thick, curly hair came out from a back room wearing a T-shirt and a flowing summer skirt. "This is Charlotte," Jasper said.

"You work here?" Marcus was pleasantly taken aback.

"No, this is my place. I don't see clients," Charlotte said, amused. "Do you guys have everything you need?"

"Bodies are out of the way in the first cabin in the drop hole Jasper showed us. We'll come back with him to take care of them," Marcus was trying to impress her.

"I'm Nora. Thank you for letting us meet here," Nora said returning from the bathroom.

"Of course. I hope for a successful journey, as well."

One of the ladies rushed into the room and whispered in Jasper's ear.

"All right, we gotta move. Possible car approaching about fifteen miles out from the south. We'll cut north and loop in. Charlotte, call me if anything comes up. You and your girls keep your guns and mace close by. Get all the SUV's underground now, except for the one with the gold trim around the plate. We'll take that one. Keep everything as normal as possible. No one in the cabins and make sure no one wanders around outside without an escort. If you need to shoot anyone, get them in the drop hole right after. And I'm serious, call if any problems come up," Jasper said.

Everyone shuffled outside as Jasper lingered about until he was alone with Charlotte. Nora caught herself glancing in from outside as he pulled Charlotte close. Feeling like a prowler, she turned and walked toward the cars. She knew Jasper wasn't right for her, not as a couple, but that knowing didn't erase their history. Her mind was all over the place. But soon enough, she was distracted as several women came rushing out and quickly got in the few military SUV's and cars and drove them into the underground lot.

A minute later, Jasper and Charlotte came outside as he pointed over to the remaining black military Mercedes G63.

"Guys, this is how we get into the Corners. Bullet proof, tinted windows, we glide in and out. Brodie and Nora, come with me," Jasper instructed. Within seconds, they had grabbed supplies out of their car and loaded up the military vehicle. "Marcus, take the car you guys came in. In about fourteen miles we'll park it in a safe lot and get it underground. Follow me in, eyes low. No contact with anyone. Make sure all devices are off or in ghost mode. Marcus is the only one online. He's got his hacker who'll be helping us get in and out. And don't fire unless absolutely necessary," he said.

Brodie and Jasper were both strong men but so very opposite. Brodie knew he could learn a lot from a man like Jasper, but being Nora's ex, it also seemed a bit of a betrayal to himself, to idolize the man. He could tell Marcus already thought Jasper was great.

"Sounds good, man," Marcus said.

"All right, Marcus. Stay close. We've got about fifteen minutes until we get there."

Marcus gave Jasper a thumbs up and hopped in the BMW they arrived in. Quickly, Nora bolted out of the SUV and hopped in the passenger side, giving Marcus some company, rather than be in a car with her ex and her boyfriend. Brodie got in the front seat and suddenly he was alone with Jasper. They all pulled off the lot, heading northwest, opposite from the direction they had arrived from. Nora and Marcus kept pace, staying close behind.

Brodie and Jasper drove in silence, but for Brodie, it felt calm.

"You know, not everyone's supposed to stay in contact with their family. Many of the people I work with haven't talked to their families in years," Jasper said. "When you do the kind of work Nora and I do, you don't have time for dysfunctional family bullshit. You know, the manipulation and games family members play with each other out of damage and habit? Kind of puts all that shit into perspective when you're saving the life of someone who was poisoned, you know?" He turned to Brodie. "Makes that stuff small. Family's great but not at the cost of your own sanity."

"I appreciate that. My sister is the last piece to my disconnection. I can't disappear without knowing she's ok," Brodie replied.

"I'm guessing that disappearing includes with Nora and you're not talking about killing yourself?"

"Right, no. I just mean disappearing from this game I've been playing with Billy. Cece will always be able to find me, but like you say, I just need to disappear from the dysfunctional family bullshit. It's time to stop," Brodie said. He caught himself getting emotional, a little irritated with himself.

"If you need work, I might be able to help you. Agents get injured. They need surgeons that keep their mouths shut and do good work."

"Thanks," Brodie said. "I appreciate that."

Hours later, the Mercedes sped along Highway 49 at a good pace. They had ditched Nora's car at a safe house and the foursome was heading straight into the Corners. The dry browns and clay reds transformed into lush and expanding greenery, pocketed with white capped mountains and beautiful waters off in the distance. As they got close to the interstate, Brodie gazed out the window, admiring the growing collage of tents. There had to be hundreds lined along the main highways and roads they passed through.

Once they cut over to Highway 50, toward Zephyr Cove, more functioning structures appeared and the protests rapidly grew in number. People carried marked up signs, some even preparing weapons and protective gear to stave off any resistance they might encounter.

"Who knew this many people would stand up and fight," Brodie said, unable to hide his joy.

"Lots have been living on the fringe in vacant homes and on abandoned farmland in the National Parks, just waiting and preparing for the revolution. There are tent encampments and cardboard counties all along the warmer southern and western state edges, too. If we hadn't taken the quieter roads, we would have seen even bigger crowds," Jasper said.

"Colorado and the region below Area 51 supposedly have complete Corners communities fully connected underground and fitted with tunnels to California, Texas and Utah in development. A fourth is rumored to go to Canada. One of my old DARPA buddies told me about it," Marcus said.

"I've heard about that madness. I want nothing to do with those smart cities. Nora mentioned you use to work for them. How long were you there?" Jasper asked.

Brodie listened from the passenger seat. He hadn't thought about it, but once he saw them interact, he knew Marcus and Jasper would be fast friends.

"Not long, five, maybe six years. I built this AI human threat based self-igniting weapon prototype. But, instead of following protocol and the rules of proprietary patenting, I went and sold it to the highest bidder," Marcus said. "I was fired before the deal even went down. I got 25K up front but before I could have the full sit down, the Government intercepted and paid the outside company to forget about the deal, turn over all the documents and sampling I had given them. Anytime I have tried to get a legit tech job, I'm treated like a drug addict. So, basically, I've been black balled in the industry. But I still dabble."

"He's made a hell of a lot of money on the dark market. Doing hack work for the highest bidder. He's made some cool gadgets, too. Intelligent clone identifiers, other crazy stuff," Brodie added.

"He's smart," Jasper looked back at Marcus in the rear-view mirror. "You're doing exactly what I would have in your shoes," Jasper said. "Why limit your talents to this country? This country charges him taxes on money he earns for services he doesn't use. Wanna do something fun? Ask the government for an itemized breakdown of where your money gets dispersed over a year's time. You'd get put on a watch list. Why not be global. I gotta get your number, man."

"No tax talk, Jasper, let's stay focused. You can continue the bromance later," Nora scolded.

Military vehicles intermingled with deluxe sedans, SUV's and sexy cars passed by, all electric, most with driverless G-Go systems. It was the law in the Corners, part of the residential contract. Brodie couldn't believe it all had taken off so quickly. Even he knew how to hack into the G-Go systems.

The busier roads meant there would be heightened security in the cities and neighborhoods, primarily in the form of street surveillance. Sure, the Corners were secure, but people wanted to feel important, too. They invested in superior sheltered basements, even gates within the gates. Brodie referred to it as security by illusion. All smoke and mirrors. If something were to happen, none of what they had accumulated would protect them much. Plus, President Boobain and his people were running strings on the residents like puppets so deep that the people subconsciously migrated their behavior to work better within the Corners systems, a human mouse trap.

"This is great. This is what I was hoping to see," Marcus said.

They all stayed focused on their goal, while appreciating the signs of the revolution. They passed a set of mangled border gates that had been destroyed. People paraded in swarms, making their way into the Corners through downed gates. Some in the Corners joined those marching, peacefully protesting for equality, while other Corners residents took the opportunity to drive past, throwing garbage and yelling expletives at the interlopers and traitors. With the revolution progressing, many of the access points into the Corners had been breached, demolished and overtaken, allowing all to enter. Military police and guards tried to hold people back, but they were outnumbered. Tear gas hovered in pockets of clouded sky down main streets. Jasper took the side streets, running parallel to the chaos, keeping an eye on what would be ahead. Brodie was happy for the distraction of people. He was trying to get motivated, stay hopeful.

An hour later, their route narrowed and the crowds thinned as cut back over to a main highway. They arrived at a fully intact, secure check point leading into one of the exclusive regions of the Corners. That was the catch, when you agreed to live in the Corners, you were agreeing to the highest standards of clean freedom, safety and opulence, but you were also agreeing to be fully exposed unless you knew the tricks to hide your secrets, unless you knew a good hacker or wanted to upgrade to the exclusive regions.

The wealthy often hired hackers on the DarkNet like Marcus to keep their activity at home running on a loop feed. An algorithm created to loop normal behavior patterns of one of several available options that would randomly scrabble for diversity. Home life algorithm hackers were a hot commodity. Brodie was good with a scalpel, but nowhere near the level of Marcus though, when it came to computers and hacking.

With his face hidden by the military issue face covering, Brodie analyzed the skills within the car. He added it up in his head to see if it equaled success. A surgeon, two fully capable hackers, two elite soldiers and marksmen, a bioengineer. He could go on. Brodie thought back to his time overseas. He knew he was capable of almost anything if he needed to be. He hated killing but it had become a necessary evil of the times. Kill or be killed. On paper, the group should be able to complete the simple task of recovering Cece with ease. Brodie was becoming more confident that the mission would succeed.

As the Mercedes reached the security gate, Brodie stayed steady and composed in the passenger seat, edging his hat down a bit over his face, doing his best to look official. Marcus put his arm over the seat and acting natural, glanced over to Brodie.

"You good?" Marcus asked. He lit a cigarette to calm his breathing, knowing the action wouldn't be construed as abnormal. Brodie wanted one, but his face needed to stay hidden and his hands needed to be ready if anything happened. Instead, he put on the mirrored aviator sunglasses he found in the glove box.

"For all they know, we've just been getting our sticks dipped," Jasper said raising his eye brows up and down.

Brodie adjusted his neck, back and forth, cracking it, just as a man in khakis and a nerdy Oxford shirt with a Corners Security logo embroidered on it walked toward their vehicle. A gun sat parked in his hip holster. Fingers limply dangling, Marcus and Brodie got their chipped palms ready for scan. The guard leaned toward Jasper's open window, assuming permission to stick his face in the car and scan the inside.

"Wrist," the guard demanded, eyeballing Brodie and Nora, still wearing their buffs. He switched his gaze to Marcus who held one palm toward the guard while the other held his burning cigarette out the window.

Though steady, as Brodie lifted his palm, he felt as if his movements appeared like that of a marionette, jerky and disjointed. Within seconds, they got the green light. Brodie hid his relief under the cover of his buff. Getting past security fueled him and only kicked him further into gear, ready for whatever was ahead.

"Shits going down. Some of the poor got in through the gates at several Corners check points and they're protesting, causing problems in the common areas. We've kept them out of the exclusive regions so far, but they're throwing garbage and stuff at the military. Just be on the lookout," the guard said, motioning them through.

The metal platform sat ahead, waiting for them to drive over it. Brodie knew the platform would scan through the underbelly of the vehicle, detecting the number of bodies, body temperature, any defects and heartbeats through sensors in the plates. The platform also predicted the gender of the passengers and scanned for cyborgs and trace amounts of human mutation. It pulled on chip data to validate identity in order for the second gate to open.

Brodie prayed silently to himself, as Jasper pulled forward over the platform. The gates slowly opened, letting them pass into the elite region of the Corners.

"Fuck," Brodie quietly exhaled with relief.

"See, piece of cake. We're in." Marcus cheered.

The guard came jogging towards the car, yelling for Jasper to stop.

"No one says a word," Jasper said. Finally, he pulled to the side and rolled the window down for the guard.

"I'm sorry, ma'am, can you just step out of the vehicle for one moment?" the guard asked.

Without hesitation, Nora hopped out of the back seat and walked around to the guard.

"What's up?" Nora had been through situations like this a million times. It was the type of thing she was well-trained for.

"Name?"

"Terry Michelson," Nora responded.

"Ok, it just said there were four males in the car." The guard was slightly embarrassed.

"The system has never gotten my gender right. They told me the algorithm for the sensor program pulls off chip data and registered name," Nora said, seeming annoyed with the glitch.

"This has only happened a few times before, certain ambiguous names confuse the internal ID AI systems. I'm sorry, you're fine to go on," the guard said.

"My Lieutenant said he put in the paperwork to get it corrected to Theresa," Nora said. "My mother put Terry on my birth certificate, was a bit of a drinker."

"Don't give it another thought, ma'am. Y'all are free to go. Just be on guard for the riff raff." The guard gave them a wave and headed back to his post as Nora hopped back in the car.

Jasper gently hit the gas, proceeding forward as Brodie wiped sweat from his brow with his coat sleeve. No one spoke a word. Jasper continued through the exclusive upgraded community decorated with fine-tuned landscape. Now through the gates, Marcus tapped intently on his laptop, sending blasts of scrambles, blocking all attempts to hack in and pick off signals from outside devices.

"The only stop we are making is to get your sister," Jasper said.

"I packed marble grenades and a few other toys to help you guys get around the building. I've been through the security structure with Brodies hacker contact, Chavo. Soon as I send him the signal, he'll shut off all cameras and the alarm systems, unlock all doors. He'll be in my headset while we track your movements He'll be one step ahead of you and I'll be in your ear, Jasper. You'll have fifteen mins, tops. All electronics need to stay in the car, turned off." Marcus turned to Jasper. "That means you, too. Seven minutes in we'll turn the power off for a diversion."

"Let's make sure it happens in ten or less. The nearest military stock is twenty-one minutes away. It'll be tight, but that's what makes this stuff fun, right?" Jasper joked.

"Definitely," Marcus agreed, rolling his eyes at Brodie, while motioning with his finger, this guy is crazy, trying to make Brodie laugh.

As they turned down a highway, the fir and fresh air swam through the vehicle's vents as a forest of trees emerged. The cooler air signaled that they were almost at their destination.

"Ok, so when we get there..." Brodie said, then lost his train of thought.

"Your sister is supposed to be in unit 807. It is a corner unit but we have to go to the south east door. Once we get your sister, we will leave down the closest stairwell exit and get the hell out of there," Jasper instructed.

As dusk approached, unlike in the Gutter, in the Corners streetlights brightened the roads as traffic dwindled. No protesters or demonstrations were visible. It was clear they were traveling through a VIP region. Some of Boobain's top men lived in the areas surrounding the building where

Brodie's sister was said to be staying so it was a fact there were more elites in the area.

They passed through a small resort town, fitted with a ski hill. Women who hated the cold and winter would pretend to be skiers just to wear the couture and mingle with the wealthy. They weren't all plastics, but to find a natural with no injections or upgrades in the Corners was not as easy as one would think. A few bourgeois elites tromped down the sidewalks in their UGG boots, oblivious to the impending revolution, hunting for the newest Tuscan Sheepskin coat, spending thousands to eat a small plate of food prepared by the finest chefs in the world.

Jasper flicked on the blinker, steering the car down a long road toward the Dison Complex. They avoided the parking garage as Jasper pulled into the surface lot on the north side of the building. They were prepped and ready. Brodie could recite the plan like a favorite song.

Jasper turned to Marcus and Brodie. "The only circumstance in which you leave is if you feel your life is in imminent danger, and by that, I mean if there is a gun in your face. Otherwise, do not separate from your partner. Especially you, Marcus. If you leave, we're fucked. So don't," Jasper said, securing his ear piece and straightened his uniform.

"Go light this bitch on fire. Alarms are off in 30 seconds, Chavo just put in the jam." Marcus was hyped, he gave Brodie the thumbs up. "I'll be here. I'm not leaving you guys." Marcus, earpiece in, sat back in the driver's seat and got comfortable, his computer hidden from view on his lap, monitoring the situation.

Jasper caught up to Nora and Brodie as they walked toward the door, chatting about random nonsense, trying to sound like they belonged there. Brodie keyed in on two armed guards just inside the main door in front of the information desk. Two guards at the north side, another two assumed to be at the south entrance. He kept everything in his peripheral view best he could. The threesome continued inside.

"Officers, here for business or a visit? We're on lock down so we have to check everyone." The guard asked them without suspicion, smiling politely to Nora.

"Business, unfortunately. We need to get to B-18," Nora confirmed. "Picking up assignment detail."

"Ah, this is the residential entrance but you can get there from here. Just go through this door, take the breezeway to the left. You'll see an archway that will direct you to elevator bank B. You'll still need to scan in again at the front once you're through the breezeway," the guard said, relaxed and helpful. "I'll walk you over."

"Cool, thanks," Jasper said as he held his palm up for the guard to scan. Jasper and Nora got through, then it was Brodie's turn to shine. Jasper looked around and located the stairwell. Brodie held his arm up for the guard to scan and got another green light.

"Follow me," the guard guided the threesome towards the breezeway as Jasper waited for the perfect moment they were out of sight and where they needed to be. Just as they went around a corner toward the back of the lobby, Jasper grabbed the guard around the neck and dragged him to the stairwell.

Once inside, Brodie covered the guard's mouth with nocturnal duct tape infused with chloroform to knock him out. He grabbed the badge from the guard's shirt and pulled his body behind the stairs, hidden from view, and took his radio. The three rushed up the stairs toward the eighth floor, Jasper leading the way. Once there, a click was heard as he pushed the door open and fired at two guards, one at each end of the hallway.

"Thanks, Marcus," Jasper said as he secured the floor.

"You got it," Marcus responded into Jasper's earpiece. "You're three minutes in."

Brodie and Nora snatched weapons and badges off the guards. Something about the bodies made Brodie take a second look as they passed.

"They're RMs, see his eyes and this," Brodie said staring down at one of the Robotic Machines. The pupils on the RM were glowing yellow. Brodie grabbed the RM's wrist and held it up, slicing through the forearm with a sharp utility blade. "See, muscle tissue braided with cable and wiring with micro transmitter coded material."

The combination created a meshed and blended silver bendable chrome fill to shape the muscle. Jasper shot the RM in the stomach where the core wiring was. Immediately, it started vibrating on the floor, as sparks snapped and shot out.

"No time for an education of things we already know. We gotta move," Jasper said.

They made their way toward room 807.

"Wait," Nora said as she motioned toward the door. The heavy thumping of bass pulsed through the door. Jasper did a one, two, three count then kicked the door open.

CHAPTER 26

L CD Soundsystem blared as Brodie's sister, Cece, oblivious to them, flailed about the room in bibs and a T-shirt, attempting disjointed dance moves. A paint splattered canvas stood, propped up in front of her. She jumped as a shadow reflected off the large window in front of her. Unsure of whether it was the drugs or not, she shook her head and snorted a line of coke off her coffee table seeking clarity. As she lifted her head, Cece saw Brodie and Jasper, guns drawn, fully covered in military attire. The glare from the red sensor of Jasper's gun glowed steady on her forehead.

"Take your gun down," Brodie demanded.

"Not until I know the scene is safe," he responded.

Nora stayed at the doors edge, covering the hallway, keeping watch for anyone approaching. As Brodie and Jasper stepped further into the condo, Cece looked up toward her forehead, trying to see the red dot. High as a kite, she tried to swat it away, then, stared directly at Brodie and Jasper, still covered by their balaclava. Brodie put his gun in its holster but Jasper kept his on her.

"Cece, it's Brodie." He pulled his mask partially down, revealing his face, then held up his arms signaling that he wasn't going to hurt her. She paced back and forth, keeping her distance, visually hunting him like a panther.

"Brodie's not military. Who are you? I can't see your full face." Cece didn't recognize him. The last time she'd seen him he was clean-shaven, with his signature brown, curly hair. Now he had a full beard, blue contacts and a platinum buzz cut.

"Lady, calm down. You just need to come with us," Jasper said, holding his aim steady on her.

"Why are you in my fucking home?" Cece grabbed a nearby vodka bottle and heaved it at Jasper. Clumsily, she dove for a gun peeking out from under a couch cushion, tumbling in the process. She didn't make it to the gun, but instead, fell to the ground, knocking over the canvas.

"It's Brodie, your brother. We have to go. You're not safe here," Brodie said.

"We got company. Take cover," Nora yelled, firing down the hall as bullets whizzed past. Jasper pulled Cece back down to the floor, behind the cover of the couch, as a bullet ricocheted into the room. Brodie went to the door and helped Nora as more guards emerged from the stairwell, now three. They took aim at the same time and soon enough all the guards were down. Nora moved forward to the stairwell, making sure it was clear, while Brodie kept watch at the door.

"We gotta get out of here. This isn't going to get better," Nora shouted. She glanced down the hallway at the simmering RMs.

"We've got her, let's go," Jasper said. He clutched Cece by the wrist, pulling her behind him. Brodie watched as she roared at Jasper, still oblivious to what was going on.

"Cece, we have to go. You have to trust me." Brodie helped Jasper get her up and to the door, grabbing her purse and phone per her shouting request.

Once in the hallway and headed for the stairs, Brodie noticed the upper sleeve of his coat was shredded. He'd been shot. His adrenaline raged as he nestled his left arm snug to his side and said nothing. Just then, the power went out throughout the building.

With her headlamp on, Nora kept her eyes on the hall behind them, as Jasper burst through the stairwell door, peering down for clearance. As Nora and Brodie held onto Cece, he fired off two shots with no response, then flagged them to go forward as he took hold of Cece, again. Brodie and Nora made a mad dash down the stairwell.

"Stay close," Nora said.

Jasper covered them as he followed Nora's lead, dragging a reluctant Cece alongside him. Without warning, just as they made it to the second floor, the third-floor door flew open as two guards fired down from above them. With cat-like reflexes Jasper tightened his grip on Cece and took down the two guards, sending one of them tumbling down the stairs.

"God dammit, put me down," Cece said, freaking out. She pounded on Jaspers back almost causing him to lose grip on his gun. Brodie's eyes were all over, trying to take cover and aim all at once. Jasper moved down to the first floor with Cece as they headed toward freedom. Nora and Brodie covered from the stairwell door as Jasper and Cece made it successfully across the lobby. Brodie ran out after them, but without warning, his path was blocked and a gun was pointed at his head.

"Not that easy," a guard said, having seemed to come out from the shadows. Brodie froze. The closeness of the gun at his temple cooled his sweat. Nora paused, lingering just inside the stairs, trying to figure the best way through this. Brodie put his hands up. "I just need the data chip, sir."

The guard didn't flinch as he spoke. His arm steady, locked in on Brodie. The two kept their eyes fixed on each other, as Cece's echoing screams trailed off outside.

"I don't have a chip. I don't know who you think I am," Brodie said.

"It was dumb of you to come when you knew people were looking for you," the guard said. "Your brother knew this was where you might come. All I need is the chip and then you can be on your way."

"I don't have any chip. I came for my sister. Shoot me and my friends will shoot you," Brodie said.

Jasper got Cece to Marcus and ran back to help Brodie, hovering at the doors edge.

"They won't save you. Perhaps you're not that special after all," the guard said, now grinning at Brodie.

Just as the guard's finger moved back to pull the trigger, Nora fired off two bullets as the noise echoed off the marble floor. The guard dropped his arm and Brodie moved away from him, sprinting toward the door. The guard fell the ground, trying to speak through gurgles through blood. Nora ran to meet Brodie as Jasper covered them while they got outside to safety.

Marcus drove the SUV up to meet them half way. Marcus had Cece in the back seat as Brodie and Jasper hopped in next to her under Nora's cover, then Nora got in the passenger side. Just as Marcus hammered on the gas, speeding across the lot toward the gates, an explosion erupted from inside the building behind them, sending the doors off and debris flying. Three armed guards stood in front of them, military weapons drawn, pointed at the Mercedes.

"Keep going, you gotta just keep driving," Jasper urged.

As the Mercedes swerved around the guards and broke through the gates, the ground shook so hard it rattled the vehicle. Brodie saw the cloud of flames bellow up behind them, as rubble from one of the buildings started to crumble. Sparkling glass, blown bits of concrete and steel, along with all sorts of personal items scattered across the lot, at times dropping in front of them as they sped off faster to avoid the aftermath. People evacuated the three standing buildings in all directions, screaming in a panic, some bloodied and confused, taking in what had just happened.

They were out. Brodie couldn't believe it. It all felt like a dream it happened so fast. As they traveled down the road at top speed, all remained silent except for Cece, who was mumbling to herself in a bit of shock. Nora and Marcus stayed alert in the front seat, scanning in every direction, while Brodie and Jasper stayed on guard in the back, still trying to calm Cece. Brodie blinked his eyes for a second, making sure the moment was real.

"Billy's gonna blow your head off for this. He is going to be so pissed, he's gonna kill us, both," Cece screamed, as she feverishly kicked her feet against the seat in front of her. "What did you do, Brodie?"

"We won't be able to handle anything that comes our way with her like that. Give her something to knock her out for a bit," Nora said. "There's a set of small syringes and a vial of liquid in my bag in a red kit. Give her half a syringe," she instructed to Jasper. "We've got two cars on our ass about a mile and a half back and who knows what's ahead of us."

Brodie held Cece still, while Jasper jammed the needle into her arm.

"What did you give her," Brodie asked.

"Just a sedative. Cece, you're going to be fine," Nora said, peering back at her. "You're gonna take a little nap. You'll feel a lot better when you wake up." Nora locked eyes with her. Within seconds, Cece's eyelids sagged, heavy on her face, as her speech began to slur. Soon, she was asleep. Jasper propped up, settling her into a gentle slumber, her head resting on Brodie's shoulder.

Jasper checked out the back window and saw two SUV's fast approaching.

"Keep driving, Marcus. We need to get to a more populated area then we'll be good. If they get close enough, we'll have to take them out," Jasper said.

"One of you should drive so I can get back on the grid. I'm pulling over as soon as we shake these two," Marcus said.

"Just wait until we're safe. The grid can wait," Brodie said.

CHAPTER 27

Inside Droshure's Colorado office, Billy scanned several monitors in front of him, hands on his hips, as mayhem was unfolding before his eyes. On screen, the citizens of America were starting their fight to regain their independence, charging into banks and businesses throughout the Corners, setting off firecrackers, trying to take over the streets. He looked out the window as thousands of protesters marched, all the while, looters and rioters making a pathetic mess. Explosions danced along the dusk horizon like fireworks on the Fourth of July. Without notice, Billy gripped his stomach in his hands and ran to the office wet bar and vomited in the sink. Nausea was a gift that all three of the kids had gotten from their mother. Billy wiped his mouth with a napkin and returned to the screens.

He was fixated on one particular monitor. The picture was grainy and unsteady, from a handheld device. He'd received the footage over an hour ago but Billy kept replaying the scene of Cece getting pulled out of the dimly lit building. Then to his short-lived pleasure, he saw a guard with his gun aimed at an officer's head, realizing it was Brodie in disguise. No matter how many times he replayed the clip, hoping for a different outcome, the guard always got shot and Brodie escaped.

"Well, look at you. Fucking up my plans yet again," Billy said pacing as he grabbed his phone. "Spider, what the fuck happened? I could care less about Cece. We don't have Brodie or the chip. That was the whole fucking point of this all."

"Billy, the team got ambushed at every turn. Someone jammed the signals. They had people protecting them from the inside. The only security footage anyone could see off site was looping episodes of *Tom & Jerry*. They didn't just hack the Dison, it was virtually every elite residence on our line within a 5-mile radius. There were no live feeds on the security cameras. This was a multilevel hack, way too smart for Droshure's people to control. Had a secretary not have recorded this on her cell phone, we'd have nothing," Spider said.

"They're probably still in California. Is anyone looking for them? They can't get away that fast with all the shit that's going on. There are traffic jams all over the fucking place. Find them, kill him and get the god damn chip by any means necessary."

"I've already got teams on it. They were in a military vehicle so it's not so easy. Tinted windows, steganographic security ink. If this chip only compromises Droshure and Boobain, I say let them fall. Let this one go. They're done anyway, there's many other things at play right now," Spider suggested.

"Hey, I agree. But until Stoyton Society gives me a green light, I have to find the chip. They are funding the bigger picture here. If anything in the data mentions them even once, I'm dead. The papers we found on that Nolan guy, it's some bad shit. Just make it fucking happen and find Brodie." Billy walked back to the window. He hit a button on his phone and instantly his music played throughout the room. *Chop Suey*, by System of a Down. He jumped up and down with clenched fists, shaking his head wildly to the music. He was getting ready for battle.

Billy picked up the receiver of a blue wall phone, just after it rang and punched in four numbers.

"Yes, sir. I'll take care of it right now. I'm on my way." Billy hung up, opened a cabinet and grabbed a blue duffle bag out. "Who knew," he said, surprised at its contents, which included a loaded gun. He left the office and headed to the elevators. As it dropped beneath the surface of the earth, to a depth much deeper than ground level, he whistled to himself, patiently waiting. The doors finally opened into an underground hallway. Billy strolled out with a kick in his step and made his way to a highly secure, luxurious, glass walled laboratory. He put his face to the FRS and waited for the doors to open.

Inside, President Boobain was in the midst of receiving a final video briefing on his escape plan, the underground speed train that was in early trials. It would take him from Colorado to safety in Canada until the unrest was resolved.

Billy sat down on a nearby stool as the video finished. A tall, bald guy in a lab coat stood in front of them pointing out a final diagram on the screen in front of them. Audrey lingered on the other side of the room near Boobain's wife, her gun resting at her side, under her gentle grip. Two stock broker suit types silently rested against the concrete wall. The well-dressed men were transporters. Across from them, on the screen, a well-lit, gleaming tunnel was displayed. It wasn't a gray, dreary, catacombs-type tunnel; it was a finely crafted, well-engineered and designed tunnel created by the finest engineers in the world. It had glow-in-the-dark, neon LED track lighting that changed color with speed and tempo, not unlike in a high-tech video game.

"No one will be hitting buttons or trying to obstruct the way. The transporters will travel with you until you reach Canada and get you above ground safely. Do you understand?" Audrey said. She spoke with a superior, methodic tone. She didn't need to intimidate anyone. Her gun was enough.

"Yes, I understand," Boobain said, nervously.

"It will take 8 hours and 27 minutes to get to Regina, Saskatchewan. The train is airtight, but you'll want to keep your mask on. Because of the depth, they are still working on the best sealant to barrier off any trace of underground gases from seeping into the tunnels and trains. I will hit the button for it to start. You don't need to touch anything. When you arrive, the train will stop and the transporters will hit the yellow button. They will take you to the..." Audrey stopped as Billy cut her off.

"I think he gets it. He can read the manual on his way. He's on a schedule. The transporters know what they're doing. It's Canada, how complicated can it be?" Billy said rhetorically.

The scientist held the manual out toward Billy, who hot-potatoed it to Boobain, laughing. Unable to catch it, the manual bounced out of Boobain's short, chubby hands, off his lap and onto the floor. Billy watched with disdain as Boobain struggled to bend down to retrieve it.

"Gotta do better than that, Mr. President. You got eight hours to sit and read, maybe do a few sit ups while you're in there." Billy winked at Boobain.

"It seems you're enjoying this more than you should be. You're sure this will stop in Regina and we'll get to a safe house? I feel like a sitting duck," Boobain said. At that point, sweat was visible on the collar of his shirt, which peeked out just above his jacket.

"You're not. Trust me. Interpol is looking for all of us right now. This is the safest way to get you to anonymity. Our people will be monitoring the train and waiting for you there. They have your ID cards and new documents." Billy tossed him a burner phone. "Call me on this when you get above ground." Billy was growing bored. He walked to the hallway leading to the train. "Come on, you need to go or this won't end well for you."

Boobain looked to Billy, then to Audrey and the two transporters, finally settling in on his wife, Gloria. She wasn't a young trick, more of an older middle-aged modern woman who had married a crazy man.

"Honey, we should go," Boobain said as he reached for her hand.

"I don't want to do this, Tim. Why can't I drive there and meet you? No one knows what I look like. I mean no one's really paid attention to me," his wife said.

"It will be fine, you're my wife. I'm not leaving you," Boobain protested.

"I'm claustrophobic. There isn't going to be anyone to help me if I have a panic attack or something. I'll be safer without you. Please, just let me..."

Billy cut her off. "Gloria, I got you," he winked at her. "New decision. We'll get her to you safely. For now, let's go Tim, this way," Billy said. Just as Boobain turned his back to Billy and took a step toward the tunnel train, Billy shot him in the back, dropping him instantly. "See?" He looked at everyone in the room, "voila, problem solved."

As Boobain hit the ground, his fingers stretched out reaching for Audrey, trying to grab her pantleg for help. She shook her leg free as his hand flopped almost lifeless, to the hard floor. Within seconds, he choked up a pie of blood, quickly fading. Audrey took Boobain's briefcases, then looked to Billy, who was grinning with pleasure.

"Jesus Christ, you couldn't have given a heads up on that one?" Audrey asked.

"Look, at this point he serves no purpose. He never liked me, anyway," Billy said.

"What if he had a gun, or worse, what if she shot me in the back?" Audrey said. She walked to a table and sat down the cases, sifting through its contents.

"Oh, calm down. The guys like ninety... maybe seventy," Billy shrugged. "Who gives a shit. He didn't have a gun and she can't stand him. She wanted a divorce. Right Gloria?"

Across the room, trying to contain her terror, Gloria nodded in agreement, yes. As horrendous as the scene was, Billy could sense a glimmer of hope trying to take over the shock that covered her face, caused by the demise of her husband.

"See, I told you. She couldn't stand him, the old fart. Gloria, you're free to go. You just have to go this way." Billy took the blue duffle bag from over his shoulder and tossed it in her direction, landing at her feet. "There's fifty thousand dollars in there. It was for him, so now it's yours. When you get to Canada, there is another two million in a bank account under the name Gloria Wagner, your maiden name. It's always been under your name for safety. The account number and everything you need is written on the third page of this. You're getting this money for your silence. They don't know who's coming through, nor do they care." Billy handed her a zipped, leather Day Runner. Gloria was in shock, as tears of both horror and gratitude slipped down her face.

"Thank you for sparing my life. Timothy was not a good man. He was a vicious and abusive human being, forceful, disloyal... and not just to me. He planned to have you killed," Gloria said to Billy. "He thought you were insane, ignorant." Gloria picked up the duffle bag, leather organizer in hand. Shaken, she stepped past her husband's lifeless body and reluctantly went toward the transporters. The doors to the tunnel opened as the transporters grabbed her bags for her.

"Don't either of you get any ideas," Billy said to the transporters. "Gloria, if you don't call the number on the first page of that organizer within nine hours, someone will hunt these two down and check the tunnel. You will be ok. I wish someone could drive you but this is how we let you live, by going into that tunnel," Billy said.

Gloria and the transporters got into the ovoid shaped tunnel train car. With a push of a button the train doors sealed shut. He gave the scientist a thumbs up, as the train smoothly shot into the tunnel as if it was being vacuumed up, with a hollow, reverberating whistle. Billy walked to the table and rifled through Boobain's belongings. The scientist headed toward the exit.

"Hey, stay put," Billy ordered, his gun still in hand.

The scientist stopped in his tracks at the words.

CHAPTER 28

B rodie and the others traveled near the California state line as news of the revolution was visible everywhere. Buildings they passed were being taken over by the masses. Crowds had taken to the busier streets, stopping traffic as the group did it's best to avoid getting stuck. By this point, the police lingered at the streets edge, allowing hordes of people to celebrate and express themselves. Brodie glanced up, watching the skies become saturated with news choppers. He hadn't seen a news chopper in at least three years. It was clear the ban on independent media must have been lifted. This gave Brodie hope for at minimum, a small victory. Whoever was in charge didn't seem to be Timothy Boobain any longer.

"I haven't seen one of those news choppers in a while," Marcus said.

"A blessing and a curse," Nora added.

"Don't be a Debbie downer. It's all over the internet, this is fucking amazing." Marcus squeezed Nora's shoulder with delight. "I never thought people would band together and make this happen," he exclaimed.

"This means we can have new elections. And just maybe, things can get things back to normal. People can get their rights back," Jasper said.

Cece stirred, squinting her eyes in hazy confusion. She glanced at Jasper, then to Brodie. "Where am I?" she asked. She looked out the window, noticing all of the activity and noise. "Brodie? What's going on?"

"You're ok. You fell asleep, again. Have some water," Brodie said.

"I mean what is going on outside? Why is there blood on me? And why is there blood on you?" Cece took the bottle of water and chugged it, then flicked Brodie on the arm of his coat, where blood was stained, as he flinched. "Why is everyone going bonkers outside, who died?"

"We got you out of the building just in time. The gates are coming down. The Corners are no more," Marcus reassured Cece. "You hungry?"

"Wait," Cece stared at Brodie, confused, then scanned the car, trying to make sense of things, landing right back at Brodie. He took her hand. At first, she drew it back, but Brodie persisted.

"Hey, you were in danger. I needed to get you out of there." Brodie kept it simple. He saw Nora eavesdropping from the front, waiting for Cece's reaction.

"Where's my stuff? I can't believe you did this, Brodie. I didn't need to be rescued." Cece grabbed around, searching for her purse.

"I did this for your protection," Brodie asked.

"Brodie, please. Just stop. Now he's not only going to kill you, but he'll probably kill me, too." Cece turned away from him. She tried to distract herself with the action outside. "It's hot in here and I want to get out of this car. I have to go back."

"Give her a Xanax if she wants or a cigarette or something. It'll calm her down," Nora said.

Cece observed Jasper more thoroughly, scanning him up and down. Now, noticing how attractive he was. "What's your name, again? Can you get me out of here? I can pay you." She scooted closer to Jasper, further away from Brodie. She was close enough to put her nose near his neck, sniffing at his aroma of clove and velvet masculinity, slightly flirty. Jasper gently shifted her back toward the middle, away from him.

"Brodie, handle your sister," Jasper requested.

"Guys, we're not out of the woods yet. They're still looking for Brodie. We have to stay diligent until we ditch this Benz," Nora said.

"There's an exit in two miles heading toward Luning, Nevada. I have a mining buddy that knows the area well. We're about two hours from the meet point. Because of the mining, Wi-Fi is sketchy and the signal sucks which will take us off grid, which is good. We'll take care of her insert there, switch cars, then I'll split," Jasper said.

Brodie could tell Jasper was ready to be done with all of this. It was a remedial event for him. Far beneath his normal scope, sloppy and dangerous. Brodie felt himself slip into embarrassment and anxiety, but quickly shook it off.

"What are you talking about, my insert?" Cece sat up, trying to assert herself through her unsteady lucidity.

"That Living Solution commercial, I saw you. What were you thinking doing that?" Brodie questioned, unaware of why Cece was getting furious.

"My fucking inserts?" Cece interrupted. "You think I have inserts? Those commercials were fake. Billy made me do one to pay a debt. The first one was me but the rest are just deep fakes. Jesus, Brodie, you think I'd let him make me use inserts? I thought you knew me better than that."

"I ran into Donte. He said you were doing tricks for Billy." Brodie felt badly stating the accusation out loud. "None of it made sense." Everything started to spin, including Brodie's stomach. Had Cece's kindness just been pity all this time, his whole life? Had she just been avoiding him?

"What else did Donte tell you? You know that guy can't be trusted," Cece was restless and growing paranoid. She wanted out of the car, too. Now closer to sobriety, what Donte said set her off. "I'm not a fucking hooker, Brodie. Jesus, you don't know what Billy is holding over me. I've been doing the best I fucking can."

Brodie watched as Cece stuck her hand in her overalls and pulled out a capsule, slickly removed the cap, but Brodie grabbed her hand. "Stop it. Take a Xanax. No more coke," he said.

"Let her be. We'll be there soon. If she wants to fly let her fly," Jasper said.

"I don't want her flying, not in this car right now," Brodie said. "Took us three hours to get you to stop swinging at us."

"Fine, then give me more Xanax cuz this shit is too much right now." Cece held out her hand. Marcus handed another Xanax back. She scooped it up and let it melt on her tongue, washed it down with the rest of her water.

Brodie couldn't stop wondering if he had he been wrong about Cece the whole time? Just then, he saw Jasper subtly signal to Nora. Brodie wanted to know what it meant, but he was tired. It didn't matter right now, anyway. None of it mattered. It would be over soon. Most importantly, they got Cece out of there. "You can tell me all about what Billy's holding over you when we get somewhere safe," he said to Cece.

Nora turned off at the exit as the car was silent, except for Cece's voice muttering through the car like a frustrated, broken heater.

"Up ahead at the fork in the road, go left down the rough dirt path," Jasper pointed. "When you see a silver mail box at the edge of the road, turn right and just drive until you see a dark blue Subaru Forrester."

They drove along the dirt road for miles, clouds of dust kicking up behind them. First, they turned at the silver mailbox which had an alien shaped face on the door. Shortly after, they saw the Subaru Forrester parked in the middle of nowhere. A dirt bike rested nearby, tipped over on the ground. A tall Native American man with a long braid and finely trimmed goatee stood waiting for them. A red backpack rested over his shoulder and his helmet sat down on the ground next to his bike.

"This is where we do it, folks. Let's get her out," Jasper said as he threw the door open and went to greet Ashkii.

Nora got out and walked around. Stretched her arms and legs, twisting at the waist side to side, stretching her hips. Brodie exited the car. Cautiously, he kept ahold of Cece's arm with the help of Marcus. He watched as Jasper gave Ashkii a huge hug.

Nora interrupted Brodie's gaze. "You doing ok?" she asked.

"I am, thank you," he said, squeezing her arm softly twice with a smile.

"This is Ashkii, he'll help with the scans and check you all for inserts and trackers," Jasper asserted as he unloaded bags from the military Mercedes and starting putting everyone's things but his into the Subaru Forrester.

"Hi guys, let's get you scanned and on your way," Ashkii said. "I'm just going to have you guys stand, arms straight out. I'll remove any gadgets we find."

"I told you I don't have an insert, Brodie," Cece whined. She was still a bit off her head but coming back down to reality. She put up a little struggle under the grip of Brodie and Marcus, but gave in quickly. Jasper paused from unloading the SUV and he and Nora got scanned first. Both clean. Soon enough, Brodie and Marcus scanned clean, too.

"If she's got one, the inserts and implants are typically behind the ear, behind the knee, at the nape of the neck, or seat of the spine," Ashkii explained, pointing at the different spots on his own body as an example.

Brodie watched as Ashkii did the thorough exam. He needed to remember the technique for himself. Out of the corner of his eye, he saw Marcus climb on to the roof of the Forrester and keep watch, scanning across the early afternoon landscape, searching for approaching vehicles. He took his shirt off, feeling the sun on his skin.

"Do you know how long it's been since I've felt the warm sun on my skin without having to worry about getting shot?" Marcus said in perfect contentment. "Fuck, this is perfect."

Brodie climbed up on top of the Subaru and stood with Marcus. Surveying the area, feeling the warmth on his face, happy to throw his face covering to the ground. He couldn't stop smiling, why would he. He glanced over to watch as his sister got scanned. Nora and Jasper held onto her, keeping her steady. Brodie didn't know if he had done the right thing, but it was done and she was safe. Just then a Firenze red Jaguar F-type R coupe appeared on the horizon.

"We got a red sports car coming this way, guys," Brodie said, shimming off the top of the Subaru.

"All good, that's my ride," Jasper said still holding on to Cece. Soon the car pulled up and as the window came down, Charlotte from the cat house peered out. She gave a quick wave to everyone, but said nothing.

Ashkii put on a slick black glove with illuminated translucent sensors at the finger points and palm. He gently patted and glided along Cece's neck and occipital ridge, her hips, trunk and lumbar region, along her femoral artery. Brodie noticed Cece smirking, seeming to enjoy the physical touch.

"What, it tickles," she laughed.

"So far, I'm not seeing anything. This will pick up everything inches deep. The sensors will turn red." Ashkii continued moving across her body. As he swept just above the back of her knee, a beeping alert sounded and the sensors flashed red. "I'm going to numb the area and make an incision. You will feel a little pinch. Just squeeze their hands if you feel any pain, it will only take seconds," he met Cece's eyes and spoke directly to her.

Brodie watched as Cece automatically held onto Jasper and Nora's hands tighter. Finally, she was beginning to trust them. He observed Ashkii as he pulled out a scalpel and made a cross incision. Instead of an insert, a large exploded beetle tracker gushed out as soon as Ashkii pinched the open cross-section. It dropped to the ground like putty. Marcus hopped down off the car and pulled out his lighter.

"Let me get that for you." Marcus leaned down and set the obsidian blob on fire as a miniature explosion zapped with lack luster reward for him.

Ashkii continued and seconds later, a silver bean shaped element was squeezed out of the same incision area. "This is a magnetic devise that can drag detected objects along the top surface just under the skin. Not sure where this little guy was but I hate to say it, someone was keeping their eye on you. These little beans, they send signals to the frontal lobe. It messes with your impulse control, which in turn, makes it easier for someone to control you, makes you more suggestable," Ashkii explained. "The beans kind of hijack self-awareness, so people don't realize they're being manipulated because they're so caught up in their own impulses. It's a pretty dangerous hack. So, if you felt a little more out of control than normal, this might be why."

"This was all planned," Jasper said. He let go of Cece's hand and walked to greet Charlotte, giving her a simple kiss through the car window. "Doesn't seem like she knew anything about it, but you were set up. Your brother did this. And I don't care what you say," Jasper said to Cece, "someone was watching you. You should thank Brodie for getting you out of there."

"I just need to treat her skin with a healing ointment. When the beetle came out there was a small amount of black staining on her dermis tissue and skin. That typically means it's malfunctioned. If you bumped your leg or had a wicked fall, sometimes that can fry out the trackers," Ashkii explained to Cece. "It can itch for up to a week but just keep putting the eater on it."

"Nora, quick chat?" Jasper stepped off to the side and she followed him.

Marcus assisted Ashkii while he cleaned the black residue from Cece's leg wound with the eater, then wrapped it with fresh dressing. Brodie stood off on his own, smoking a cigarette, distracted by Nora and Jasper's conversation that he couldn't hear. They had their backs to the group. There were no lips to read.

"What's up?" Nora asked.

"Something doesn't feel right about all of this. Just watch your back, ok?"

"Jasper, he felt she was in danger. It's his sister, she's the only family he has."

"All I'm saying is be careful with this whole thing. Someone was tracking her and messing with him. Just remember, this isn't a mission. No one has your back," Jasper asserted.

"Jasper, I'm good. I'm protected," Nora assured him. "My team should be done decoding the chip. Everyone's trying to track some kid down in Europe that has a final key. Christopher Scott, some hacker kid who's tied to Nolan Petri. My team said what they found in the first twelve hours is enough to confirm the first list of Stoyton members to be charge, about four so far. Most of it is stuff on Boobain, but Stoyton is our goal. This president has just been a sideshow distraction," Nora said.

"This is why I don't do agency work anymore. Everyone is shady on all sides of the square. Whenever you want out of IBI, I'll help you transition. You can work for yourself, like I do," Jasper said. By the look on his face, Nora could tell he was done with agency work for good.

"This is big. They don't go after one, they want to get all of them. Not all of Stoyton are corrupt, but the ones that are, are very dangerous," she said. "After this, I may take you up on your offer and retire from the agency." Nora waited for Jasper's response. No matter how many missions she did, how smart she was, she still looked up to him as a mentor. She would never admit it out loud, but he gave her a sense of security, stopped her from second guessing herself. "Jasper, tell me the work I'm doing is important."

"The work you're doing is important. It's very important. You're a much better agent than I ever was, so stop questioning yourself. All I'm saying is, get out while you're still young and you can enjoy a normal life, whatever you want that to look like," Jasper said and put his hand on Nora's shoulder. "The thing I need to know before I leave though is, are you sure you can trust Brodie? He pulled you into this," Jasper said.

"He didn't pull me in, I wasn't going to let him do this alone. I'm as safe with him, as I would be without him."

"Nora, that's so not true," Jasper said. "I don't see this ending well. His brother has it out for him. If he's behind all of this he has an agenda, Corners or no Corners. It doesn't stop just because he got her out of there. And I'd keep my distance from her if I was you, even if she didn't have anything to do with any of this. Call me you get back home. And if anything comes up, call me right away. You know I have your back for life." He held Nora's gaze, winked at her and then gave her a hug.

"Fine, thank you. Seriously. Now get out of here. We'll be safe," Nora said, a bit emotional.

Brodie saw them embrace, then watched Jasper kiss her on the cheek. Nora jogged back over to the Forrester as Jasper spoke with Ashkii and handed him a package. After they shared a quick hug, Jasper waved to the group then stopped.

"Marcus, mi amigo, give Nora your info and she'll get it to me. I know several that could use your skills," he said, then hopped in the passenger seat of the Jaguar. The door shut and the car raced off down the dirt road, eventually disappearing into the cloud of dust it left in its wake.

"All right guys, head out that way," Ashkii directed. "Just stay on that road, it will eventually take you to the interstate. My guys are on their way. We'll take care of the Mercedes."

CHAPTER 29

The Subaru Forrester pulled off, leaving Ashkii and the military Mercedes as they headed down the road through the lingering cloud of dust.

"I didn't know I had that in my leg. I swear to God," Cece said. The truth was sinking in, becoming visible as she tried to force the pale glow from her face. "I'm not saying this to freak you out, but just promise me you'll be careful. Billy is a loose cannon."

Brodie didn't respond. They were all exhausted. Then Brodie put his hand on Nora's shoulder.

"You holding up ok?"

"Yes, I'm good," Nora said, keeping one hand on the wheel, reaching back to meet his hand with her other, reassuring him. "We made it through this. I really wasn't sure we would," Nora smiled, finally taking a moment to relax.

The Subaru sped along the highway as they made their way into Salt Lake City just before dusk. Soon, they were engulfed in a large fog of tear gas, as hundreds ran the streets with bandana's tightly snug around their faces, protecting their nose and mouth. Some ran with jugs of milk, others with backpacks and supplies, all making a mad dash toward one of Droshure's manufacturing facilities at the edge of town. Car loads passed them driving in the opposite direction, heading into the Corners.

While Boobain's military police tried to maintain control, even rubber bullets weren't enough to keep the growing crowd of people contained. Many celebrated in the streets, toting signs with slogans demanding freedom, filling the air with camaraderie and cheer. Nora watched a wave of people rush the doors of the facility, together, in perfect unison. Instead escalating their force, the mob was met with the parting of police, giving way, creating a path for the anarchists and revolters.

"Holy shit, they let them through," Nora said.

"That's awesome. Yes," Marcus cheered as they made their way back toward the highway and away from chaos.

Brodie leaned forward in his seat, squeezing Marcus on the shoulders with cheer. He was happy. Even happier seeing Nora smiling. She hadn't smiled like that since their night alone. He nudged Cece playful.

"This is pretty cool, it's good," he said to her. Cece couldn't help but laugh and join in the celebration.

Their Subaru was one of a dozen vehicles making their way through the jubilant crowds that were heading in the opposite direction, into Salt Lake City and headed for the Corners. Many were on foot, while others were out of their cars having climbed on top of them, blocking parts of the highway, doing anything to be a part of the growing celebration. There was a part of Brodie that was excited to be traveling right through the action. He had avoided crowds for so long, it felt good to pass through as an unknown and be a part of something good, for once.

Marcus rolled down his window, pumping his fist in solidarity, celebrating with the crowds as people high-fived him along the way. A gorgeous woman with thigh high boots on and a long sweatshirt, sunglasses covering her eyes, thrusting a *Fuck Boobain* sign high in the sky, deviated from the large group to high-five Marcus. She planted a lipstick filled kiss smack-dab on Marcus's lips. He grinned as she gazed into the car, winking at him. Brodie smiled in celebration.

"Get her out, gun. Close your window!" Nora yelled, seeing the woman reach for something nestled inside her thigh high boot, in the passenger side mirror.

"For Joke." She quickly drew a small hand gun up and tried to get aim at the back window toward Brodie.

Instinctively, Marcus threw open his door into the woman, knocking her over, causing her to fall back, firing off two unsteady shots into the sky. Marcus got his window up, as Nora honked the horn and hit the gas, maneuvering through the now chaotic crowd best she could. Brodie gave her a thumbs-up signaling that he was ok and checked on Cece. Nora looked at Marcus, watching him inspect his arm.

"Marcus," she yelled, "are you ok?"

"I got shot," Marcus said, touching his arm, seeing blood on his shirt. "Holy shit," Marcus laughed.

Brodie scooted up and carefully examined Marcus's arm best he could. It had been grazed by the stray bullets when his arm was out the window. Nora honked the horn again, moving through the last of the packed streets and then picked up speed. With all the crazy shit Marcus had done and all the fights he'd been in, Brodie realized he'd never been shot before.

"Are you ok?" Nora and Brodie asked, Brodie trying to lock eyes with Marcus to get a read on him.

"I'm fine, but shit, it fucking hurts. At least I got a kiss out of it." Marcus winced through an attempt at laughter. Brodie treated and wrapped his arm, as Marcus held pressure on the wound. Cece kept a hand on Marcus's shoulder.

"No open windows. Not until I say," Nora said. "And Brodie, keep your buff up. We can't take any chances. Like your sister said, your brother's goons are probably still looking for you."

"I'm sorry. I didn't know that would happen," Marcus said.

Cece grabbed a water and held it forward to Marcus, "here."

Brodie watched him take it. Marcus and Cece's history may have been their saving grace.

They got out of the city limits and picked up speed, more vehicles passing them, going in the opposite direction, heading straight into the action. As they got onto a quieter highway, Marcus shifted in his seat, trying to relax his body. Cece was falling asleep in the back next to Brodie.

"Hey, can I see your tablet?" Brodie reached his hand forward waiting for Marcus to hand back his portable.

"Here, you gonna do a live stream or something?" Marcus asked.

"I didn't do that stuff before all of this, definitely won't be doing any of it now. All that social media crap is what paved the way for this bullshit in the first place. I just want to see how the international news is reporting on things," Brodie said. "Maybe the UN will start sending help now that Boobain is nowhere to be found." Brodie keyed in to the tablet and searched for BBC, then Aljazeera news. He skimmed his eyes across the screen, seeing both mayhem and merriment replayed in front of him.

"The UN is helping, just not in a way the general public needs to know," Nora added. "With Boobain out, hopefully they'll let the US back in fully and remove the aid restrictions."

"Just over one thousand people reported dead at this point. Three skyscrapers imploded in Texas, a few more in California and Chicago. Some looting and fires. It sounds pretty bonkers in the Corners, but it also sounds like our side is winning," Brodie said. "I hate that people are getting killed because of this. I know it's for the greater good though, it just sucks. Haven't found any news on Billy or anyone else for that matter."

"Maybe he's dead. Cross your fingers," Marcus chuckled.

"It's too much for my brain," he said. "Can we turn on the radio, maybe find some music?" Brodie shut the tablet and handed it back up to Marcus.

Nora flicked on the radio and found a random 80's rock station. They settled in, still alert but relaxing more and more with each moment. Before they knew it, they were all singing along to *'Tainted Love'* by Soft Cell. They would be to the first safe house within three hours.

After taking refuge in a safe house for a few hours of rest, food and aid, the Forrester zipped along the highway continuing forth toward Chicago. As they crossed the Mississippi River, the last of the red clays from the western states disappeared from view of the rear-view mirror, replaced by the flat browns of winter leaves and dying grass on lawns. Sporadic dustings of melting snow jumped out into view. Nora felt comfort in seeing more open signs on store fronts than she had in years.

The revolution was still going on and a win wasn't a sure thing, but all signs were fueling positivity in the Gutter. Some people were out walking in the early morning. It wasn't as busy as it was before the split and people were still cautious, but they wanted to get back outside and back to their normal lives.

"Fun fact, my grandfather, Marvin's, best friend swam most of the Mississippi River," Marcus said. "It touches 10 states. It took him eighty-four days and he stayed in the coolest places at each stop, including my grandfather's tricked out VW bus in Vicksburg. That dude was in phenomenal shape. I only met him once when he was like seventy-eight." Marcus sat back, trying to stay comfortable and keep his arm up.

"I remember my mom and dad talking about that," Nora interjected, "when someone swam the whole thing. That's pretty cool. You know Marcus, you're that guy that on the surface everyone thinks is an annoying stoner, but I have always found you to be fantastically interesting," Nora said sincerely.

"Oh, don't go starting rumors, now," Marcus laughed. He liked getting compliments from Nora. She wasn't one to say nice things unless she meant them so he knew it was genuine.

A few hours later, in a high-end suburb just outside Chicago, the Forrester approached a large, colonial estate at the end of a cul du sac. Several parked cars lined along the horseshoe driveway and both sides of the street. The lawn was plain and dressed down as was every other lawn in the neighborhood. It was a much more elegant neighborhood than many in the slums, but the residents did their best to remove any signs of elegance and wealth.

As they pulled in the drive a woman in her late fifties came jogging out in jeans and a sweatshirt. A joyous grin covered her face as she gleefully waved the car forward, up the drive and through a gate. Once in they traveled down a long private drive to a large car port. They parked and she met them at the car as they now realized the house they'd seen at the edge of the road was just the front guest house. What now sat in front of them was an enormous mansion, a true estate.

Seconds later, three strapping college-aged kids rushed out to the car as Brodie, Cece, Nora, and Marcus exited. Nora kept her gun holstered and held a watchful eye on Brodie

CHAPTER 30

Billy drew his head up from the table in the back office of Current, the restaurant, as he snorted up a thick line of the mighty white dust. Omari stood across from him with her arms crossed.

"This is it, Billy. I don't want you doing drugs in here anymore. Besides, I thought you had a big meeting," Omari said. "I wasn't expecting you."

Billy shook his head back and forth as if to sprinkle the coke throughout his cranium. He took Omari by the waist, although she pulled back, resisting him.

"Baby, you do drugs in here all the time," Billy said. "This is the biggest meeting of my life and I need to be confident and ready to roar. A win for me is a win for you." Billy leaned in to kiss her but she pushed his face away with the palm of her hand.

"I don't need your wins," Omari scoffed. "Lord knows what trash you keep company with when you're not here. This whole thing you're doing whatever it is, it's changed you." Omari furrowed her brow at Billy. "You need to get your shit together. There's a lot of people looking for you. They come in asking for you."

Just then Future Islands started playing throughout the restaurant. Billy fought to pull Omari in close again and looked her in the eyes.

"Just give me today. I'll straighten out, get rid of all the other girls. Just you and me," Billy said. "We can take off and get out of here. Away from all of this. Come with me?"

"We open in an hour. You should go," Omari said ignoring his questioned.

Billy held an unreturned gaze, waiting for a smile that never came, then bellowed an ironic chuckle. "I'll call you later." He grabbed his suit coat and dragged his finger along the table where the coke residue sat. He fingered the rim of his gums, garnishing them with the remaining cocaine. "Don't want to waste any of it."

"Billy, come on," Omari said. She held the office door open for him. "Go out the back."

"I know you're an agent. I've known since the first time you slipped me your number here two years ago. It's part of what makes you so fucking hot. It's part of why I'm so over the moon for you, baby," he said with an overconfident smirk.

"Leave, Billy. Get some help," Omari said, not surprised by his accusation. It fit right in with all of his delusions.

"All this time you could have turned me in," Billy stood in the doorway, "but ya never did." He winked at her and left out the back alley before she had time to react. He checked his watch, made his way to his car and sped off.

Two hours later, Billy drove along a private gravel road heading up the base of Mount Lukens. This meeting was the most upper crust Billy had attended. He'd never been to this location. He'd only found out it existed the day before. The security was at the highest he'd experienced, but after all, this was Stoyton, the Order of the Realm, not the second-rate superstar hacks Boobain and Droshure had tried to be. Stoyton Society controlled the world.

As Billy pulled up to the gate, a bin kicked out toward his driver side window. He rolled it down.

"Name?" A voice asked over an unseen intercom.

"Billy Wessner." He loosened his tie and the neck of his collar. Billy was growing nervous and could feel his body heating up, pulsing with perspiration.

"Place all weapons, your phone and all other communication devices in the bin. They will be returned upon your exit," the voice from the intercom ordered.

Billy grabbed two guns, a 6-inch Bowie knife strapped around his leg, and two phones and placed everything in the bin, then looked at the intercom, waiting.

"How will you know these are mine?" Billy asked.

The gates simply rose for his entry. After a beat he realized no response was coming. Billy pulled forward and drove up a long and curvy drive.

Finally, he came to the side of the mountain with no other direction to drive. As he crossed a point, a camouflage door revealed itself and opened. Billy drove into a large, inground parking lot and parked in the first open spot he came to. As the hidden door closed, Billy got out of his car and was greeted by a sharply dressed man wearing dark glasses. A visible bullet proof vest sat over his black collarless shirt.

"Good afternoon, Mr. Wessner," the guard said. "The meeting will be commencing in twenty-seven minutes. I will be escorting you in. Once in the room there is a kitchen where you can collect a beverage if you so desire and a snack of your choice. The meeting will start promptly at 5:00pm. If you need to use the bathroom please do so before the meeting starts. There will be no exit and reentry. The meeting will be approximately two hours depending on title and clearance, with a dinner to follow. Do you have any questions?" the guard asked as he continued walking Billy toward the cafeteria area.

"Um, not right now. Will I be able to ask questions in the meeting or anything?" Billy asked.

"Sir, this is a closed meeting. You will receive an envelope upon departure and be informed of where and when you will receive your pay and next instruction. Your level is 'Pigeon' so when there is instruction for that title you will want to pay attention."

"I'm a Pigeon? No one's ever told me my level is Pigeon. Why Pigeon," Billy sarcastically laughed.

"Sir, I am only instructed to inform. Should you have further questions, please contact your Stoyton mentor after the meeting," the guard said. Finally, he led Billy into a large auditorium-style meeting room. "The cafeteria is just there, to the right. You'll find bathrooms there, as well. Good luck, sir. Oh, and please don't deviate from the designated areas."

As the guard walked off, Billy made his way to the cafeteria. Once inside, he assessed every single person his eyes could find. He recognized no one. He could no longer boost his stock by making them look weak, he'd accomplished that already. The game was leveling up. Billy grabbed an energy drink, took a piss and made his way to the auditorium and sat down. He guessed the crowd to be around one hundred people, a mixture of men and women, but mostly men. A few minutes later the lights flashed on and off, signally that the meeting would start soon.

Finally, the lights around the auditorium stayed dimmed and the stage became highlighted. Richard Stoyton, Dexter Maxwell and Tevin Labrossa walked out to center stage in such unison it was as if they were in a chore-ographed dance troupe. All three men stood, allowing for a brief applause. It was clear Tevin Labrossa was a hippy genius who could afford to walk on stage in jeans a T-shirt and flip flops. The other two men were well-dressed and well groomed, very focused on appearance. While Richard Stoyton had to be in his sixties at minimum and Tevin close behind him, Dexter was closer to his thirties. Dexter Maxwell walked to the front of the stage, the two other men standing on each side of him.

"Welcome ladies and gentlemen," Dexter announced. "Good afternoon. None of you are under punishment so let's all take a deep inhale, then ex-hale." He paused as the audible exhale was heard from the crowd, followed by refreshing laughter. "You are all here because of your successful roles in a global venture that will sustain our planet and level it up as the premier master of the galaxy. To my right and my left are two of our twenty-nine directors. You all know who this man is, Richard Stoyton, son of Sylvester Stoyton our founding father, and Tevin Labrossa. Let's give them both some much-deserved applause for all they have done for those of us in the room." Dexter stepped to the side clapping, as Richard took the podium.

Billy shuffled in his seat, sizing up the competition sitting around him. Soon, Richard Stoyton cleared his throat, then rattled off one name after another in some type of a promotional ceremony as different people came to the stage for acknowledgement. Billy was growing bored, unsure of why he was there and what the purpose of this whole circus really was. Forty-five minutes in, just as Billy released a yawn, he heard his name.

"Mr. Billy Wessner, Pigeon, please come on up," Richard Stoyton said. The audience continued with the obligatory applause that had been carried out throughout the ceremony.

Billy straightened his tie as he made his way up to the podium. As tall as Billy was, Richard Stoyton still had a few inches of height on him. He was even more intimidating to share a stage with than Billy could have imagined, especially since this was the first time Billy was meeting him in person. Billy extended his hand to shake and was met with a large paw of a hand with the grip of a pit bull. Richard Stoyton shook his hand and patted him on the back, a gesture he had done to none of the other recipients. Billy still wasn't sure what was ahead, but he stood, ready for all of it. His demeanor shifted as a grin covered his face. He was near the end of the awards, they always save the best for last, right?

"Ladies and gentlemen, the man before us has flawlessly assisted with the execution of the successful rise and removal of the buffoon we have all come to know as one Mr. Timothy Boobain and his lapdog Jacob Droshure," Richard Stoyton said. "Billy Wessner has successfully parlayed the creations of those two men, eliminated them from our quest like the removal of two annoying flies. He has delivered the dribbling leftovers of their corporations along with full ownership rights into the hands of the Stoyton Society. Jacob Droshure signed the papers yesterday from an undisclosed location. As we sit back and watch as the reestablishment of the country takes place, Mr. Wessner will be leading two of our significant Phase 3 projects. Because of your successful efforts we award you, Billy Wessner, the leveling up to Raven. We have only had five previous associates who have jumped in status this quickly since Stoyton's establishment eighty-four years ago." Richard Stoyton stepped aside with a genuine, yet ego-filled grin.

Billy couldn't help but be exhausted and bored with the long-winded feather fluffing bird talk Richard just bellowed out. While he was comfortable as an ally of Stoyton, his only reason for the partnership was the power and the invitation to be a member which had nothing to do with birds. Pheasant, Pigeon, Raven... none of that shit mattered to him, but he would oblige as long as he would eventually become a member. He wanted to be one of the true two hundred and twenty-nine members of the Order of the Realm. They were like Gods. All this bullshit was simply arrogant dick pulling.

"Thank you so much for the opportunity," Billy said, playing the game as he was handed a small envelope. "Working with you and having your protection throughout this objective is what has made me successful, Richard. The support of yourself, along with the rest of the Stoyton members has allowed me to put some of my best skills to use. I am just happy to be a part of the greater cause. I look forward to our continued work together," Billy said. He walked over and shook the hands of Dexter and Tevin.

"You're a fucking fraud Wessner!" A male voice yelled from the back of the room.

It stopped Billy as he scanned the crowd, along with many in the audience, trying to see where the voice came from.

"You're a lazy hack riding on the coattails of natural stup..." the man continued, completely unseen by Billy due to the lights on stage. He could hear a brief scuffle as security wrangled the heckler and two others out of the room.

Two security guards walked Billy off stage as he received his ceremonial backpack of goodies and gadgets. He was escorted to a back room then into the hidden parking lot by two security guards.

"Thank you for coming today, Mr. Wessner. The Stoyton Society members appreciate all you do for them," one of the guards said.

"Wait, this is it? Those people could be waiting for me," Billy said, confused by the abrupt dismissal. "I thought there was a dinner after this?"

"Sir, it is in the best interest of Stoyton Society if you remove yourself from the premises," the guard instructed. "The members, while they hold you in high regard, don't like any unsettlement. Again, congratulations sir." The guard then extended his hand toward Billy's car, signaling for him to leave.

"So, I'm rewarded with a backpack then kicked out. This is rich," Billy said, frustrated.

"Sir, this is for your protection, as well. Not all Stoyton participants see eye to eye on tactics used. This isn't an uncommon occurrence."

Billy got in his car and pulled to the edge of the parking lot as the camouflage door opened to the outside. He sped up to the gate where his phones and weapons were to be returned. When he pulled up, the bin opened and everything was in a secure pack waiting for him. He took his phone and checked to make sure everything was in place. It wasn't.

"Hey, where's my SIM card?"

"Upon commencing the next phase of your role, you will be given a new SIM card. SIM cards are removed at the completion of each phase. It's listed in your contract laws and paperwork. Should you desire to file a complaint, that instruction is also in your contract paperwork," the voice on the intercom stated. "Thank you for all you do, Mr. Wessner. Have a good evening."

CHAPTER 31

B rodie got out and walked over toward the fifty-something woman as joy covered his face. A beautiful sunset cast over them in full motion.

"Guys this is Winston. She's a good friend of mine," Brodie said, introducing Nora and Marcus. "And this is my sister, Cece." He went to Winston as they met with a euphoric embrace. The three college kids stood waiting for instruction.

Winston gave everyone a wave hello.

"She's the one with the tracker wound?" one of them asked.

"Yes, get her inside and give her a full scan, clean and dress her wounds. We need eyes on her at all times. She's going to be detoxing, so only the proper meds and antibiotics. Put her in private med-den in the back and wait for us. We'll be there in a minute," Winston said.

Brodie watched as Cece threw her arms around the bulky college kids as they helped her limp towards the door. He felt bad. He knew she was exhausted, no longer resisting. Hopefully with her sobriety would come some answers. Cece turned back to Brodie as he met her gaze, unsure what she would response with.

"I'm sorry I didn't go with you right away. I promise you I had no idea Billy was watching me. I didn't know he was this desperate to get to you," Cece said. "He was paranoid you had something on him but I didn't know he was using me like this."

"Everything will be ok. It will get figured out," Brodie said reassuringly.

He made sure she got in safely. He had almost forgotten about his own wound as his wrapped arm pulsed with a throbbing pain. They were all weary and hungry, so happy to have successfully arrived at their destination.

Finally, Brodie paused, looking up to the trees and sky as the setting sun hit his face. He hated to admit it, but he was relieved to get time away from Cece. He needed to do a mental review of everything that had happened. He took a deep inhale, smelling the brisk fresh air.

Marcus and Nora walked around the car to meet Brodie and Winston.

"We did it, you guys. Rumor has it, new elections within six months. No one can find Droshure and Boobain is dead. That fucker is dead," Winston said, unable to contain her joy. "A bunch of Splitters found his body dumped in the Gutter somewhere in Detroit. They carried it out into the streets. I am speechless." Winston was ecstatic with excitement as she grabbed Brodie and pulled him in for another hug. Finally, he broke away, unable to wipe the growing smile from his face. "We gotta get you inside and take care of that arm," she said.

Brodie thanked her for the refuge, but he knew it was visible that he was fading. He was only half there. Knowing that he could finally rest, it took an effort for him to keep his eyes open, even with all the excitement. He felt unsteady, not in posture, but of mind. Then, as if in slow motion, he turned at the sound of Winston's voice as it slowed down like a distorted record.

"Brodie has been talking about you for the last four years almost non-stop. You must be…" Winston's voice faded as Brodie passed out.

When he came too, Brodie was lying in bed surrounded by Nora, Winston and two nurses.

Forty-five minutes later, he was back up on his feet with his arm freshly wrapped and in a sling. He and Nora wandered through the maze of a manor with Marcus joining at their side as rooms were abuzz with jubilant activity. Some feverishly typed on laptops, tracking data and sending correspondence. Others chatted on phones, talking with politicians and international delegates with a gallant fundraising effort, all prospective allies and supporters. Brodie was on information overload, as several TVs in the main room regurgitated robotic news feeds for national and global media. As they wandered past the back med den, Winston was lingering inside.

"There you are. You guys doing ok?" Winston stepped out asking them.

"I'm just a bit exhausted. I think these are the first moments I haven't had anxiety spinning in my head," Brodie said.

"Well, you're safe here. Get some rest and we'll get you all in good shape," Winston said. "Marcus, let's get you checked out." She guided Marcus over to a nursing attendant. She stood back with Nora as the nurse removed the original bandage from his arm. Brodie looked around in a daze, mentally fried, just taking it all in. The med den was staffed with four doctors and several nurses, as ambient music played in the background. He found it all relaxing.

"No one can find Droshure. Some of his systems are active but our hackers can't track his location yet. We figure someone is purposely scattering it," Winston said.

"They'll find him. I got word from my team that his data track last went to a flight, then cut out midair. He's either dead or got a flight scoop and hc's being moved to a protected location which is fine. On his own, he's harmless and useless," Nora said.

"I agree. I'll get an update from my people and keep you posted." Winston took a breath. "For now, help yourself to food, drinks, shower. My home is yours. There are rooms upstairs if you need privacy or want to get some rest. But, if the door is closed, please leave it closed. I'll be back to steal Brodie in a little bit."

"Sounds good. I might take you up on one of those rooms. I need a minute, anyway," Nora said.

Brodie watched as Nora left the room. He was afraid if he let her out of his sight, she might disappear. All the time he avoided her out of fear, now he was afraid that at any turn, she might decide to run. He sat down and rested back in a chair by Marcus, keeping him company while the nurse cleaned up his wound and got some fresh bandages on.

A little while later, Winston came back for Brodie. She took him by the hand, breaking him from thought. She led him away from the hustle and bustle. As the celebratory noise dulled, they reached a private back patio with a closed door. She knocked twice, then slid the pocket door open revealing another med den, but this one looked out on a beautiful garden. Several nurses tended to a few high-profile celebrity and political patients.

A college age female sat in a chair next to the bed Cece rested in. A refrigerator and counter sat along the wall with several waters and juices available. Winston went to speak with the nurses, while Brodie sat by Cece. Groggily, she tilted her head in his direction, exhausted.

"Is this why you got me, you thought I needed to detox?" Cece questioned.

"Cece, you kept called me, several times. Never said a work, it was always just breathing, sometimes dead air. You're saying that wasn't you?

I couldn't get ahold of you. What was I supposed to think?" Brodie spoke but she stopped him.

"Brodie, I'm sure this is for the best, but I didn't call you. At least not those calls. I couldn't get a hold of you, either. I left you messages, but just that I hoped you were safe and to call. I figured you were being you, just taking some time. I mean, I haven't seen you for a while. You kind of chose to do your own thing when the split happened. We just lost touch," Cece said.

"I didn't get any of your messages, not since we last talked a few months ago. Then, when I saw Donte, I got worried. I should tell you, he's dead," Brodie confirmed.

"Billy got me a new phone and took my old one. Maybe he's been fucking with us, both. I gotta rest, this is all too much. Can we talk more tomorrow?" Brodie walked over and hugged her. "Go," she whispered, exhausted

"Ok, I love you," Brodie said, taking the cue. "I'll check on you in a bit." Brodie joined Winston in the hallway, shutting the door as he left.

Nora wandered around the estate, seeking a quiet place. Ultimately, she came upon a vacant room and stepped inside, locking the door behind her. She stood, embracing the silence, then covered her face with her hands, feeling the warmth on her skin. Patiently, she tried to slow her breathing, inhale, exhale, hoping her body could return to its natural patterns. She replayed all that had transpired over the last few days. Her eyelids rested shut.

Nora's contemplation was interrupted as cheers echoed from the main rooms of the estate. The noise only aggravated her. She couldn't stop thinking about that chip. Last she knew, her team was close to decoding it. She couldn't contact them where she was now. It would jeopardize them. They were already tracking Christopher Scott. Who was he and how was he involved? She couldn't talk to Brodie about it, these were things she could only talk to Jasper and her team about.

She tried to imagine a moment where she and Brodie could live a 'normal' existence, but the picture was still blurry. She loved him, but the word normal gave her anxiety now more than ever. She didn't want normal, nor did she know how to be it. Overanalyzing got the best of her. She needed to think about something different. In her dysfunction, Nora dialed up a number.

"Hey, it's me. I just wanted to let you know we got here. We're still getting checked out but we made it to the safe house. Thanks for all of your help." she hung up.

Nora held the phone in her hand, questioning the emotion she felt inside her. She didn't know if she would be able to settle down, she was afraid. She wanted to be with Brodie, that she knew. She loved him more than anything. She hoped that she would be able to give him what he deserved, her time, her focus. She wasn't sure she even knew how to give that to herself, though. If there was one thing she did know, it was that she would try her hardest.

Outside the window, she saw the beautiful snow frosted greenery along with a covered pool and dazzling patio, closed for the season. To have all of this, she thought. To be in one place without a mission, have a garden. She definitely knew she wanted one, even one much smaller. Maybe even a small hanging garden from a window sill in Spain or even San Diego.

Finally, out of her head and into her heart, the edges of a smile stretched across her face as she watched a bunny spring along outside.

A knock on the door caused her to flinch. She drew her gun, keeping it behind her as she opened the door. It was Marcus. He was bandaged up and bursting with confidence from the journey. He scrunched his eyes when he saw her return her gun to her holster behind her.

"Are you ever going to relax? We're safe here," he assured her.

"Sorry, I know. It's just habit." Nora showed both her hands, holding them out in front of her, steady. "I'm just fried. How are you not exhausted?"

"I totally am, but we made it through all this shit." Marcus watched as Nora gave him a smile that held so much peace within it. But then, she looked down, still holding back. "Hey, one of the guys in the med den has some really good edibles, it's already taking the edge off."

"Fine, I'll take a few. How'd you know I was in here?"

"I was coming to talk to you early, but then you shut the door when you walked in. I figured I'd give you some time. Come here," Marcus held his arms out for her to come in for a hug. She obliged, feeling the unconditional warmth in his hold.

"It was a stupid idea for us to do this," Nora said, stepping back and looking him in the eyes. "His brother isn't going to stop looking for him."

"You and I both know he would have gone without us. There's no way I would have let him do that. He's my best friend. I think what we did only affected everything for the good," Marcus said. "You gotta try to see things from a hopeful perspective sometimes, Nora. Not everything is a start and end mission. You don't always have to be so serious. I like you best when you're not," he laughed. "You still have to enjoy your life."

"I know. I'm just a little worried," Nora said. "That chick wherever we were, the one that shot you. We aren't going to be able to protect him from stuff like that all the time".

"Nora, it's not your job to save his life. It's not mine either. We have no control over his fate," Marcus said. "Try to just stay in the moment. If you take any advice from a stoner like me, that would be it."

"You're right. I hope you know how much I love you. You're really a good friend to me," Nora smiled, stretching her arms out to hug him once again and they shared a good calming squeeze. "So, what's next for you?" Nora asked, finally allowing herself to calm down.

"I'm going to get nice and high tonight and relax. Get some decent sleep. These guys that are back from the field, they have some insane stories. Then, I'm heading out with one of the teams in the morning. I want to do my part with the restoration. And as soon as the borders open and I can get on a plane, I'm going to see my sisters. So, you headed back to your headquarters wherever that is?"

"I need to check in. Stoyton is still our target. But I'm going to take your advice and see if I can get some time off with Brodie." Nora nodded her head yes, knowing that wasn't just what Brodie needed, she needed it, too. "I'm just glad both of those psycho's are out of power," Nora said.

"Things are still crazy and there's a lot of work ahead, but the takeover efforts are going in the right direction. Unfortunately, people in the Corners are starting to arm themselves," Marcus said. "Some don't want the gates down. The guy I was talking to outside said there's already rioting and escalating violence in the bigger Corners cities. The team I'm going out with is set to temper it. Create some sense of calm and organization for the path ahead. That's something everyone wants." Marcus carried with him a look of contentment. "I feel like I have a sense of purpose after stoning around for the last few years. If I have any ability to help keep the borders down, so everyone has access to good health care, clean water, electricity for god's sake, then I should do it."

"It's good of you to go. I'm glad you were with us, Marcus. Jasper really likes you," Nora laughed. "I'm not surprised. You two have a lot in common. I'll send him your info."

"I like that guy, too. He's intensely smart. All right, I'll give you some space, I just wanted to check in. You're my sister, the third one, the special one," Marcus laughed, then kissed her on the cheek and headed for the door.

"Thank you." Nora found herself oddly calm. Marcus was right. One day at a time.

Brodie hung back in the doorway as people rushed past him into the large media room awaiting news.

"We just got word that the main residential building where several of Boobain's top men stayed, along with the two RM plants have been blown up. Sixty-four injured, but only four fatalities which is good," a man in a jogging suit said. The room erupted with cheer. The camaraderie in the room was unifying.

Brodie watched Winston from across the room. He could see a cautious shift in her demeanor, but she winked back at him, reassuringly.

"We have two teams leaving later for California and three more heading into Chicago, Texas and New York to help with restorative efforts and clean up. It's important to remove the trash and restore the electrical grids and waters systems in the Gutter. We have health clinics, businesses and corporations that are waiting to reopen in the areas deemed hot spots. We have so many partnerships in this effort to get communities back to a healthy, functioning level." The man continued on, but Brodie was already heading out of the room. His part was done. His sister was safe and the chip was out of his hands.

Brodie slipped out and headed back to the med-den to see Cece. As he approached, he could see her nestled in and comfortable, sober, and resting. He peeked his head in.

"She'll sleep for a while. Rest is good for her. We were able to get the residue out and extract most of the infection from the tracker. We're still treating her with an antibiotic though, it will help clear out most other things lurking. Winston said she wants her here for at least six weeks." The nurse stepped out of the med-den and took Brodie aside. She leaned in close. "She wants her here that long in case she has information. Any time there's a rescue they have to go through like, a protocol, gentle interrogation I guess you'd say. She needs to detox for thirty days before they can assess her legitimacy, anyway. I'm sure you understand," the nurse whispered. Brodie nodded yes.

"Makes sense. Thank you. The main thing is she's safe," Brodie replied, grateful. He made his way towards the stairs. It all felt surreal. Not even 24 hours ago they were being shot at. As he walked through the halls, he heard different bits of news and conversation leaking from different corridors, followed by the eruption of cheers, all on repeat like a touchdown during a football game.

Brodie was happy about it all, but he still liked his world small. He didn't want to be around a bunch of people, especially one's that he didn't know. And the unfortunate thing that weighed on him, was that Billy was still crazy. That hadn't changed. After searching around, Brodie saw Marcus lingering about and caught up with him. Marcus smiled wide and placed a packet of edibles in the palm of Brodie's hand. "Time to relax, my friend. 15mg's of Indica will take the edge off, there's fifteen in that packet. I'm going to chill here tonight, then head out in the morning and help the teams. You hanging for a bit?" Marcus asked.

"Yeah, it's all just still kind of hitting me. It felt like it took so long to get to Cece, now it feels like it happened so quickly. It will be nice to stay with her."

"We did good. We got her out of there. No matter what she says, you and I both know you saved her life." Marcus gave Brodie a sentimental hug, mindful of their wounds.

"You're my best friend, Marcus. My ride or die. I owe you my life," Brodie said.

"Just keep yourself in one piece. Life's too short. We have too many fun adventures ahead for that shit," Marcus affirmed.

Slowly, but surely, Brodie snuck his way up to the second level to take a moment for himself. He popped one of the edibles into his mouth and peered over the rail. He saw Nora below, lingering about. The sight of her made joy take over his face. He playfully whistled to her.

"Hey," Nora smiled, mouthing the word up to him. She grabbed on the hand rail and jokingly hauled her tired body up the stairs.

"Hi." Brodie pulled her in as soon as she reached the top and kissed her on the lips, almost disappearing into her. He closed his eyes, holding on to the moment of calm. Nora followed him as they searched for an open room with a bed. Finally, they found one and Brodie flopped back onto the queen mattress like a little kid.

"Come here," Brodie playfully held his hand out for her. "Stay with me. I need to sleep a bit," Brodie requested.

Nora took his hand and snuggled up with him, playing big spoon to his little spoon. She gently kissed him on the side of his neck.

"I love you," Brodie said almost in a whisper. With his eyes already closed, he took her hand around his waist and held it. Before he knew it, he'd fallen into a sweet slumber.

CHAPTER 32

Six Weeks Later

Many of the people staying at Winstons, like Marcus, had left for the Corners, the Gutter or returned home. Winston, Brodie, Nora and Cece, along with a few others sat in the living room watching the TV. On screen, Denny Lochardt, a handsome man in his sixties and his wife stood outside on a stage in Central Park. The area was overflowing into the streets with people from all walks of life. Massive waves of sound rolled across the park from the roars of the crowd. But then, Brodie noticed Billy lurking near a tree, almost hidden within the masses. An MC stood at a podium speaking, hyping up the crowd, getting them excited for the future of the country. Brodie kept the sight of Billy to himself. All it meant to him was that Billy was still alive.

'*And with the recovery of President Boobain's remains, several organizations, both national and international, are covering every angle of this catastrophe to identify and locate all those involved in his execution. Stolen classified documents were also recovered from his property and several of Droshure's Corporate offices. President Boobain's wife is still missing, along with many others that worked alongside him, including his business partner,*

Jacob Droshure. I think we all feel much more confident that they will be found and held accountable for their crimes,' the newscaster reported on screen.

The small crowd in Winston's living room erupted with cheer. 'In four months, to the day we will be holding our next presidential elections. Soon, Denny Lochardt came to the stage. The MC shook his hand, then gave Denny Lockhardt the stage. Denny Lochardt, who put his hands up with a smile, waved his wife, Mona, over to join him at the podium.

'Good morning and thank you, thank you all for everything you have done. Thank you for raising your voices and demanding your rights as listed under the United States Constitution. You are the people that have made this happen. You are the people that never lost hope and stood up, continued to fight for what this country is truly about, freedom unity and equality,' Lockhart's speech trailed on.

Winston jumped up, invigorated, and ran around the room high-fiving everyone. Brodie hugged Nora, cheerful from how much progress had been made in just six weeks. He was finally feeling more like himself, not so paranoid and angry. Cece, now up and about, couldn't help but join in with everyone and celebrate. The energy was contagious.

"I told you everything would get better," Brodie said to Cece. She didn't speak, she simply opened her arms for a hug with a look of happiness. Winston disappeared from the room, only to return with a cart filled with bottles of Champagne.

"Ladies and gentlemen, we are getting our country back. Let's celebrate." Winston held up a bottle and popped off the cork, then started passing out glasses.

A week later, Brodie held onto Nora's hand as they walked out the front door of Winston's home. Cece, Winston and her husband stood outside, popping tiny plastic bottles of confetti. Brodie and Nora finished packing up a Nissan 370Z, tossing two duffle bags in the trunk, carrying a bag full of snacks for the front seat.

"Drive safe and enjoy. We'll get Cece to the airport tomorrow," Winston said.

"You sure you're going to be ok? You'll call when you get there?" Brodie asked.

"Yes, Brodie, I'll call as soon as I land," Cece said. She took the snack bag and put it in the backseat of the car for them.

"Thanks. Now promise you're going to stay away from Billy?" Brodie pleaded with her.

"Brodie, stop. I'll be fine," she said making a crisscross motion over her chest. "I'll already talked to him. I promise I will be removing him from my life very soon."

Brodie was nervous about leaving her alone and couldn't stop talking. Nora watched him, seeing how much he cared about his sister. Nora, on the other hand, still wasn't sure Cece could be trusted. Yet, she got all the answers she could get from Cece earlier. She gave her a hug. As she did, Nora attached a beetle track onto Cece's shoulder, something she would never tell Brodie she was doing.

"Take care of yourself and call if you need anything," Nora said as she backed away.

"Thank you. Now, you guys just have fun. I mean shit, the California coast sounds perfect. Now get out of here, enjoy your trip," Cece demanded.

Several hours into their drive, Nora and Brodie inched along in the Kansas City afternoon traffic, appreciating the sounds of a normalcy, the simple pleasures of life. The sound of honking horns, people biking and walking outside, along with the sing-songy whistle of spring birds filled the air. Visual symbols of the slums improving and the poverty declining appeared all around them. Tent cities were being revamped with more safety and cleanliness until assisted housing could be provided. Some businesses reopened. Others were in motion, getting ready to bring their hometowns back to life. Cleaning, construction and repair crews worked around the clock, making their way through the states to get street lights working again and road repairs underway. The Department of Housing hired thousands of people within each state to go through vacant and abandoned homes to remove the squatters and get them assistance at shelters or contact the police to take them into custody if necessary. Brodie was silently reflecting on it all.

Finally, there was a break in traffic and they were on their way, again. Brodie gazed over at Nora, took her hand as he rested his head back, felt the warm sun on his face.

"I'll find something on the radio. Man, that feels weird to say." Brodie put his hand out of the window as the breeze swam through his fingers.

"This seems too perfect." He took Nora's hand and kissed the top of it with a smile. He fuddled with the radio, finally landing on some Van Morrison.

"It's real, no dream, my love," Nora said. "You know Van Morrisons my favorite."

"That's why I stopped on it." Brodie took a pause. It was moments like this that he had waited so long for. "Are you really going to go active, again? You could be a housewife, I could knock you up, have a few babies," Brodie teased. Nora raised her eyebrows at him.

"Stoyton is still out there and I still don't trust your brother. IBI has one or two agents trying to track him and until he's..." Nora turned to Brodie. "Do I have your permission to kill him?"

"Sure," Brodie smiled. "But I need you to promise me you're going to relax on this trip. Turn work off, at least for a bit."

"I will, I promise, and after your brother is dead and Stoyton's dirty players are caught and charged with their crimes, I promise you I'll quit. I know you don't want to hear this, but I actually love what I do, it helps people, it helps whole countries sometimes. Besides, I'm pretty sure I can't have kids, but I'll welcome your efforts," Nora laughed.

"Plenty of effort coming your way," Brodie said.

CHAPTER 33

Late the next morning, a black town car pulled up to the O'Hare Airport departures in Chicago. The driver hopped out and opened the back door. Looking more put together and healthier than ever, Cece stepped out, well dressed in heels, casual trousers and a magenta dress coat. He took her bags, a backpack and her purse from the trunk and handed them to her. She flung the backpack over her shoulders and took her purse and bag, then handed the driver a fifty. She walked into the airport, waited for the driver to leave, then went back outside with her things to have a cigarette, but no sooner did her phone ring.

"I've been calling you for the last three days. Is it done?" Billy barked the question into the phone.

"Jesus, Billy, yes. Hi, how are you? Remember pleasantries? My flight leaves in an hour and a half. Are you back in California?" Cece asked, annoyed.

"Yes, I've been back for two weeks dipshit. We've talked four days ago. I'll send a driver," Billy said.

"Don't bother. I have a friend picking me up," she said, then relaxed a bit. "This is it then, right? I don't owe you anymore? You'll give me my file?"

"Well, slow down. You did what I asked?" Billy probed.

"I said yes," she announced. "Why are you so obsessed with him? Just leave him alone now. Stop calling him from my phone. He's knows everything."

"I just want to know what he's up to, don't worry about it. And don't get lippy. If it hadn't been for me bailing you out that night, you'd be living on the streets, or in some chick's prison somewhere," Billy said.

"Had I not been with your idiot friends who were so drunk they couldn't see and for you forcing me to get them to their hotel, none of it would have ever even happened. It's kind of your fault, too."

"Oh, is that what Brodie programmed you to say? Now you're this strong fucking, whatever. I just want to know what he's up to."

"I'm pretty sure he's up to his girlfriend and relaxing," Cece said, lighting a cigarette. "We're square now, don't ask me to do anything else for you. You put me in such an asshole position with this," she grumbled.

"I didn't know he was coming for you. But he got you, it was an amazing opportunity, it's the cleanest way," Billy said. "I'll get rid of any paper trail of your accident. As soon as the signal is 100%, you can do whatever the fuck you want."

"You're a dick. I found the tracker and the insert, so don't act like you're innocent here. A fucking insert, Billy, really? If you keep fucking with him, the chick he's with is elite. She'll kill you. He's got a whole team of people. Just leave him alone now."

"Don't lecture me. I'll see you when you get back," Billy said.

"Billy, he's still your brother."

"Nope, maybe yours, not mine," he replied.

"Billy, please, just stop already. I gotta go." Cece hung up the phone, not waiting to hear Billy's response. She shook her head with frustration.

She finished up her cigarette and had a chat with one of the security guards standing outside. She paused for a moment, filling with doubt and regret. She pulled her phone back out and scrolled to Brodie's number, then flicked her cigarette butt into the road. But, if she told Brodie, Billy would get her put away. She didn't care, anymore. She should have never given Billy this much power over her. She dialed Brodies number and waited, but it went to voicemail.

"Brodie, call me when you get this. Billy wanted me to put a track on your car. I told him I did, but I didn't. I promise you. Just be careful. I'll try you again, when I land," Cece said. "I love you." She put her phone away and went inside.

Cece strolled through the terminal and headed to her gate, O'Hare to LAX, but not before grabbing a coffee. She took a sip, then without warning, rushed to the nearest bathroom and threw up. She cleaned herself up and looked in the mirror. Staring back at herself, she instantly felt guilty. She put her ear buds in and sunglasses on, in full 'ignore strangers' mode and got to her gate. She was ready to go home.

CHAPTER 34

J ust inside the city limits of San Luis Obispo, Nora came trotting out of a gas station carrying some bottled water, a pack of smokes and a bag of green gummy frogs. She shook the bag at Brodie, then tossed it to him through the driver's side window.

"Lunch of Champions," he laughed. A map sat open on his lap. "Last leg, baby. We should be there by 4 at the latest."

"Ah, this is perfect," Nora said, popping a frog in her mouth. "This is such a beautiful ride. Thank you for driving," She took the map from Brodie and glanced at it. He leaned over and pointed to a spot.

"We're here. Once we hit the 1, just wait, it only gets better." Brodie pulled out of the gas station and Nora pointed to the sign directing them towards Highway 1. "Just remember, we agreed to quit smoking when we get back."

"No one likes a buzzkill," Nora said, then kissed him on the cheek.

They drove along the windy road, passing Morro Rock, catching a glimpse of the huge mound. They rounded the curve and were met with the rich and luminous blues of the ocean on one side. On the other side, roaming green hills balanced with wild flowers periodically visible in full bloom, scattered in bundles, letting their beauty be known. Nora sat with her toes resting on the dash, painting them a vixen red.

On occasion, she'd place a gummy frog in Brodie's willing mouth, then enjoy two for herself. Eventually, she let her feet dangle out the window, catching the breeze, drying her toes as the tepid air brushed against her feet. They drove, windows wide open, at the oceans edge. With the radio on low and the map put away, Nora was in the midst of a perfect day.

Brodie caught her eye as she held his hand, resting it just inside of her thigh. The move piqued his interest.

"Want me to pull off somewhere? Cruz I'd really like to pull off," Brodie laughed.

Nora nodded yes. They continued driving until they saw a break in the trees and turned down a dirt road for a bit, then found a secluded area and parked. Brodie got out, took Nora's hand and led her along a path, then off the path to a hidden area where they could hear the waves crashing along the nearby cliff. She pulled off her shirt and went for Brodie's belt as their lips met.

Thirty-five minutes later, Nora pulled her shirt over her head and got dressed. Both flush with satisfaction as they walked back along the path to the car hand in hand. Brodie drove back onto Highway 1 heading north along the oceans edge. Nora put her arm around him, massaging his neck.

"I didn't think we'd ever get to this point. You're here with me and this is all so much more gorgeous than I remember," Brodie said.

"Your eyes have been clouded in hell for the last four years," she laughed dramatically, then kissed him on the cheek.

Just past Lucia, Nora let her eyes close, drifting off as the gentle wind lulled her to sleep. Brodie took the moment alone as an opportunity to truly feel joy. Never in his mind did he think things would get this good, go this smoothly. He gazed out at the waves crashing against the rocks and stones. The oil rigs that decorated the ocean just off the coast line, transitioned to yachts and beautiful sailboats leisurely resting on the water. Brodie glanced at Nora's resting face as she hummed a sweet, barely audible, snore. He put his hand on her leg, just to feel the warmth of her skin. She opened her eyes slightly and gave him a wink, then drifted off, again.

Moments later, a strident zip, as if a match was being lit off cement, howled through the car. Brodie turned at the sound, trying to identify it. He felt an aggressive sting in his back, and almost immediately, he felt a burning dart-like pain in his shoulder blade. His vision started to blur and he was no longer certain of the lines in the road. His hand clutched Nora's leg as tight as he could, unable to speak. He did his best to slow the car, trying to wake her.

She jolted up from the sound of the back window shattering and looked at Brodie as his body tightened. It was hard for him to turn his head to see her.

"I, I...something..." Brodie coughed the words out through a newly forming gurgle of blood. His hands couldn't keep steady on the wheel, as Nora scrambled to grab it. His head gently bounced off the wheel as Nora saw the open wound on the back of his neck near his ear. She guided the car to the side of the road, pressing her foot on the brake.

"Brodie... Brodie no! No, no, no don't do this. Stay with me, stay with me." She put the car in park and rushed to the driver's side, opening the door to Brodie.

Nora grabbed her sweatshirt, holding it to the wound just below his shoulder, nervously close to his neck. She keyed a number into her phone. She scanned the hills and mountains behind her, searching everywhere for any movement. There were no homes to see, hidden by the landscape. Then, just as soon as she saw a shimmering reflection from the top of a peak, it was gone. No one was coming in either direction. Everything moved in slow motion as she looked at Brodie sitting almost lifeless in the car. His left shoulder was now covered in blood. One of the gunshots had punctured the seat. He'd been hit twice. Nora stood up, staggering about in shock, waiting for the person on the other end to pick up.

"I need your help. I need immediate medical extraction," Nora said waiting for the voice on the other end. "No, there's no time! Do you have my coordinates, tag my phone," Nora pleaded. She looked down at Brodie. "Ok, just hurry!" She lifted him by the armpits and pulled him to the ground, propping him on his side into the recovery position. She quickly ran to the trunk and grabbed a flare, releasing it into the sky, then knelt by his side. "Stay with me. Come on, Brodie, stay with me," she said through tears. She held his hand, cradling his face, rocking him in her arms as the seconds felt like hours.

The throbbing pump of helicopter propellers caught her off guard, as she looked to the sky. She jumped up to standing, frantically waving her hands.

"We're here, we're here. Please!" Nora begged.

Seconds later, a medevac rescue litter shimmied down from the helicopter, dancing its way down toward Nora.

CHAPTER 35

Later that night, a two-tone black Mercedes Maybach S-Class pumped down the Los Angeles freeway with the bass banging against the frame, sending vibrations and tremors against any car that got close. Neon silver rims spun like a roulette wheel, and tinted windows blocked out the city as the moonlight added an impressive dazzle to the smiling chrome and body of the car.

Inside, Billy drove while Spider, the Splitter, sat next to him in plain clothes, puffing on a joint. He passed it back to Cece, who was sitting in the tight back seat next to Audrey.

"My guy said he got her. Said they were one of the only cars on the road. Not a hard target," Billy said in a hushed voice. He didn't want Cece to hear. Spider shifted in his seat, uneasy with the whole situation.

"I don't know if it was the smartest thing to do, Billy. Might be some repercussions," Spider warned. "She's an international agent. I don't know that Stoyton gets off on this kind of stuff as much as you do."

"You think I care? Stoyton is funding me. They need me. Besides, I knew I couldn't trust that one to do a fucking thing," Billy nodded his head back toward Cece. "This is how I know she's full of crap, listen," Billy alerted

Spider. "Hey C, how was Brodie and the chick when they left? They seem suspicious of anything?"

"I told you I'm not talking about it. You were supposed to leave me alone, leave me out of all of this. I didn't want you to pick me up." Cece paused. "You know, he told me you called him from my old phone, the one you said was broken? Something is seriously wrong with you," she insulted.

"Don't worry about it. Anyway, most importantly, you're sure you couldn't find any info on where the chip is?" Billy's demeanor tightened up and got serious with the question. He looked over to Spider, seemingly proving his point.

"Billy, enough. You're supposed to be driving us to a fucking party that you couldn't handle me not being at," Cece said. "Stop talking about this. Jesus, I need a break," she laughed, mocking his obsession.

"Doesn't matter, he's fucked now," Billy snickered, sticking his fist out for Spider to meet, which he didn't. "What the fuck, dude?" Billy looked to Spider who quickly met Billy's fist with his own.

"What are you even talking about?" Cece was stoned and having trouble determining the purpose or point of Billy's conversation.

"Don't worry about it, Bozo," Billy patronized her.

"Spider, let me see your gun," she said, changing the subject.

"Here," Spider took the bullets out and handed back the sexy Smith & Wesson Performance 500. She held it by the grip, pointing it out the window at nothing.

"This is a nice gun." she said, now pointing it toward the back of Billy's head, then pressing the nozzle into the back of his seat. Spider watched her, turned on by the action. Cece knew he was growing bored with Billy's revenge game.

"Give him back the fucking gun. I can see what you're doing." Billy swatted the gun from the back of his head.

"She's just playing around. I have the bullets, Billy," Spider said.

Cece gave Spider his gun back. She wrapped her arms around his neck and kissed him on the cheek. Billy was growing paranoid and irritated with Cece. He raised his brows at her.

"Stop fucking around, Cece," Billy said.

He turned up the deep, thumping house music, drowning out all conversation. The car sped off into the night, heading to their party. Cece and Audrey created their own dance party in the backseat.

Cece felt her phone vibrate and paused from her dancing. She read a message on her display, drawing her phone closer to make sure she had seen it correctly. She was frozen, her behavior abruptly shifted from joy to sober devastation. Spider took the phone out of her hand, trying to see what happened.

"Let me out of the car," she said flatly as her face grew pale.

"Right here, now? You gotta wait," Billy said.

"Let me out of the fucking car, now," Cece demanded with a thunderous rage Billy had never heard before. She grabbed at the door but Billy had them locked from the front.

"What the fuck is your problem?" Billy asked.

"Brodie's dead. What the fuck did you do?" she screamed, now feeling trapped in the vehicle. "Let me out." She grabbed the phone from Spider and responded to the text, soon the whole message dissolved from her view.

"What are you talking about? Who told you that?" Billy turned down the radio and gave Spider a furious look, then looked to Cece in the rearview mirror. "Are you being serious?"

"His girlfriend just texted me. Let me out. I can't be around you. You're a fucking lunatic. Stop the fucking car." Cece slapped at Billy, trying to get the door open, disregarding the speed of the car.

"That's awful. And so weird, don't you think, Spider?"

"Fuck you, let me out. I'm done, Billy. Let me out or I'll call the FBI, again," Cece demanded.

Billy swerved over to the side of the road at the first opportunity.

"Go with her Spider before I fucking shoot her," Billy barked.

"I hope you die," Cece said to Billy then walked away from the car. Spider hopped out of the car and went to her.

"You say anything to anyone..." Billy yelled after her. He pounded his fists on the wheel. He wanted to chase after her and figure out a way to keep her quiet.

"Let me out. I'll make sure she's ok," Audrey said.

"Your serious? Well fine, all three of you can get the fuck out. I knew you'd betray me," Billy said to Spider. "That's why I got someone else to do what I knew you wouldn't. If you're going to side with her, you can get out, too. Watch your back!" Billy threw the verbal threat at Spider.

Audrey got out and rushed after Spider and Cece. Billy peeled off, squealing down the road. She, Spider and Audrey walked stoned but steady, just off the shoulder, in the grass along the highway toward the exit.

"You didn't have to come with," Cece said. "I'm fine."

"Hey, easy. You can't say that stuff out loud. Just give this some time," Spider said, taking her hand.

"Are you fucking kidding me?" Cece stopped and turned to Spider. "He had my fucking brother killed. You said it yourself, he wanted you to have Nora killed. You said you lied to him. That no one was going to do anything."

"I didn't have anything to do with this. He must have checked my phone and hired someone himself. I swear to God. I wouldn't have let him do this if I knew it was his plan," Spider pleaded with Cece. "You have to believe me."

"Look, let's get off the road. It's the middle of the night and standing here isn't safe," Audrey said.

"You've never cared about me before, why be nice to me now?" She didn't even look at Audrey as she spoke, just kept hold of Spiders hand, occasionally wiped away falling tears. Audrey slowed down a little and pulled out her phone. Cece looked back and saw her stopped. "Well, come on, if you want."

"Look, I'm sorry about Brodie. I never understood Billy's obsession with him," Audrey said.

"You didn't even know Brodie," Cece said. "You could have stopped this."

"Could I? How? I did everything I could to get him to leave Brodie alone. I even smashed your old phone so Billy couldn't call him anymore," Audrey said.

"You mean you knew and you never said a fucking word to me? What the fuck is wrong with you."

"Come on, let's get off the highway. This isn't the place for this," Spider said, trying to temper the situation.

The three walked in silence. Finally, they made their way off the highway. Audrey stopped.

"I've been trying to break up with Billy for two months," Audrey confessed. "He's gone totally off the rails. I'm truly sorry about Brodie. I mean it," Audrey said.

"Killing Brodie was never part of any of this. Everything got way out of hand. Billy has a way of threatening people without threatening them. I put myself on the line to lie to him to save Brodie and his wife. I didn't know he'd get someone else to do it. He never said anything about killing Brodie," Spider said, sincerely.

"You guys wanna get drunk with me? Cuz, I feel like I need to get wasted," Cece said through tears to them both. It was the only truce she could offer. She motioned toward the street lights of a busier area.

"Absolutely," Spider said.

The three made their way to the closest dive bar and once inside, they grabbed a seat near the back. Soon enough, each sat with a shot and a beer in front of them. Cece lifted her glass.

"Brodie was my protector. He made me laugh and smile all the time," Cece said, tears falling from her eyes. "I had to go with my dad. I didn't have anyone and I didn't have any money. Brodie was overseas. I fucked everything up. I let him down. I should have just stayed and helped my mom, but Billy wouldn't let me. This is all my fault." She started to break down.

Spider and Audrey rallied around her. "None of this is your fault, Cece. Don't take this on. This is how Billy is. Once he wants something done, there's no stopping him," Spider said.

"What do you even see in Billy, anyway? He's a loser, a snake. You seem too smart for..." CeCe's inquiry was interrupted as Audrey's phone rang.

"Yes?" Audrey held her finger up to Spider for him to wait. "Well, is he going to be ok?" Audrey said somewhat panicked. "Where is he? We'll be right there." Audrey hung up her phone and grabbed her coat. "We have to go. That was your dad. Billy got hit. Someone smashed into the driver side of the car. He blew a light or something, I don't know. I have to go," Audrey said. "Please understand." She got up and went outside to wait for a car.

"Let him die. I told someone where he was going," Cece said to Spider.

"Do you know how many people want him dead? Do not think you are first in line by a long shot." Spider didn't move. He locked in on eye contact with her. "I'm with you. I'm not going anywhere," he said.

Days later, Billy walked through his house, getting used to the heavy cast on his foot and the crutches nestled under his armpits. He sat down and took a gulp from a nearby beer. He grabbed his phone and made a call.

"Yes?" Nora answered on the other end of the phone.

"Hey peanut, just wanted to say nice try. Your little car crash didn't work. Now it's your turn to try to stay alive. But don't worry, I'll make it fun for both of us. Love you bunches, Nora." Billy made a kissy noise into the phone, but she had already hung up.

CHAPTER 36

Four Days Later

B ack in Milwaukee, Nora stood behind the bar in a daze. Brodie was a constant on her mind but she needed to remain patient. Since getting the call from Billy, she let the necessary contacts know that her phone may have been compromised. She turned both her private and work phones over to her handler, to which she was promptly issued replacements. Her mission would continue with the corrupt members of Stoyton Society, but her primary target was Billy. Nora's higher-ups gave her the green light to utilize him as a reluctant informant. Billy was the perfect pawn to get inside Stoyton's 'Order of the Realm' undercover. Once her team got the information they needed, Nora received the go-ahead to dispose of Billy as she pleased.

She wiped down the counter for the third time that morning. Portishead somberly echoed throughout the bar. Motor sat in a booth eating a burger. They would open within the hour. The bar phone rang, startling her. She picked up the receiver to the seemingly obsolete wall phone.

"Shadow Box," she answered, waiting for the caller to speak.

"Nora?" the male voice questioned on the other end.

"Who is this?"

"It's Jasper," he responded.

"It's been four days. I'm going crazy. Is he ok?"

"My dear, you are a bit of a liability for him at the moment. I got your message that his brother called you. Is this line safe?" Jasper asked.

"My team wiped everything after he called and heightened the security wall," Nora assured him. "We're good. But Jasper, please, how is he?"

"He's pretty doped up on meds. Won't shut up about getting a new skateboard," Jasper laughed. "How soon can you get to Madrid?"

Nora covered her mouth, overcome with joy, catching her breath. "Is he really ok?" she asked, wiping a rogue tear from her cheek. She pulled out a palm size device and eagerly searched for flights. "I can be on a flight tonight. Is that where he is? You're with him?"

"Yes, to both. We can regroup once you get here. He has one more surgery tomorrow, but he'll be ok. He's been talking about going after his brother."

"Good, that's my plan, too," Nora firmly stated.

"I figured as much. I've got somethings in motion you'll be happy about," Jasper said. "Book two other flights to wherever. Scatter your plans in the event that you're being watched. Do a switch while you're in transit just in case. You know how this goes," he said. They'd both been through these scenarios on missions hundreds of times. "Turn everything off before you leave the bar. No trace until your plan lands. Text me when you arrive and I'll pick you up or send someone."

"Thank you." Nora hung up. For a moment she stood in disbelief. She wiped her tears and walked over to Motor. "He's alive," she said as a smile ignited across her face. "I'm going to kill Billy. Can you watch the bar?"

"You sure?" Motor asked.

"It needs to happen now, before he moves up in rank with Stoyton," Nora said, "before they start protecting him. Jean Luc will contact you with any further details for my absence."

"All right then, Godspeed," Motor said with confidence.

"Thank you," Nora replied, sincerely.

She ran upstairs and quickly packed a duffle bag full of clothes, along with the necessary items for vengeance - her knife and two favorite pistols. She went to the bathroom and looked at her reflection in the mirror. With a finger, she pulled down on the drooping dark circle under her right eye. She looked tired, but strong. Nora was exhausted, but knowing Brodie was alive gave her a renewed sense of energy.

"You got this," she said to her mirror image. She clapped her hands together, grabbed her things and rushed down the stairs.

O'Hare Airport, Chicago

Several hours later, Nora was at the airport. She paced back and forth near her gate with a dark, short-haired wig on. She wore Capri pants and a sweatshirt with a beach scene on it. She looked like she was waiting to board a geriatric cruise through the Caribbean. The disguise was a good distraction. She had her headphones on low playing calming music. Then, across the concourse she saw him.

Marcus came trotting towards her with a backpack looped over his shoulders. She couldn't help but go to him as they embraced.

"Hey, girl it's good to see you," Marcus said.

"You got my message, then." Nora was overcome with joy in seeing him. She couldn't help but cry a little. Happy tears.

"You bet I did. He's my best friend." Marcus leaned in and kissed her on the cheek. "And you are, too. Come on, let's get on this plane before anyone sees us."

The End - Part One

Acknowledgements

Continuous thank you's to my wonderful and supportive parents, Jim and Sue, who started out as my audience in my youth and morphed into my readers, editors and fans. Thank you for eagerly reading all of my sweet, scary, weird, hilarious and wild stories. Your love and encouragement is appreciated every day. Thank you for exposing me to the Arts at such a young age. The films, music, plays and literature you introduced me to has remained constant fuel for my imagination and creativity.

Many thanks to the readers who took a chance on my debut novel *Scrapers*. Readers give writers the gift of their time, patience, praise and forgiveness. For that, I am grateful.

Many thanks to my story editor and mentor, author Robert Eversz, for your education, guidance and continued support of *Scrapers*. To Leah Dobrinska, you are a guru and one of the kindest guiders of light through the daunting journey that is self-publishing. Thank you for lending your wisdom and time. To my copyeditor Kristen Holt-Browning, thank you for your keen eye and sound work. To my good friend Ted Torcivia, thank you for your reading, feedback and support throughout this journey.

Special thanks to my friends, both social and industry, that read *Scrapers* in its many shapes and drafts over the last 25 plus years: Jenny Wood, Mike Hanson, Sue Schramka, Yukie Fujimoto, Mary Flynn, Erik Kritzer, Mike Wanger, Katie Biever, Julie Zanoni, Jim Staahl, and Leon Williams. Reading the work of others can be a daunting task so thank you for your time and motivating feedback.

Many thanks to those that have been constant motivators and the cheer squad for my writing quest: Sarah Wagner, Julie Tarney, Ann Foley – the best and coolest teacher, Nicole Engelken, Andrea Bell, Lori Lester, Chris Drotzur, Matt Collison, Dave Vollmers, Adam Werther, Greg Haag, Shelly Parda, Carri Torcivia, Sharon Oswald, my amazing GBG squad, Sue Bella, Betsy Albert, Ro Hanus and Patty Byrne. A big thank you to my Hannah, Austin and Lexi, follow what brings you joy.

A big thank you to music. As a sufferer of tinnitus, I often write with music on. Because of that, I am grateful for the bands that guided me through creating the atmosphere and story of *Scrapers*: Boards of Canada, Portishead, Stereolab, Echo & the Bunnymen, Trampled By Turtles, Amon Tobin, Front 242, and Killing Joke, along with the best DJ in Milwaukee, Dori Zori. Music holds the power to open the windows of the imagination and let creativity soar, for that I am forever grateful.

A wide reaching thank you to all of the people whose names I am forgetting, the people that have shared their optimism and support of my writing over the years that aren't mentioned. I do remember and appreciate you.

About the Author

Remi Zorne graduated with an English Degree from UW-Milwaukee and continued creative writing studies at Columbia College in Chicago and the UCLA Extension Writers Program. She works in Finance, but enjoys doing freelance work as an editor and ghostwriter.

Some of her literary influences include Claude Baudelaire, Dorothy Parker, and Gil Scott Heron. The fiction works of Gillian Flynn, Toni Morrison, Anthony Burgess and Margaret Atwood. The novel *The Warriors* and the film *Blade Runner* had a big impact on Remi and served as catalysts for the development and writing of *Scraper's*.

Remi feels the films of 1979 are some of the best as they had a significant impact on her life and creative imagination. In her free time she enjoys time with her nieces and nephew, along with good friends. When not writing she relaxes with travel, meditation, tennis, hiking and music.

Made in the USA
Columbia, SC
08 April 2024

34110206R00186

Made in the USA
Columbia, SC
08 April 2024

34110206R00186

About the Author

Remi Zorne graduated with an English Degree from UW-Milwaukee and continued creative writing studies at Columbia College in Chicago and the UCLA Extension Writers Program. She works in Finance, but enjoys doing freelance work as an editor and ghostwriter.

Some of her literary influences include Claude Baudelaire, Dorothy Parker, and Gil Scott Heron. The fiction works of Gillian Flynn, Toni Morrison, Anthony Burgess and Margaret Atwood. The novel *The Warriors* and the film *Blade Runner* had a big impact on Remi and served as catalysts for the development and writing of *Scraper's*.

Remi feels the films of 1979 are some of the best as they had a significant impact on her life and creative imagination. In her free time she enjoys time with her nieces and nephew, along with good friends. When not writing she relaxes with travel, meditation, tennis, hiking and music.